monsoonbooks

A YELLOW HOUSE

After a childhood spent _____ nd
Europe, Karien van Ditzhuijzen settled in Singapore 12.
Karien has a degree in chemical engineering, but gave up her
career developing ice cream recipes to become a writer. She now
dedicates her life (in no particular order) to advocating migrant
workers' rights, her family, her pet chicken and being entertained
by monkeys while writing at the patio of her jungle house.

In 2013 Karien joined Singaporean charity HOME to support
domestic workers staying at their shelter. In 2014 she founded the
MyVoice blog, a place for migrant workers to share their stories.
Karien created and edited the book *Our Homes, Our Stories*,
an anthology of 28 real-life stories written by migrant domestic
workers, which was published in March 2018.

As a freelance writer and blogger Karien contributes to several
publications in Singapore and the Netherlands. In 2012 she
published a children's book in Dutch recounting her childhood in
Borneo. *A Yellow House* is her first novel.

www.bedu-mama.com
www.myvoiceathome.org

A
YELLOW
HOUSE

Karien van Ditzhuijzen

monsoon

monsoonbooks

Published in 2018
by Monsoon Books Ltd
www.monsoonbooks.co.uk

No.1 Duke of Windsor Suite, Burrough Court,
Burrough on the Hill, Leicestershire LE14 2QS, UK

ISBN (paperback): 978-1-912049-34-9
ISBN (ebook): 978-1-912049-35-6

Cover design by Cover Kitchen.

A Cataloguing-in-Publication data record is available from the British
Library.

Printed and bound in Great Britain by Clays Ltd, Elcograf S.p.A.
20 19 18   1 2 3

Happiness that we want, will happen, but briefly.
There is a limitation in everything. I keep trying to evaluate
every situation, but it's not us. Because our fate is in your hands.
That is the reality. That's how we are. The migrants.
Bhing Navato

Every night, pain moves into my eyes
I don't even know how I can survive
It's so hard to set aside
The loneliness I feel inside
Rea Maac

Acknowledgements

Although *A Yellow House* is a work of fiction, and the character of Aunty M is completely made up, there are many real women in Singapore who inspired me to write her and they deserve to be mentioned. I grew up in Malaysia and the Middle East with domestic workers in the house, and as an adult found I had so many questions about them that - unlike Maya - I had not even begun to imagine as a child. So when I moved to Singapore in 2012 with my own family I joined HOME, a local charity that supports low wage migrant workers. I have been part of HOME for the past five years in many capacities. I managed volunteers, the shelter, a befriender program. I taught creative writing and empowerment classes, and created the MyVoice blog and the book *Our Homes, Our Stories* to showcase their work. Not only did I learn a lot about the plights and rights of migrant domestic workers, I also met a large number of inspirational and strong women.

The HOME helpdesk has given direct support to roughly 2000 migrant workers per year since 2004, and their shelter houses around sixty domestic workers that have run away from their employers. Some are abused, others simply ill-treated, exploited, or not paid. A few are accused of criminal offences themselves. All the cases of domestic worker ill-treatment and abuse in this book are based on actual cases I encountered through HOME. The details of the cases were adapted, to protect the privacy of the individuals involved and to fit the plot of the book.

HOME's helpdesks could not run without the amazing contributions of both the staff and the team of volunteers. Many of the women that volunteer with HOME are domestic workers themselves; they spend the little free time they have to educate themselves and help others. They man the Sunday helpdesks, answer calls and messages during the week, and comment on questions in our online support groups. They organise events and activities, and run a Sunday school. Together they offer a community and support network for tens of thousands of women from different countries that left their families behind to work in Singapore.

This book is for all of them, to honour their good work. These women are not afraid to speak out for themselves and their peers. They show us that migrant workers are not victims, but strong women that have the courage to move overseas on their own to do this challenging work. Many of them became my friends, and shared the stories of their lives with me.

Novia, Cute, Bhing, Lita, Emi, Ei Phyu Tun, Moe Moe Than, Kina, Rea, Miriam, Gilda, Jo Ann, Chusnul, Juliet, Jinky, Jenelyn, Fitri, there are too many of you to list here, but you know who you are and I am grateful and happy to know you!

I'd also like to mention the Singapore Ladies Book Club, that helped nurture my love for Asian literature, and that has been nothing but supportive in my writing. I particularly like to mention Audrey Chin and May Murayama, for reading early versions of my manuscript, and Raelee Chapman for her never-ending advice and support. I'd also like to thank Sari Sudarsono, Juliet Ugay, Marion Kleinschmidt and Soojata Samy for giving feedback on my manuscript from their unique perspectives.

And last but not least thanks to my husband – who's feedback I do appreciate even when it seems I don't – and Indah, who puts up with my less-than-domestic-goddess style management and runs my household like clockwork. Indah is the owner of the original yellow house, that she built years ago in central Java with the money she made working in Singapore.

1

The first time I saw her she was dripping wet. Dashing the fifty metres in the barrage of rain from the car to the entrance of our block's tower had made her purple shirt cling to her body, revealing a black lacy bra underneath. She didn't look at me or Dad, just stared down at the puddle that grew around her feet. I followed her gaze, watching the rainwater creeping over the shiny white tiles, its wet arms moving towards my toes. I backed away and turned to Dad, who was shaking his umbrella just outside the door.

'What's that?' I pointed at the water spreading across our living room floor. When wet, the tiles became as slippery as the ice rink in Jurong mall.

'What? You mean who. This is Merpati. We told you about her, Maya. She's from Indonesia.'

Yes, you told me, but I made sure I forgot. I wanted to melt into my own puddle on the floor.

Dad continued, 'Merpati is your new nanny. Maid, helper, amah, domestic worker – whatever they call it these days. She's going to take care of you and Chloe when Mama goes back to work.'

She still stared at the puddle around her feet.

'I don't need taking care of.' Other words bubbled from my belly but I swallowed them down; if I said them, I might cry. Instead I glared at Dad. 'I can take care of myself.'

He smiled indulgently. 'What about your baby sister? What about school? No, you girls need Merpati.' He shoved the umbrella in the red china vase.

'She can't stay. She doesn't even have luggage!'

'Shoot! I left her suitcase in the car. All that rain...' Dad went back out to the corridor, leaving wet footsteps behind him.

The woman in wet purple finally looked up. I narrowed my eyes, watching the drops of rain that slid from wisps of dark hair and ran down her cheeks.

She smiled.

Even years later, I would not have been able to tell you the meaning of that first smile. I could not have told you if it was a smile that wanted to please, or a genuine one that wanted to get to know me. But even then, staring back at her with pursed lips, I watched the wet crack of her lips widening and could see the light in her eyes, where the real smile lived, fading away.

I ran to my room.

I didn't need another person to come into my life then turn her back on me. I didn't need a dripping wet whatever-they-call-it-these-days to replace Mama and my dead PoPo. That's why I'd pushed thoughts of her to the place I put all the difficult ones; behind a special wall in my head. I built it as solid as the concrete of our Singapore condo, with its rising towers whitewashed and bright. If the gardeners ever neglected their endless pruning, tropical creepers would climb up the lower floors, pushing into the stone with green, prodding arms. Her smile felt as intrusive as those creepers.

I struggled to remember her name anyhow. *Merpati*. What kind of a name was that?

When I saw her later she was drier. Her purple shirt was hanging on the drying poles on the balcony behind the kitchen. Her black lacy bra was there too. *On our poles.*

She'd changed into shorts and a faded green shirt. Her black hair, still shiny wet, was pulled into a pink clip. It was a pretty clip, with tiny fake diamonds along the edge. It annoyed me. It clashed with her shorts and T-shirt, the standard uniform of all the helpers in the condo. Plain and boring, they disappeared into the background, unnoticed unless needed. On Sundays they transformed into butterflies, flying out in skirts and dresses, their eyes painted. On Sundays they became women – at least, the ones whose employers allowed them to.

I didn't see much more of her that day. Mama, Dad, Chloe and I went out for satay and fried rice at the food court, and Dad said she had better stay at home to get settled, since it was Sunday and technically her day off anyway.

The next morning Mama wanted to head off for work straight after breakfast. Dad had left already, which meant I'd be left with this woman I didn't know. *She* had arrived two weeks late because of problems with paperwork. There'd been no time for *getting used to each other* – Mama's words. As if two weeks would have made a difference. The only one who'd met her before she arrived was Dad. He'd done all the interviews and hiring papers – he said

Mama wasn't ready to cope with such a thing yet.

I blocked the door in my pyjamas. 'You haven't combed my hair or made my pigtails yet! You can't leave us alone. Chloe is only nine months old!'

And I'm only ten, I wanted to add, but didn't. Mama knew how old I was.

'You won't be alone,' Mama said, patting my hair. 'Mer – erm – Merpati is here. She'll take care of you. I'm sure she can do perfect pigtails.'

'I don't need her. I can take care of myself!' I shouted. 'I just don't want to do it alone.'

'Honey, I can't be late on my first day back at work. Don't make a scene. You're a big girl. Look at your little sister.'

Chloe was sitting on the rug throwing toys against the wall. The door slammed behind Mama, the sound pulsating in my ears. I wanted to cry; I badly needed my PoPo. Instead, I turned around and was confronted with *her*. I stared at her until her stupid smile slid away.

I was sulking on the sofa in my pyjamas when I heard her come up behind me. She stroked my hair and I froze in my seat.

'You have pretty hair,' she said softly. 'Let me make it nice.'

I grunted. First smiles, now flattery. I wouldn't fall for that.

But I couldn't do my own pigtails yet, so I let her get the brush and the elastic bands from my room. I closed my eyes and tried to enjoy the fingers caressing my scalp. It was so different from the way Mama did it, pulling hurriedly and cursing me for not using enough conditioner. My hair wasn't black and sleek like Mama's, but lightened by Dad's blonde, frizzy and tangly. Now I imagined it wasn't a brush that slid through my hair but a shell with long teeth, sweeping it out in long, wavy locks like a mermaid's. I felt my limbs loosening with my hair.

When I looked in the mirror it was terrible. The pigtails were all wrong. They were too high. Too far to the front. And too tidy.

Thirty minutes in a school bus with Jenny, Meena and these pigtails would be thirty minutes of pure hell. I felt a surge of panic. It was all *her* fault. She was smiling at me again, but I was sure now the smile was fake. How could Dad have hired her? She and her shitty pigtails had to go.

I pulled the elastic bands out and rubbed my hair into a sticking-up mess. Then I ran to my bedroom, locked the door and built myself a tent of sheets. I retreated inside it to read my library book, ignoring her pleading knocks until I knew for sure the school bus would have gone.

Mama was blazing when she had to come back to drive me to school; but even though she yelled at me, I could tell she really wanted to yell at *her*. *She* seemed to think so too, because when Mama dragged me by the arm to the car, she flinched as we passed, as if scared that Mama was going to hurt her. It was the first time she didn't have a smile for the occasion.

As Mama pulled me over the threshold I turned back and saw her raising her hand at me. Was she miming hitting me in revenge? Did she plead for my help? Or was she merely waving goodbye? Mama's strong hold pulled me out of sight to the elevator before I could decide.

In the car, when Mama asked why, I mumbled, 'Because of the pigtails.'

Mama clenched her jaw. Then the shouting started.

'You're such a drama queen. Seriously, make me late on my very first day? There I was, hoping to come home early today for you girls! Well, that's not happening now. I hope you're happy. If you pull this again tomorrow I'm not driving you. You can stay home and fail school! Drop out for all I care! Go work in a hawker stall frying noodles! It would serve you right. Stupid pigtails. Seriously, you think it's easy being a woman? You'll find out one day. Trying to raise two daughters and have a job? No, not a job, a career? Deal with an irrational boss while your boobs leak? Fucking pig. And only to bump your sleepless head against the glass ceiling. No, you wouldn't know, you just care about your bloody pigtails...'

Mama had said fucking. *Wow.*

Mama continued muttering under her breath, but when we got to school she combed out my hair in the parking lot, pulling painfully yet pleasantly at the tangles. Then she hugged me. 'I know this is difficult for you, Maya, but you're a big girl now. You understand that I need to go back to work, right? Merpati will be alright. Trust me.'

She kissed me and zoomed off in the car. Only then did I realise she'd forgotten to redo my pigtails. In the school bathroom, staring at the mirror, I thought back to the scene by the door and suddenly saw them: the two red elastic bands in *her* upheld hand. I stood pondering this, considering shaving my head, when the door opened. I froze. Jenny and her minion Meena stood on the doorstep.

Jenny let out a long hiss. 'Hello, Cockroach.'

2

There was a large bowl of goreng pisang on the table when I came home. I rushed over to it without taking off my shoes or backpack.

'Watch out, pisang is hot,' she who cooked them called out, but I knew goreng pisang was worth burnt fingers. I paused momentarily, telling myself I shouldn't fall for her trap, for her trying to buy me with sweet stuff. Then I ate six pieces of the fried bananas. I needed something to cover up the wriggling in my stomach that Jenny and Meena's sneers had caused.

When she said, 'Let's go to the playground,' I curled up in my chair. No. *No, no, no.* I tried to run to my room, but Chloe was already in the stroller, blocking the way.

'I'm too big for the playground,' I said. 'The playground is for babies.'

When she ignored me, I rubbed my belly and told her it hurt.

'Too many pisang,' she smiled. 'Need to work that fat.' She slapped my behind and shoved me towards the door, pushing Chloe in the stroller. The imprint of her hand felt warm on my back, annoying me more than I cared to admit. I wanted to call after her, but had forgotten how to say her name.

Our playground was fine, as condo playgrounds went. It

served all five blocks and there was a climbing frame, a slide, some spring riders and a see-saw. When I was younger, I went there every day. The floor was made of that stuff they used for playgrounds everywhere, soft when you fell but still hard enough for Jenny's brother Harry to break his arm when he tumbled off the top of the slide. If you picked at it hard enough you could loosen whole slabs – good fun, as long as the parents or security guards didn't catch you.

Luckily, most of the time there were few parents around – and while some of the aunties were just as bad, others never paid attention; we, of course, knew exactly which ones. Some kids had grandparents supervising playground visits, but they had become more and more rare. Had they all died, like PoPo?

Most of the day the playground was scorched by the Singapore sun, but in the late afternoon the sun slipped behind the trees and the towers and the playground filled with shrieking kids. When I was younger, I'd been part of my own gaggle of condo children, meeting every day after school, climbing, running, yelling, doing what kids in playgrounds do. We'd been like family.

Now, as we walked down the concrete stairs, everything looked the same as it always had. The gaggle of kids, the swings and slides. They hadn't changed, but I had. I was older now. Many of my friends had moved away or just stopped coming. Of our group, only Jenny and I still came regularly, and the boys who played their eternal games of football on the asphalted square at the side.

I really only came for one thing: the swings. I loved swinging, the feeling of flying, of taking off and knowing the only things still connecting me to the world were two pieces of rope. I secretly hoped one day the rope would snap and I would be catapulted into the sky. It was something Jenny and I'd had in common, our love of the swings. Why else had I been friends with her? I found it harder and harder to remember all the fun we'd once had; it seemed to have faded away, as if it had never taken place at all.

Today, like most days, there were children and aunties. And Jenny, but no Meena. Jenny was hanging around the bushes with some kids I didn't know. I felt a dark shape in my belly move and stretch its legs.

I looked around for *her*, but she had taken Chloe to the bench in the corner and was chatting to the other aunties, feeding Chloe apple slices. I considered making a dash for the swings, but they were in full view of Jenny. Instead I crouched down behind the climbing frame and watched the group of aunties.

I'd never seen *her* talk so much. At home, she just smiled in silence and spoke when spoken to. Now, she chatted and giggled. It had taken her exactly five minutes to make friends in my playground. Life was easy for some.

Suddenly, her lips froze and she bit them together under a frown. Curious, I was about to sneak up and try to listen when I felt a tap on my shoulder. 'Roach, we're playing hide and seek,' said Jenny. 'Now. You're it.'

The thing in my stomach jumped up and down and I had to force down the *no* that was on my tongue to quieten it. I shrugged. 'Okay.'

I counted to ten, slowly. 'Ready or not, here I come!' I yelled.

When I opened my eyes, Jenny and the others were nowhere to be seen.

I started looking, looking for the catch that wasn't there. They'd gone. Relieved, I strolled over to where *she* was sitting, still chatting to her new friends.

'Have you seen Jenny?' I asked.

'The girl with the red dress?' I nodded. 'The girl went home. Took her bag and go.'

Her stupid smile was back. Grateful that Jenny was gone, I smiled too.

I sat on the swing. The afternoon had turned out to be not too bad. I rocked back and forth, swinging higher and higher. I tried to keep the good feeling, but slowly it slipped away. I swayed along to the rhythm of my thumping heart as the images slowly pushed themselves up from the dark thing in the pit of my stomach. And, after the images, the acrid taste I couldn't get rid of.

Things had been good before Meena moved into our condo. Jenny had still been Jenny – not the easiest friend, and a bossy one – but my best friend all the same, as I was hers. With Jenny you could never be bored; she could create the best games out of nearly nothing. Until the day her imagination had turned against me.

Swinging my legs up to reach for the sky, I tried for the millionth time to make sense of it all. What had I done wrong? It had been so unfair. The double standards. The stupidity. What had Meena done right, besides standing at the side-lines laughing? I was the one who'd tried to be original and brave, and Jenny chose her anyway. Jenny chose Meena. After she made me do that shameful thing, even more shameful because I'd been the one to suggest it.

I'd got the idea from PoPo. PoPo was, had been, *is* Mama's mother. PoPo was grounded in Singapore, like she really belonged.

PoPo told me stories about when she was a child in the war, when the Japanese ruled Singapore and everybody was hungry. So hungry they had to eat chichak, the tiny lizards that walked our ceilings and made their presence known by their clicking 'ci ci ci' sound. PoPo had grinned when she told that story. I liked chichaks, walking upside down over the ceiling like that, catching flies and mosquitoes. But eating them? No way. But PoPo had said they were quite tasty when deep fried, just like ikan kuning, the little fish that are served with nasi lemak, fried to a crisp so you can eat them with head, bones, tail and all. Ikan kuning are yummy.

And, PoPo had added slyly, some people had been so hungry they ate cockroaches. Her brother had once. Raw, straight from the floor.

'Think of that next time you're hungry,' she'd said, 'if you're ready to eat cockroach, your hunger is for real.'

I'd hoped I would never know hunger like that.

When Jenny said Meena and I needed to prove to her who was the best friend, the bravest, the friend that was for real, I was ravenous to please her. Meena had just chuckled.

On my swing I kicked my legs higher, kicking myself for not seeing they would have betrayed me anyway. Instead I had scuttled around on my knees to find a cockroach, presenting it proudly on the flat of my hand. What had I been thinking? That Jenny would just laugh, flip it back on the floor and hug me tight? I should have thrown that cockroach in her face shouting, 'You eat it, bitch!'

Instead I ate the cockroach. At first, it didn't taste that bad; the worst bit was the wriggling legs on my tongue. But then I bit through something and a sharp bitterness flooded my mouth. I wanted to retch but didn't. I thought about PoPo's brother and a Japanese officer hovering over me, and I swallowed. The taste lingered in my mouth a very long time.

I don't know what I'd expected, but it wasn't what happened. Jenny and Meena just stared.

'That's sick,' Meena said, pulling Jenny's arm. 'Let's go.'

They said I was too disgusting to play with. And my hunger was still real, only not the kind any food would fix.

Afterwards I'd run back inside to PoPo, but when I started to tell her what had happened she just coughed and coughed. That evening Dad took PoPo to the hospital and she never came back.

Mama puked through the whole thing. In those days she did nothing but puke. She was pregnant with Chloe but it wasn't normal puking. It was a disease: Hyperpuking gravid-something, they called it. Mama puked and PoPo never said a word about her own pain. She just slowly withered away in the background, while I was too distracted with Meena moving in and upsetting my life with Jenny to even notice.

PoPo was gone and Mama could barely stop puking long enough to cry. Even during the funeral she puked. Dad told me to be nice to her and not to burden her. But even if I'd wanted to tell her what had happened, PoPo's contorted face when I told her about the cockroach was etched in my mind forever. I knew I could never, ever tell anyone. I had to keep it inside.

In the playground, I kept swinging up and down, trying to fly away from it all – but the cockroach in my belly weighed me down. Every time I reached the highest point of my swing bile rose too, and only swinging towards the ground again could push it back to my stomach.

I swung until the cockroach was deep down where I couldn't taste it anymore.

After that, I'd had enough of the playground for one day. 'I want to go home,' I grumbled.

She shook her head. 'Already? We just got here.' But something in the way I looked at her made her get up and fasten Chloe in the stroller. 'Okay, but let's not go home yet. Let's go explore the condo. Come on.'

Who was she to boss me around? I followed grudgingly.

We took the elevator back up, but when we got to our floor it kept going. What was she up to?

We got out several floors up and I had a strong sense that we were wrong to be there. Was it trespassing if you lived in the same building? We walked away from the elevator, past doors and more doors. It was pretty much like our corridor: some houses had tidy lobbies with shoes and slippers stacked neatly in layered shoe racks; another had a row of colourful scooters.

'I know these people,' I said.

She ignored me and stared up at the numbers above the doors, as if she had some kind of plan. Suddenly she stopped.

The door before us was open but barred by a metal grille that ran from the floor to the top of the doorway. We had grilles like this too – they let in the air whilst keeping out unwanted visitors. Ours were shaped like flowers in the middle and were always left open with the door shut, because Mama preferred air-conditioning to a breeze. These were just straight vertical bars.

We peered through the doorway into an empty living room. From the back of the apartment came the sounds of someone shuffling around. I reached out and pulled at her shorts. *Come on, let's go before they see us.* But she stayed put.

A figure was approaching the grille and I tugged again. Still she didn't move. Who was this person heading towards us? I darted sideways and hid behind her back as the figure stepped into the light.

3

The woman who appeared behind the bars was dressed in shorts and a t-shirt. I allowed myself to relax – another aunty. Did we know her?

The two of them started talking in a language I didn't understand. There was a lot of headshaking. The aunty inside the apartment reached out and rattled the bars with both hands. Then she shouted in English, 'This prison! I want out!'

She gaped at us aghast, then shot a glance to the closed door behind her. 'Shush! Ah Mah sleep.' She continued in a whisper, staring straight at *her*. 'Merpati, tolong aku.'

I looked at her too – at Merpati, whose name the strange aunty had pronounced in a way that made it difficult for me to forget or ignore it again. It wasn't just the way she rolled the *r*; suddenly the name seemed connected to a real person.

I tugged at her shorts again, scared now. She gave me a half smile. 'Wait just one minute.'

The other aunty started talking in a hushed voice. My feet were getting itchy so I pushed the stroller with Chloe in it towards the elevator. As we approached, the doors opened and a teenage boy stepped out. He was looking at his phone, and only just managed to sway past without bumping into us. We were inside before the doors pinged shut.

We went straight home, and I retreated to my room and my book until Dad called me downstairs for dinner. Dad and Mama were already sitting at the table, while Chloe hung back in her highchair, jamming at her plate with her spoon. Through the open door I could see Merpati in the kitchen, rinsing pots at the sink. Dad and Mama chatted as if everything was normal, *more* normal than normal. They talked about the on-going downpour as if the rain was something miraculous, as if the Singapore skies did not always dump a flood on our heads every day at this time of the year.

I said nothing.

Finally, my parents fell silent too. Mama shifted in her chair and started fiddling with her fork. Dad leaned towards her and nodded in Merpati's direction. 'Do we need to ask her to join us at the table?'

Mama sighed. 'Must we? I suppose her room is so small, she'd have to eat on her bed with her food on her lap. We need a larger kitchen. We can't even fit a table in there. These modern condos are so squashed.'

Dad just shrugged. Our dining table was small too. If I'd been talking I could have stated the obvious: there was no space for her.

Dad's phone beeped and he glanced at it. 'Hold on,' he mumbled, 'This one's important.' He pushed back his chair. Apparently, now Merpati was there, Dad could go back to putting his job first. He pointed at me as he left the room. 'Fetch another chair, Maya.'

I put the chair between Chloe and me and shuffled my own as far away as I could. I figured Chloe would swiftly get rid of whoever sat there with a well-aimed flick of her spoon or a handful of rice to the face.

I refused to acknowledge Merpati as she sat down. She, in turn, said nothing, just smiled and made cooing sounds at Chloe. Chloe returned to hitting her plate with rhythmic beats, making the food dance. *If only we'd had peas instead of broccoli today,* I thought, grinning on the inside. Peas would have hip-hopped off the plate and Merpati would have had to bend down to retrieve them. Maybe she'd even have banged her head on the way back up. Instead, the broccoli just jiggled up and down.

Chloe, realising nobody was impressed with the banging, picked up a spear of broccoli and stuck it in her mouth, fluffy side out. She started sucking it with squished cheeks. Mama leaned over the table and pulled it out.

'Don't play with your food.'

It was sort of funny, the broccoli dummy – but Mama's tone had been icy and nobody laughed. Only Chloe didn't seem concerned. The rest of us sat there watching her in silent suspense, as if Chloe were the queen, deciding which of our heads would roll.

She grabbed another piece of broccoli, and looked back at each of us in turn. Finally her gaze fell on the intruder, who sat with her wanting-to-please smile frozen on her face.

Next to Mama, Merpati looked frumpy. Her hair was drier and duller than the day she'd arrived, whilst Mama's was the same almost-black colour and shone even when dry. Merpati's diamante hair clip only made the contrast worse. As for their clothes – even without her career-mama outfit of pencil skirt and blouse, Mama's casual shorts and shirt dazzled next to the ugly, faded ones Merpati wore.

Chloe looked back and forth one more time. Then she drew back her arm, took aim, and hurled her piece of broccoli straight at the interloper. Yes, at Merpati! I had to glue my own arm to the table to stop myself pumping my fist in satisfaction.

The broccoli bounced off Merpati's nose and onto her lap.

I looked over triumphantly, but to my shock the wanting-to-please smile was breaking into a laugh. More worrying still, across the table Mama snickered too. Still laughing, Merpati picked up the broccoli as if it were an honour bestowed on her, speared it with her fork, and held it in front of Chloe's face. Chloe opened her mouth wide and took a big bite.

I watched in horror as my baby sister leaned back in her highchair with bulging cheeks. Merpati looked equally satisfied, smiling as she picked up the spoon and started feeding Chloe rice porridge. Chloe, who would normally have protested the bland goo, took spoonful after spoonful, her hands for once still, whilst Mama looked on approvingly. Mama was always happiest when everybody got along; it was as if she didn't realise that she was the one who was difficult.

Chloe grinned around at everyone, yet I didn't blame Chloe; I never had. Everything had started to go wrong when she'd made Mama's stomach heave then swell, yet I'd loved her the instant she was born. So I didn't blame her; but I couldn't eat a bite after that.

Chloe was chewing happily until Mama asked, 'Aren't you eating, Merpati?'

Merpati put down the spoon and Chloe responded by splashing her hand in the rice porridge then rubbing it in her hair. Merpati looked at her, then at the napkin on the table, hesitating. 'Yes Ma'am. I thought maybe I eat after.'

I rarely saw Mama indecisive. 'Maybe that's better. But eat with us today. It will be good to get to know each other. I have to go to work early again tomorrow.'

The porridge had made Chloe's hair stick up in a quiff. Mama looked on in silence while Merpati got up and combed it with her fingers until it was tidy again. Then she wiped her hands on the napkin and turned to Mama. 'Yes ma'am. Which are my plate and cup?'

Mama blushed. 'Sorry, I forgot to set a place for you. I mean, I forgot to, erm, tell you to do it... I mean...' Mama stuttered, 'They are in the first kitchen cabinet on the left.'

Merpati walked to the kitchen, opened the cabinet and stared inside for a while. She came back empty handed. 'Ma'am?' she asked.

Mama looked up from her plate. 'Yes?'

'Sorry, ma'am, I don't know which are mine.'

Mama looked nervous again. 'What do you mean, which are yours? Just pick any. There are plenty there. Cutlery is in the top drawer.'

When Merpati looked at her blankly, Mama got up and went through to the kitchen. She grabbed a plate, cup, spoon and fork and tried not to slam them on the table. 'Are these ok for you?'

she asked, sitting back down.

'Yes, ma'am, thank you,' Merpati nodded. 'Shall I keep them in my room?'

Mama shook her head. 'No. Why? Just put them back where they came from. Who keeps china in a bedroom?'

Now it was Merpati who blushed. 'Sorry ma'am. My ma'am before, she did not allow me to use the family things. I kept my own in my room. One time I used hers, she scolded me badly. She said if I break it she will take it out of my salary. She bought me cheap ones.'

'That's crazy!' I cried out, forgetting I was being silent. 'That's crazy, right, Mama, to not be allowed to use the plates?'

'Shush, Maya, don't judge people you don't know,' Mama said, smoothing back her hair. 'Well, Merpati, ours are hardly gold plated so just use whatever you like, wash them up carefully, and try not to break too many pieces.'

Merpati looked down at the empty plate in front of her. 'Yes, ma'am. Thank you.'

When Dad came back, Mama pretended nothing had happened. After the weather, she moved on to talking about work. It seemed that her first day back since Chloe's arrival had been a bigger deal to her than the birth itself. Mama started a rant about her boss; he held her long leave against her, she said.

Mama didn't say it, but I knew she'd taken much longer maternity leave than usual because of PoPo. If your mother dies when you're seven months pregnant, you can't cope with work or with your nine-year-old daughter. Mama had retreated into herself and that big belly, and later all she seemed to care about was the gurgling and wailing thing that kept her up all night. 'I don't want help with her. She keeps my mind off things,' Mama would say from beneath the bags under her eyes.

'We have to give Mama the space she needs,' Dad had told me. He took time off work, taking me to theme parks and the zoo. Giraffes to replace Mama and my PoPo. And now Merpati was here to replace the giraffes.

Mama was still talking about her boss. He was a male chauvinist pig, she said. I'd never met this boss, but I imagined him as a chubby little man with an upturned snout, prickly moustache, and a curly tail poking from pink buttocks. In his hand he had a pencil with a sharp point, which he kept poking at Mama. I managed to suppress a giggle, and went back to being stern and quiet.

I made a pizza from my rice as Mama talked, flattening it with the round end of the spoon and arranging the broccoli and meat on top. Nobody told me not to play with my food. When Merpati took the rice pizza away without comment, I realised I would be hungry later.

It made me sad that nobody noticed I didn't say a word. Mama and Dad didn't know how good I'd become at being quiet. That was a skill I'd learned on the school bus.

4

That week we visited the grilled apartment several times. The aunty behind the bars was called Sri and came from Central Java, just like Merpati. She didn't speak much English but, like Merpati, she smiled at me a lot. One day she showed me her arms. They had a pattern of dark purple and brown stamped on them. I looked at Merpati for an explanation. 'Ah Mah does not know her strength,' she said. Another day Sri had a bruise on her cheek.

Sri and Merpati chatted in Javanese, but occasionally she would say a few words to me in English. Some days Merpati would slip her phone through the bars, and Sri would bow gratefully and chat on the phone in even faster Javanese. Those conversations always ended in tears.

I didn't see the ominous signs; I was too focused on keeping Merpati out to let Sri in. Or maybe ignoring the questions our visits to Sri raised, the questions that resonated in my underbelly, was easier than ignoring the taste of the cockroach's bitter bile in my mouth. I went along with Merpati, but I didn't stop to think about what it all meant.

One day, Merpati was squatting beside the grille chatting to Sri while Chloe and I were practising walking in the corridor. Chloe was the one person who always made me feel happy. Her little pudgy arms, the warmth oozing from her tight hugs; she was full of love in a way I knew I could never be.

Her sticky hand held on lightly to my little finger as she toddled along. Every time she fell on the cool, smooth marble she cooed, stretching out her arms to me: *again, again!* We had gone up and down at least fifty times and were starting to get bored when the elevator bell rang and a lady laden with shopping bags stepped out.

As soon as she saw Merpati she started shrieking. 'Aiyoh, what you doing? Who you talking to lah? Finish chores already meh? Better be. I neh pay you to talk to your friends!'

She waved at Merpati, shooing her out of the corridor towards the elevator. 'Why you don't do your job? Who is watching this kids, making noise in the corridor? Noise will wake up my mother-in-law and who will get the blame?'

I wanted to point out how quiet we were, that all the noise was hers; but my mouth was too dry to speak. Besides, we weren't quiet, not anymore. Chloe had started wailing. I picked her up, hugging her tight, and ran to the elevator.

The lady shouted after me. 'See gin nah! Girl, you watch your maid better. Keep out of other people lives liao?'

We walked to our apartment in a silence only broken by Chloe's muffled hiccups, me cradling her while Merpati pushed the empty stroller. I said nothing, angry as I was at Merpati for dragging me into this and getting Chloe all upset. When we came back the next day, Sri's front door was closed. It stayed like that for the rest of the week.

Sri's closed door kept popping up in my head, and that weekend I told Dad about her. He scratched his head for some time. He asked what floor she lived on, and what unit number. 'So this woman, Sri, you think she has suspicious bruises? And she's not allowed to use her phone? And they lock her inside?'

I nodded.

'What about Sundays? Maybe she can come here next Sunday? We can talk to her? See if we can help.'

The whole world felt a little better when he said that. But then Dad's phone rang. He answered briefly before covering the mouthpiece with his hand. 'You know, I'm not sure I should interfere. I'm a foreigner here. They don't like it when foreigners, well...' Dad stopped talking for a few long seconds. 'Ask your Mama,' he said, and left the room, phone to ear.

The Sunday after that conversation Dad had to go abroad for work, so Sri couldn't have spoken to him anyway. But I didn't want to ask Mama: we hadn't really spoken since the pigtail incident, except about food or tooth brushing.

I did ask Merpati about the Sundays, but she just laughed derisively. 'Sri does not have off-day.' She shrugged. 'Sri is always inside.'

That night in bed thinking about Sri, her bruised arms and never being allowed out, I felt sad and frustrated. I needed someone to talk to about it all. Merpati seemed to have it all figured out, but I needed to keep her at a safe distance. Mama was obsessed with work, and I instinctively felt she should still not be burdened. Now Dad had dismissed me too.

I started to cry. I needed my PoPo. How could I make sense of the world without her? I buried myself in my bed tent and stared at the dark between the sheets. I tried so hard to remember her, to repeat all she'd told me – but it kept slipping away. Then in the distance I heard a comforting sound. It was a rhythmic clicking and it stopped every minute, only to start again as if it had needed a moment to catch its breath. It was a sound I recognised.

I'd first heard it just after PoPo died. Then I'd listened to it night after night, not scared but comforted, and when one night I didn't hear it I couldn't sleep. Neither Mama nor Dad had any idea what it was. I started guessing: an insect, a lizard, a bird? Dad had laughed. 'More likely some piece of equipment upstairs. It reminds me of the sound an old fashioned traffic light makes, when you have to wait for green. I don't know, what does it matter? Just go to sleep, sweetie.'

But I lay awake many nights listening to the weird sound, which I called the traffic-light-bird. One day it had simply stopped and I hadn't heard it again until now. I'd missed my traffic-light-bird like I missed PoPo, and hearing it now it was almost as if she had come back to me again.

PoPo had grown up in a house on the East Coast with a real garden. In those days there weren't condos all over Singapore like there are now. No eternal rows of grey-white Housing Development Board flats – or HDBs, as they're known. The green spaces weren't just neatly mown patches of grass interspersed with concrete drains and waterways. Old Singapore was dotted with kampongs, villages where people lived side by side in small wooden houses surrounded by plantations, bushes and undulating rivers.

PoPo's house was called the Blue House. I would have given my little finger to see this mansion, but it had been torn down to make way for a shopping centre years before I was born. I didn't even know whether it had really been blue; PoPo had never said, and I'd forgotten to ask. She told many stories, yet so much remained untold. Listening to her tales always made me feel more whole, more *me*.

Right now, I remembered the frogs.

'Tell me about the Blue House,' I begged PoPo.

'Aiyoh, no! Just an old house. Why do you want to hear that lah?' PoPo muttered, but her eyes shimmered. It didn't take much to get her started. 'Sayang, listen, I will tell you. I was about your age. In the garden there was a lotus pond. Early one evening, after the rains, there was a strange noise by the pond.'

PoPo had demonstrated the sound, a low, bellowing whoop, a bit like a donkey. The haw without the hee.

I told her that, and PoPo nodded. 'Like a donkey, but no donkey by our pond. I kept hearing: *Bu-wrahhhhh. Bu-wrahhhhh.* My skin got goose pimples, like this.' PoPo rubbed her lower arms, making the hairs stand up. 'I was afraid to go closer to the pond, so I asked my brother James, and he said it was Hantu Katak.'

PoPo had said the word in a low, chilling voice, drawing out the syllables: *Hantuuuukathak*. I sucked in my breath. Hantu meant ghost. I wanted to ask, *who, what?* But PoPo had already moved on.

'Hantu, what hantu?' I asked my brother James. And James told me that after the rains the frog phantom comes to look for revenge for her children. Hantu Katak, she is angry, because people eat the zui keuh, water chicken.'

'Water chicken,' I'd interrupted, 'what's that?'

PoPo grinned. 'Water chicken, you know. We eat them in Chinatown. You like them.' Did I? 'Frogs. You bodoh, you know frogs. As in frog porridge. You like it, is it?'

I shuddered. 'Frogs? I don't like frogs. Ugh.'

PoPo kissed her fingers. 'Frogs are shiok. De-li-ci-ous. When you were little I took you to eat frogs in Chinatown. You loved them. But the bones are so small, aiyoh, so difficult to eat for you. You called them baby chicken. Baby chicken legs, hehe! The Chinese call them zui keuh, water chicken. I'll take you again. You'll see.'

I was sure I didn't like frogs, but I wanted PoPo to go on so I nodded.

'So,' PoPo continued, 'I ate frog just the week before, and ran to my room to close the window to make sure Hantu Katak could not come in. But still, I could not sleep.

'The air was so thick I opened the window again, and the bu-wrahhhhh was in my bed. I was convinced Hantu Katak would come for me in my sleep, so I stayed awake until the sound died. The next evening we sat on the patio for drinks before dinner. We heard nothing but the hammering rain on the roof. After the rain stopped, it started. *Bu-wrahhhhh*. I went pale and still.'

PoPo fell quiet, remembering. I waited.

'My father asked what was the matter, and I whispered to him, it was Hantu Katak. My father did not understand, and James laugh laugh, and father cannot hear it, so I tell him, "Hantu

Katak is coming to eat me." Then father laughed too, and said there was no such thing as a frog phantom, I should not listen to James. He said, "Do you want to see what makes the sound?"'

PoPo paused. 'Yes, I want to see! Please, go on,' I begged her.

'My father took my hand and walked me to the pond. "There," he pointed, "There is your Hantu Katak." In the pond swam a frog, brown with red on its sides. Normal frog, no hantu. Father and I squatted, waiting, my heart beating in my throat. Suddenly, the frog changed. Sucking up air, it blew into a ball. Then, like a squishy toy, it squashed empty again, and a big bubble inflated from its mouth: *bu-wrahhhhh*. It puffed up again and blew, *bu-wrahhhhh*. And again. *Bu-wrahhhhh*. So funny I forgot I was scared!

'Father and I watched the frog for a long time. Father knew about animals. He told me how that frog, the chubby frog, bellows to call females. And that the females liked it too.'

PoPo smiled at me. 'Frogs are mad lor.'

I lay in bed half-dreaming of the mad frogs and listening to the traffic light sound, waiting to be tucked in by Mama. But Mama had gone out and it was Merpati who came that night. I put my finger to my lips when she tried to speak, and when she looked back puzzled, I held out my finger to the still open window until she heard it too. 'It's the traffic light bird,' I said groggily.

Merpati smiled in the near dark. Without me even asking, she told me it really *was* a bird, a large brown one. 'Burung malas,' she laughed, 'Lazy bird'. Then she bent over me and whispered into my ear: 'It is a gravedigger bird. It lives in the cemetery.'

She closed the window and turned on the air-conditioning. The hum hid the sound of the bird.

Had Merpati wanted to scare me by talking about graves? Her tone had been friendly enough. But if that's what she'd wanted, she'd failed. Every time I heard the bird after that, I felt like it brought news from my dead PoPo. Merpati couldn't ruin my memories. They were my heritage from PoPo. My PoPo, whom she could never replace.

5

Not long after the cockroach incident Meena and Jenny had squeezed on both sides of me on the back row of the school bus.

'Good morning,' Jenny said.

Meena laughed, like she laughed about most things Jenny said, even if they weren't remotely funny.

'Morning,' I mumbled.

'So, you know, we've finally figured you out,' Jenny said.

'Oh, really, have you?'

'Yes, we have. You see, Meena here, she's Indian. I'm Chinese, I mean, real Chinese, not a stuck-up Singaporean. But you? We weren't sure at first, but now we know. If you mix a number of stinky nationalities, stir well, and add a bit of cowardice and dirty feet, what do you get?'

I kept quiet.

'Well?' Jenny insisted.

Meena answered for me. 'A cockroach, of course! You're a cockroach.'

Their comments hit a raw nerve. Maybe they were right. I was a mix of so many nationalities I felt like nothing. How could I be sure I wasn't a cockroach? They say that when you mix all the colours you can make white, but it's not true; I'd tried with my paints, and it turned out a muddy brown. Cockroach brown.

The bile rose again from the pit of my stomach. The ghost of the cockroach would never leave me alone now.

PoPo had known exactly who she was, and she knew all about Singapore and its creatures and history too. The Singapore it had been before it was bulldozed and covered in concrete. That was because PoPo was Peranakan, and being Peranakan meant you had belonged here for a long time. Peranakans were the ancestors of the first Chinese settlers of Singapore that had married Malay women. As long as I remembered PoPo's stories, I had proof I belonged here too. But what if I forgot? Looking around me it seemed most people never looked back. My parents didn't, for sure. Neither did kids like Meena and Jenny, nor others at my international school who weren't even born here, who seemed to belong everywhere and nowhere at the same time and were perfectly comfortable with that.

PoPo's great, great – I wasn't sure how many greats – grandfather had come from Southern China to Singapore. Her family stopped speaking Chinese and used Malay instead, Baba Malay. It was a local version that PoPo still fell into when she got excited, the words mixed with her mother's Cantonese in a hotchpotch I struggled to follow. My parents always spoke English to me, but at school they made me learn Mandarin Chinese, even though I was rubbish at it. When I tried to read it, the characters crawled in front of me and off the paper like ants. Mama spoke it quite well, and insisted I learned. I wanted to learn Malay, like PoPo, but Mama said Malay was a pointless language. Everyone in Singapore spoke perfectly sufficient English, she said, and Malaysia was a dirty and dangerous country, so why go there? Mandarin Chinese would be much more useful for when I grew up and had to do business with China.

I had no intention of ever doing business with China.

Mama always told PoPo off for speaking Malay to me. 'Speak proper English to the girl,' she'd say, 'or Mandarin if you want to teach her something useful.'

But PoPo didn't speak Mandarin, just Malay, English and Cantonese. She said Mandarin was nobody's language in Singapore, and that the government just promoted it to suck up to China. That first part was true: most immigrants spoke Hakka, Teochew, Hokkien, Cantonese, or other Southern dialects. The Northern tones of Mandarin did not suit our tropical island, and to spite Mama PoPo would change from her normal speech to a thick Singlish, the pidgin version of English commonly spoken in Singapore. Mama was too modern for Singlish, and would tell me off for replying with a curt 'can' or 'cannot,' or when I added 'lah' to any of my sentences. I secretly loved Singlish, and hoped speaking it could make me a true Singaporean. Unfortunately nobody spoke it at international school, so it was hard to pick up.

PoPo's stories recounted her childhood, but she never told me anything about her life after her early teens. I had to piece together the rest from snippets of overheard conversations between my parents, and the basic facts of my mother's life.

PoPo had grown up to marry an older Indian man, Mama's appa, against the wishes of her family. She moved from the East Coast mansion to an HBD flat in Ang Mo Kio, one of Singapore's new high-rise heartlands. My mother said that growing up there was a hell of concrete dullness. The rows and rows of identical apartment blocks, built to replace the bamboo and attap-palm leaf huts of the kampongs, were solid, with good plumbing and electricity, but offered little space or freedom. Our modern condo was just a more luxurious version of the same.

Simple maths told me my mother was not born until PoPo was forty, and appa had died when Mama was little. Mama barely remembered him or his family, and PoPo raised her as a single mother. Occasionally I had been taken to Deepavali celebrations with people PoPo referred to as aunties, uncles and cousins; but they seemed too distant, too different, too much like real Indian people to be connected to me. When PoPo took me to see my Indian cousins, Mama stayed at home. 'You go,' she said, 'I'll come next time.' But there never was a next time.

Mama's Indian and Peranakan Chinese mix made her the most beautiful woman I ever saw. I knew I would never be stylish like her. Her looks turned heads on any continent, and people would guess at her racial heritage. They usually got it wrong, and she loved to keep an air of mystery. 'I am a proud Singaporean,' she would say, 'or better yet, a global citizen.' Maybe that was why she'd married Dad, who hailed from Europe. His parents, Grandma and Opa, lived in England, but Opa was from the Netherlands originally. In my case, the effect of mixing all those nationalities was muddled, rather than mysterious: burnt caramel skin, the double folded eyelids the Chinese craved but looked plain on me, and mousey hair that twisted in ways I didn't want it to.

PoPo said it didn't matter where your parents came from. Peranakan meant 'local born,' and since I was born in Singapore, I qualified. She said Peranakans had always mixed with other races, Indians as well as Europeans. PoPo's stories made me Peranakan too, which felt good; but now she was gone and the feeling had gone too.

If I didn't fit anywhere else, maybe I really was a cockroach. And if so, I could act like one too. I might not dare to fight Jenny and Meena, but I could fight *her*. I wanted Mama and Dad back, so Merpati had to go. Merpati and those smiles of hers I still couldn't figure out.

Mama was strict with what we ate. We were allowed only fruit, biscuits and crackers for our after-school snack. She particularly hated lollipops – oh, the danger of those sticks! – and hard boiled sweets. I had some sweets stashed in secret, the leftovers from a party-bag; I would offer them up to use against *her*.

Just before Mama came home, I ate four of them and dropped the wrappers on the living room floor, next to where Chloe was sitting. Merpati was in the kitchen, so there was no chance of her seeing them and tidying them up before Mama came home.

Mama spotted them straight away. 'Maya, who's been eating sweets?'

I lowered my eyes. 'Sorry Mama, Merpati gave them to us. I should have said no.'

Chloe, beautiful ally, picked up one of the colourful papers and stuck it in her mouth. 'Please tell me Chloe didn't have any. You know she can't.'

'I know Mama, but she had them before I came home. Don't worry, she didn't choke.'

Mama turned purple. 'Merpati, can you come here for a minute?' She came over from the kitchen. 'Merpati, did you give Chloe sweets?' Mama's voice was sharp. 'My instructions were quite clear on what they should have after school, and that sweets were not on the menu. Don't you know how dangerous it is to give a baby sweets? They can choke on them.'

Merpati bent to pick up the wrappers from the floor and wrestled the remaining paper from Chloe's fist. She shook her head and then looked at me.

Mama followed her gaze. 'Maya. Did you...?'

Mama looked from me to Merpati, trying to make up her mind. I felt myself shrink, and wondered if I'd get small enough to run and hide under the sofa, like a real cockroach.

'Maya?' Mama asked again.

'No ma'am,' Merpati said, 'I'm so sorry. I gave them the sweets. I did not know, I did not work with kids before.'

Mama started a lecture on health and safety, muttering that one could not leave anything important to a man, who'd hire someone without experience to watch their children. Merpati swallowed it like I'd swallowed the sweets. Chloe, not understanding what was happening, held on to Merpati's leg. That switching of allegiance hurt most of all.

When Mama left the room, Merpati said nothing to me. She just went back to the kitchen and dropped the sweet wrappers in the bin. I followed, feeling I had to say something – but I couldn't say it. I could no longer remember why I'd started this, nor what

I'd wanted to happen. Instead I asked, 'Did you really never work with kids before?'

Merpati turned around, that sad look back. 'No, never in my work. I wish I knew more about ten-year-old girls. If I did, maybe I could...'

She stopped talking and looked past me, sad, as if she wasn't thinking about me at all. I'd tried to hurt her, but now I worried whether the fact that she hadn't got angry meant she didn't care about me. Who or what was she thinking about?

Merpati said abruptly, 'But I do know babies. I did tell your Dad that.' She looked like she wanted to say something else, but didn't.

I felt utterly confused. My plan had succeeded in making Mama angry with Merpati, so why did I feel like I had failed?

6

On a hot afternoon, about a week after the showdown with Sri's employer, we were back at the playground. I loitered about, not knowing where to put my arms and legs. The voice in my head said I should just go and play, but boredom surrounded me like a cocoon. It wrapped itself around the cockroach in my tummy. Bored was better than bullied.

Anyway, there was no one to play with, only babies like Chloe. I told myself I didn't mind.

I hung around the aunties, where Merpati had slid into the posse as if she'd known them forever. Even though being her friend was the last thing I wanted, I secretly craved to be part of their group. The aunties at the playground were mostly Filipina and Indonesian. They spoke English together, so eavesdropping was easy. Most of the time they spoke of tedious things – boyfriends, dresses, the weather. Condo gossip was better. Today, it was a long moan about their employers.

Jenalyn's employer first. Jenalyn looked after two toddlers, twin boys who were goofing about on the see-saw. I didn't know their mother. She was pregnant again, Jenalyn said.

'She always complains, she sooo tired, the boys so tiring,' Jenalyn said. 'But why is she tired? She lies on the couch, she does nothing. I have to get up, run after the twins, clean the house, cook food. Wait on her, bring water to the couch. Charlie wakes up in the night, and now, now she asks me to sleep in the boys' room. She sleeps all day, and all night too.'

The others echoed, 'So lazy.'

They switched to another. Jinky's employer always cooked her own food, so Jinky never got to cook.

The others looked at her, baffled. 'You are lucky you don't have to cook,' Mary Grace said.

'I know,' replied Jinky, 'but she makes a mess! She drops the peel on the floor, splatters tomato soup on the tiles. She burns the bottoms of the pans black. My fingers are red from scouring. And I have to eat her food. She always cook potato. I don't like potato.'

Jinky wrinkled up her face in disgust. Everyone laughed. I grinned too. I quite liked potato. Dad did too, but Mama hated it and she set the menu. Only on my birthday would she ask me what I wanted. I wondered whether Jinky would get rice on her birthday, but couldn't ask since I was eavesdropping.

'So never rice?' Merpati asked instead.

Jinky shook her head. 'I cook for myself, sometimes only. She gives me good food, meat as much as I want. How can I tell her I don't like it?' She fell silent, her hands on her stomach.

'I had a friend,' Jenalyn said, 'before, when I lived in Tampines. She was never even allowed rice in the house. The ma'am hated the smell. If she got it from her friend she had to throw it in the garbage chute. My friend lost fifteen kg.'

Life without rice in Asia was impossible, even I knew that.

Jenalyn continued, 'Some employer so stingy. You must take what you need if they don't give. Mine is ok, just lazy. But at night, I always take from the fridge. When Charlie is finally quiet, I can't go back to sleep. So I tiptoe to the kitchen. Ma'am got this chocolate from Australia last week, from her family, it was so good. She thinks sir ate it.' Jenalyn laughed and patted her belly. 'That's why I'm so fat. It's Charlie's fault for waking me up all night.'

'Did you hear about Wati, from tower four?' Khusnul said. They hadn't. 'She has a new boyfriend again.'

Another aunty, Maricel, joined the group together with her dog, Toy-toy. 'Who has a boyfriend?' she asked.

They gossiped on about the boyfriend until, becoming bored, I started to drift towards the slides. Then Merpati, who had so far said little, finally spoke. 'Actually, I wanted to ask. Have any of you spoken to Sri this week?'

I instantly felt a jolt in my stomach and an urge to hear the answer. I crept back and sat behind the aunties' bench, pretending to be engrossed in making patterns with the leaves on the ground. Meanwhile, Khusnul was telling the aunties how she'd seen Sri from the balcony.

'Our tower is opposite, same level. I can see her, I can shout her, but she cannot hear me. So I wave, she waves back.'

'Do you think she is ok?' Merpati asked.

Khusnul shook her head. 'I think she has black eye. I could not see for sure, but she pointed at it. I tried to throw her a note, but I can't throw that far. The paper flops,' she mimicked a downward loop with her hand. 'I had to go down to pick them all up. Maybe someone find them.'

Mary Grace said, 'The door has been closed all week. No one can talk to her.'

They all sat quiet.

'It is our fault,' Merpati said finally. 'Her ma'am caught us talking to her in the hallway. She closed the door.'

The cockroach scuttled its way up, and I hadn't even thought of Jenny or PoPo. I shuffled the leaves again.

'How to contact her?' Maricel asked.

Surprising myself the most, I ran around the bench. 'I know. We can try a paper airplane!'

The aunties gazed at me. 'How did you throw the note?' I asked Khusnul.

She looked at me suspiciously. 'I made it like this,' she demonstrated, making a ball from her hand. 'But too slow.'

'No, it would be,' I said. 'But if we fold the paper into an airplane, it will glide. Like this.' I tried to demonstrate with the large leaf I was holding, but it broke when I tried to fold it. 'With paper it works, really.'

Khusnul stood and looked down at me. 'Sweetie, I don't think games will help Sri.'

Merpati stood up too. 'I think it's a great idea. Let's try now.' She nodded at Khusnul. 'Is your ma'am out?'

Khusnul looked thoughtful. 'Yes, she is, but we need to be careful. Many cameras in my place.'

I was intrigued by that, but right now Sri was more important. I felt more energised than I had in a long time.

Three aunties, six children, and two dogs thronged together

in front of Khusnul's apartment, and I peeked inside. It was just like ours but tidier, even though her employers had two small children. Besides the children, Khusnul looked after Snoopy, a yappy cotton wool Maltese who was fussed over more than the kids.

'We better stay in the kitchen,' Khusnul said, 'No camera there. I'm not sure they like me bring people over.'

I was still thinking about that camera when Maricel shooed me, Merpati and Khusnul inside. 'I'll stay out here with the kids. You go fly planes.'

Khusnul took paper from a drawer and Merpati wrote the note. Khusnul and I went out to the back balcony behind the kitchen.

'There,' Khusnul pointed across the stretch of grass to the next block, 'that's her place.' The blocks mirrored each other, and other kitchen balconies were opposite Khusnul's. Laundry hung there and aircon fans puffed out hot air noisily. There was no one on Sri's balcony, but the door was open.

The distance between the two blocks was bigger than I'd expected.

'Who lives next door?' I asked, pointing at the apartments whose balcony adjoined Sri's. From there we would be able to talk to Sri over the concrete barrier.

'I don't know,' said Khusnul. 'No one is ever there.'

Merpati came out and started arguing with Khusnul in Javanese. I grabbed the note from Merpati's hand. 'Write some more,' I said to Khusnul. 'We'll probably need more than one go.'

I folded the paper into a plane and threw. Time after time,

Khusnul and Merpati wrote, and I threw.

None of my airplanes got close to Sri's balcony.

When we got home, I felt sheepish, as if I'd been playing with a toy that was too big for me. Khusnul had been right: it had all been a game to me, some fun to be had since I was a sorry person with no friends. When they'd spoken about how their employers treated them like irresponsible children, I'd felt a connection between us. I'd been so excited when I imagined I could help. It had made me forget everything else, and the excitement had felt close to happiness.

But the way they'd all looked at me afterwards showed how wrong I'd been. Of course, they were friendly and polite; after all, my parents and people like them paid their salaries. They kept saying it didn't matter, and how sweet it was that I'd tried. I understood then that the only real child there was me.

I made more airplanes, different models, and threw them out of my window over the parking lot. Some actually went fairly far. But none went far enough.

7

That night Mama was home early from work, so Mama, Merpati, Chloe and I ate together. Dad was away on business, and when he was away, Merpati usually ate with us. We had rice and stir-fried beef with green beans, which Merpati generously dosed in ketjap manis, an Indonesian sweet soy sauce which had fast become the family favourite. We ate rice most nights, and I figured that Merpati would not have to lose fifteen kilograms in our house.

Mama was in a chatty mood. Work must be going well. She asked how school was.

'It's ok,' I said.

'How is your new class? Have you made some friends? Such a shame you're not in the same class as Jenny now. But you see her on the bus, I suppose. Does she still come to the playground, or are you girls too big for that now?'

'I don't know. She's busy, you know. Homework.'

'There should be plenty of time after. They hardly give you any homework at that international school.'

Please, let it go, I thought, and Mama did. But she found a new bone to pick.

'Did you make any friends yet in your new class? Why don't you ask someone over for a playdate?'

I kept quiet for a bit. I'd been in this class for months, so it was hardly new. There was no one I wanted to have over, let alone anyone who'd want to come to me.

I said: 'Yes, I'll ask someone. Maybe next week.'

Mama seemed satisfied and turned her attention to Merpati. 'And how are you settling in, Merpati? Have you made any new friends? There are nice helpers at this condo, Indonesians too.' Merpati nodded, but Mama was on a roll. 'Your English is very good Merpati. They always say Indonesian helpers speak bad English. How come yours is so fluent?'

Merpati turned red and gave a shy smile. 'Actually, my first ma'am – no, my second – she was an English teacher. She taught at a school for girls. A very famous school. The Raffles one. You know it?'

Mama nodded. 'It's a well-known school.'

'My ma'am, she taught me better English. She gave me lessons, and many books to read. Her kids were big already, so I could borrow theirs. I still like to read English books. My ma'am said reading was the best way to improve your vocabulary.'

Mama nodded. She pointed at our bookcase. We had a lot of books. 'You're welcome to read our books in your free time,' Mama said.

'Thank you, ma'am,' said Merpati, looking not at the bookshelves but at her plate. She picked up Chloe's spoon and scooped up some finely shredded beef.

'Was she the one who didn't let you use her plates?' I suddenly needed to know.

'Yes,' Merpati said. 'That was her. She was a good employer, a good woman.'

'How could she be good when she didn't want to share her stuff?'

'Maya,' Mama said, 'Let it be. I'm sure Merapti isn't comfortable discussing this at the dinner table.'

Merpati shook her head. 'It's ok ma'am. It's like this, Maya: she is very particular. She needs things to be done exactly how she wants them. But she is generous too. She bought me everything, because I did not have off day, and at first, I had no money.' She giggled, reminiscing. 'The first time she bought me bra, it was the wrong size. I was afraid to say, so I wore it until it spoilt already.'

Mama seemed interested now. 'Why did you leave?'

'I wanted to have off day. So I asked for the transfer. I told you, she was a good woman. She let me go.'

'How long did you stay with her? And how long have you been in Singapore?'

'Over eight years now, ma'am. I stayed with her for four years, then with another employer, also for four years.'

'But your first employer? Did you not stay long?'

Merpati shook her head. 'No ma'am. The sir, he always stared at me in the wrong way. I went back to the agent. The third employer, I looked after Ah Kong, the grandfather, until he passed away. The last one, I stayed four months only.' Her face clouded over.

'Why did you leave?' I asked.

'Ma'am was bad. Very fussy. Always shouting at me. One day she screamed so loud and she hit me.' Merpati rubbed her cheek.

I wanted to ask more, know more; but Mama's look stopped

me. 'And what about your family in Indonesia? Are you married?'

'No, ma'am, I'm separated.'

Mama ignored that. 'Do you have any children?'

Merpati beamed. 'I have two.'

'You have kids?' I blurted out. 'No way.'

'Maya, don't be rude. Of course Merpati has children. What do you have, boys, or girls? And where do they live? Who looks after them?'

'One girl, she is twelve, one boy, he is ten. They live with their nenek, my mother.'

'How nice,' Mama said, and speared some more beans on her fork.

Nice? How was that nice?

Everyone was silent for a while. How come nobody had known about Merpati's kids? The thought of them infuriated me. And Mama had stopped me from asking more. I looked at the two of them, eating quietly. Merpati alternated her own eating with feeding Chloe.

'Merpati did make a lot of friends today,' I said. 'All the aunties at the playground like to sit and gossip. Merpati too.'

Mama looked angry, but not at Merpati. 'And who likes telling tales? Nobody likes a tattletale. Do you know what your PoPo would do when I would swear or tell tales when I was little? Rub chilli on my mouth.'

A much more uncomfortable silence ensued. Merpati looked at her plate again. Finally, Mama spoke. 'But nobody likes a gossip. I don't want my family business out on the playground. And don't tell me gossip either. You know, this happened to my friend. Her helper told her about a neighbour's husband having an affair. What was she to do with that information?' Mama looked around the table, facing blank looks. 'God, I wish we could have some adult conversation sometimes. It must be the main reason to go back to work, so I can use my brain rather than lose it.' She sighed. 'Anyway. How was school?'

'You asked already, Mama,' I said.

'Oh. Well, you start a conversation then.'

Her happy mood had evaporated. I racked my brains, going over the day, the playground, the paper planes, the aunties.

'Mama, why do we call aunties that? They aren't actually our aunts. Not like Aunt Lauren.' Lauren was married to Dad's brother.

We were back on neutral territory and Mama's face cleared. 'It's a sign of respect. Like you call the lady in the school bus aunty, or someone who works in the shop. Anyone older than you. It's friendly. I would say aunty to a friend of my mother. Or an old lady at the market. Or uncle to the guard or taxi driver. It's a Singapore thing.'

I knew that. I'd been calling people aunty and uncle my whole life. I could still feel my mother's hand on my back, urging me to speak the magic words: *thank you, uncle*. But that didn't explain it. I wanted to ask again, but thought better of it. Mama's moods were fragile.

Merpati, emboldened by Mama's improved humour, spoke instead. 'Chloe has been talking very well today ma'am. Show Mama, Chloe. Show her how you can talk.'

Chloe piped 'Mama,' obediently.

'Now me, Chloe, say Maya,' I asked.

'Ma-ya,' Chloe said. She smiled proudly and so did Merpati.

'Such a good girl!' Mama walked over to Chloe and Merpati's side of the table and kissed her on the head. 'Can you say dad, too?'

Chloe obliged. 'Dada.'

Smiles all around. Chloe was the one thing we all loved.

'That's not that special. She needs to say something harder,' I said. 'Come on, say Aunty Merpati.'

It was a difficult name – even Mama still called her Merapi or Mertapi sometimes. Chloe would never manage it. I said again: 'Aunty Mer-pat-ti.'

Chloe pursed her lips. 'An-tee. An-tee Ati.'

'No, not just Aunty. Aunty Merpati. It's with an M. Aunty M-erpati. With an M.'

Chloe pointed at Merpati. 'An-tee M.'

Mama laughed. 'Aunty M. Sounds sweet.'

So that's how Aunty M got her name. The problem was, Aunty M would prove much more difficult to hate than Merpati.

A name defines you, and my own name had no flavour. Mama said they had chosen Maya because it was used in many cultures and was 'nice and generic'. Generic? What did that even mean?

What could you make from it? Ma? Ya? When I was a baby, I used to call myself Yaya. When I was a bit older, maybe seven, I decided Yaya would be my real name, and I started writing it on all my notebooks. When PoPo saw it, she laughed. 'Heh, you ya ya? Ya ya Papaya!'

'What's so funny?' I asked angrily.

PoPo called out to Mama, 'Your girl, look at her yaya-ing around. She a little ya ya papaya already.'

Mama walked into the room and laughed too. I sat there, looking up at the two of them, feeling very small. They give me a stupid name, I pick a better one, and now they laugh at me?

Mama glanced at my notebooks and nodded, still smirking. 'All right, miss. We'll call you Yaya from now on. It really suits you.' She left the room with a bounce in her step.

I looked at PoPo, close to tears. 'What's so funny?' Why were they talking about papaya? I hated papaya, with its mealy texture and flavour that was both bland and too sweet.

'You know what it means, ya ya, in Singapore?' PoPo said.

Obviously, I did not.

'How to explain,' PoPo pondered. 'When someone is a bit up in the sky, high and mighty, feeling better than others, we call them ya ya. Or, in full, ya ya papaya.'

I thought about it for a while. I liked to be up in the sky, but the fruit was so yuck.

Mama and PoPo called me Yaya for a few weeks after that, always sniggering when they did. It was one of the few times I heard Mama use Singlish like PoPo; but when she did it, it didn't feel cosy.

PoPo sometimes called me sayang. I had forgotten that until one day, out of the blue, Aunty M said, 'Sayang, please can you get me a cloth? Chloe is making a mess with her porridge but I can't leave her.'

I froze. Sayang was my special name, my PoPo name. Aunty M had stolen it!

I dragged myself to the kitchen, fetched the cloth, and handed it to Aunty M. 'What did you call me?' I asked her, my tone hostile.

Aunty M did not look up. 'Sayang, sorry, I needed a cloth. I can't leave Chloe, it's not safe.'

She'd said it again! I stalked off.

Ten minutes later, Aunty M followed me to my room. 'Maya?'

I huffed.

'Sorry I asked you, but you know, Chloe is small. We need to help each other to look after her.'

'I know that. But don't call me that word.'

'Call you what?'

'Sayang. It's my special name. From PoPo. Where did you get it?'

'Sayang? Did I call you that?' Aunty M's face hazed over. 'I didn't.'

'Yes, you did.'

'Oh. I'm sorry.' She was silent for a while, and I could see all sorts of thoughts running over her face, good ones chased by bad ones. Then she said, 'Why don't you like it? It is a nice thing to say.' She looked at me in a peculiar way. 'I call my daughter sayang. It means dear, or sweetie in Indonesian. It's the same in Malay. If your PoPo called you that, then...'

'Then what?' I sneered.

'Then she loved you a lot.'

I didn't know what to say. 'You can't use it,' I mumbled, and buried myself in my book.

8

The next afternoon I was still in a huff when Aunty M asked me to come to the playground. She hadn't used that word again.

'I can stay home alone. I'm ten already.'

'I know, and I think you can, but I need to check with your Mama first. I'll do that tonight. Then you can stay home tomorrow.'

'Can't you check now?' I pointed to the phone Aunty M held in her hand.

'Do you think your Mama will like it when I call her when she is in an important meeting? She will be much marah, very angry. She'll say no, because she don't want to think about it now. Better ask tonight.'

I hated it when she was right. 'There's nothing for me to do there. Only babies go. Can I bring my book?'

'Sure.'

I collected my book and hoped I would be lucky, that she wouldn't be there.

When we arrived I could smell in the friendly air that Jenny wasn't there. I sat down behind the benches and leaned against the trunk of an orchid tree to bury myself in my book. I remembered all too clearly how the last time I'd tried to fit in with the aunties had ended.

Suddenly, all the aunties started twittering. I couldn't help myself; I was in too good a position not to listen. And as long as I kept my eyes on my book, no one would suspect. But the commotion died down quickly. It had had something to do with Wati and her boyfriend, who had asked her to marry him.

'Only together for a few months, how can?' Jenalyn cried. 'Anyway, maids cannot marry, can we? It's not allowed. Need to wait two years.'

'I hear he's an Ang Moh. With Ang Moh can.' Maricel responded. 'Cannot marry Singaporean, but foreigner ok.'

'Wah,' said Jenalyn, 'Will she hire a helper herself? You know, my friend Marilyn, she has a friend, I forgot the name, she married an Ang Moh. These white foreigners, very good husbands. Anyway, after she married, she had a baby. So she hires helper. You think she treat the helper well?' She paused, building up the suspense. 'No. She was nasty! So when Marilyn visits, you know, this helper, Pinoy too, from the same area as Marilyn, she complains to my friend. Her friend so bossy!'

They all laughed.

Jinky tutted. 'She should know better. Did she at least give off-day?'

Jenalyn said, 'I don't know. Maybe not.' She frowned. 'You know, my boss, when she has the baby, she wants to cancel my off-day. Can she do that? I don't want her to.'

Jinky said, 'There is this new law, you know. Can't you say no?'

It was Aunty M who replied. 'Yes, the new law says everybody has the right to the day off. You can agree to work on the Sunday, but they need to pay extra.'

'I don't want extra money,' Jenalyn said. 'I want my off-day.'

'You can refuse,' said Aunty M.

'I told her already I don't want to, but she said she would hire someone else who did. She says she cannot allow a transfer, because she needs me. If she sends me back to the agency, she cannot hire someone while I am there. She says she will hire someone else, and send me back to the Philippines when the new one starts. I don't want to lose the job. What can I do?'

'No choice,' Jinky shrugged. 'At least you have had the off-day. And maybe when the baby is bigger, you will get again.'

'You have a day off, don't you?' Aunty M asked.

'More like afternoon off,' Jinky answered. 'I need to make breakfast, clear up, and be back in time to help cook the dinner.'

Mama always made me set and clear the table for Sunday breakfast, and for dinner we ate out more often than not. I figured the kids Jinky looked after were too young to help.

One now toddled dangerously near the edge of the climbing frame and Jinky jumped up to save him. The aunties returned to the subject of Wati's boyfriends and I went back to my book, the trunk of the orchid tree rigid against my back. I hated that I hadn't been able to stay in my room today. Being an aunty was as bad as being a child; you always had to do what other people wanted. I'd be better off as an investment banker like Mama when I grew up.

I tried to imagine what I'd do if, like the aunties, I never had a day off. My life at school was horrible – the whole cockroach thing had been escalating rapidly – and the idea of not having the weekend to recover before going back there again was unbearable.

The mention of Khusnul's name roused me from my thoughts, and for the first time I realised she wasn't there. Something had been on my mind ever since that afternoon in her unit, and before I could think better of it I had gone up to Aunty M.

'Aunty M, those cameras in Khusnul's house – is that allowed?'

Aunty M thought for a while. 'I read in the Straits Times about a case where the employer put a camera in the bedroom of the domestic worker, and also in the bathroom. The employer was convicted for outrage of modesty. If a male employer watches a woman undress, domestic worker or not, that is indecent behaviour. They can go to jail. But it's ok to check what your domestic worker does in your living room, especially when they take care of young children. So I think in Khusnul's case, where the camera is in the living room, it is allowed.'

My sudden pluck had alarmed me, and I nodded and retreated quickly to the swings.

9

The next day there was no school. It was a teacher training day, and Aunty M and I went to the market with Chloe in the stroller. We walked in silence.

The concrete was boiling; it seemed like the rainy season was finally coming to an end and coils of heat crinkled off the pavement. I let my hand drag through the bushes on the side. They had pretty red flowers, breaking the grey of the noisy, smelly road and the sleek condo towers behind.

In the distance big clouds of white billowed over the pavement, like fog in the countryside Singapore style. Aunty M held out her hand to stop me. 'Wait. They are fogging.'

The poisonous smoke was meant to kill the mosquitoes. Not that it worked, there were still mosquitoes aplenty. The acrid smell wafted over us and I coughed, just because I could. We waited for the clouds to dissipate.

I don't know whether it was the toxins from the fog, but suddenly I could take it no longer, the silent treatment I'd been trying to give Aunty M. I knew exactly what it felt like when nobody talked to you, or worse, nobody listened to you; it was as if you didn't exist. My relationships with the other kids in my class had got worse, and it wasn't just Jenny and Meena who called me Cockroach now. Everyone did.

At home, it wasn't much better. Chloe couldn't speak more than seven words, Dad only spoke on the phone, and Mama spoke at me, not with me, moving on without listening to my replies. I felt like talking, shouting, making noise – anything to make my presence known.

Aunty M was paid to listen to me, wasn't she? So I asked her about her children.

She didn't seem surprised or pleased. She showed me photographs of them on her phone. A girl with dark hair like hers in a pink, frilly dress, and a smaller boy with a clip-on tie.

'They look pretty. Was there a party?'

'Yes,' Aunty M said. 'Nurul had her graduation at primary school.'

'Really? Did they celebrate like here, with a stage and performances?'

Aunty M turned red. 'I think so. I wasn't there.'

'Ok. I see.' But I didn't, not really.

Aunty M stared at the photo. 'I got her the dress, sent it from Singapore. She adored it. My mother said she did not want to take it off that night. She slept in it. It was all wrinkled the next morning.'

'When did you last see them?'

Aunty M took some time to work it out. 'About two years ago now. Adi had just turned eight.'

I stared at her in horror. Aunty M looked back and stroked my hair. She laughed. 'Nurul could look just like that.'

Suddenly I felt weird, in a way I couldn't tell was good or

bad. Aunty M must have felt the same because she turned away from me and fingered some orange spiky flowers on the side of the road.

I needed a different subject. What would PoPo do? She'd taught me that food was always safe. She said, 'In England, if you don't know what to say, you talk about the weather. In Singapore, you talk about food.' PoPo had never been to England, but she knew Singapore and it sounded like solid advice.

'Aunty M, do you like beef rendang?' I asked.

The air cleared, and not only from toxic fog. 'Yes, I love beef rendang.'

Since PoPo had died, food in our house had become a lot more boring. PoPo had been a good cook, each dish more fragrant and flavourful than the last. Mama was such a bad cook she couldn't even tell Aunty M what to make properly, always picking the same, safe dishes. 'I have failed in your upbringing,' PoPo would lament to Mama. 'What woman cannot cook?'

Dad, on the other hand, was a good cook. He used to let me help, and together we'd make the biggest mess. His specialty was risotto and he called me his sous-chef, which is French for helper cook. But these days he was always too busy with work.

For some reason, the blander our food became, the more stiff and boring dinnertime was too.

PoPo's rendang, sweet beef curry, made both your eyes and mouth water, but she never wrote down her recipes. They were a pinch of this and a handful of that. Mama had not even tried to cook it since she died.

'Can you teach me to cook beef rendang?' I asked Aunty M.

'Sure. Do you have a recipe?'

'No,' I said, 'Don't you? It's Indonesian, right? Did your mother not teach you?'

Aunty M smiled. 'No, she didn't.'

'Why not? What did she teach you then?'

'We grew tapioca in our garden. We would make curry from the leaves, singkong lemak, with coconut milk. The roots are starchy, we ate them fried. And we got salted fish from the market. Very salty, that fish. You had to soak it for hours but it always stayed salty.'

'Tapioca?' I asked. 'Like tapioca pudding?'

'Yes,' Aunty M said, 'like tapioca pudding.'

'And then you had it with rice.'

'Actually, you know, rice was expensive. We could not always afford it. Tapioca every day, when I was your age. I hated it. When we had rice we were very happy. Even if we only had it with garlic and chilli. For special occasions we would catch a chicken, we had plenty of kampong chicken running around. Village chicken meat has the best flavour, like it's concentrated in their scrawny bodies. Not like those ones you buy in the NTUC supermarket, fat but bland. My mother could fry up a chicken, so good. Just like I do now, the one you like. Yes, she taught me that.'

Aunty M looked like she could almost taste that fried kampong chicken. And I had to admit, her fried chicken was good – much better than Mama's, although I was not yet ready to admit it was better than PoPo's.

Aunty M said, 'But you know, beef, beef is even more expensive than chicken. So how can my mother teach me to cook beef rendang?'

'I see,' I said, and this time I did.

'You know, sweetie, we will buy beef today and we will cook rendang together. We can figure it out.'

'And then you can teach your daughter too one day,' I added.

I thought it was a nice thing to say, but Aunty M didn't look happy. She walked in silence for a minute. Then she stopped and smiled. 'Yes, I will, you are right. You know, I am very lucky: I have a job. My children eat good food every day.'

We didn't have a recipe, so Aunty M had to guess what ingredients to buy. We got beef, spices, and vegetables, as well as everything else on our list. Then we had thosai for lunch, the Indian pancakes I always had when we were at the hawkers' stalls. We hadn't been there often since PoPo died.

On our way back Chloe, full of thosai, fell asleep straight away. At the gate of our condo we saw Sri's employer drive past in her car. Immediately Aunty M pushed the loaded stroller towards the elevator. 'Come Maya! Hurry up, before she gets back.'

As always, Sri's door was closed. Aunty M knocked softly but no one answered. She knocked again, a little louder: 'Sri, it's me, Merpati.'

We heard shuffling behind the door, then a muffled voice.

'She can't open the door, it's locked,' I said.

Aunty M squatted, pressing her lips as close to the slit under the door. They spoke in Javanese.

Suddenly, the door next to Sri's opened and a teenager came out. I jumped up before Aunty M could stop me. 'Hi, can I ask you something?' The teenager grunted something that sounded like yes. 'We need to speak to your neighbour. Can we use your balcony? This door's locked.'

He looked at me dubiously.

'Please,' I said. 'It's important. A matter of life or death.'

'Sure,' he said, laughing as he opened his door for us. 'But be quick, I need to go out.'

I pulled Aunty M's sleeve but she pointed at Chloe. 'She's asleep,' I said, 'Come on, let's go.'

Aunty M shouted something through the door, and when we got to the balcony behind the kitchen we could hear Sri already on the other side. The teenager handed Aunty M a chair. She climbed onto it and hung over the wall separating the two balconies to speak to Sri.

After a minute the guy became impatient. 'Why are you doing this? Why can't she open the door?'

I explained that she was locked in, and very lonely, and that we had talked through the grille until Sri's ma'am caught us.

The guy seemed to wake from his zombie state. 'That's ridiculous. She should leave that place.'

I reminded him that the door was locked. 'They shout at her too,' he said. 'We hear it all the time. My mother always complains about it. She called the police once, but they did nothing. They couldn't act unless they beat her, that's what they told us.'

I told him about the bruises, and the black eye Khusnul thought she saw. 'You'll need to prove that, though,' he said.

Aunty M was still talking to Sri, and we could hear sobs from the other side of the wall.

'Sorry, but I need to go or I'll be late. If you want to come back any time, be my guest. Come in the afternoon. I'm usually home alone.'

When we got back, Aunty M started to unpack the groceries. She didn't mention what had happened or compliment me on the presence of mind I'd shown in asking the teenager to let us use his balcony. That put me in a huff. We shared an important secret – surely we should discuss it? There was an invisible thread that tied us together now, yet Aunty M ignored it.

But I needed some nice thoughts after the week I'd had at school, so I suppressed further worries about Sri; and when Aunty M said, 'Let's make the rendang. It needs to cook very long,' I smiled at her.

Aunty M put Chloe in her cot and we googled recipes for beef rendang, which Aunty M studied carefully before finally picking one. We chopped and pounded ginger, turmeric, galangal, garlic, chilli and lemongrass together for the rempah, a spice paste that we fried till the house smelled like the hawker. Next we added the beef, coconut milk and more herbs and spices. We chatted about nothing as we worked, and I felt light and happy.

'Now, sayang, we leave it to simmer,' Aunty M said. I shot her a look and she clasped her hands in front of her mouth. 'Sorry, sa… sweetie.'

I gave her a tiny smile and went to my room to simmer too. I felt a lot better after my day with Aunty M. The talking had done me good, and now it was time to think. Finally, I allowed the thoughts I'd been suppressing to bubble to the surface.

What had changed at school? It had never been this bad before. Other than the daily trial of the bus ride, my school days had been mostly comfortable. My classmates were nice enough, maybe not my friends but friendly. Now the silence in the bus was worse than the bullying had been, and in class no one spoke to me either. A while ago, people had sniggered behind my back, but now even that was over.

Had Jenny and Meena gone around school telling people to stop talking to me? Or had just sharing the cockroach story been enough?

At international school everyone was supposed to be different, but they all seemed the same to me. Happy. Talking. Sociable. Not liking me. No one sat next to me in class or at lunch. If someone had to team up with me in a project they'd roll their eyes, sigh, and be as economical with words as they could to get the work done. No chit-chat, no *how was your weekend,* or *did you see that movie?* I ate lunch alone too. Quietly.

I could smell the rendang cooking, but I needed something stronger to cover up the cockroach flavour. I summoned up the memory of the pineapple tarts PoPo and I had made together for Chinese New Year. PoPo was a good cook but not a good teacher. It had made me try to be a better student, and I had jotted notes in my Hello Kitty notebook constantly. PoPo kept pushing the notebook away.

'Don't write. Knead. Feel with your fingers.'

I kept asking how much, how many, how long – but PoPo shook her head. 'You need to *feel*. Feel with your fingers, smell with your nose. And then think with your brain. No book.'

She threw in ingredients in portions she described as handfuls, pinches, big spoons, small spoons. The most specific measure was a cup, but it wasn't always the same cup. 'No scale in my kitchen,' she'd said. The pineapple tarts had tasted amazing.

I searched my drawers for the Hello Kitty notebook, then leafed through it until I found the pineapple tart recipe, or what passed for it. I folded the rendang recipe and slipped it inside next to it. It wasn't long now until Chinese New Year.

Mama looked startled when Aunty M put the rendang on the table.

'Maya and I made it together,' Aunty M said.

Mama stared at the pot for a few seconds, then raised her face and forced a smile. 'I'm glad you're starting to get along,' Mama said.

I was too, I realised – but Mama didn't need to know that so I looked away. When I turned back to her, Mama didn't look glad either. She asked a few more questions – about the beef rendang, about how our day had been – but she didn't really listen to the answers. She was staring at a spoon full of rendang held just in front of her mouth, as if hesitating to eat it. She inhaled the flavour and a small tear formed in the corner of her eye. I hadn't seen Mama cry, ever.

Mama finally put the spoon in her mouth, closed her eyes, and chewed silently. After she swallowed she wiped her eye and looked guilty. 'Wow. A lot of spice in there. It tears up my eyes.'

'Do you think it's a bit like PoPo's?' I asked.

'It's different, I think,' Mama said, heaping another scoop into her mouth. 'But very nice,' she added hastily, her mouth full.

I felt bad that our rendang had upset Mama. I decided to change the subject. 'So how was your day, Mama?'

She swallowed her food and dropped her spoon on the table. 'It was horrible. I don't know how to do this, seriously. This guy Chua – I mean, what does he think he's doing? Why does a boss feel it's ok to interfere with the way an employee does her job? I can't really tell you, you're too little, let alone your sister. You wouldn't understand.'

She started off on one of her rants. I should never have asked.

'And it's not just work stuff. Where does he think he gets the right to an opinion on my marriage, my children, my pregnancy, even my mother dying? You know what's next? He'll decide how to do those bloody pigtails of yours! That would be the end. Can't people just stick to their own stupid lives?'

It was clear she didn't want an answer.

'As if I don't have enough on my mind, enough to deal with, without having to worry about how he feels about it! If I deliver my targets, that should be good enough. I make tons of money for his bonus! Work is work and my life is my life.'

She was unstoppable. I wished Dad were there. Aunty M was quiet and Chloe just kept wiping her greasy hands in her hair.

'Girls, I'll tell you something. You stick to your own shortcomings, don't bother about other people's. Let them live their own lives. Don't try to help. Helping is just a euphemism for interfering, no matter what they tell you.'

Eu-what? Mama caught sight of my puzzled face and seemed

to remember who she was talking to. 'Don't worry, girls. I'll raise you to not put up with this kind of crap.' She laughed a weird, crooked laugh. 'One day I'll just quit. That will teach him!'

Was a bland, boring dinner better than one that was too spicy?

I thought about Sri. Why didn't she just quit, like Mama had threatened to do? Could we make that happen? Get her out, over the balcony, and away? The excitement I'd felt before rose inside me again – but then something Mama had yelled stuck like an extra hot chilli padi in my throat: helping was just another word for interfering.

The following Friday afternoon, when I was just back from school, I remembered those words when Aunty M's phone buzzed. It was Khusnul. Aunty M exchanged a few sentences with her, grabbed Chloe, and shoved me towards the door.

'Come, quick, it's Sri.'

10

We hadn't gone to see Sri at all that week. I wasn't sure whether Aunty M had visited when I was at school, or whether she had taken Mama's *helping is interfering* to heart too. I had no time to remind Aunty M of those words now; she was already striding towards the elevator with Chloe in her arms.

It took me less than a second to run after her. I jabbed at the buttons, willing the elevator to go faster. Neither of us spoke.

Downstairs, we ran to Khusnul's block and took another elevator to her floor. Khusnul opened the door to us pale and shaking, and pulled us inside. 'Come look. Quiet, the kids are sleeping.'

From Khusnul's kitchen balcony we looked across to Sri's. It was empty.

'No,' Khusnul pointed, 'There, below.'

Our condo was made of large slabs of concrete, piled together like play blocks. They jutted out irregularly, as if someone had thought that adding a pinch of creativity could break the monotony of the concrete towers. Here and there, narrow ledges had been formed between the slabs. On one of them, just below Sri's apartment, lay a dark shape.

'It's her!' I cried.

Sri was lying face down, unmoving, like a mosquito squashed on the dirty white concrete. Aunty M started talking to Khusnul in Javanese.

I pulled Aunty M's sleeve. 'We need to go. We need to rescue her.'

Khusnul nodded. 'I can't leave the kids. You go.'

We went back outside, and it seemed the elevator was even slower in coming this time. Why did our condo have so many floors? I started pushing the buttons again, but Aunty M snatched my hand away. Finally it arrived and we descended and ran back to our block. The doors of the second elevator opened immediately. My finger hovered above the numbered buttons. 'Which floor?'

'Sri is on the sixth floor, right? So we need fifth.'

'But how will we get in?'

'Just try,' Aunty M said.

We rang the doorbell of the apartment we guessed was the closest to where Sri lay. Yet another aunty opened the door. I hadn't seen her before.

Aunty M said, 'We need your help. It's an emergency. Is your ma'am home?' The aunty looked at us blankly. She shook her head. 'Do you understand what I am saying?'

She shook her head a second time. 'No Eng-lis.'

The aunty was still blocking the way and Aunty M grabbed her hand. 'You, need, to help. Help. You help us?'

The other aunty nodded uncertainly and Aunty M pushed her aside. She placed Chloe in the middle of the floor and turned back to me. 'You watch her.'

I picked up Chloe and followed her to the back balcony. Aunty M started calling softly over the concrete wall. It was lower on this side of the ledge; the other side was high, like the wall between the balcony of Sri's apartment and the one where the teenage guy lived. I remembered that day, and how I hadn't gone back to talk to Sri since then. I felt a pang of guilt.

Over the concrete wall we could see Sri huddled on the ridge across the gap. The other aunty saw her too and pointed, shook her head, then nodded. She hurried to fetch a small stool and climbed over the barrier onto the ledge beyond. She looked over her shoulder impatiently.

Aunty M followed. 'Sri,' we heard her calling, 'Sri,' then something I couldn't understand.

Slowly Sri turned to face us. I felt my pulse hammering in my throat.

Aunty M spoke to Sri softly in Javanese. The gap was not wide, but Aunty M stared down at it anxiously. We were on the fifth floor, the ground far below. Looking up, I was glad that Sri didn't live higher - our condo counted 20 stories.

The other aunty didn't hesitate. She stepped across to where Sri lay, then stooped and rubbed Sri's back. Sri slumped further down. When she saw that, Aunty M stepped over too.

Together they pulled Sri to her feet and over the gap to the ledge nearest the balcony. My breath came in ragged bursts and I swallowed it down. I held my hand over the wall.

'Can she stand?' I asked.

Sri's leg was hanging at a weird angle. Between us we helped her over the barrier and inside to the sofa. The aunty got Sri a glass of water.

'How long had she been there?' I asked Aunty M. 'Is she ok?'

'Not long, inshallah,' said Aunty M. 'She was lucky Khusnul saw her.'

She and Sri started talking in Javanese again. I tried to listen but couldn't understand what they were saying. I turned to the other aunty, who stood there, her face a cross between a smile and a frown. 'What's your name?' I asked. 'I'm Maya.'

She pointed at herself, and ejected a rush of words that sounded something like *winter thing*.

'I'm sorry, what did you say?'

She said it again, slower this time. The first bit was Win, the rest of it I couldn't catch. I repeated it back to her and she shook her head. She said it once again, and when I repeated it she grinned. 'Can I just call you Win?'

Win nodded. 'Win. Win ok.'

'Where are you from?'

'Myanmar.'

It seemed we had exhausted Win's limited vocabulary, so I turned back to Aunty M and Sri. 'How is she? Is she ok?'

Aunty M said, 'She must have broken her leg. She needs to go to hospital.'

I looked at Sri, and it seemed there was more wrong than just the leg. She had another fresh black eye and more bruises on her arms. Her eyes seemed the most broken of all; they stared into thin air, looking right through me.

Aunty M said, 'She tried to escape, she tried to jump down to this floor. Look at her, what Ah Mah did to her. Her ma'am knew and did nothing. She is the one that locked her in.'

'Did Ah Mah do all that?' I asked, pointing at Sri's bruised face.

'Yes. It's her sir's mother. Old lady stay with them and Sri has to take care of her. The old lady is evil. Every time Sri makes a mistake – pulls her hair when combing, does not pick up something fast enough – Ah Mah hits her.'

Sri still looked through me into nothing, but now she was nodding.

'Not only Ah Mah is mean,' Aunty M added. 'Her son does not stop her, and sometimes his wife hits Sri too. Sri said the worst part was being alone. They took her phone so she could not call home.'

'Lonely,' I responded. 'She was lonely.'

Aunty M nodded. Why hadn't we gone to see her sooner? Maybe we could have got her out before she'd got hurt. Was Mama wrong about helping?

'Should we call an ambulance?' I asked.

'No,' Aunty M said. 'We'll take taxi. We can ask someone to go with her. Maybe Mary Grace or Maricel. Maricel ma'am and sir never home before dinner. I could watch the dog for her.'

Aunty M and Win each took one of Sri's arms, supporting her weight as she hobbled down the hallway and into the elevator.

I waited with Sri in the lobby while Aunty M called Mary Grace. Her employer was out, but Mary Grace said she wouldn't mind anyway. Mary Grace might not speak Javanese or Indonesian, but she had no children to look after and was free to go.

'Does she have money?' I asked Aunty M. 'Shouldn't we call

her employer? Who will pay?'

'I gave Mary Grace money for the taxi already,' Aunty M said. 'And the employer did this, didn't they? Why call them? It's the police we should call!'

Sri straightened at the word police. 'No, no police. Police trouble for me. Please, no.'

They spoke some more in Javanese, and then Mary Grace arrived, a red taxi behind her. We waved at them as they left.

Win pointed after the taxi. 'She ok, yes?'

Aunty M gave her a hug. 'You were great, thank you. Thank you so much. I'll stop by sometimes, yes? You my friend?'

Win nodded. 'Friend.'

I felt like hugging her too, but didn't dare. Instead I just smiled.

Win smiled back. 'Friend,' she said.

We took Chloe home. Win's final word had left a warm glow until I remembered Sri. 'What's going to happen?' I asked Aunty M.

'I don't know,' she said. 'Let's wait till we hear from Mary Grace.'

She didn't say much more, and when we got home she told me to do my homework. 'I need to cook dinner.'

I went to my room and sat down feeling good. Then I felt bad for feeling good. Hadn't I just witnessed a horrible thing? Shouldn't I feel upset? I didn't. I was happy Sri was finally out of that house, and that I'd helped, and that I might have made a new friend in Win.

When Mama came home I was on the sofa playing on the

iPad, and I just nodded when she asked me if I was going to greet her. I couldn't look her in the eye. Aunty M said nothing about Sri at dinner, and I didn't either.

After she had cleaned up, I saw Aunty M furiously messaging on her phone. I hovered, and when I was sure Mama was out of earshot I asked whether there was any news.

'She broke her leg bad. They will operate tomorrow. She is still in hospital. She bruised some ribs too. And the doctor called the police. They took photos. Not just of her leg, but her eye and arms and everything. They said they can press charges for the hitting.'

'Wow. Do we need to testify?'

'I don't know. I will visit on Sunday, and ask her.'

Today was Friday, so Sunday wasn't far off. 'Can I come?' I asked.

Aunty M looked at me like she wasn't sure. 'That is sweet of you. Maybe next time?'

I realised I'd have to tell Mama and Dad if I wanted to go, so I shrugged. 'Ok. Tell her I say hi.'

'I will, sayang. Good night.' She turned back to her phone.

But there was still something on my mind. 'Aunty M,' I said. 'Yes?'

'Why did Sri not just quit?' Like Mama, who I still hoped would do as she'd threatened and quit the job that took her away from me every day. The job that had made her stop liking me.

Aunty M pondered for a while. 'I don't know,' she said. Then, 'No, actually, I do know. We have a contract. It is for two years.

Maids cannot break it, only the employer can. So Sri needs to finish her contract.'

I repeated the words in my mind, making sense of them. They were mama-words. Contracts and investments. Would the same apply to Mama? Would she have to finish two years? In two years I'd be in secondary school already. I wanted her to quit now.

But Aunty M was already continuing. 'Also, she had to pay a lot of money to get this job. Eight months' deductions. It is her first job in Singapore.'

I didn't understand. 'What's a deduction?' I asked.

'You have to pay to the agency that got you the job. But if you don't have the money, they take it from your salary. The first eight months, sometimes six, you get no salary. You only get allowance, maybe twenty dollar, to buy toiletries. Sri has worked six months, so she still owes the agency two months' worth of money. She can't go home.'

'So she didn't get paid?' I asked.

'No, not yet. Maybe next month. She needed the money. She needed to stay.'

I started to understand. 'And what about you, do we pay you? Do you have this deduction?' Aunty M had been with us less than six months.

She smiled. 'I only had to pay two months of salary because it was a transfer. I worked in Singapore before. Your dad paid the rest. And I had some savings. Don't worry about my salary, it is fine.'

I felt relieved. 'But Sri did not get any money. And she got beat up. That's not fair.'

'No, sayang, that is not fair. And that is why she jumped.'

It seemed some things were simply not easy to fix. At least the hospital called the police. Someone knew what was right and wrong.

The words fair and unfair kept popping up in my head throughout the evening. Eventually, as I was getting ready for bed, another thought drove them away: Aunty M had called me sayang again.

11

The beef rendang, which had worked perhaps too well in loosening up Mama's emotions, had taught me the power of food. I wanted to try again. It was almost Chinese New Year but no one seemed in a festive mood. Mama had decided we'd go away for the holiday: without PoPo, she said, there were no family obligations important enough to stay in Singapore. PoPo had loved family traditions. Mama treated them as a chore.

'We won't need to have a reunion dinner or New Year's Day visits this year. Won't that be great? We did Christmas dinner already – that's enough elaborate cooking for a year for me. We'll go to a beach resort, and we won't have to do anything except relax.'

I pointed out that Aunty M could do the cooking – she could do Chinese food as well as anyone – but Mama ignored me. She had booked this place in Thailand that looked flawless, with a pristine stretch of beach bordering turquoise sea, lined by palm trees, and backed by a resort with a shiny blue pool and yellow parasols. The photos looked way too good to be true, but I did not say that. Aunty M would stay at home.

I pretended to love the idea, agreeing with the stupidity of reunion dinners. In a way Mama was right: our reunion dinner would be pretty lame. Mama was an only child and Dad's brother was far away and probably had no clue what a reunion dinner was anyway. Both my great-uncles had died before PoPo, and without her we had lost the link to their families. Would they even visit us for New Year if there was no PoPo? Would we visit them? I hadn't seen any of them since the funeral, and it was better not to risk disappointment.

I wondered whether Mama had planned it like that on purpose. It was what I did at school: better to pretend you didn't care so that after a while you could convince yourself you were fine on your own. Then again, perhaps Mama genuinely wanted to get away from it all, away from her pig boss and from Aunty M. And away from home, PoPo's absence would be less noticeable.

I wanted to cheer up Mama, that's why I asked her about the pineapple tarts. We had never had Chinese New Year without homemade pineapple tarts. PoPo wouldn't allow it. The taste of shop bought ones was unacceptable, she said, and experiences were better when you put in more effort. To my surprise, Mama agreed and sent Aunty M to the market to buy pineapples.

When I brought out my Hello Kitty notebook with the notes on PoPo's recipe Mama's eyes filled with tears she didn't try to hide. 'She made the best tarts, didn't she? I didn't know you had this, PoPo's own recipe.' She hugged me, and I could already taste the tarts.

When Aunty M came home with the pineapples, I thought Mama was going to flake and tell her to cut them up; but instead she asked her to take Chloe to the playground. 'Just me and my big girl,' she said, squeezing me in another hug. She hadn't hugged me this much in months. My plan was working.

Dad was out playing tennis with friends. He would be amazed if – no, *when* – we pulled this off. He loved pineapple tarts. Dad had been away a lot lately. I felt he needed a reason to be home more often. Perhaps good food would be the thing. And Chloe's first ever pineapple tart would be a proper one, not store bought. PoPo would have been pleased. She always said nothing conveyed love like a home cooked tart.

I opened the notebook. 'We need to clean the pineapple first.'

Mama picked up a pineapple, and turned it in her hands. I could see she already regretted sending out Aunty M. She pondered the fruit for a while, then took a big knife and started peeling it.

I read out my notes. 'Peel the pineapple then remove the seeds.' Pineapple seeds are on the outside and are a pain to get out.

Mama did not clean the pineapples by cutting a curling downward spiral along the sides, like PoPo and Aunty M did. She just hacked at the seeds, cutting away a lot of the flesh. I bit my lip.

'Then we need to shred it, very fine,' I added. 'PoPo used the big cleaver for that.'

Mama looked horrified. 'I remember that cleaver. She never let me touch it when I was little. Then all of a sudden I wasn't a real woman if I couldn't handle it. Well, you know, there's more to being a woman than handling big knives.'

She rummaged in a cabinet and dug out the blender. 'This is

the twenty-first century, Maya. No need to be stuck in the middle ages.'

I could hear PoPo breathing down my neck. *'Never grind a sambal in a blender, Maya, you kill the flavour.'* She would spend hours pounding spices on her flat stone pestle and mortar. She didn't kill the flavour, but it must have killed her back. Aunty M mixed her sambals in the blender, and they tasted fine to me.

I wasn't even sure if PoPo's old grinding stone was still there. Had Mama thrown it away with PoPo's clothes and other stuff? Only a few weeks after PoPo died I had come back from school to find her colourful things vanished, her room painted over in a pale pink with white furniture, a crib with dainty trellis bars in pride of place in the centre.

I looked over my notes again. They said nothing against the use of blenders in the case of pineapples, and I couldn't remember PoPo mentioning it. I wanted the tarts to be perfect, just like PoPo's. But I had to keep Mama in a good mood too, so I stayed quiet.

Mama chopped the pineapples into coarse cubes and blitzed them to a pulp in less than a minute. I remembered PoPo shredding patiently and figured the blender had its advantages. We put the pineapple pulp in a pot with sugar and brought it to the boil.

Mama rolled up her sleeves. 'One down. Now for the pastry. What does she say?' She took out the large mixing bowl and looked at me expectantly.

I referred to the notebook. 'Flour, four cups.'

'That's easy. Look, we have a cup measure.' She got a set of six plastic cups in different sizes out of the drawer and started measuring from the largest one. 'Three, four, done. Now what?'

I wasn't sure. PoPo had used an old teacup with roses to measure the flour. But that had disappeared too. So I read on: 'Butter. One pack of butter.'

'Pack of butter,' Mama muttered. 'What kind of measurement is that? What brand did she use?'

I couldn't remember. 'I don't know. It doesn't say.'

I had jotted down all sorts of comments, like 'use cool hands' and 'work fast' and 'can add spice to the jam. Clove, cinnamon.' I remembered what PoPo had said after that, the words I hadn't written down. 'But your mother likes them plain, so that's how I make them.'

'This is a pretty normal sized pack,' Mama said, chucking the butter in the middle of the flour. White clouds puffed up.

'Wait,' I yelled. 'We need to soften it first. To room temperature.'

Mama shrugged. Too late for that.

'Ok, never mind. Then, ten spoons of sugar.' I recited the rest of the ingredients from my list. 'Two eggs, two spoons of corn starch, but a different spoon, and a pinch of salt.'

'Thank you PoPo, for your clarity,' Mama said. 'What does she mean, different spoon? What kind of an instruction is that? Was the spoon for the corn starch bigger, or smaller?'

'I can't remember. Sorry.'

'My mother, seriously.' She took out a smaller spoon and measured out the corn starch.

Reading back, I suddenly realised we were supposed to have rubbed the butter and flour in to a crumbly mixture before adding the rest of the ingredients. I hoped it wouldn't matter.

'Now, we need to knead it, I think.' I said.

'You think? Or do you know? Read, Maya, don't think.'

I read out loud: 'Knead fast, a few times, to get rid of the crumbly bits.'

Mama looked at the bowl in despair. 'What crumbly bits? It's all still there. There's a big chunk of butter in a pile of flour.'

'Just knead, I think – I mean, I know. It says so.' I hoped I was right.

Mama started kneading, covering the kitchen in a thin layer of flour. 'How can I get this smooth fast? It's all lumpy and dry.'

This I could answer. 'It says here, if it's too dry, add some water.'

I added a couple of spoons of water and Mama kneaded on. 'Now it's very sticky,' she said. Her voice started to sound tired. 'Very sticky, Maya.'

She stopped kneading. 'Oh, seriously. Why on earth did I think we could do this? We need PoPo for this. Why...' Mama looked like she was going to cry again.

Because we can, I thought. *Because we have to if we want to honour PoPo's memory.* I read over my comments again, swallowing tears of disappointment, trying to make sense of PoPo's advice. Last year it had seemed so easy.

Mama stopped kneading and stood frozen over the bowl, eyes closed. Suddenly she started. 'What's that smell?'

I ran to the stove where an ominous smoke came from the pan with the pineapple. I turned off the gas and looked inside. The pineapple had turned golden. It looked lovely but smelled horrid.

I looked at the clock in the corner. 'We left it too long without stirring.'

Getting carried away with the pastry I'd forgotten the bold, underlined writing at the top. *Low heat. Stir the pineapple jam regularly.*

Mama looked at the clock too. 'Shit! I have a hairdresser's appointment in fifteen minutes. I'm going to be late. Fuck. Why did I even try this? I should have known better. I can't cook. Don't ask me again!'

She looked at me as if it was all my fault, as if I had purposely lured her away from what was really important for something as stupid as pineapple tarts; as if I were just a silly child. Mama could be very eloquent with her looks. And she had really taken up swearing recently. PoPo would have rubbed chilli on her mouth, but now no one did.

'I can't do this, not without PoPo,' she said, softer now. 'Please don't make me.'

She shook the sticky dough off her hands and scrubbed them in the sink. She didn't look at me again.

'I'll send Aunty M back from the playground on my way,' she yelled, taking her purse and slamming the door behind her. I stared at the closed door. Conjuring up PoPo to get the real Mama back had failed. Mama really had to quit that job; it was the only solution left.

I stood above the mixing bowl and tried to knead the sticky dough into a ball, like PoPo had. Tears wetted the dough even more. I shook in more flour, and kept kneading till I had something that could be rolled into a sticky ball, which I stuffed in the fridge. I washed my hands, ran to my room and played with the iPad under my covers. When I heard Aunty M come home and rummage in the kitchen, I ignored her.

A while later, she knocked on my door. 'Maya, come. I need your help.'

I tried not to respond – it wasn't as if she actually needed me – but after a while my curiosity got the better of me.

In the kitchen, Aunty M had scooped the pineapple jam onto a plate and set it to cool. It was thick and solid, like it was supposed to be. What had she done to it? It still smelt a bit smoky though. The pan stood soaking in the sink, black-crusted bottom and all.

She had rolled out my dough on the counter top and pointed at a round cookie cutter lying next to it. 'You make the circles, I'll spread the jam.'

I cut out circles and Aunty M laid small blobs of pineapple on top. We worked in silence until the baking tray was filled and the dough finished.

Aunty M popped the tarts in the oven and gave me the remaining balls of pineapple jam. 'Here, eat those, sayang. It will make you feel good.'

They tasted sweet, fragrant, fruity – and burnt.

Aunty M hadn't realised she'd said sayang again, but suddenly I felt I didn't mind that much. She could never replace my PoPo. But she could be my Aunty M.

When Mama and Dad came home, the tarts cooling on the rack made the whole house smell like Chinese New Year. Dad had a big smile.

'That's coming home. Can we eat them?'

PoPo always made us wait until the actual New Year, but we weren't going to be home for that, and neither Mama nor Aunty M said anything. But if Dad tasted the horrible flavour of the tarts, everything would be spoilt. 'No!' I yelled.

Dad paid no attention, grabbed one, and bit into it greedily.

'Almost as good as PoPo's,' he grinned. 'Just a bit smoky. And a bit salty. Did you make them?' he asked Mama, with a wink.

'No, they did,' she said, pointing at Aunty M and me. She went upstairs without tasting the tarts, and without berating Dad for not noticing her new haircut or the red rims around her eyes.

I ate a pineapple tart too. It tasted burnt and I had to drink a big glug of water to keep it down. Was this why most people these days bought their pineapple tarts, because they were no longer capable of conveying love? Couldn't you have an important career and bake pineapple tarts too? And if you couldn't, what made Mama pick the bank over the kitchen?

If I couldn't make Mama see sense and quit her job, I had better stay away from her.

12

Chinese New Year turned out surprisingly well. I had to admit Mama had a point: for a small, confused family like ours it could be good to let old traditions go. The important thing was to make new ones, and it seemed that instead of pineapple tarts, our new tradition involved Thai pineapple fried rice, served exotically in the hollowed out fruit. We had ordered it the first day and all of us, including Chloe, wolfed it down. After that, we had it every day.

The resort was as good as promised, and Mama and Dad acted normally most of the time. We were us again, an average family of four. Only once did things threaten to go wrong. Chloe had wanted Mama to build a sand castle for the umpteenth time, but seconds after Mama had made it, she smashed it and decided she preferred to swim instead. Or no, actually, another ice cream. Then she started pulling Mama's hair when she couldn't get one.

Mama *growled*.

She had begun doing this weird thing when she got really mad; she started to act like a monster, like she'd been taken over from the inside by another creature and the real Mama had disappeared. Her voice changed, her face got distorted, and her mind seemed to leave her body with the screams. I called it the

Mamamonster. It was scary when it happened, but after, when I looked back and thought of her bulging eyes and imagined clouds of red smoke coming out of her ears, it was quite funny.

This time, Mama realised all the other guests were staring, so she swallowed down the monster and muttered under her breath that she'd been stupid to leave Aunty M at home. But I loved it being just the four of us. Apart from that one incident, it felt like we were a family that could cope without PoPo. PoPo wouldn't have liked it there anyway.

There were plenty of children at the pool and beach and we all played together – tag and ball and the sort of games that no one can explain but all the kids understand anyway. Life was easy. At breakfast Mama, Dad and I debated the important decisions of the day. Swim at the pool or the beach? Have lunch at the restaurant or beach bar? Go back to the buffet for more eggs or stay where we were? There was a guy that would do your eggs any way you liked them. I loved that guy. For a few days I had fun, but then I started dreading the inevitable return home. I could see Mama felt the same. The shadow of the monster was behind her eyes again.

On the plane back I felt like a snail slowly retreating into its shell. I pushed all the wonderful tastes and smells and feelings of the holiday down into my stomach: the pineapple rice, the fruit juices in the pool bar, the chargrilled jumbo prawns. I hoped I could preserve them there as long as possible, and that they could keep the nasty, bitter cockroach flavour in check. But as soon as the plane wheels hit the Changi concrete, it crept its way up. The bus would be there the next morning, eight o'clock sharp.

When we came home Chloe rushed straight into Aunty M's arms. 'Auny M, Auny M!' Aunty M picked her up and hugged her tight. 'Can I put her to bed, ma'am?' she asked Mama. She stuck her nose in Chloe's hair, breathing in her scent.

Mama nodded and started to unpack.

I followed Aunty M to the bathroom, and while Chloe was in the tub I asked her for news of Sri. She'd had surgery before we left but had still been in the hospital. The fracture had been more complicated than they'd first thought.

'Is she still in hospital?' I asked.

'No, her leg is much better. She can walk, but only slow.'

'So where is she? Did they send her back to her employer? ' I hoped not. She might jump again. 'Or did she go to Indonesia?'

'No, sayang, she is staying at a shelter. They are helping her.'

Who is helping? I thought. *Weren't we doing that?* I felt a stab of anger.

'The police said Sri cannot leave Singapore as they need to investigate. She can't go back to the employer either. They gave her a special pass so she can stay but cannot work.'

'What do you mean, a shelter? Is she in the forest?'

I pictured a piece of tarpaulin stretched over rope somewhere in the wood, like when we'd built a shelter once at summer camp.

'In the forest? No, what do you mean? The shelter is a house. There are many women staying there, all domestic helpers, all being investigated.'

'Were they all hit by their employers?' I gasped.

Aunty M laughed. 'No, not all. But they all ran away. The people at the shelter, they help them. They have a helpdesk. I'm going to work there too.'

Her words tightened my throat. No, no, no. Aunty M worked here, with us. Chloe loved her. Mama and Dad needed her. I was almost used to her. Then I felt relief. She was not allowed to quit, not for two years. All of a sudden that seemed a lot less unfair. I was sure Mama wouldn't let her go.

'You can't go!' I blurted out. 'Chloe would miss you too much.'

Aunty M laughed, and hugged me. 'Sayang, I'm not going anywhere. I'm staying with you. I'm just going to help them on Sundays. Other maids come there for advice. They gave me training. I can help people like Sri.'

I was relieved and annoyed at the same time. We'd helped Sri together. I didn't want to be left out like a small child. Whatever Mama said, helping made me feel good. Besides, Mama needn't know. It was obvious Aunty M saw that too.

'What about me? I want to help as well.'

'I'm sure we can find a way.' Aunty M lifted Chloe out of the tub. 'I'll tell you all about it tomorrow. Now, I need to put Chloe to bed. It's late. You have a bath too. The water is still warm.'

The next day at school I didn't understand why things were so different to the way they'd been in Thailand. At the resort I'd played with other kids, kids who seemed to think I was normal and fun to be with. Here, I was back to being nobody. I decided that *nobody* was not required to do her best in class. I just sat there waiting for the time to pass so I could go back and ask Aunty M about that helpdesk.

But on the bus home, I suddenly ceased being nobody.

'Hey, Cockroach,' shouted Jenny when I slung my backpack on the back row. 'You look nice and tanned. You're starting to look more like a real cockroach every day, with a brown face like that.' The holiday had given me a healthy blush. 'Did you go partying with the other cockroaches for New Year? In the sewers, heh heh. Must have been fun, to spend some time with your own kind?'

Yes, it was actually, I thought.

Then some big guy from secondary butted in. 'Hey, you know what a female cockroach is called?'

'No,' Meena said, looking straight at me. 'Tell us.'

'A cuntroach!' the guy hollered.

Jenny and Meena folded double in their seats. 'Seriously, I'm wetting myself! Maya is a cuntroach. Hilarious,' Meena hiccupped.

They all loved it, even the little ones who didn't get the joke. I wasn't sure I got it myself. But the laughing was contagious. I might even have joined in myself if the joke hadn't tied my windpipe in a knot. If I'd been able to laugh too, would I have become one of them?

The laughing subsided until another kid, a boy in the year above me, added, 'I killed a cockroach yesterday. So sorry Maya. It might have been your uncle.'

By now the whole bus was in fits. 'Don't kill too many,' Jenny said. 'Maya will starve as she'll have nothing to eat.'

Laugher roared again. I wanted to disappear, but there was nowhere to hide in the bus, not even a toilet.

'Do you know,' the boy went on, 'I heard cockroaches can survive a nuclear blast. So after a blast, when everything else is dead, the shitty buggers still crawl out of every hole.'

I huddled down in my seat, trying to ignore them whilst they threw cockroach jokes back and forth. I wished I had a switch in my mind that I could just flip, so all the sound was gone. Then they could say what they wanted and I would be nobody again.

I wondered whether it was true, whether cockroaches really could survive a nuclear blast.

When I got home, Aunty M asked whether I was ok. 'You look pale,' she said. 'Are you tired?'

What was I, brown or pale?

'I'm fine,' I answered, pulling myself together. I needed something else to think about, something to distract me from the cockroach inside me. 'Tell me about the helpdesk. And the shelter.'

Aunty M sat across from me at the table and pushed a glass of Ribena my way. 'I saw them at the hospital. They came to pick up Sri. She could leave the hospital but she had nowhere to go. She cannot leave Singapore, as the police are still investigating. They say if she was beaten, it's a criminal offence. But they need to prove it first.' She raised her hands. 'But who jumps off a sixth floor balcony for fun?'

I nodded in agreement.

'The police called the shelter. I'm not allowed to visit, but the officers also got Sri's phone back.'

'Had the employer stolen her phone?'

Aunty M laughed. 'Stolen, ha! Taken away for safekeeping so that Sri could focus on her work. At first she was allowed to use it one hour every Sunday, but later they never gave anymore. Remember how we gave her my phone to call her family?'

I remembered how Sri had cried on the phone. 'But now you can call her?'

'Yes. They even have wifi so we just whatsapp. And as soon as Sri is well enough to go out, I can meet her. And I'll go to the helpdesk again too. I went last week to have training. I learned about the rights of the domestic worker and the employer. You know, you can complain to the MOM if you are not happy with the way they treat you.'

'What's MOM?' I asked.

'The Ministry of Manpower. They issue the work pass, and they have rules that employers have to stick to.'

This sounded much more interesting than maths and the iPad. In any case, a nobody like me didn't have to do her homework.

'So, we need to let all the domestic workers know that they can complain to this MOM?' I asked.

'Yes. But they need to be careful. You need to have a serious complaint and be able to prove it to MOM. Running away will make an employer angry. The employer can send you back to your own country.'

I was starting to get this. 'And they don't want that, because of the deductions.'

Aunty M nodded. 'Exactly. Well, some do want to go home, but others want a transfer instead.'

I was learning a lot here. 'What do you mean, transfer?'

'To quit and change jobs, get a new employer.'

'But you said before that quitting isn't allowed for maids, right?'

'Correct. Normally, you can't, but you can if MOM or the employer says you can. So you need to prove to MOM that your employer did not stick to their rules. Or make sure your employer likes you, so they will allow the transfer.'

'Why wouldn't they allow a transfer?'

'I don't know.' Aunty M considered for a while. 'I think, some prefer to send her home, to protect other employers from a bad maid. Or they want to keep her, because they have invested a lot in the maid. The agency fee. And time and energy to train her.'

Investing, that word I knew. Mama had tried to teach me about it once. 'You need to realise how important it is as a woman to provide your own bread and butter,' she'd said, and when she'd lent Jenny and me money to buy limes for our very own lime juice stand by the playground, she'd insisted we pay her back with interest. Mama had taken more than she'd given us, and the word 'investment' acquired a citrusy, sour taste.

Now I savoured that flavour again. It was turning from acid to acrid.

Was this the same problem the aunties were having? Could the employers keep the aunty until the interest had been paid? I felt a light switch on in my mind. The deductions! Were they the interest? But after the deductions had finished, they still couldn't leave. There was also the contract. It was all so complicated

The aunties couldn't leave because of the deductions, and

the employers would keep them because of the investment. I was almost there. But aunties weren't limes.

'How can the employers keep them?' I asked. 'Aunties aren't things!'

Aunty M laughed. 'No, we are not. But still, some employers feel that way. They call themselves owner, not employer. Because they paid good money.'

'But I thought the maid paid the agency? The deductions.' I really didn't get this.

Aunty M looked pensive. 'Yes, they do. I don't know.'

We were quiet for a bit. Then I said, 'Will Sri be allowed a transfer now?'

'I hope so. But they say it can take very long for the police to investigate. A judge needs to decide if Ah Mah is guilty, and the son and daughter-in-law who locked her in. They say it can take years. And Ah Mah is very old. Maybe her brain is no longer good.'

'Years? But isn't it obvious? They have the pictures of the bruises. Why should it take so long?'

Aunty M sighed. 'I don't know. That's just the way it is, they said.'

'And what will Sri do in the meantime?' I asked.

'She can stay in the shelter while she waits. She has no money to send to her family now.'

'And who pays for the hospital? The shelter people?'

'No,' Aunty M said, 'they don't have a lot. She has medical insurance. The employer got that for her. But the insurance people they say they won't pay because it is her own fault. She put herself in danger by climbing out that window. Legally, the employer is responsible for the medical costs.'

Aunty M gave a knowing smile. 'The hospital is expensive.'

Watching Aunty M smile now, I realised something had changed. It was not that she smiled less often, or that her smiles were more sincere; but they were different in a way I couldn't describe. It seemed that that was *more* to her now, and the only way she could show her new powers was with those tiny muscles around her lips and the determination in her eyes.

I don't think Mama or Dad noticed. Neither did they notice the invisible thread that connected Aunty M and me since we had started helping Sri.

13

After that first day with its nuclear bus ride home, the rest of the week at school was slightly better. But still I had a nervous knot in my windpipe. What if they started again? At school there were escape routes. I could move around, hoping people wouldn't notice me. I could read in the library, or spend forever in the toilet. But on the bus it was them and me in a space that was much too small.

Every afternoon I hoped something exciting would happen, that the helpdesk would call Aunty M and we'd have to rush out to save someone. But Aunty M said that wasn't the way it worked. She was just there on Sunday to help and advise people, and during the week they had staff to rescue women and help those who were staying in the shelter. Besides, she had her own job to do.

'But if you really want to help, I have an idea. Do you remember Win?'

Oh no, Win! I had forgotten all about her. No wonder I had no friends. 'Yes. Win. Of course. From Myanmar.'

'She needs to learn English. Maybe you can help? Her employer is always back late, she is alone in the afternoon. She finish her work by then. You can visit and talk to her.'

That evening I dug out some easy reading books and put them on my desk. There was a tingle in my tummy. Would I manage to make a new friend? The next day at school passed even more slowly than usual. I wanted to make this work but was worried I'd screw it up again, like with Sri. What if I was doomed to be a horrible friend? And what if Jenny and the others found out that I was friends with an aunty? I had to hope for the best.

Finally I was home and could take out my books and visit Win. I had a drink and snack, shouted to Aunty M that I was leaving, and rushed over there. I remembered reading somewhere that if you smiled you'd automatically feel better, so I curled up the sides of my lips like Aunty M always did, and rang the doorbell.

When Win opened the door she didn't seem surprised to see me. Aunty M must have told her I was coming. She smiled, and I stared at her. Her face was painted with swirls of a yellowish creamy stuff, like she was ready to go on the warpath but in a friendly way. She smiled all the way to the dining table, where she had set out drinks and biscuits for me.

I thanked her and sat down, pulling out the books I had brought and a notebook.

'What do you have on your face?' I asked Win, pointing at the swirls. 'Your face, what is it?'

Win grinned. 'Thanaka,' she said.

'Thanaka?' I asked. 'What is it?'

'Thanaka good,' she said.

It was as if a face painter had used a crude brush to decorate her face. 'Is it like a face mask?' I asked. 'Good for your skin?'

If that was it, wouldn't she have covered her whole face, like

Mama did?

Win nodded, 'Good skin,' she repeated. 'Feel good.'

'Is it cream?'

'No, no, thanaka,' Win replied.

On a blank page of my notebook she drew a tree. I looked at her, not understanding. How did Aunty M communicate with her? She must have told Win I was coming. Did she manage all that via whatsapp, or had she seen her this morning when I was at school? And how could I teach her anything if I couldn't explain things?

I looked at the picture of the tree again. It had curly branches and three round leaves. 'What has the tree to do with the stuff on your face?' I repeated the last word. 'Face? Why?'

Win got up and left though the kitchen. A minute later she came back with a piece of wood, a stone and a dish. She rubbed the wood over the stone, grinding the bark into a soft powder in the dish. Then she added a few drops of water, and swirled it into a paste.

'You?' she asked.

She pointed at my face. Did she want to put the stuff on me? Lesson number one, I decided, would be body parts.

I nodded. 'Do my cheeks first,' I said, pointing at the appropriate bits.

With her fingers she made what felt like two large circles on the side of my face. 'Cheeks,' she repeated.

The paste felt cool and soft. 'And now the nose.' I pointed again.

Win giggled. 'Nose,' she said after me, 'Thanaka nose.'

She put her finger in the paste again and smeared it in a long line from the bridge of my nose down to the tip. She ended with a dot. 'Nose.'

It tickled.

I pointed at her nose. 'Your nose.' And mine again. 'My nose. Now do your nose.'

She draw a line on her own nose. 'Your nose,' she said.

'No, no, when you say it, it should be my nose,' I corrected her.

After a few more attempts she got it. Up next was the forehead, then the chin. When we got to the ears we both giggled, unsure if we should put the paste there too. Win shook her head, so we carried on without. We visited all the body parts down to our toes and back up again, repeating, testing, until she knew them all.

When we were done, Win got a tissue and removed the paste from my forehead, chin and nose, leaving just the two circles on my cheeks.

I left the books with her. She stared at them for a while, until I realised she didn't know our alphabet. I wrote it out for her in the notebook. I told her to practise by copying the letters. I mouthed the sound of each one to her, and she repeated it back to me.

'Just practise on your own,' I said. 'I'll be back.'

When I got home, Mama was already there. I didn't understand why she was looking at me strangely until she pointed at my painted cheeks. 'What's that?'

I'd forgotten the paste was still there. I had to recover quickly. 'Oh, that. Jenny has an aunty from Myanmar. They put that on their faces, like a beauty mask. It's made from tree bark.'

None of that was a lie. Jenny had an aunty from Myanmar. Her name was Moe Moe and her English was only slightly better than Win's. Jenny called her stupid. Mama looked amused, and before she could say anything else I left for my room. On the way I passed Aunty M, who stood there looking at me with her lips pursed. I smiled at her and realised that my afternoon with Win had made me feel happy. I wouldn't let a white lie to Mama spoil that.

Win always had snacks when I dropped by – iced gem biscuits, ginger snaps, and on some days even home baked chocolate chip cookies – none of which she touched herself. It was as if my presence was her treat, one that she savoured. Slowly, Win started to pick up some English, and we were able to have simple conversations, more signs than words. Every time I left she hugged me and thanked me profusely, more than I felt comfortable with as I had done so little. Win had blossomed just by being my friend, and that made me feel good too. I was starting to think that Mama must be wrong, about helping and interfering making someone's life worse. But I would not risk telling Mama this.

Helping wasn't all pink puffy clouds anyway. From her helpdesk, Aunty M had dark stories that nibbled at my happiness: stories of maids that had their hair cut off against their will, who got only a few hours of sleep every night, who had no breaks, or got treated worse than the dog. One had to look after sixty cats in her employer's house. Another had an employer that punished her for mistakes by dipping her hands in bleach. They were stories of loneliness and sometimes cruelty. Most wouldn't make the front page – many maids who approached the helpdesk were merely shouted at, overworked, or so homesick they wanted nothing more than to go back to their own country.

The heroines of Aunty M's helpdesk stories were at the mercy of their employers, who, in my mind, took the shape of evil kings and stepmothers, like those in the fairy tales PoPo had sometimes read to me. Aunty M's maids became modern day Cinderellas, forced to clean all day but never allowed to go to the ball, or Snow Whites, made to drudge first, then sent away to foreign shores when the employer-stepmother felt unsatisfied or threatened.

Listening in on their playground talk had shown me how these women, living in a faraway land, would fantasise about romance with men from this different world. They were just like the little mermaid, hoping for men who would sweep them off their fins, give them legs, and take them to live happily ever after. I too wanted to live a fairy tale life. Were my own problems horrible enough for me to deserve a happy ending?

In reality, not many of Aunty M's stories ended that way. Neither had many of Grimm's or Andersen's, for that matter – but I still believed in the Disney version of the world, even if my daily examples showed that real life wasn't like that.

The more Aunty M went to the helpdesk, the more she learned, and in turn she told me about the laws in my own country. MOM had rules to protect domestic workers, but the problem was, the workers didn't know about them. How could someone who wasn't allowed to leave the house go to MOM to complain about their treatment?

By now I understood what a contract was. The problem was, said Aunty M, if you didn't know much English, how could you know what was in it? And because of the deductions, not signing the contract wasn't an option.

I sat and listened to Aunty M, amazed to learn all this, and amazed at Aunty M too. She did all her helpdesk work and still looked after me and Chloe. The house was clean and the food was good, all of which kept the Mamamonster at bay. Aunty M obviously loved Chloe, but how did she feel about me? I wanted to love her, but not if she couldn't love me back. And not if she would leave me again one day. So I had to keep her at arm's length, always making sure I didn't care too much.

Aunty M loved teaching me things: about the helpdesk, the cases, cooking. She would look at me with all her different smiles, many of which I didn't understand at all. Sometimes when she smiled at me, her eyes were full of sadness. When I had a new dress, or did something special at school and rushed over to tell her first, before Mama came home, she was never as proud as I'd expected her to be. She would nod and say, 'Well done, Maya. Why don't you show your mother tonight?' And she would do that smile.

I did my best to be good and help her with her cases. Learning about the domestic workers, I couldn't help wondering whether other people knew how they were treated. Not other kids, of course, but grownups like my parents and their friends. I absorbed all that Aunty M told me, and mulled it over. If I couldn't be Prince Charming on the white horse, at least I could be one of the dwarves in the wood that offered food, friendship and advice. But how?

People started to seek out Aunty M for help. We noticed it first at the playground. All of a sudden everyone had a friend or cousin, an old neighbour or aunt, who had a problem. Aunty M made a note of them all and handed out her number. I was always there – after all, I didn't have much else to do. But I craved to do more than just sit and listen.

14

One day, Aunty M took me to meet a friend of a friend of Mary Grace's, who lived just opposite our condo in a landed house with a small garden. Bella was a large, pretty girl. She cried when she saw us, smiling through her tears.

'You are Mary Grace's friend? You can help me?'

We sat at the back of the house on a small concrete stoop. In front of us drying clothes flapped on washing lines in the breeze of a standing fan. Chloe toddled underneath them, catching drips of water in her outstretched fingers. I wasn't sure whether I was supposed to say or do anything, so I kept silent.

Aunty M pointed at the washing. 'It will dry fast, outside like this.'

Bella said, 'If it doesn't rain. Always, when I put the laundry, it rains. Five people in the house, plus me. So many laundries.'

She held up her hands for Aunty M to see. I couldn't really see from where I was sitting, but I didn't dare say anything. 'This is my problem. The laundry,' Bella said.

Now she turned to me and I saw her hands. They were red and blistered. Bits of skin flaked off around her nails. 'The laundry hurts my hands. I cannot take it anymore.'

Aunty M took Bella's hand in hers and tracked the palm

with the tip of her finger. 'Why?' she asked. 'You have a washing machine right? Why does it hurt your hands?'

Bella shrugged. 'My ma'am, she says I am stupid. Every day she says this. And that I am lazy. She does not want me to use the machine because I am too stupid. The last maid broke the machine. I need to do the laundry by hand to spare the machine. And to spare the clothes. Only sheets and towels can go in the machine, ma'am will turn it on herself. But even if only clothes, it's five people. So much. That's why my hands hurt. I am not lazy. I am tired, all the time. I start at five, because so much to do. A big house. All the washing. Ma'am works different shifts. And the kids make everything dirty. And they always eat. Always hungry.'

'What does your ma'am do, that she works shifts?' Aunty M asked.

'She is a nurse. I showed her my hands, she gave me this cream.' Bella disappeared inside and returned with a small pink tube. 'But it does not work. When I do the washing or cleaning, it comes off. I asked for a doctor, but she says no need, she is a nurse. Doctor is too much money.'

'Wah,' said Aunty M, 'Such a big house, and no money for a doctor?'

Bella shook her head. 'Always they pay my salary late. Maybe they have no money? I don't know.'

Aunty M took a moment to answer. I tried to take advantage of the pause but I didn't know what to say.

'Did they ever not pay your salary?' asked Aunty M. 'You know, you can complain to MOM if they don't pay you.'

'No,' Bella shook her head again. 'They always pay late, but they pay.'

'And what about the food?'

I thought Bella looked pretty well fed.

'The food is good, but many times not enough. Three boys, big boys already, they eat so much. Not enough is left for me. I eat after they finish.

'I always work, work, work. And still they call me lazy. And stupid. Always shouting at me, *stupid, stupid*. What can I do? We are here to work, and I am trying my best to do all my tasks in the house. But I am also a human being. How difficult the work is, still I force myself to do it. But how come my employers feel it is all not enough, my hardship? Why do they still scold me?'

Aunty M nodded. 'For some people, it is never enough. Other employers are better. Did you ask for a transfer?'

'Yes,' said Bella. 'I asked, but they said I have to finish my contract. One more year. I don't want to. What can I do? Can I complain?'

'I am not sure,' Aunty M said. 'The washing by hand, there is no rule that says it is not allowed. Any safety issues? Do they make you clean the windows upstairs? You might get hurt.'

'Yes, they do!' Bella jumped up. 'Can I complain? Will it help me to transfer?'

I had surprised myself by jumping up too. Embarrassed, I sat down again.

'I don't know,' said Aunty M, 'Maybe. MOM takes safety very seriously since some maid fell and died. You are not allowed to clean windows without grilles.'

Bella pointed to the windows at the top floor. 'Look, the

third floor, very high. Sometimes, I stand on that ledge to clean better. My employer says, "Just be careful, don't fall, don't give me trouble." It is not allowed?'

'No, it's not allowed, said Aunty M, 'but that does not mean MOM will give you the transfer. Better you call the helpdesk for advice.' She handed Bella a piece of paper with a phone number on it.

'What if I run away? Will they help me?'

'Yes, they will help you. But it is better to ask your agency to help. Don't make your employer angry.'

'Ok,' said Bella.

'You can also come on Sunday, if you don't want to call.'

'I don't have Sundays off,' said Bella.

'Then call,' said Aunty M. 'We need to go home now.'

We didn't speak much on the way home. When we were almost there, Aunty M asked me what I thought. I was full of questions about what had happened, but there were too many in my head for one to come out of my mouth. When I spoke it was about how I felt.

'I didn't do anything,' I said.

Aunty M smiled. 'That is ok. This was your first case. You need to learn. You learn by shadowing me, the more experienced one. That is how we do it.'

I marvelled at how fast she'd become the expert. To follow her example, I would need to let her teach me.

Aunty M sighed. 'Poor Bella. Many girls like her. It's too much.'

Too much what? I wanted to ask; but Aunty M was busy stopping Chloe from climbing out of the stroller.

The following week Aunty M heard that Bella had run away after all. When she first showed up at the shelter, she slept for two days straight. Bella had then gone to MOM to complain about the hand washing, showing her rough, chapped hands to the officer in charge, pleading with him to give her a transfer. She brought up the window cleaning too, as Aunty M had suggested. They took the case, and told Bella to wait. When the employer found out Bella had gone to MOM, they got scared, and said that if Bella would drop the charges, they would allow the transfer. But by the time the agency passed on the message to Bella it was too late. The complaint had been filed and could not be cancelled. All anyone could do was wait and see what MOM would rule.

It was my first real case, if I didn't count Sri, and it left me confused. This employer, what was she thinking? I realised I needed to see more, more cases, in order to be able to process this properly. But I was starting to see one thing already: the domestic workers were left to the mercy of others. They had to put their faith in either their employers or MOM.

As for me, I had my own dilemma. The bus rides hadn't improved, and I dreaded the twice daily test of endurance. The key question was whether my parents would, or could, help me. Just like the domestic workers were afraid to go to MOM in case it backfired, I didn't go to my parents. And where the workers had the helpdesk to advise them, I didn't think to confide in Aunty M. She must have suspected what was going on, but she never mentioned it. We both wanted that distance between us to protect us from getting too attached.

Aunty M got more requests for advice like Bella's. She sometimes went out in the mornings, taking Chloe in the stroller. If she went to see someone in the afternoon she would let me join them. Other afternoons I'd go and see Win. I happily neglected my homework. As a nobody, I wasn't bothered about my own future.

Win told me about life in Myanmar – or Burma as she called it – about her father who was a farmer, and about the rain that had been so much one year that all the rice drowned. That was why she'd come to work in Singapore, to help the family to eat. Her stories made me curious about Aunty M's life. I knew she was from Java, Indonesia, but that was all. One day when she was cooking soto ayam, an Indonesian chicken soup, I hung around in the kitchen.

'Aunty M?'

'Yes, sayang. What is it?'

'Can you tell me about your hometown? What is it like?'

'Sure. What do you want to know?'

'Everything!'

'Everything?' she laughed. 'Where to start?'

'At the beginning?' I offered.

'I come from a village near Salatiga, central Java. It's beautiful. Green rice fields as far as you can see. And there is a lake that is like a mirror. A big fire mountain hangs over the lake. You can see it two times, in the water and above. Gunung Merapi.

Sometimes it spits flames and hot ash. You know why they made the mountain?'

What did she mean? Could you make a mountain? 'No, why? And how?'

'The island of Java is very big. Much bigger than Singapore. In the beginning, it was not balanced. It wobbled.' Aunty M demonstrated with a ladle full of stock. 'There was only a mountain on one side. So the gods, they decided they needed a new mountain in the middle. They wanted to move a mountain from the sea to Java. But where they wanted to put it, there were two – how do you call that? – iron-makers.'

'Blacksmiths?' I said.

'Yes. So, the iron-makers were making a keris, a magic knife, in a big fire. These men did not want to move for the mountain and they got angry. The gods got angry too, and then they put the mountain on top of the iron-making fire. So now it's a fire mountain. Sometimes the spirits of Rama and Permadi, the iron-makers, they get angry and the mountain bursts out in flames. So we need to keep the spirits happy.'

The smell of spicy boiling chicken was filling the kitchen. My stomach rumbled. 'How do you keep a volcano spirit happy?'

'Food. Every year the people offer from the kraton, the palace in Jogja where the sultan lives. The sultan rules the land, the spirits rule the volcano. Everyone climbs up the mountain and throws food into the crater, for the spirits.'

Wow. The island of Singapore did not wobble. Everything was clean and organised. Not a blade of grass was out of place. Lakes in Singapore were ponds, or reservoirs filled with water we had to drink and were not allowed to play in. The only thing towering above the land were the stacks and stacks of apartment blocks and high-rise condos. I loved Aunty M's land of fiery mountains, sultans and spirits. It was like PoPo's Singapore of old, colourful and exciting. Now that Singapore was buried under slabs of grey concrete. No looming danger of a fire mountain, just the fear of failing a school test. A fire mountain was so much cooler.

'Does it ever erupt?'

'Yes, a few years ago. Many people died. My village was evacuated. Afterwards, everything was covered in dust.'

Ok, not so cool. 'No way! Was it very scary?'

'I was here, I just saw it on the news. It was a long time before I could speak to my family, no hand phones then. But my village is not very close to the mountain. I was sure they were ok.'

Aunty M looked less sure. Even years later I could see the leftover worry in her eyes. What was better – safe and boring, or the excitement that came with fear?

'And your family, what do they do?

'Do? What do you mean?'

'I mean,' I said, 'what sort of work? How do they make a living? Like your dad. Your mother.'

'Ah. That. My mother does a lot. Get fire wood, work the garden, tend to the chicken, the tapioca. Sometimes she sells some produce at the market. My father does not have a job. He has a bad leg. Before, he would try to find work every week. Sometimes in the sugarcane factory. Sometimes on a paddy field. We have some land too, we grow rice. But now my father can't work it. So we rent out the land, others plant it. But it is not enough money.

That is why I came to Singapore.'

It was always about the money. The investment. The deductions. Why did people need so much money?

'And what about your husband? I mean, the father of your kids. Doesn't he help?'

Aunty M laughed heartily and the whole story gushed out. Her husband was unemployed, a good-for-nothing. Unhappy with both his life and his wife, he had left home and hadn't been heard of for a long time. A year later they got divorced. Aunty M said he had remarried, and wasn't interested in his children. She had heard rumours he had a new baby.

'And your kids? How does that make them feel?'

Aunty M started stirring the soup vigorously. 'I don't know. It has been a while since I spoke to them. Especially Nurul. She is angry with me.'

I wanted to ask more but she kept her back turned to me as she hacked at an onion. 'Don't you have homework?' she said.

15

I'd started to forget about school. I still went, of course, every day. What I mean is that I'd stopped thinking about it. Nobody spoke to me, and in class I did the bare minimum to make sure the teachers didn't notice me either. Recess was the worst. For someone without friends, it lasted forever. Often I would hang around the library reading, or if I was fast enough, I could snatch a spot at one of the computers. My mind was never at school. As for the bus rides, the other kids had got tired of the cockroach jokes and had gone back to ignoring me.

I didn't care, I was excited to go home. I had a secret life.

One Saturday, Aunty M took me to see Sri in a park near the shelter. When I saw her, I ran to her and we hugged. We'd seen each other often when she was still in our condo, but had rarely spoken or touched. The metal grille and her lack of English had been physical barriers, my distrust of Aunty M a barrier in my head – they had all prevented me from really connecting with Sri. But that day when we found her on the ledge had changed everything. Sri's eyes had seemed empty to me then, but she cried when she looked at me now. Her English had improved, and with Aunty M's help we managed to chat. Aunty M seemed to know more about Sri's case than Sri herself. Did Sri understand what was happening to her?

'Will the police throw Ah Mah into jail?' I asked.

Sri shrugged, and Aunty M answered for her. 'The police are still investigating. They will hopefully decide soon whether they will press charges. Not just against Ah Mah, but the daughter too.'

'But it's been months!' I cried.

'Police very slow,' said Sri. 'Need to collect evidence. I had to do polygraph test last week.'

'How did it go?' asked Aunty M.

'I don't know. I very nervous. They said, practise first. They ask these questions, but even with translator, so difficult. They say, no worry, stay calm. Just say yes or no. Maybe I did wrong?'

Aunty M shook her head. 'You cannot do it wrong, as long as you told the truth.'

I added, 'That's why it's a lie detector test. If you tell the truth, you pass.'

I didn't actually know this for sure, but it sounded right. With Sri it was easier to say something than it had been with Bella. After what we'd been through together I felt part of her case, and the way Sri had hugged me back showed me she felt the same.

Sri still looked nervous. 'But, if me not sure which one truth, yes or no? Is that a lie?'

None of us knew. 'I think the photographs of your arms and face don't lie, and the doctor's report,' said Aunty M. 'They should be enough, right?'

Sri shrugged again. 'I want go home. I want drop charges. How can, Merpati? If I tell lie, that Ah Mah never did bad thing to me, can I go home?'

Aunty M shook her head. 'You can't now. You have to wait for the police to decide whether they will move on with the case. It is them against the employers. You are just the witness.'

'I don't want!' said Sri. 'Annaliza, in the shelter, you know. Same same case, also employer beat her. She already in shelter three years! I don't want to stay in Singapore three years. I need money. In shelter, I no money. I better go home Indonesia.'

Aunty M looked at Sri. 'You don't have a choice anymore. It is in the hands of the police. I thought you liked the shelter? The other women, the activities? Look at you talking English to Maya. You learned that already there.'

Sri told us about English classes and yoga lessons, but also bedbugs and bickering women. I was so curious about this place, but visitors were not allowed. Even Aunty M had never been.

It was nice to see Sri again, and to see how she had changed. Not only did she speak English, her face was full and healthy again. She was still nervous, moody, and insecure about her case – but she was different. It was like she was a real person now, no longer a vague character in a fairy tale. Before I had thought of her as poor Sri, poor victim, someone that needed helping. Now she had a personality of her own, and it wasn't just her improved English that had made the difference. I wondered whether Sri would grow even more if she left the shelter, went home to Indonesia.

As the aunties became more and more real people to me – much more real than Jenny, Meena or the bland kids at school – my interest in them grew. At the playground, there were always friends and acquaintances of the aunties needing counsel. Slowly

I started to feel I could contribute during our visits.

Julia lived on one of the highest floors of our condo. We didn't know her, as she was not a playground aunty – the children in her family were at secondary school. But she was a dog walker, and Mary Grace knew her. All the dog walkers got together in the morning by the benches. Mary Grace didn't even have a dog but she often joined them, joking she needed the exercise.

I started to notice that life was easier for the aunties that had a dog or small children to look after. They came out to walk the dogs and supervise the children playing, so they made friends quickly. Friends for gossip and boyfriend chat. The ones that had to stay inside all day, like Win and Sri, were lonelier. Maybe the work was lighter, but they couldn't go out. Some went to the market to shop. Others never went anywhere.

Mary Grace took us upstairs to meet Julia. The three aunties talked, first about Bella. The big news was that MOM had agreed with her complaint. The employers had received a warning, and Bella was allowed to transfer.

But after that, they started talking about the same boring stuff they talked about in the playground. I got impatient and pulled Aunty M's arm. Julia noticed me and suddenly pulled her shirt up and her shorts down to show us the reason she needed us. The skin on her torso had stretches of dark brown, almost black, with red and purple pimples. In places, it was broken and scabbed. Julia told us the rash covered her private parts, and hurt most when she used the toilet.

The horror of it shocked away my shyness. 'Have you seen a doctor?' I asked. I knew from Aunty M that the employer had to send her there and pay for her treatment. But Julia said her employers didn't believe in medicine.

'Don't believe in medicine?' Aunty M asked.

'Not modern medicine,' Julia said. 'They have their own.'

Julia's employers apparently didn't believe in medicine for themselves either. Their three teenage sons had never seen a doctor unless their school required them to, but then they just went to get the necessary certificates and flushed any medicine down the toilet.

'But what do they believe in?' I asked.

'Nan yan,' Julia said, but none of us had heard of it. Julia wasn't even sure how it was spelled.

'They go this place, with other people, where they worship together. This lady supplies them with a holy water that is a cure for everything. Like magic.'

Every day, she told us, Julia had to sprinkle the house with the liquid. She showed us the bottles standing outside the kitchen. She also had to put stickers on the mains water pipe so that all the water would be infused with the power of light, impregnated with holiness.

As a cure for the rash, Julia had to bathe in a special basin filled with water, salt, and some of the holy water. She had to drink the holy water too.

'It tastes just like water. Do you want to try?' We shook our heads.

Once, when she had started to lose her hair, the employer had taken Julia to see a regular doctor. The doctor had said it was stress, that the hair would grow back, and she was prescribed some cream for the rash. Julia was allowed to keep the cream, but it was a very small tube. The rash spread.

'What about your medical check?' asked Mary Grace. 'You need to have it every six months? If you skip it, MOM will complain to your employer.'

'I always go, but the last one was a long time ago, it was not so bad then. Only the last few months it got worse. The itch. I can't sleep. I worry. My employer shouts at me, because my work is slow now. They say my brain is upside down.'

'It's their brains that are upside down,' said Mary Grace.

Aunty M grew serious and said this was medical neglect, and that Julia should not accept it. MOM would help her. Or the agency.

'But who will hire me like this?' Julia said.

'We need to get you medicine first,' said Aunty M.

MOM could force the employers to pay for it, so she needed to file a complaint. The rash spoke for itself.

I wanted to know more about this mysterious lady with the holy water. 'Where are your employers from?' I asked.

'They are Singaporean, Malay.'

'So is this holy lady Malay too?'

'I don't know. They only took me to the temple one time, but I stayed outside. Many people were there. Korean. Chinese. White people.'

'And she was called Nan Yan?'

'I don't remember. It sounded like that.'

It all seemed so random. Julia had got an employer with weird beliefs, and because of that she had to live with those rules too. I knew that children had to take on their parents' beliefs. My parents didn't really believe in anything – well, Mama believed in money, and Dad was originally a Christian but never went to church. PoPo had practised some Confucian rituals and Aunty M was Muslim, but I never saw her pray and she ate pork. She said her previous employer ate pork every day, and she had started eating it because she was afraid to ask for beef or chicken. She said she hoped Allah wouldn't blame her.

I wasn't sure about God, but I figured life might be easier if I had one of my own. But which one? Would Julia have started to believe in the crazy lady herself, had she stayed long enough? And, if your former best friend believed you were a cockroach, would you eventually start to believe it yourself too? Would you become one?

'So what will we do now?' I asked Aunty M.

Aunty M said that Julia could run away and approach MOM herself if she wanted to. Or she could confront her employer and demand to see a doctor. When Julia said she'd had enough, she agreed to meet Aunty M on Sunday, her day off, at the helpdesk office.

'Bring your luggage,' Aunty M said. 'They will take you to the shelter, and send you to MOM on Monday.'

'And a doctor.' I added. It was really a question, but I said it like I knew they would. Thankfully Aunty M nodded. 'And a doctor.'

I was proud of myself for speaking out, and I hoped Julia hadn't sensed the inexperience I'd tried to hide. Aunty M had been supportive when I'd spoken to Julia, which strengthened my resolve to be the best helpdesk assistant I could be. Later, I tried to find out more about the strange religion on the internet, but I couldn't find anyone with that name. I tried different spellings. The Chinese name for South East Asia was Nanyang and many things in Singapore were called Nanyang – universities, schools, shopping centres. But no crazy holy women.

Dad would help, I thought, if I told him it was for a school project. We googled together, and came up with nothing. 'It sounds like a cult,' he said. 'None of the common religions would be that extreme.'

I didn't know what a cult was, but Dad went on, 'Religion is supposed to bring people together, but it usually does the opposite: anyone who isn't a believer is out. And a cult is an extreme form of religion. It brainwashes people until it is no longer a way of thinking, but the *only* way.'

We had fun fantasising together about washing our brains with holy water, and how smart we would become, or more likely, how crazy. I played with the idea of telling Dad the truth: about Julia not having a choice, having to wash herself with the holy water to cure her rashes, which only got worse. But he would of course tell Mama. And Mama was busy with her career, being stressed, and she hated busybodies. They would argue, and it would end with them forbidding me to go with Aunty M and telling me to focus on my schoolwork.

If only Dad were around more. He would have been a good help with our cases. Dad knew a lot, and everything he didn't know, he could find on google on his phone. Unfortunately, most of the time that phone would start ringing and Dad would be back at work. PoPo used to say life was much better without mobile phones. Dad would laugh and agree.

16

I had plenty of opinions about Mama, and if I listened to her talk for long enough they'd always be confirmed.

One Saturday afternoon I was playing a game of Monopoly with Dad. Mama had some friends over and they were sitting on the patio, chatting and gossiping. Dad had to leave the room halfway through the game to deal with a phone call, so I hung back, eavesdropping on Mama and her friends. They were gossiping about their helpers.

Linda had a new one, her third in a year. 'I don't know why I'm so unlucky. I always get the bad ones. The first one couldn't clean. I had to point out every single bit of dirt! She was so short, she only cleaned up to here.' She pointed halfway up the wall. 'Everything above that, she couldn't see. And what dirt she couldn't see apparently wasn't there.'

The friends hung on her every word – even Mama, who wasn't interested in anything about cleaning.

Linda rolled her eyes. 'And the next one, she couldn't handle the boys.'

No shit, Sherlock. Linda had three sons, and not even Linda could handle them. They were vicious. Nobody commented on that, but every single one of Mama's friends tried to speak next.

Nadia won. She had just hired a Filipina maid, who had said she could cook Indian food as she had worked for an Indian family for eight years.

'So, I ask her to make chapattis, and she looks at me if I am crazy. "But ma'am, where is the electric chapatti maker?"'

Everyone laughed. 'So lazy,' cried Cynthia.

Nadia continued. 'She is nice though, good with the children and willing to learn. But she does not know how to make vegetarian food. I am sending her on a cooking course next week. Spice Kitchen. Have any of you tried them? It's supposed to be good.'

'Mine is so stupid,' Cynthia butted in. 'No cooking course could help her. She did tell me she didn't cook at the interview, but I thought, how bad can it be? I don't like to pay for so-called 'experience', which is really just bad habits taught by former employers. I cook myself, and I train her so she learns my way. Much better. Fresh maids, I tell you. But this one, she beats it all. So, I asked her to boil some eggs. Hard-boiled eggs. You can't spoil that, can you?'

Everyone nodded. They sat back, and Cynthia helped herself to more biscuits. Aunty M and I had baked them together the day before. We baked a lot now, after the debacle of the pineapple tarts, and I was becoming good at it. Mama offered the plate to Mei Li and Linda.

'No thanks, I'm gluten free. No biscuits for me,' Linda said.

'Really?' started Mei Li. 'I was thinking of that. How do you feel? Do you have more energy?'

'Hello,' Cynthia cut in, stuffing the remains of her biscuit in her mouth. She wagged her hand to keep the others quiet while she chewed. Finally, she swallowed. 'Wasn't I in the middle of a story? Can I finish?'

Mama looked sheepish. I knew she didn't like Cynthia, who acted as if she were better than us. She had a big house and two cars. Her kids were stupid and shy, but she still bragged about them. I didn't understand why Mama had invited her to tea.

'So, I asked her to boil the eggs while I went to lie down for a few minutes. I must have fallen asleep, and before I knew it, I hear this knock, very softly. She can't even knock properly. "Ma'am," she is calling.'

Mei Li stared at the uneaten biscuit in her hand, while the others tried to look attentive.

'"Ma'am, can you help with the eggs, I maybe did it wrong," she says. So I haul myself out of bed – I mean, they can't ever do anything right, can they? So I go into the kitchen and there is this burning smell. How on earth you burn a boiled egg, I ask you?'

Mama looked up. 'Burn a boiled egg? No, even I don't do that.'

Cynthia looked around the patio triumphantly. 'Yes. She had burnt it.'

'How is that possible?'

'There were two eggs in the pan and they'd completely boiled dry. She'd only put them in half an inch of water. She boiled them for an hour. The water had gone, and the pot just boiled dry. Pan all black, spoilt. How stupid is she? I'm taking it out of her wages.'

Everyone agreed, very stupid.

'Hadn't you explained to her how to boil an egg?' Mama asked. 'Maybe she only ever ate them fried?'

'Explain how to boil an egg? Do I need to explain everything? How to wipe her own bum? She should know this. And if not, she could have asked, right?'

I imagined being Cynthia's maid. I wouldn't dare ask anything.

Linda said, 'Mine isn't stupid. But so slow. She drives me crazy. Sometimes I watch her do it, and think I could have done it in half the time.'

When you're eavesdropping you can't say anything, but it doesn't mean you can't have an opinion. I kept mine to myself. But Mei Li finally put down her biscuit. 'You should just do it yourself. I fired my maid last year, and it's such a relief. I don't have to get annoyed anymore, or be polite, or take her into account.'

Cynthia reeled in shock. 'Be polite? Why would you be polite to your maid? You spoiled her, I suppose. I make it a point never to spoil a maid. Last week, mine asked for strawberry jam for her breakfast. I bought her pineapple jam. I mean, she has to eat, but a maid should not be able to choose her own food. What kind of a signal would that be?'

'Isn't that a bit mean?' I felt warm inside: My mama was the one asking that question.

'Mean? Mean, that is not mean. The pineapple jam was good quality, it cost more than the strawberry jam. I take good care of my maid. But she should not get an attitude. I make sure she doesn't. Would you let your maid pick?' she snapped at Mama.

Actually, Aunty M did all the groceries, and Mama let her buy whatever she wanted. Aunty M had gradually become the one who decided what we had for dinner. She would show her shopping list to Mama, who would glance over it for appearances' sake then nod. What would Mama say about this to Cynthia?

'Oh, Merpati is great. She does all the groceries. I have no idea what she has for breakfast. My new role at work doesn't leave me any time at all. Did I tell you about that project we are starting, in Myanmar?' Mama's face seemed to glow. 'I'm hoping to be the project lead. It will be amazing, not just the financial side, but the human angle. Going into a country like that, that is genuinely developing, and at such a pace. We can make money and help the community at the same time. It's amazing.'

Watching Mama blossom as she told her friends about the project, I was confused. I thought her work made her unhappy? This excitement wasn't what I wanted. She had to hate it! She had to quit.

Mama's friends asked some polite questions, but their lack of interest seemed to disappoint her and she smiled uncertainly. Cynthia didn't even pretend. 'Yes, yes, your work, very important and all, but let's talk about that maid. While you're out squeezing money from Myanmar, if you don't pay attention she'll be ripping you off. Do you keep a tight rein on her? Do you check her shopping lists? You need to know how much cash to give her.'

Mama turned red. 'I gave her a bank card.' I could see Mama was getting irritated. 'I check the receipts, of course.'

Aunty M always put them on top of the kitchen cabinet, but I hadn't seen Mama look at them for longer than a few seconds before tossing them into the bin.

'You need to check thoroughly, or your maid will start taking advantage of you,' Cynthia said.

'You know what, Cynthia, I trust Merpati with my most treasured possessions, my daughters. Why would I not trust her with a bank card? It's just groceries. She's meticulous.' Mama's tone had become high-pitched.

I thought about the aunties in the playground, and how their lives seemed to be ruled by their employers so that they couldn't make important choices for themselves. Aunty M had become quite independent, and this worked well for our whole family. I leaned back, proud of my mama and my aunty, who seemed to have worked it out so well.

But Mama was less content it seemed. Her face clouded over and she lowered her voice. 'No, I trust her. But you know what the problem is with Merpati?'

I shrank back, trying to make myself invisible.

'She is, like, too good. She is worse than my own mother, who at least talked back to me. Sometimes I feel like I'm living with Mother-bloody-Teresa. Always nice and polite. She's a great cook, and doesn't hesitate to show it. The house shines and sparkles. Do you know what she said the other day? That she likes the floors to be so clean they squeak when she walks on them with bare feet. She mops the whole house every single day. Even though I told her it wasn't necessary.

'My husband, kids, they all love her, making me feel like a bad wife and mother. My mother always told me I cannot cook, and that that makes me less of a woman. Do I need her to look at me and think the same? Bad mother, bad cook, bad wife. A mother that loses her temper and shouts at her kids. As if I don't have a high profile banking job. I'd like to see her do that for a day. My maid is little miss perfect. Always helpful. Always right. It does my head in. Always on the lookout to help someone in need. Busybody bitch. *I hate those holier-than-thou types!'*

Mama's voice went up with each new sentence, until her screeches echoed through the room. She stopped and looked up in shock. Her friends stared at her. Mama had never shown the Mamamonster outside the family. But there it was, in plain view, saying bitch and all. No-one spoke until Dad came back, cutting through the stillness with, 'Well Maya, let's see about that Chance Card.'

Into the broken silence Mei Li said, 'Well, you're lucky, you know? Count your blessings.'

Mama sighed. 'I know. More biscuits, anyone?'

After Dad had crushed me at Monopoly I went to my room and googled Mother Teresa. She had been a nun in India, but left the convent to help poor people. The poorest of the poor, as she said herself. That did sound a bit like Aunty M, who was always helping people too. Did Mama suspect that Aunty M worked for the helpdesk? She hadn't mentioned it in her tirade. If she knew, she wouldn't like it one bit. But then she'd told off Cynthia for being mean. Was one the real Mama, the other one the Mamamonster? Which one could I trust?

If I wanted to be grown up and independent I needed my own opinion on matters, so I read more about Mother Teresa. She had grown up poor herself, having to beg for food and clothes. According to Wikipedia, she'd said that her mission was to care for 'the hungry, the naked, the homeless, the crippled, the blind, the lepers, all those people who feel unwanted, unloved, uncared for throughout society, people that have become a burden to the society and are shunned by everyone.'

We had not really helped the naked or blind, but we had seen our share of women who were hungry, unwanted, unloved, uncared for. What were lepers?

I wasn't sure what shunned was, or a burden to society, but if I understood this correctly, Mama was right. Aunty M and I were acting a bit like mother Teresa, and I liked it. It made me feel good. By taking action the part of me that felt ashamed of living in a country where people did this was overshadowed with pride, pride that like Mother Teresa we were trying to make things better.

But Mama hated Mother Teresa. I still wasn't sure what I thought, but I knew I couldn't ask anyone. Just before I closed my laptop I noticed a quote tucked away in the corner of the screen. It read, 'Forgive others not because they deserve forgiveness, but because you deserve peace.' I went to bed with that thought on my mind.

17

I had started to go to the playground again with Chloe and the aunties, eavesdropping and playing the good big sister at the same time. But when we arrived one afternoon, I felt the air leave my lungs. Jenny was there.

She was sitting on the ground behind the swing, fiddling with a bag. I decided to be big, ignore her, and went to sit with the aunties. Mary Grace was handing out iced gems, so I hoped it didn't look like a weird thing to do. With any luck, Jenny wouldn't even notice me at all.

Of course she did. She wandered over and grabbed more than her share of the iced gems. 'Alright you girls, go off and play,' shooed Mary Grace.

'Yes, let's play,' singsonged Jenny, grabbing my hand and skipping towards the bushes, to what used to be our favourite secret spot. Her good mood made the tiny cockroach feet inside my stomach jump for joy. I turned to Aunty M for help, but she looked at me encouragingly. I eyed the gloomy bushes and hesitated. The quote I'd read about forgiveness came back to me. I felt I deserved peace, so should I forgive Jenny? Just like that? And, the bigger question, could I trust her? I decided yes to the first, but to be careful with the second.

'Let's go to the swings,' I said. In plain sight, in safety.

'No, let's go there,' said Jenny, pointing at the bushes behind them. 'I have some fun stuff in my bag.'

Jenny's idea of fun wasn't mine, and I pulled my hand free. 'No. You can't make me.'

Jenny looked at me. The suspiciously sweet expression she'd worn earlier had gone. 'Come on. We were friends, weren't we?'

'Yes,' I mumbled, 'but Meena is your friend now, not me.'

'Do you see Meena? No. Meena went to India. Her grandfather is ill. Come on. *Please?*'

I shook my head again.

'Are you going to make me beg? Look, I got some new make-up.'

She showed me the contents of her zip bag. There was an eye shadow kit with at least twenty colours. And lipstick. And little jars of glitter. Cute brushes with sparkles on the stems and fluffy bristles. We'd begged our parents for this kind of stuff for years.

'It's the Stargirl set,' Jenny pointed out unnecessarily.

She smiled again and the dancing sensation in my stomach subsided. 'Ok,' I said.

We disappeared behind the bushes. It was dark there and the air was still, cooler than where the aunties sat but stifling. A butterfly fluttered past, its fragile wings shimmering in a single ray of sun that had broken through the branches. I felt a few more flutters inside, and managed to convince myself that was a butterfly too.

We crouched on the ground, laying out all the products in a line before us.

'Where did you get it?'

'My mum went on a business trip. A lot of them actually. I guess she felt bad.'

Jenny's mother's career always seemed even more important than Mama's. Her dad was home a lot though. He didn't speak much English. I fingered the products jealously. Mama hardly wore eye shadow or lipstick, just mascara and concealer under her eyes. PoPo had said that painted faces were ghostly. Dad said I was too young.

Jenny thrust the eye shadow set in my hands. 'You do me first.'

'Ok. What colour?'

'Purple,' she said, squatting down in front of me. 'With pearl glitter.'

I picked up the brush, and swept it over the palm of my hand. So soft. I felt the butterfly flutter again.

Gently I painted Jenny's eyelids in three tones of purple, finishing with a small dab of the glitter. Jenny opened her eyes. She took out a compact mirror from our line of goodies and stared at her reflection. 'Not bad. More glitter on my cheeks.'

I obeyed. When Jenny finally approved my work, she pushed me to the floor. 'Close your eyes.'

She didn't ask what I wanted, but I didn't really care. I felt the brush tickle my eyelid and tried to suppress a giggle.

'Sit still.' The brush caressed my face. 'I'm going to do this super make up on you,' Jenny said. The brush now stroked my forehead too. 'I saw it in a magazine. They did it in a fashion show. Super wow.'

She stopped to admire my face with a snigger that squeezed my throat shut. The air around me seemed suddenly hotter and hard to breathe. I opened my eyes and grabbed the compact.

Jenny had made dark brown circles around my eyes, spotted with little yellow dots. On my forehead two antennae pointed up to my ears.

Jenny's giggle rang out louder. It echoed all the way down my throat to the pit of my stomach, stirring up the cockroach flavour.

How could I have been so stupid? I ran away.

As soon as I'd left the bushes it was as if taps had opened in the corners of my eyes. I kneeled, sobbing, and rubbed the tears over my face, trying to scrub off the insulting brown. A loud wail built up inside me but I tried to keep it in – Jenny was just behind me. I swallowed and swallowed until I felt sick. I struggled to my feet and crashed headfirst into a squishy stomach.

'What's the matter, girlie?' asked a soft voice.

From the pink flip-flops with the daisies on them, I could tell it was Mary Grace.

I hugged her midriff like it was a stuffed animal, and let her cushiony softness envelop me until I managed to swallow the bile. I sniffled.

'Hey, you make my shirt wet. Come on.'

Mary Grace pulled me to the barbecue pits on the other side of the playground, out of sight of anyone else. She handed me a water bottle. 'Drink. You lost a lot of water.'

With a tissue she wiped my face and nose. Slowly, with a last few hiccups, the tears subsided. 'What is going on, baby girl? You are all brown smudges. Do you want to tell Aunty Grace? Or do you want me to call Merpati?'

I shook my head violently. I liked Mary Grace. She always treated me like a grownup. With Aunty M you never knew – sometimes she did, sometimes she didn't. Besides, I'd seen enough to know that in some cases she just couldn't help. I was her assistant, not her client.

Mary Grace was a mother hen, always fussing about everyone else. Before Aunty M came, she was the one everyone turned to. These days, Mary Grace sent many women to Aunty M and me, and came along on some of our visits. But she didn't talk about herself much – she obviously didn't need any advice. Sometimes she could be a bit rough around the edges, telling people not to moan. I wasn't sure how she'd react to me crying my eyes out all over her shirt and leaving brown streaks down her white top. But Mary Grace ignored that.

'I am a good listener, you know, and it can really help to have someone listen to your problems.'

I knew that, it was one of the things Aunty M and I did a lot, especially with the cases we knew we couldn't help. But Jenny was my secret. I hadn't told anyone about what she was doing, and I wasn't ready to make it feel more real by changing that now. I'd rather hear about someone else's ugly truths. I said that to Mary Grace, and she laughed.

'You know, you are right. I am the same. Focusing on someone else takes the attention off you. I do it all the time. Why do you think I keep busy?' She hugged me. 'You know what? I'll tell you my story. That will make you feel better.'

Mary Grace grinned, and a cascade poured out. She had grown up in a village in the Philippines, on a mango plantation. After marrying young, she now had a husband and a fifteen-year-old daughter and, like all the other domestic workers, was in need of money. This was her second job in Singapore, but not her second as a domestic worker.

'You always think, *I am so lucky, have such a good employer* – but, you know, it wasn't always like this. I have had it both. Good and bad. Being a maid, it is like a lottery.'

'Yes,' I said, 'Like the birth lottery.'

'Birth lottery?' Mary Grace asked.

'Yes, we covered that at school. It's like a lottery where you are born, and from which parents. Like, some people are born in a rich country from rich parents, so they're winners. But others are born in a poor country, or from poor parents, or in a country where there's a war. So they're the losers of the birth lottery.'

'Ah. That's a good way of putting it. First, we maids, we lose already – born in a poor country from poor parents. Then we make it worse by picking the wrong husband.'

Mary Grace laughed a throaty laugh. 'Actually, no, my husband used to be ok, before I left him alone too long in the Philippines. It's my own fault. But he didn't make enough money. So I went to be a maid. I played the maid lottery a few times. Sometimes I win. Sometimes I lose. Now, I won top prize. My employer is very good. After this, I go home. No one wins the jackpot twice.'

Before coming to Singapore, Mary Grace had worked in Kuwait, with a Kuwaiti family who were very nice to her. She was treated like part of the family, going on trips and eating nice food at the table with them. But as their children got older, she was no longer needed. She then found a job in Qatar with an Egyptian family. They beat her when she made mistakes. Mary Grace had escaped and flown back to the Philippines, black eyes and all. She hadn't wanted to deal with the police in Qatar. 'Qatari police is not interested in domestic workers that have problems,' she said. 'It's not like Singapore where the police can help you when your employer beats you up.'

After that, Mary Grace had gone home for healing rest, and then decided to try Singapore. The money was better here. And maybe the treatment too, so Mary Grace hoped. But she got unlucky again.

She told me about her first Singapore employer, how she'd had to work long hours helping the family business by wrapping up parcels on top of her regular work. That meant she ended up with very little sleep. The food was bad too, and whenever she was given something decent to eat, she was told how expensive it was, and how she ought to be grateful.

'You know, Maya. I have this dream. I'm not going to be a domestic worker all my life. I have plans. I wanted another chance, a decent employer, just for a year or two, so I could save some money for my own business. I don't need a perfect employer – I'm not perfect myself – just someone who treats me as a human being.'

Mary Grace told me how her husband worked filleting tuna, and how he loved his job. They wanted to invest in more equipment, so he let her go again reluctantly. 'Take good care of yourself,' he had said when she left and he stayed. But Mary Grace's plans did not stop at fish-filleting. Together with her mother she had a business selling bottled water, buying in bulk and delivering it to people's houses. 'Never give all your money to a man, Maya. That's my advice, and I'm happy I took it.'

Suddenly Mary Grace was the one crying. I felt confused. Mary Grace was the strong one, always giving a shoulder to cry on. So I did what Mary Grace always did. I got up and hugged her.

Mary Grace sniffled. 'I told myself, I only want to ask the Lord for another chance, just one more. What did I do? Did I commit some sin that this happens to me?'

'What happened?' I asked.

'I asked them for a transfer, and first they said no. Then I asked my agent. They did not want to help either. So I threatened them. I told them I would make trouble for them with MOM, because it was not allowed what they asked me to do, help in the family business. I got a new employer, and bingo. Now, I have a good life. I will stay a few more years, I cannot leave ma'am Tan. She is so sweet. She needs me. I sent the money home to my husband, to put in the business.'

Mary Grace started crying again.

'But he... the bastard. I did it all for him. But I should not have left him alone so long.' Mary Grace broke off and looked me in the eye. 'You're a little girl. Let's stop talking about me.'

I still didn't feel like telling Mary Grace my problems. Why would I bother her? She'd just laugh. I'd always thought it was normal the way we lived, in a condo with a pool and a playground, going to a good school. I knew about people in poor countries living in bamboo huts and being hungry and all, but they were no more real to me than Harry Potter. I felt ashamed. I had to stop feeling sorry for myself. But was it my fault I'd been born here and not there?

I didn't think I'd said anything out loud, but Mary Grace answered anyhow. 'One person's problems are not worse than someone else's. They are all bad. Bad employers, bad husbands, and bad friends. You have a bad friend back there, don't you?'

She pointed behind the bushes I had come running from. 'She's not my friend,' I grumbled, 'Not anymore.'

'Good. Never waste your time on bad friends,' Mary Grace said.

'Or bad employers. Or husbands,' I added.

Mary Grace laughed. 'Those too. Do you want to tell me what she did?'

'Most of the time she doesn't really do anything. They all just leave me alone. And that's fine by me.

Mary Grace looked at me in a way that showed she knew I wasn't telling the truth. 'No. Not fine.' I corrected myself. 'Before, Jenny was my friend. Now, she's Meena's friend. But today, Meena was away. And Jenny was being nice, so I hoped. Hope is so stupid.'

The tap started dripping again. I told her about the bullying in the bus. The way they made everyone ignore me at school. That I had no friends. That I maybe won this birth lottery thing, but I was still a loser. Not because of the ticket I got, but because of who I was. And I told her that she could never, ever tell Aunty

M. Because she would tell Mama, and then she would go talk to Jenny's mum and everything would get even worse.

'So there really is no solution, you see. This is my life. I can't go and complain to MOM, now can I?'

Mary Grace shook her head.

'You know,' said Mary Grace. 'Another thing I learned: some problems you can't fix. You have to sit them out. This is your life now. This is not your life forever. Things will get better.'

But when, I wanted to ask – but before I could, Aunty M saw us and called me over.

'I need to go.' I gave Mary Grace a last hug.

Aunty M stared at my puffy, brown-blotched eyes but didn't ask any questions. When we got back, I went straight to the bathroom. I took Mama's cotton wool and make-up remover and it wasn't until I felt the sting that I realised it was nail polish remover instead. I took a long, long shower with the water falling on my face, waiting for the tears to clean my eyes. I cried for Mary Grace, for myself, for PoPo, Mama, Dad, Aunty M, Sri, for all of us. A few years ago, life had seemed so simple.

Getting older, I'd expected to understand things better, but I just found it harder and harder. All those different kinds of people struggling. Moving around, exploited as 'foreign workers', or others who were 'expats' like Dad. What was the difference? At school most people called themselves expats, but nobody said that about Mary Grace and Aunty M. Instinctively I felt the difference: the lives of expats were easier than those of the foreign workers. They were in control of themselves, made their own choices and lived with their own families. Like Sri, waiting for the police to decide on her case, the aunties had placed their destinies in someone else's hands when poverty pushed them to pursue an unpredictable career abroad. Their families stayed behind, which presented a whole slew of different risks. We were all humans that moved around the globe, but we were not the same.

All types of migrants had to leave the country as soon as they finished their contracts, but thankfully Dad was PR, a permanent resident. How come people still called him an expat? Could he ever become Singaporean with his blonde hair? And the most difficult question of all: where – if anywhere – did I fit in?

I was born here, so why did it seem so unclear? Was it the international school? Or was I homesick for PoPo's Singapore of old? I had so many questions but no-one to ask for answers.

If only PoPo hadn't died. Aunty M could never replace PoPo, I told myself; but deep down I knew that was what had been happening. Aunty M was here, PoPo wasn't, so I had to make do with her. I needed to have Mary Grace's perseverance.

But Aunty M could never help me feel like I belonged; I needed PoPo's memories for that. 'If you are forgotten, you are really dead,' she used to say. That's why the Chinese had ancestor tablets in shrines. PoPo used to have one on a small shelf in her room. Now we had no shrine, but I did have a picture of PoPo and me on my dresser, with a little tea light in front of it. I would keep PoPo alive.

When I saw Mama she commented on my red eyes. I told her Jenny had a new make-up set, and that I'd accidentally used nail polish remover to take off the eye make-up. Again, it was all true. She was extra sweet when she put me to bed. We read together and she crawled into bed with me for a cuddle. I didn't tell her anything.

18

Half asleep, I tried to forget the cockroach that kept biting at my eyes. Another insect popped into my mind, one that was green, luminescent and sparkling like the colours in Jenny's eye shadow box. PoPo had told me about the green beetle on the string. Now it flew around my head, fluttering its shiny wings but never managing to get further than the string's length away.

When Meena first arrived, she was nice to me. Nicer to me than to Jenny, in fact. One day I had been at the playground with Meena, when we saw Jenny approaching in the distance. Meena tugged my arm, and whispered we should go to the bushes. But that was our special place – mine and Jenny's, so I shook my head. 'Let's wait for her.'

Meena smirked. 'Don't you think Jenny is a bit childish? Let's go before she sees us.'

But I refused. That afternoon, the three of us played together awkwardly, whilst I took care not to suggest doing anything Meena would think was childish. The week after I saw their hunched, hidden shapes behind the bushes; but I didn't dare follow. Somehow I knew it was no game.

I went back home instead, and hung around PoPo moping. When she said I couldn't go on the iPad, I asked her to tell me stories instead, stories of the old days, when she was a little girl like me. But PoPo had been in a mood. 'You kacau me all day. Go play,' she said. 'What am I here for, your entertainment only?'

I didn't move and PoPo kept grumbling. 'These kids these days, they do not know how to play. Itchy backside lor. So many toys, cupboards full, lego, playmobil, games, Barbie dolls, all these things, and madam is bored. You all malas, lazy, ah. She thinks I am just like that machine, lah, that flat computer thing, that she can turn me on, flip a switch, and I will start entertaining her? Don't I have chores to do? Her mother spoils her, lazy child. Go fly a kite.'

I had no kite, nor did I know how to fly one. But I did know exactly which buttons to push with PoPo. 'PoPo, when you were a little girl, was that what you did? Did you fly kites? Please tell me about the games you played.'

PoPo put down the laundry she was folding, and looked at me. 'We knew how to play, sayang, not like you modern girls. A little ya ya papaya, nose-in-books girl like you. What do you know?'

'Then teach me, PoPo,' I implored.

PoPo settled in her chair and looked around. 'Why you so kaypoh? But not your fault, really. This flat, you know, it's too small. No garden. The playground, the pool, not leave anything to imagination. In the kampong, we knew how to play. Boleh. I will tell you.'

'But PoPo,' I said, realising I was skating on thin ice, 'You did not live in the kampong, did you? You lived in the Blue House?'

PoPo's stories had started to become jumbled those last months. Her speech had changed too, more and more colloquial Malay and Singlish slipped into her sentences, and other words that sounded Chinese but were not the Mandarin I learned at school.

'Of course, I'm not kuku, I know where I lived. But the kampong is ulu, the best for playing wild. At home, I had to do chores. You know, we had two amahs, a cook. The amahs can do chore lah, but no, my mother made me too. Not spoilt like you, always need to focus on school work.' PoPo paused and sniffed. 'I sneaked to the kampong at the end of the road. My mother did not like me to go there, we were not kampong.'

'What did they play there, PoPo?'

'Last time in the kampong, life was free. No amah to check on you. The kids had no shoes, but the boys played football. My brothers always play football. The kampong boys were happy when my brothers came. They had a real leather ball.'

Football. The condo boys still played it now, and at school too.

'And they played chaptek. And goli. I liked goli too.'

'What are those?'

'Goli, are – what do you call in English? Marbles. Little glass balls.'

Marbles I knew, I had a jar full in my bedroom. But apart from arranging them in pretty patterns, I wasn't sure what to do with them.

'Sure, marbles, I have those. But what's chapter?

'Chaptek,' PoPo said. 'Well, chaptek, you know. It's this thing with feathers and you need to kick it, keep it in the air, lor. Like a football. The kampong boys made from old tyres and chicken feathers. My oldest brother was neighbourhood champion. He had one bought in the store, but the kampong boys made better so he'd trade for goli marbles. Marbles they could not make.'

'Did you play, PoPo?'

'How can? It is for boys, is it? Like kite wars.'

'Kite wars?'

PoPo told me how in the windy season her brothers and friends all flew kites, and the kampong skies filled with colour. Kiting was not a friendly game. The boys would stick glue to the kite string and add ground glass, so the string got sharp as a knife. They would fly their kites, high, steering to cut through the string of others so that the loser's kite blew away in the wind.

'My girlfriends and I, we would watch and chase runaway kites,' PoPo said, her eyes hovering around the room. 'The one who caught it could keep it. Sometimes they would fly for miles, and we'd follow the sungei, river, until it got stuck in a bush or tree. My mother would scold me if I came back dirty. Girls like me were supposed to stay clean. So we had other games.'

'What else did girls play, then?'

PoPo contemplated her answer. 'Hopscotch. You must know hopscotch.'

I did. But you needed friends to play it.

'And masak masak. Play cook. We pick grass, leaves, colourful seeds, and pretend campfire from sticks. We use empty tins as pots, and boil soups, stews.'

Childish. I did that when I was, like, five.

'You know,' PoPo sat up straight. 'You know what your mother loved? Zeropoint!'

I had never heard of it. I waited, knowing PoPo would explain if I said nothing.

'You don't know zeropoint, or yay yay? What do you girls play these days? You just want this make-up, computer games, stick glitter on fancy paper lah, but no-one plays good game with yay yay.'

'But what is it?' I asked.

PoPo spread out her arms wide. 'You need a lot of rubber bands to make a rope. These ropes, they are very good. You can use them for skipping too.'

'I have a skipping rope, PoPo.'

'No, no good,' she shook her head. 'No good. For zeropoint it needs to be elastic. We need to make the rope first.'

PoPo got up and started rummaging in kitchen drawers. 'I can't find anything here. Where are rubber bands?'

I had an idea. 'We can use my rainbow loom.'

Rainbow loom had been a craze the previous year, and Jenny and I had spent many a rainy afternoon using it to make bracelets from rubber bands. When we'd made more than we could have worn in a hundred years we created figures, dolls and animals, all from those colourful bands.

I ran to my room and brought out the loom and stash of rubber bands. PoPo eyed them suspiciously.

'Why so small lah, too long time to make the rope? My fingers don't fit.'

But PoPo's fingers were slender, and after some fiddling she strung the loom bands together with surprising speed. I used the plastic loom and we competed to see who was fastest. She was.

Whilst I concentrated on my fingers on the loom, PoPo spoke more about kampong games. When she broke off, I told her how you could make everything you wanted from loom bands. I showed her the little figures I'd made, which she looked at as if she'd never seen them before. PoPo abandoned her rope to inspect the lizard that had been my favourite creation. She said nothing, didn't even compliment me for finishing the complex design.

Instead, she said, 'You know, I used to collect chichak eggs. I bred them in an empty matchbox so I had baby chichaks. My brothers said I had to catch flies to feed them, but I did not know how, so I would let them go, find new eggs, and start again.'

She cradled the lizard in her hands and picked up a snake.

'My brothers kept a zoo in little boxes. Grasshoppers, and spiders that they trained to fight. At the kampong, they held fights; pretend cock fights with grasshoppers and spiders. I could not watch. Many of their insects lost legs.

'But once, they had this beetle. It was the most beautiful thing you ever saw. Bright green and shiny, like a jewel. Gold sparks shone on its shield.'

PoPo eyes sparked too when she looked at the rubber lizard in her hand.

'I wanted one of those, to keep in my own box and look at every day. A beetle like that was a treasure, hard to find. My brother bound a string to one of the beetle's back legs. The beetle would fly and he would let it go, and then, when it reached the length of the string, bang, stop. My brother would take it for a fly, like walking a dog.'

'Wasn't that cruel?' I asked.

'Of course. People were cruel to animals then. People were cruel to people. In the war...'

PoPo stopped.

'What, in the war?'

'Never mind lah. You know, one day, I cut the string. The beetle flew off, like a runaway kite, happy as a bird, a length of string still stuck to its leg. My brothers were, oh so mad. They broke my favourite doll in revenge.'

PoPo sighed. 'I have not seen a beetle like that since I can't remember when. That day, maybe.'

She looked at me wistfully. 'Can we make one?'

'What, a beetle? From rainbow loom?' I said.

'Maybe. But how to do it?'

I took out the iPad and we googled instruction videos. We could not find any for jewel green beetles, but there was one for a ladybird.

'If we do this one in green, with some of the glow in the dark yellow for the spots, it will be bright like that,' I said.

PoPo nodded, excited like a little girl. I was happy to show her that I had good things to play too, that I could match her kampong games with my loom.

We set the bands on the loom as in the video and PoPo looked on, following every movement of my hands. It took a long time, and PoPo sat with glistering eyes while I worked, commenting on my moves, trying to make out that she was the one in charge;

but this was my time. When it was done, PoPo brought out a matchbox, threw all the matches in the bin, and put the beetle inside. 'I'm keeping it,' she had said.

Then she put the matchbox in her pocket, and transformed back from little girl to old lady in an instant. She picked up more laundry to fold.

'But PoPo,' I said. 'What about the zeropoint?'

'Ah, yes, can. The yay yay.'

PoPo put down the bed sheet, picked up the rope we made, my loom-made one tied to her handmade version, making one long, colourful string. She looked at it thoughtfully, and her enthusiasm faded.

'We don't have enough people,' PoPo said. 'You need three: two hold up the rope, first low, then higher. And then the third one has to jump over. There are seven levels. You can't touch the rope, not at all for the first levels, not with your hands with the higher ones.'

You jump over? How? Why? I wanted to ask more, but PoPo had taken the matchbox from her pocket and was staring at the beetle again. We'd spent all that time making a rope for a game we couldn't play.

Can you miss a country that you've never been to, one that no longer exists even though you're living in it right now? As I lay in bed nursing my painful eyes, I imagined that beetle whizzing around, tethered and frustrated. I wished I could have seen the real thing. We only had mosquitoes and ants. And cockroaches, of course. Would people love cockroaches too, if they were green and shiny, like a jewel? I slipped into dreams where I was the beetle, my swing like its string, going up and down, back and forth, until PoPo cut the rope with her glass-tailed kite and released me high into the sky.

The next day, I rummaged in my cupboard and found it all, all but the beetle: the loom I had abandoned when the craze ended, the bracelets, the lizard, and even, to my shock, the rope PoPo and I had made. Even without the beetle I remembered the excitement in her eyes that day, as well as my disappointment when we never played the games she'd described.

I ran out to Aunty M and asked her if she knew zeropoint.

'Zeropoint? What is that?'

I explained it was a game and showed her the rubber band rope.

Aunty M exclaimed, 'Lompat Tali! Yes, we played that in our village.'

She knew exactly how to play, just by a different name, and that afternoon we took the rope to the playground. We took turns in playing, two of the aunties holding the rope, higher each level, me and the others jumping over it on the padded surface of the playground. Most of the aunties were better at giggling than jumping, and Mary Grace sat on the ground rubbing her sore knee, unable to stop laughing long enough to get up.

Nobody managed the highest levels. Afterwards we played with the little ones, the rope at ankle height. When they kept falling they got up and tried again and again.

PoPo's magic, her stories and ways of reviving the old times had worked to bring people together, even after her death.

Perhaps I should give Mama a zeropoint rope to use at work? Mama would come home happy, just like the aunties had that day. I giggled as I imagined going one step further: what if we gave one to all the mean employers in Singapore and let them play with their helpers?

But then I thought about school, and how I would never, ever dare bring a yay yay there to make friends. I could hear the jokes already.

The thought weighed me down, and I didn't even ask Aunty M what her daughters played in Indonesia, whether they played zeropoint, or if they had a rainbow loom – or any toys for that matter. If I'd had their address, I could have sent Nurul my old loom and the spare elastic bands. But I didn't ask.

19

I was helping Aunty M to do the dishes. My mother had decided I risked becoming a spoilt expat brat, so forced me to do chores like setting the table and making my own bed. I hoped she'd get over it soon. I was a Singaporean, not an expat.

Aunty M had been quiet all evening – but then Mama was home, and she was usually quiet around Mama. She had this multiple personality thing: she was one person with Chloe, all cooing and sweet, and another with me, friendly but strict. She was chatty and gossipy with the other aunties, and subdued around Mama. With Dad she was neutral. And when we had visitors, she just blended into the background as if she wasn't even there.

At dinner she'd said less than she normally did, not even when spoken to. Now, when it was just the two of us, she said nothing at all. She'd been on the phone just before dinner, and I was curious if something was up.

I broke the uneasy silence. 'Are you ok?'

'Of course I am. Why wouldn't I be?'

I carried on drying the plates whilst working up the courage to ask about the telephone call.

'Who was on the phone? I mean, earlier?'

Aunty M started. After another pause she cleared her throat. 'It was my daughter.'

After the zeropoint afternoon I had banished Nurul and Adi from my mind. Aunty M was mine now, and thoughts of those distant kids upset me more than I cared to admit.

'Oh. Nurul. Is she ok?'

'Fine.'

'Ok.'

Aunty M scrubbed a large pot fiercely. 'Actually, I don't know. We only spoke a few seconds. She did not say much.'

That must have run in the family.

'Then she hung up on me. Again.'

'Why would she do that? Isn't she happy to hear from you?'

I always chatted forever when Dad called from one of his business trips, until he'd say he was busy and had to go. We exchanged more words on the phone than in real life.

'No. She is angry with me.'

We finished the dishes in silence. But when I was done and about to leave, Aunty M turned to me. 'You know how you are mad at Mama sometimes? When she is busy with work? Or comes home late? That's why Nurul is angry with me. I have been away since she was four.'

She left the room, a broom in her hand.

The horror slowly sunk in. Now, at last, I saw the real Merpati. I couldn't believe she'd had me fooled all that time. She was as bad as Mama. Putting the money first. A mother for everyone but her own children. It was good I hadn't asked her what games Nurul and Adi played in Indonesia – she wouldn't have known. The fact that Nurul had more reason to be mad at her than I had only made me more angry. I hated Nurul, but I decided to hate Aunty M more.

One Thursday evening not long after that, I could sense Aunty M was nervous. We were at dinner – she often ate with us now, even when Dad was home. When she found a gap in the conversation, she drew herself up straight. 'Ma'am?' she asked.

Mama looked up from her plate.

'Ma'am, sir, can I ask a favour.'

Mama shrugged in Dad's direction. 'Sure. What's on your mind?'

'My cousin, she lives in Singapore too. Next weekend, her employer is away. She is afraid to be alone in the house, it's big house. She asked if I can stay with her Saturday night. After work is finished, of course, so no trouble to you.'

Dad halted his fork in mid-air. 'Sure, why not.'

Mama cut in, 'Well, because these people may not like that? What about the employer?'

Aunty M said, 'Her employer said it was ok, they don't mind. They said you can call them to check, if you like.'

Dad looked at Mama. 'That's fine then. Honey, can you call these people?'

Mama nodded absentmindedly. 'Sure.'

I had learned a lot from Aunty M's helpdesk stories. I said, 'Actually, I don't think that's allowed.'

'What do you mean, not allowed? By whom?' Dad asked.

I felt my anger at Aunty M bubbling up in my throat. I said, 'By the government.'

Dad looked surprised. 'What do you mean?'

I was on a roll now. 'MOM says she has to stay with us. It's one of their regulations.'

Dad looked at me strangely. 'Where did you get that from?'

'School,' I mumbled, avoiding Aunty M's gaze. 'We did this project on laws, and erm, foreign workers and such.'

I briefly caught Aunty M's shocked look, and hesitated. 'It is, like, a very unfair rule.' I looked at my plate. 'But the rule is there.'

Dad looked thoughtful. 'It could be true. I saw something like that in the online course for new employers I had to do.'

I glanced up from my plate to see Aunty M staring at hers. My anger mingled with shame and I pursed my lips tightly together. *Shut up, Maya.* But the cat was out of the bag now.

Dad pulled out his phone. 'Would it be on the MOM website?' He fiddled with the phone for a while. 'Aha. Here we go. A domestic worker needs to reside in the house of the employer. Clear enough. It should be fine for her to stay with her cousin.'

'No, wait, what do you mean?' Mama looked confused. 'That means she can't, can she? She has to be here.'

Dad looked at Mama and gave a small shake of his head, as if afraid to do so openly. Aunty M continued to look at her plate. After a pause, Dad said, 'No. I reside here, but I can still go on holiday. That doesn't mean I don't reside here. If you reside somewhere, it just means you have to be there most of the time. Check a dictionary.'

'I don't think that's what MOM means,' Mama said. 'I'm sure it's not that simple.'

I wanted to say something too, but then Dad got angry and

I was glad I'd kept quiet. 'If you know for sure, why did you ask me?'

'I didn't,' Mama retorted. She turned to Aunty M, who had been staring at her plate without eating ever since she asked the question. 'I need to think about it. I'll let you know.'

After dinner, Mama's phone rang. When she came back to the living room where we were watching TV she said, 'Cynthia says I'm crazy if I allow that. She says Merpati might as well be staying with her boyfriend. They could give us a fake number, just another friend who says what we need to hear.'

Dad paused the film we'd been watching and looked at Mama. 'It doesn't seem like Aunty M to do that. Don't you trust her?'

Mama sighed. 'I think I do. I mean, she's married and all.'

'Actually, no,' I said. 'She's divorced, remember.'

Mama looked at me suspiciously. 'Maya, I think this is an adult conversation you'd better stay out of.'

It had slipped out before I realised what I was saying. Now I was really angry – at myself, Aunty M, and Mama too. I was young yes, but, I knew much more about this than she did. I was close to blurting it all out, everything I'd learned about all the aunty issues. I wanted to march out to my room indignantly, but my curiosity won out.

Mama continued talking to Dad, her back to me. 'But you know, what if she does have a boyfriend? Or gets into some other kind of trouble? What about the security bond?'

'She can have a boyfriend. Why not if she's divorced? She's a grownup.' Dad came to a halt, as if something had occurred to him. 'Would we really lose the bond if she gets pregnant? I thought you said we got insurance against that?'

This bond thing was new to me, and I made a mental note to ask Aunty M about it – but then I realised with a shock I couldn't do that now. I had betrayed her. I was alone again.

'Yes, we've got insurance,' said Mama. Then, 'No. I'm not sure. I'd need to check the policy.'

'What would be the point of insurance if it didn't cover that?'

Mama sighed. 'I don't know. Why do they make it so darned complicated? I'm trying to remember. I think they changed the rules for the security bond. I think we only lose it if she goes missing. Disappears or something. I'm not really sure. Cynthia says we're legally responsible for her, and that's why she has to stay at our house so we can keep an eye on her. She says it's definitely not allowed to let her stay anywhere else.'

'I wouldn't take any advice from Cynthia. I'd much rather go with what the MOM website says,' Dad argued. 'Why on earth would Aunty M go missing? She has a good job, right? Why would she risk that by disappearing?' He went on, 'Do you know what I think? I think MOM couldn't care less where Aunty M sleeps, as long as she keeps out of trouble. They keep the rules vague so people don't understand. It makes them insecure so they take fewer risks and lock up their maids just to be on the safe side. Let some urban myths go around on social media. So civilised.'

Mama's eyes started to bulge. 'Oh, don't get all Ang Moh on me. Does it feel good, being so superior? Your country is doing much better! You just want to close up all the borders and let nobody in. Britain for the Brits. Talk about an isolated island. At least we keep the causeway open for people who want to work. And we're honest in what we promise.'

Dad turned back to the TV, and pushed the play button. 'Do what you like. I don't think you want my opinion at all.'

'Thanks for nothing. Don't act like I'm a monster just because I want to be careful. I mean, Cynthia says...'

Dad interrupted: 'Why do you even listen to that woman? You hate her. You're not a little girl anymore, you don't need her approval. I can't understand why you want to be friends with someone like that, with how she treats you, the things she said about your mother...'

Mama's eyes became teary. 'Why on earth do you bring that up now?' She marched out of the room, just like I'd imagined doing, and slammed the door behind her.

Dad seemed suddenly to remember that I was sitting there. He looked shocked. 'Sweetie, you mother... You know she's still hurting, right? We need to be understanding when she acts like that. And try to be nice to her.'

I could have pointed out that he was the one who hadn't been nice, and that perhaps he should start by being home more, that that would be very nice, not just for Mama but all of us... But I felt I'd said enough already that night. Without Aunty M and Mama I needed to stay in Dad's good graces. So I just nodded and we went back to our film.

Aunty M slept at home that Saturday.

20

Dad was home and excited. Today was Opa's birthday. We were going to call him on Skype at 7 pm – evening for us, morning for them. I had made Opa a drawing and Chloe had poked at a sheet of paper with some crayons too.

Opa and Grandma were sitting in front of their computer wearing broad smiles. Dad and I sang *Happy Birthday*, Chloe humming along and waving from Dad's lap. Afterwards Opa and Grandma asked about school, about my friends. It was easy to pretend life was great.

They were nice, but they were never going to replace PoPo. How can you have a real conversation with two cameras, a second's voice delay and a little sister who always screams through everything you want to say? And Dad was always there too when we Skyped.

Grandma didn't understand anything about me, not like PoPo had. Last summer we'd spent a few weeks in their cottage in Kent, and the year before we'd gone for 'a proper British Christmas.' The tree, food and presents were good, but it was way too cold to really enjoy it. There wasn't even any snow. It had rained most of the two weeks, and my cousins and I spent our time on the PlayStation.

With PoPo gone, it felt like we were unconnected, floating in space. Our concrete, glass and marble condo didn't help. And at international school, instead of asking each other 'Where are you from?' we asked what our 'passport country' was. We learned about our different cultures, all those represented at the school. Only one country was blatantly underrepresented: Singapore. Real Singaporean kids had to go to local school, the government said. I was only allowed to go to the school because I had two passports.

When we'd had to dress up for World Day, I'd had no idea what to wear. Dad suggested an English football kit, and laughed at my horror. But PoPo had bought me a Singapore Airways stewardess outfit, and the batik sarong kebaya had fitted me like a glove. Mama had beamed and hugged me. 'You're my Singapore girl.'

But when I looked in the mirror I wished I had the sleek black hair and poise of a real Singapore girl, not the mousey frizz my mixture of genes had produced.

Aunty M hadn't spoken to me since that night at the table, other than necessities like 'Here is your lunch,' or 'Pick up your shoes.' I was glad. She was a terrible person. But she was also my link to the aunties. They were my friends now, and I missed them. Helping them gave me a purpose; it was my lifeline.

As for Aunty M, a question kept buzzing around my head like an annoying bee. I struggled to hate her without at least knowing the answer. Remembering the anger in her eyes the last time we'd spoken, I'd been bracing myself to ask it. One afternoon, at the table for after school snack, my growing unease finally forced the question out.

'Aunty M,' I said, 'Why did you leave Nurul when she was four?'

She looked straight at me. 'Not just Nurul. Adi too. He was only two.'

Two was not much older than Chloe was now. A baby, really. How? Why? Just for the money?

'How could you do that?'

Auntie M went to the kitchen and started rummaging in the cabinet under the sink. Just when I thought she wasn't going to answer she came back and sat down in front of me. She was silent for a minute, then started to speak.

'Their father was not a good man. We separated. I did try to make it work for a while, more than a year. I had a job in a factory, a noodle factory. But it was not enough. Nurul was about to start primary school and she needed uniforms, books, pens. Adi needed milk. My ex-husband did not give us any money. He remarried very fast. He does not care for my kids anymore.'

She paused. I said nothing, not wanting to interrupt her thoughts.

'A friend of mine had gone to Singapore to work. From her salary she built a nice house, a stone house. She painted it yellow. Nurul thought it was so pretty, the yellow house. She wanted a house like that too. I felt like a bad mother, that I could not give her a house. A yellow house.'

Aunty M studied her nails.

'Many women in Indonesia go abroad. In my village, some

people have nice houses. They work in Hong Kong. Dubai. Qatar. And Singapore. Only a few stay behind, you can see; they are in bamboo huts. The roofs leak in the wet season, the wind blows through slatted walls. Stone houses are better. But, on Java, there are not enough jobs, and the pay is low. So we leave. We remit the money back home. This is how we do it in Indonesia, same like Philippines, Myanmar. We work in other countries and send the money back. Sometimes the men go, but mostly the women. The women need to provide. I came to Singapore to build a yellow house for my daughter.'

What Aunty M told me made me forget about the hate. I asked, 'So, in Indonesia, it's the women who have careers?' Mama would like it there, I thought. 'What do the men do?'

'Yes, a career as a *maid*. Super career. The men work abroad too, but it is difficult for them. There are not so many jobs. Some in construction, but they prefer Indians and Bangladeshis for that. Men can't do domestic work.'

'Won't do domestic work,' I echoed Mama. 'Well, cleaning, anyway – although Mama doesn't like that either. And Dad is a better cook than Mama.'

Aunty M laughed. 'But they would never get a work pass in Singapore. Do you know anyone with an uncle instead of an aunty?'

We both cracked up. 'It would be so cool,' I hiccupped.

'Well,' Aunty M continued, 'My friend told me I should go to Singapore to make money for my girls. For their food, their education. She put me in touch with her agent. My mother took the kids.'

'Did you ask them what they wanted? Nurul and Adi?'

'Sayang, they were four and two. How did they know what they wanted? Nurul wanted the yellow house, did she not? How else could I build it?'

I was fairly sure Nurul hadn't realised the house came at such a price. But I didn't say that.

Aunty M continued: 'I am their mother. It is not about what they want, but what they need: food, school, and a safe place to stay.'

So I asked, 'Did you build the house?'

'What house?'

'The yellow house.'

Aunty M broke into a smile. 'I have enough savings now. Building will start soon.'

'Cool. Can I visit when it's finished?'

'Of course you can, sayang.'

I hugged Aunty M. I sucked at hating. She hugged me back, but something in her expression made me think she hadn't yet forgiven me for something.

Now I knew why Aunty M had left Nurul and Adi: to build the yellow house. She hadn't left because she didn't care, she left because she *did*. It was hard to wrap my head around this; it was wrong, but she'd meant well. To forgive her would not only give me peace, but all her lessons and companionship too.

Forgiving my own mother was much harder. Why did Mama need to go back to work when Dad was providing for us? I had a good school and plenty to eat. We had a house already, even if it was a stupid condo. But I suddenly knew that what I really, really wanted was a yellow house. A yellow house just like PoPo's blue mansion, with a garden and a lotus pond. Most of all, I wanted Mama to want it for me. I wanted her to understand me.

After our reconciliation, I asked Aunty M what had been happening that week. She told me she'd heard from Julia, the aunty with the rash. A week after we'd seen her, Julia had told her employers that she really needed to see a doctor. Eventually, they'd given in – Julia was given more cream and a week to find a new employer. A week to find a new job would have been a challenge even without a disgusting looking rash. After the time was up without luck, Julia was sent back to the Philippines. She was better and she kept texting Aunty M, saying that she needed a new job.

'What am I, an agency?' Aunty M complained.

21

Every other Sunday Aunty M went to the helpdesk. On her day off she'd go shopping, to the cinema, or have a picnic with friends. Sometimes she'd just spend the whole morning in her room. Maybe she was on the phone or her laptop; I wasn't allowed in her room on a Sunday, so I didn't know. If I passed her in the hall on Sundays she would barely greet me, as if I didn't exist. It hurt. It was like she only cared on workdays.

Mama was in a foul mood again. She hadn't got the Myanmar job and she was furious. 'Because I've been away so long, he said, people don't know me anymore in the company. I need to "up my profile" first. Seriously? I've worked there for over a decade. They say you lose your brain when you get pregnant, but I remember all these stupid people perfectly well.'

Dad agreed, but there was nothing he could do. He tried to cheer Mama up the way he usually did, trying to take her mind off things. He started planning Sunday outings again – the zoo, the beach, museums, Gardens by the Bay. Maybe the thing I hadn't said, the one about him being there for Mama and for all of us, had reached him telepathically. He still needed to be away a lot for work, but he tried to make up for it by making what he called 'quality time' for us at home. We all had to join in, and like it too. Or at least pretend. Mama wasn't always good at that.

'Remember what PoPo used to say?' Dad asked one Sunday at breakfast, 'About eating wind?'

'Eating wind?' I said. *What on earth?*

Mama laughed. 'You mean makan angin. A Malay expression.'

I was glad to hear Mama laugh. She usually looked so sad whenever PoPo was mentioned that I didn't dare bring her up. I worried I would forget her and she would cease to exist.

'Yes, that one. Where you go out for a stroll – the park, seaside, anywhere. I love that saying. In England, we say go out to get fresh air. But then again, the air is fresh in England.' He paused. 'Here nothing is fresh, apart from the air conditioning.'

I didn't remember PoPo talking about eating wind. I liked the expression. I was hungry for fresh air. It might blow away some of the stuff in my head.

'There isn't much wind in Singapore,' Mama commented. 'All those high rises, they block everything.'

'True. But there must be somewhere. What's that place, the one behind "Satay by the Bay"? The place where everyone flies kites?'

'Marina Barrage?' Mama said.

'Yes, exactly. That field on top of the building. Let's go there. We can have satay afterwards.'

Wind and satay. That sounded promising. 'What's a barrage?' I asked.

Mama said, 'It blocks the sea from the Marina, I think.'

Dad shook his head. 'That's rather simplistic.'

Mama looked grumpy again. 'Ok, you explain it.'

Dad put on his teacher face. 'You know how Singapore needs

to store water, right? We have so many people for such a small island, and we can't just rely on imports from Malaysia. That's why we have all the reservoirs – McRitchie, Seletar, Pierce.'

He'd dragged us around McRitchie reservoir in the boiling sun just a few weeks before, giving us the same lecture. So yes, I knew.

'Singapore is full of rivers, but they all flow into the sea. The Singapore River now flows into the Marina reservoir instead. It's closed in by land reclaimed from the sea and the barrage. Water from the rivers can flow out when the reservoir is full, but when there's a dry period they close the sluices. That means the water level in the bay is always the same.'

Dad's paramount idea of fun was sharing the entire history of something. I wasn't sure if he researched everything secretly on his phone before he made plans, or just knew all these things already.

'You see, Maya, Singapore likes to control things,' Mama added, 'So the government built this dam.'

'You have to, if you live with so many people in such a small space. That's why this country works,' Dad said.

All this boring talk made me long for wind more than ever. 'Are we going to fly a kite?' I asked.

'We don't have a kite,' Mama said.

'Well, we can always watch,' said Dad.

'And there'll be satay,' I added.

'Stay,' cheered Chloe, and that decided it.

Mama's laughter had given me courage to mention PoPo, so

in the car I told her and Dad about PoPo's brothers' kite wars. Mama had never heard the story before, and Dad said he was tempted to try it, sneaking up on others, making the kites of the barrage *really* fly. Mama looked at him sideways from the passenger seat, as if to say *don't even try it*.

When we arrived at the barrage the parking lot was chock-a-block. We weren't the only ones keen to eat some wind. I stepped out of the air-conditioned car and felt the sweat form on my skin. Mama put on her sunglasses, and grabbed hats from her bag. 'Maya, Chloe, hats on. This sun is lethal.'

I couldn't feel any wind yet, but above us the sky was dotted with colourful shapes and figures.

'Look, that's a giant octopus,' Dad said.

'And there, a Minion kite,' I pointed.

We walked around the barrage building to find the part where we could make our way up to the roof, where the kiting took place. I looked through the glass walls and saw huge pumps inside.

'Look, there's a visitor centre,' Dad pointed. 'We can learn all about the barrage and the water.'

'Weren't we here to makan angin?' Mama said. 'I didn't dress to go inside in the cold. Anyway, you taught us everything already this morning. I have a better idea.' There was a playful gleam in her eye. 'There's a kite shop over there.'

'Yes, a kite! I want a kite!' I yelled.

Dad gave in. 'Ok, let's get one.'

I was allowed to pick, and I chose one that looked like a giant yellow butterfly. It had a long green ribbon tail. The lady from the shop helped us put it together and tie a string to it.

The barrage building was something special. It was oval, all glass, steel and concrete, with a hole in the middle bigger than a house, as if the building were wrapped around itself. The roof was made of grass, a large field that caught all the wind that blew from the sea towards the city. To get there, we had to spiral up a winding grass slope. When we reached the top, Dad and I stood there for a minute, facing the entire skyline of Singapore.

It was amazing. Then and there I understood that new things in Singapore could be beautiful too. Dad was right: this country worked, even if it was in a roundabout way.

There was the Marina Bay Sands building, the flagship of Singapore's skyline. Even though it had only been there a few years, I couldn't imagine the city without it. It looked like a surfboard positioned atop three skyscrapers, a sky boat lined with palm trees. I knew it was a hotel, and the palm trees were for the guests to lie under as they lazed around the pool. It had won many prizes, as had the Supertrees and Flower Domes of the next-door Gardens by the Bay. They would have been made, of course, by foreign workers, and Dad had told me the architect was American; but someone in this country must have come up with the idea. Someone here had made it happen.

We found a quiet corner. Mama, pushing the stroller, was still somewhere on the path out of sight. I had never flown a kite.

'How do we do it? Do you know?' I asked Dad.

He looked as if he didn't know either, but would never admit it. 'It's been a while, but yes. You stand over there. Hold the kite, like this.' He stretched out his hands to demonstrate. 'Wait, no. I'll hold it. Give it to me.'

Reluctantly, I handed over the kite. 'But I wanted to do it.'

'Exactly. That's why you need to hold the string. When I let go of the kite and say go, you need to run.'

I looked around to find a space to run into. Mama had arrived and taken Chloe out of the stroller. She'd spread out a rug and now sat there sipping water, looking hot and flustered. I waved at her. 'Are you joining us, Mama?'

'Darling, let me cool down first. I had to push your sister up that hill.' She looked at Dad meaningfully.

Mama really looked like she needed a rest so I turned back to Dad, who was still holding the kite. Suddenly, he let it go. 'Go!' he shouted.

What did I have to do again?

'Run!' Dad yelled, 'You need to run, Maya!'

I made some hesitant steps but now Dad yelled again. 'No! Not now. It's too late. Wait. Let's try again.'

He walked to where the kite lay on the floor and picked it up. Holding it above his head, he pushed it into the air and yelled 'Go!' again, and I tried to run. Concentrating on where I was going, I couldn't see the kite flopping behind me, pulled along the rooftop like a dead dog. When Dad yelled 'Stop!' I looked behind me. The line had got tangled in the wheels of the stroller.

Mama unpicked it. 'You're useless,' she told Dad. 'This is a woman's job. Let me have a go.'

She shoved Chloe into Dad's arms, then turned to me. 'Look at me when you run, Maya, and start earlier.'

I tried looking at Mama, but walking backwards was slow and I almost stumbled over my own feet. The second time I bumped into Chloe, who had toddled into my path. Then, Mama and Dad tried together. Mama held the kite, Dad ran, and the kite went up. It flew for a few seconds, floundered, then tilted and dropped down.

Mama looked from the kite to me. 'Where's Chloe?' she yelled. 'Maya, I told you to watch her!'

I wanted to say, 'No, you didn't,' but thought better of it. I looked behind me and at the far end of the field I saw a red dot, which could have been Chloe's dress. I ran over and carried her back.

Mama muttered under her breath, but I couldn't hear what she said. Dad was trying to stay cheerful, but Mama was turning red under her hat, and it wasn't from the sun.

She had the beginnings of the Mamamonster about her, but instead of yelling out in the wind and the crowd, she seemed to scream on the inside. Her sunglasses protected me from her deadly looks.

By now Dad was rolling up the string. He tossed the kite on top of the stroller and sat down. 'Why can't we ever act normally? We were just trying to have fun.'

I thought Mama was going to implode. Then Chloe pulled the kite off the stroller by its tail.

Mama jumped up. 'Stop it, Chloe. You'll break it.' She looked at Dad, but didn't scream. 'Am I the only one looking after her?'

I drank some water and looked up at the sky. It was full of kites. I opened my mouth and tasted the salty sea breeze blowing in. Hungry for the wind, I swallowed big gulps.

Mama drank some water too. It seemed to cool her down. 'Why don't we ask someone for help? That guy?' She pointed at a man a few yards away, who had an impressive array of three different kites up in the sky. One was the giant octopus we'd seen from the parking lot.

Dad said, insulted, 'No, we'll do it, won't we, Maya?'

Mama put Chloe in the stroller. 'I'll take her for a walk, see if I can get her asleep.'

After three attempts, Dad and I had the kite up in the air, at least five metres. I ran as fast as I could. Then I felt the line snag. I pulled harder until I heard shouting.

It was the man from the octopus kite. 'Hey, girl, your kite and my kite langar. What you do?' Looking up, I realised my kite was strung around the string of the octopus. Dad came running, full of apologies.

'Give me that string lah.'

The man snatched it from my hand. He walked up and down, fiddling, and suddenly the kite flew free. It went high up, settling under the octopus.

The man grinned. 'You need to practise lah. You do it all wrong.'

Dad grinned uncomfortably. The man pulled in the kite, elbow by elbow of string.

'No!' I exclaimed. It had finally been up! 'Please don't.'

'Don't worry,' he said, 'We'll get it back up. I'll show you. I'll hold it, you take this.'

He handed me the end of the string, took Dad by the arm, and walked the other way. 'Look,' he said. 'You need to go downwind. He pointed in the sky. 'The wind, where does it come from?'

Dad looked around, uncertain. I opened my mouth again and tasted the wind. 'That way,' I pointed.

'Correct,' the man laughed, his thumb up.

'So I stand that way. No need to run. You just pull gently. Pull, let go, then pull again. No hurry.'

He let go and I pulled. 'Right. Just let go and pull, hand over hand.'

I felt the kite tug the string. It was going up!

I tugged back, and slowly the kite soared. 'Not too fast, be patient,' the man warned me. 'Now, you can walk. And just ease out the string, so it can get higher.'

I looked at Dad proudly, and he grinned.

'Look, Mama, I'm flying the kite!'

Mama, sat next to the stroller with a sleeping Chloe, looked up from her phone and smiled too. 'See, when you ask for help you get it.' She jumped up. 'Wait, stay there. This is an amazing shot.'

Behind us was the skyline, and in the air above me, all the kites – including my yellow butterfly with the green tail. In spite of the string, or perhaps because of it, the kite flew happy and free. I felt like I flew too, but when I turned my head to smile at Mama's phone, the pressure dropped from the string. 'Look out!' Dad yelled. 'Keep walking.' Then, 'Why is everything a photo for you? Just learn to enjoy,' he hissed at Mama.

I ran, and the kite soared again. Mama ignored Dad and gave me a thumbs up and a big smile.

We flew the butterfly some more. Once it came down, and Mama and I managed to get it up again together. Afterwards we walked back to where we could see clouds of fragrant smoke billowing from the coal fires where rows of satay were being roasted. Dad ordered fifty sticks, and we ate till we burst. I thought that any country that had satay like this not only worked, but had to be the best in the world.

When we were almost home, Mama said, looking at her phone. 'That photo got seventy-six likes already! Wasn't it an amazing afternoon?'

Dad and I said nothing. Chloe slept.

22

Surprisingly, school was getting better. Bus rides were still bad – Jenny and Meena alternating snide cockroach remarks with ignoring me – but the rest of the day was ok. In my class people treated me almost like normal.

Although my own life was bordering on boring, terrible things were happening to other people. You would think getting involved in such misery would make a person feel worse, but I experienced the opposite. Even if we could help an aunty only a little – by offering a listening ear, a shoulder to lean on and, where we could, some straightforward advice – I could see some of the strain leaving her face. And every time we made someone else feel better, I felt a little better too. And when I felt better in myself, people at school seemed to treat me better. It was like a spiral that started so deep down, in such shitty stuff, that there was no way for it to go but up.

Not that the stories we heard didn't affect me. Often I lay in bed at night mulling them over in my head, trying to understand why these employers did what they did. I understood them even less than I did my own mother.

Aunty M was turning into an expert in domestic worker issues.

Was she really a busybody? The helpdesk people had told her off for dealing with cases on her own. She told me about it and said she'd do better, stop meddling outside work. But she didn't. The aunties kept calling her.

'When they ask for help, how can I not give it?' she asked, raising her hands skywards. I agreed. 'And you, you are such a good helper.'

We had become closer than ever. It was as if we'd both realised we got along best when we talked about other people, not ourselves. I didn't mention Nurul again. And Aunty M never mentioned Jenny.

When we visited others, my role was mostly to sit and listen. Now and again, though, I pitched in. I was better than Aunty M at remembering all the rules, the details of what had been paid, by whom, what was said, who did what. Aunty M could mix things up. She would look at me, checking that she'd got her facts right. I would make notes in my red notebook – not the Hello Kitty one; that was so childish – but a new one I'd picked specially. If we revisited someone, I'd look up the details beforehand and share them with Aunty M.

We now knew everything about deductions, the payments that the domestic workers – Aunty M and I had learned not to call them the derogative name maid – had to pay when they started a job. Some agencies called it a loan, or savings, or any other name to make it sound nicer. The government only allowed the agencies to ask for two months of recruitment fees on a two-year contract, so they had to be creative in order to charge much more. When we visited someone and it was about salary, or she hadn't been in Singapore that long, I tried to make a summary of the salary she'd received. Often it took a while to get the numbers straight. The aunties had no idea how to manage their finances. If they did get their salary, many sent all of it straight to their home country.

'Write down when you get your salary each month, when and how much,' Aunty M would exclaim. 'How can you say your employer is not paying you, if you don't know what they give you?'

Many of the women who called for help had only been in Singapore a few months, and hadn't finished paying off the loan. But sometimes they weren't even sure how much they'd been charged and how much they still owed. My notebook would be full of scribbled numbers and question marks. Debt, contract, transfer, investment, deductions, remittance, agents; I wrote the words in my little notebook. Whenever a new one came up I didn't understand, I would ask Aunty M for an explanation. Or even Mama or Dad, pretending it was for school. Mama was quite proud that I'd taken an interest in economics, and I didn't correct her.

The stories from Aunty M's helpdesk piled up: stories about woman having their hair cut off by jealous ma'ams; employers hitting women; even one where an employer let her kids hit the maid while she looked on. The realisation that adults could bully other adults scared the hell out of me.

Sri was still in the shelter. Another couple of months had passed without any progress on her case. After the lie detector test, she hadn't heard from the police again. The helpdesk people said they were gathering all the evidence and would soon decide whether they would press charges against her employers. Sri wasn't sure what she was hoping for now. She mainly wanted to go home. If the police decided to press charges, her employers might get punished, but Sri feared that justice would come at a cost. If the case went ahead, Sri was the main witness and wouldn't be able to leave the country until it was over. She had made friends in the shelter that had been stuck in Singapore for years, as court proceedings and appeals dragged on and on. If they got permission from the police they could work under a temporary job scheme, but they weren't all brave enough to do so. Nor was it easy to find an employer. Some women got financial compensation for their long wait without income, but many did not. How much was justice worth to Sri? And could her family in Indonesia hold on that long without her sending any cash?

She struggled to understand what was happening, even with her improved English. Many times she begged Aunty M for help to stop the case, to cancel the charges. Aunty M couldn't get her to understand that that was the prosecutors' call, as it was a criminal case. It was out of Sri's hands now.

Aunty M was worried about Sri; she said she was getting depressed. She had made a good friend at the shelter, but sunk in silence again when that friend went back to Indonesia. There was nothing anyone could do but wait.

I started to think I needed to become a lawyer when I grew up. I'd speed things up. But Aunty M said I was only a little girl, and had no understanding of how things worked in the world of courts and lawyers. She became bossy. When she was like that, I felt much tinier than ten.

The stories we heard at the playground or our house visits weren't as bad as Sri's and her friends' in the shelter, but there were so many of them. Domestic workers not getting enough sleep, having to sleep in a living room where teenage sons played computer games all night, being called stupid over and over again, taking extra deductions from their salary as punishment, not getting paid at all, or too late, being made to cook for a catering business, days off that were promised but not given. Women having to do complicated nursing jobs they weren't trained to do, then getting told off when they didn't do them properly.

I did wonder sometimes about PoPo, and her old Singapore. She had let slip things about cruelty, about the war; yet to me her version of Singapore seemed a lot friendlier than mine. Had people been nicer in the past? I had some inkling there could be cracks in the picture, that reality wasn't black and white like an old photograph.

PoPo had told me about Ah Feng, the old Chinese woman who looked after her when she was little, and I wondered whether she had been anything like my aunties. Had she left a husband and kids behind? Had she gone back to China after PoPo was big enough to look after herself? Would Mama know? Could I ask her without making her sad?

One day, when Mama was in a particularly good mood, I asked. Mama reacted very differently from what I'd expected. She beamed. 'Ah Feng, PoPo's old maid, yes. Did you know, I met her once? She must have been close to ninety then. She stayed in this old people's home, paid for by the uncles. They loved her. In those days, servants were part of the family. Amahs, they were called.'

'Amah? Like in grandmother?' I asked.

'No, that's Ah Mah. Some still call their maids that, amah, or ayah. Ah Feng was sharp as a nail, even at that age. A feminist avant la lettre.'

I didn't get it, and looked blankly at Mama.

'A feminist is someone who wants equal rights for women. Before, women were supposed to get married, have kids, do the housework. But a feminist thinks that women can work, have a career, choose their own life, make their own decisions.'

'Like you?' I said.

Mama was overjoyed. 'Yes exactly, smart one. And you too.'

Me? I wasn't so sure. 'And Aunty M?' I asked.

'I suppose yes, Aunty M too. She took responsibility for her life in her own hands.'

'But she does housework.'

'You can do housework and still be a feminist. She makes money, right? Feminism is about financial independence. About women being able to make their own money. Having your own money makes you free.'

Oh joy. We were back on the old theme, money. Housework was a job if it made you money. I didn't want to be a feminist now, even if I liked the idea of being able to make my own choices, unlike children and domestic workers. As always, money ruined everything.

'So why was Ah Feng a feminist?' I was surprised that Mama had got excited about an old maid, even if she was a feminist.

'In university I wrote a paper on early Chinese feminism; let me see if I can find it. I interviewed Ah Feng for it.'

Mama went up to her room and came back with a thin binder. 'Here.'

We pored over the words together. There were a lot.

'Wait, you sit down, I'll read out the highlights.' Mama reclined in her chair and leafed through the binder. 'Ah Feng was born in the Pearl River Delta, in Guangdong province, early in the century, but she didn't know exactly when. Her family were silk farmers. Then, in the nineteen twenties, the Great Depression hit.'

She looked up from the pages. 'That meant that all over the world businesses crashed and people lost their jobs. People stopped buying expensive silks.'

She flipped through the pages again. 'Ah, here. *Women in the delta traditionally had a high level of freedom and autonomy. Due to a shortage of men, female labour was required at farms. Unmarried women lived together in girls' houses, where they formed sisterhoods with fellow lodgers.*'

Ok, I had not understood a single word. Mama looked up from the paper to explain. 'They couldn't just leave the women at home to do the housework. They needed them on the fields. And the ones that did get married wanted to keep some of those freedoms. But many others refused to get married. They stayed together in these sisterhoods. Ah Feng didn't like men.' Mama laughed. 'She felt they were more trouble than they were worth.'

That sounded a bit like Mary Grace.

'Instead of a wedding they did a special hairdressing ceremony to show they were bound to their sisters. This way, they were allowed to get a job that paid wages. Some people say that before, women didn't work. But that's nonsense. They worked very hard. They just didn't get paid for it.'

'So Ah Feng got married to her friends, instead of to a guy?' I giggled.

Mama nodded again. 'Yes, something like that. She told me she had seen a lot of bad marriages, and didn't see the point.'

Mama read some more passages of the paper for herself. 'After the Great Depression, since there were no jobs in China, these women came to Singapore to work. They also called them Samsui women. Some worked in construction, factories, or other jobs usually done by men. But Ah Feng arrived later and ended up doing domestic work. Interestingly, around that time, the British colonisers had banned new Chinese men from coming into Singapore. They felt there were too many Chinese men and not enough jobs. But they forgot to take the women seriously. It must have been men that made that rule!'

We laughed together. I wondered whether that made me a feminist? If it could make Mama laugh with me, maybe I needed to embrace feminism. I liked the idea of being free, of not having to answer to anybody. But I hated feminism if that too was all about money.

'Ah Feng stayed in another sister house here. Until she found her first job, as a live-in amah. Do you want to know what her first salary was?' Mama flipped through the document frantically. 'Here. Five dollars a week.'

'That's nothing!'

'It was a lot more in the nineteen thirties. And she was live-in, so she had no other costs. And no family to support.'

No remittances, I thought. No daughter to build a yellow house for. She could spend all her five dollars on herself.

'I wonder what she spent it on?'

'That's a good question,' Mama said. 'I never thought to ask that.'

'The interesting thing is that when I wrote this, in the nineties, people felt very strongly about these Chinese amahs. I interviewed some old employers too – they all raved about them. They were so loyal and devoted. They called these amahs 'superior servants', as if they were better than the Filipina and Indonesians that came later.

'But Ah Feng was not so bothered by loyalty. She worked hard and picked the employers that suited her. She preferred to work as an amah, which meant she had to do everything, from cooking to cleaning and laundry, to child-minding. She said that if she was in a bigger household with more servants, she'd have to listen to others instead of being in charge herself. She felt no one could do it better than she could. She took a lot of pride in her work. Did you know she worked for PoPo's family for twenty-five years?

'Ah Feng insisted she didn't owe anyone anything in her life. That was what she was proud of. Her independence was the most important thing.'

Mama let the pages slip through her fingers. 'I was used to getting all my information from a book. PoPo insisted I did some fieldwork and speak to Ah Feng. She was right.'

I wondered whether Mama would be interested in doing

fieldwork on the lives of aunties like Aunty M, who came from Indonesia and the Philippines. The un-superior servants. Could they be feminists if they'd got married?

'Do you think they really were superior to the maids we have now?'

'No,' Mama shrugged. 'That's nonsense. When people look back they like to think everything was better in the past. They apply a rose-coloured filter. Like, they see it as an Instagram shot. I'm sure they weren't much different. People these days like to complain.'

I thought about the aunties I knew, the ones who'd become my friends. They were, most of them, hardworking. 'I think so too.' I said. 'But maybe there was one difference.'

'What's that?'

'The aunties now, they usually have a family, children back home. They send all their money there.'

'Well observed,' said Mama. 'You'll make a good field worker one day. You're right, their loyalty is torn between their job and their families. They're never fully here; their hearts are still in their home countries. They remain foreigners, whereas Ah Feng eventually became a Singaporean.'

I pondered that for a while, wondering what that meant for someone like Dad, whose heart, I hoped, was here with us. Would he eventually become a real Singaporean? But there was another question I wanted to ask Mama first.

'You said that Ah Feng picked who she worked for. That means she had a choice. Is that right?'

'Yes, she did,' said Mama. 'In China, in the old days, they had mui tsai, bondmaids. They were women who were owned by their employers like – well, like slaves, I suppose. Parents were so poor that they sold their children when they couldn't feed them. Little girls as young as five or six were brought up as housemaids in rich families. Bondmaids like that couldn't leave their employers, not as a free woman like Ah Feng could. I believe some bondmaids existed in Singapore too, but thankfully that type of thing isn't allowed these days.'

'I'm not so sure,' I said. 'It's a bit the same for the aunties. They have no money to feed their children, but instead of selling them, they leave them behind. And they can't quit their job either.'

Mama looked surprised. 'Where did you get that idea? What nonsense. MOM has plenty of rules in place to protect the domestic helpers these days.'

I couldn't give away more about my work with Aunty M and the aunties, so I just shrugged. I didn't say what I thought, which was that those rules might be there, but did anyone check whether employers stuck to them? Like when my parents said, 'Do your homework,' and never checked whether I did it or not. So I might be in a lot of trouble at school, and they'd never know until a teacher called them.

Mama handed me the paper. 'Here, why don't you read the rest if you like? It might be a bit difficult for you still, but I'm happy to explain more. But don't lose it. It's the only copy.'

I tried reading the report, but there were so many things I didn't understand that I didn't even know what questions to ask Mama. I hadn't had a conversation like this with her since I couldn't remember when. But somehow it had fallen flat when we started talking about the aunties of today.

How were they different? Were they less interesting? The things Mama had told me mixed with what I'd learned from Aunty M, and not all of it added up. The good feeling I'd had during our talk faded away. I didn't want to become a feminist. I wanted my mother to build me a yellow house, like the one Aunty M would build for Nurul; or even better, like PoPo's Blue House.

But Mama didn't care what I wanted. *But honey, we have a house! Isn't this a beautiful condo?* I could already hear her reply. And then she'd say something about financial independence being more important than a house. Would we ever understand each other? But if feminism was what it took for me to get Mama back, perhaps I needed to make an effort.

I showed the paper to Aunty M but she barely looked at it. 'Superior servants. Pah! The Chinese look down their noses at everyone else.'

'Hey, I'm part Chinese,' I reminded her.

She looked at me without a smile.

23

Just as I was starting to feel accepted by the aunties, something happened that changed everything. It started at the playground. Maricel was telling us about her friend Ronalyn, who was in trouble.

'What's the trouble?' Aunty M asked.

Maricel gently kicked Toy-toy, who was biting her toes. 'Shoo, Toy-toy. Aunty's talking.

'The trouble is Ah Gong,' said Maricel. 'When Ronalyn started working there, the ma'am, Ah Gong's daughter, already said that Ah Gong was naughty. That's why they had to let the last maid go, she said. Ronalyn needed the job. Her son has medical problems, so she took the job anyway. Ah Gong was eighty-four. How naughty could he be, she thought. But now she is late.'

I was about to ask what she was late for, when Aunty M exclaimed 'Maricel!'

'What?'

Aunty M pointed at me with the top of her head. Maricel covered her mouth with her fingers.

'Go play at the swing, Maya,' Aunty M said.

'I don't want to. I want to sit here,' I sulked.

Aunty M knotted together her brows like Mama usually did.

I'd tried raising my brows like that on Chloe, but it didn't work. It worked when Aunty M did it to me, though, and I pottered to the swings, brooding.

Why didn't they trust me? Why couldn't I hear about a naughty old man? I tried to listen in, but every time I approached the benches – from the back, from the side, on my tippy toes – they stopped and changed the subject. I felt the pitter patter of tiny cockroach feet in my stomach again. It was something I hadn't felt for a long time, and the only way to squash it was by going to the swings and swinging as high as I could.

When we got home, I asked Aunty M why I couldn't hear the story of naughty Ah Gong.

'Sayang,' she said, 'If your mother found out about you listening to a story like that, she would fire me on the spot. And she would be absolutely right. You are ten. You are too young.'

I left to sulk. I knew Aunty M had visited Ronalyn without me when I came home from school the next afternoon. She must have taken Chloe, so why was that ok? Chloe, who wasn't even two!

I could tell Aunty M wasn't going to tell me anything, so I thought of visiting Win. I hadn't been to see her in a while. But something held me back, made me stay in and do homework instead. I sat there at the dinner table twiddling my fingers, dawdling, pretending to read. When Aunty M's phone rang and she took it into her room, she left the door ajar. I snuck over and crouched in front of it.

I was in luck: it was Maricel on the phone, and Aunty M was giving her a full update on her visit that morning. She'd done some sort of test. False alarm, it turned out, and Aunty M sounded relieved.

'I'm happy for her. It saves her a lot of trouble. She would have lost the job if MOM found out.'

Found out what? That Ah Gong was naughty? That Ronalyn was late? How could you be just late? You had to be late for something. Was Ah Gong angry that Ronalyn brought him his porridge late?

Aunty M's hushed yet excited tone pointed to something different, and I started to get a hunch about what was going on. Ronalyn's problems must have to do with *that*. With *it*. Something I had little clue about yet.

'She said she wanted to go to the police if it had been positive. But now, I don't know if she will.'

How did the police come into it? Into *it*?

Aunty M was quiet for a while. Maricel must have been talking.

'Yes. I know. They will say that. Ugh. Ah Gong is wrinkly and old. It makes me sick.'

Another silence.

'A charge will never stick. Not without proof of violence.'

Aunty M hmm-ed in response to Maricel. Then, 'No, she didn't fight. She was changing his bed. He was sitting in a chair, and he just grabbed her from behind. Yes, she is stronger, but she did not want to make trouble. She has her son, remember, and doctor's bills. She thought it would just be kissing.'

Maricel shouted so hard on the other side I could hear it, but not what she was talking about.

'She kept silent first, when he kissed her cheek. Then her mouth. She still kept silent. Then he went too far.'

More noise from Maricel. How far did Ah Gong go?

'She still kept silent. Until she freaked out when she was late. He told her he was too old for that, that it wasn't him. But she had not seen her husband in over a year...Yes...Of course, she panicked...She's asking whether she should still call the police.'

Chloe walked towards me, stretching her hands. I put my finger to my lips. I wobbled, and almost tipped against the door. Inside, Aunty M talked on.

'She would have lost the job anyway. They would have found out at the medical and sent her back. Now, she doesn't know what to do. It hasn't happened again, no.'

Chloe toddled up noisily. I wasn't sure why I was still listening. I could feel this Ah Gong's smelly lips and prickly whiskers on my own cheek. It made me gag. But my feet stayed glued to the floor.

Aunty M was now debating with Maricel what Ronalyn should do. Leave the family, said Aunty M. It seemed Maricel disagreed.

'Yes, I know he should be in jail, but that's not going to happen, is it? She weighs twice as much as he does. He is eighty-four. She is never going to convince a police officer she could not have fought him off. She has been stupid. Very, very stupid. She needs to go home.'

I couldn't listen any longer. My feet had fallen asleep and my head spun. I toppled over, crashing in front of Chloe on the floor.

Aunty M rushed out of the room. 'What are you doing here? How long have you been here?'

'Chloe and I were just playing, I didn't know you were in there,' I lied unconvincingly.

Aunty M said into the phone, 'I need to go now. I'll call you tonight.' She turned to me, 'Are you sure? You ok?'

I picked up Chloe and took her to the Duplo blocks. 'Sure.'

If Aunty M would lose her job if Mama found out about me being involved in this, whatever it was, I'd have to be ok. So I put on an ok face.

Chloe and I built a tower; that is, I built it and she kept pushing it over as soon as it was as tall as she was. I tried hard not to think about what I'd heard. Whenever I did, a wave of panic rolled up inside me. Usually when we encountered something terrible, Aunty M and I would deal with it together, and it would feel ok. Now I was alone. I had no idea what to do with the information I'd just heard, half of which I didn't understand, and the part I did understand made me feel sick. I was supposed to do nothing, know nothing, and this helplessness made me feel very, very scared. When Chloe and I had finished playing, I tried to bury the whole thing deeply under all the colourful blocks in the box.

The next day, Aunty M took Chloe to the playground. I stayed home, claiming homework and tiredness. The truth was that I couldn't bear to be around the aunties and risk hearing another word about Ronalyn. The prickly whiskers of Ah Gong tickled as badly on my cheeks as the cockroach feet had, first on my tongue, and now in my stomach. The cases of the aunties, the helpdesk, Aunty M herself – they had been my escape from Jenny, Meena, from my unhappiness at school, the Mamamonster. But my safe place now proved not that safe after all.

I sat on my bed, trying to read, but I felt so nauseous I had to run to the toilet and vomit until I was completely empty. I must have fallen asleep afterwards, because Aunty M woke me, asking how I was feeling and whether I was well enough for dinner. I wasn't, and I slept on until Mama woke me for breakfast in the morning. She was kind, and kept talking about a stomach bug going round, and said that I should stay home from school that day.

I felt lonelier than I ever had. I had no friends at school and none at home either. I had to avoid Mama in case I became weak and told her everything, and got Aunty M in trouble. Who could I talk to now about the things that upset me? I lay in bed trying to ignore the wriggle of the cockroach and the tickling of the whiskers. It took a few sleepless evenings until the cockroach won out, and Ronalyn's story sunk out of sight. The cockroach, my only friend now, guarded the story like a fierce little dragon. The one thing that managed to get past him was a question that had surfaced in my mind: could feminism help Ronalyn?

24

Suddenly, fate decided I needed a break: I got a friend.

In international school, kids came and went all the time, and your best friend could move out any day. Or move in. Her real name was Cathelijne, but no one could pronounce that. Our teacher called her Cathlyn, which was the closest she could get without breaking her tongue, she said. Her parents called her Lijn, which sounded like *line* to me, odd but cute, and she said I should call her Cat. She said she liked being a different person to different people.

Cat blew me away. To start with, her names were cool and original. Not like Maya. Maya, as Dad had explained once, was international, not really linked to any country. Perfect for someone like me, who came from nowhere. I hated it. I'd once googled the meaning: it was *illusion*. I wasn't sure what illusion meant, so I googled that word too. Many synonyms came up, amongst them phantom, and figment of the imagination. That really helped my sense of self.

Cat's family obviously didn't care about whether everyone would be able to spell or pronounce her name. Her last name I could never remember. It was a jumble of unintelligible letters and she laughed if anyone tried to pronounce it. 'Just call me Jones. Cat Jones. I am going to find a man named Jones to marry when I grow up.'

Cat was amazing. She was Dutch but had never lived in the Netherlands, the same country Opa was from. Cat didn't need to have a country to belong to; she seemed to belong everywhere. She'd lived in a village in Borneo before moving to Singapore. Her dad was an expert on monkeys with exceptionally big noses.

On her first day at school, Cat had come up to me and bluntly said: 'Why do they call you Cockroach?'

At first, I felt like a nest of baby cockroaches had hatched in my stomach. They crawled up my throat and filled my mouth so I couldn't speak. But Cat looked at me in such a way that I spat them all out. And I told her. Just like that.

She was cool about it. Cat told me that lots of people ate insects. In the jungle they ate special ants to get vitamin C. She said they tasted nice, a bit fruity, like orange.

'Did you try them?' I asked, impressed.

'Of course. Insects are protein. And vitamins. I have eaten,' she counted on the fingers of her left hand, 'ants, mealworms, snails, flying termites, and crickets. But I've never had cockroach.'

She said it as if she was in awe of me.

Cat went on: 'Grasshoppers are the best. If you deep fry them, they get crunchy, and very, very lekker.'

'Lecker?'

'Delicious, I mean. I've had them a few times. In Vietnam they put them on a stick and grill them.'

'Grasshopper satay.' We both giggled. 'Did your parents know? Did they let you?'

'Yes, it was my mum's idea. She's really into that sort of thing. Alternative sources of protein, saving the world. She doesn't eat meat. But she still ate the grasshoppers. We had a scorpion once too. It was covered in chocolate, but it still tasted weird.'

I said that cockroaches tasted vile, nothing like fruit at all, nor crispy, but like something that should be stuck to the bottom of your shoe. We looked at each other and doubled up laughing.

'Did you ever eat chichak?' I asked.

'The lizard? No, have you?'

I told her PoPo's story, how they ate them in the war.

'We should go and catch some,' she joked, and then we were friends.

Cat's dad was with Singapore University now, doing important research on the funny nose monkeys, which were really called proboscis monkeys. Cat said they had some in the Singapore Zoo, and she would show me one day.

I was jealous about almost everything in my new friend's life. She lived in a house next to a nature reserve, and when you were there it felt like you were in the jungle. A jungle in Singapore, just a few minutes from the city. It was a revelation you could live like that, away from concrete or manicured parks. We had been to that nature reserve, hiked around the reservoir, but we always stuck to the boardwalks. Someone else, someone who'd just moved here, had to show me my own city.

Mama said Cat's family were maladjusted. I wasn't sure

whether that was good or bad. Dad had laughed then, and said they were just a bit wild. He said he'd take Cat's dad out for drinks, but he never did.

I would have loved to live in a house like Cat's. Dad was all for it, but Mama said it would be full of snakes and bugs. I vehemently denied that when Mama said it, but later Cat admitted it was true. She'd seen two snakes since they'd moved in. As the daughter of a biologist, she could name them too. The first was a bronzeback tree snake, long, thin and pretty, curled around the bars of her sister's bed frame. When I asked whether her sister had freaked out, she shrugged. Tree snakes, she said, were only mildly venomous. By bedtime, this one had long since vanished into the garden. The other snake had been a house wolf snake, again mildly venomous, curled around the base of the toilet one morning. Cat said that pythons could climb up through the pipes and bite you on your bum. I wasn't sure if that was true, but I was always nervous when I used the toilet in her house.

They had monkeys too. Normal monkeys, not proboscis monkeys, roaming over the fence, not understanding the difference between nature reserves and human streets. They swung through the trees in a troupe, some with babies clutching to their bellies. Cat and I would sit watching as they filed by in a row. They scaled a large palm leaf, one at a time, waited for it to sway and tilt, and then jumped off to the next tree, the leaf swaying back to its original position so the next member of the family could jump on. We would watch in silence, our flow of words temporarily halted while we sipped our Ribenas and looked on.

Cat's mother said the monkeys were a pest, and that she was

tired of hiding all the food. Now that they'd learned to graze from human bins, they wouldn't stay in the forest. One day, when I was there, she scolded Cat's little brother Oliver for losing the toothpaste yet again. 'Can't you ever treat your things, our things, with some respect? What did you do to it?'

We found the empty tube in the garden. It was only when Cat picked it up to bring it inside and incriminate her brother that we noticed the two large punctures in the side. Cat and I imagined a monkey, high up in the trees, snickering at us with a pearly white grin, wide as the Cheshire cat's.

Cat laughed when I said she lived in a jungle. 'This isn't a jungle. In Borneo there's jungle.'

Cat's mother didn't work outside the house. Anna, Cat's older sister, spent most of her time in her room on her iPhone, unless her mother got too annoyed and confiscated it. Anna would be in a huff all afternoon if that happened, and still wouldn't come out and play with us. They did have an aunty: her name was Mimi, and she was from Borneo. Mimi blended naturally into the jungle background, and didn't speak much English. She'd been with the family since Cat's little brother was born, which was longer ago than Cat could remember.

Mimi was homesick often. In Borneo her whole family had lived together in the few small rooms that had been allocated to her behind Cat's house, and she wasn't used to living alone. Her husband was a policeman, and when he had lost his job they couldn't afford to say no to the Singapore dollars Cat's mother offered her if she'd follow them here. The money was good, but Cat worried Mimi would go home soon. She was lonely, and always looked sad.

Cat's brother Ollie was wild as a wolf, running amok in the greenery. He loved his catapult. He was only allowed to use it with the seeds of the large oil palm, not stones, as he promised his mother without looking her in the eyes. The monkeys grinned down at Ollie from the same palm he foraged under for seeds, but his catapult shots helped keep them under control.

The monkeys ate the palm seeds and everything else. Bare green stalks adorned the side fence, where Cat's mother's orchid collection became monkey food as soon as their petals unfolded. The baby papaya tree was chomped up, stalk and leaves. In season, the monkeys hung out in the rambutan tree, throwing the peel and seeds on our heads.

The best thing about Cat was that she could act as if I, not she, were the interesting one. It made me feel warm inside. But I much preferred listened to her telling me about Borneo, the proboscis monkeys, the snakes. She was a talker, bubbling like a cauldron. I used to be a talker too, before Jenny and the cockroach; but being ignored had turned me into a nobody, an observer, a listener. And nobody listened to a nobody, so what choice had I had? Cat was an asker too. She asked and asked till I spilt. When I told her about the kids on the bus, she said that I wasn't the loser, they were. And she said what I did with Aunty M, helping the aunties, was the most phenomenal thing she'd ever heard.

I loved being interesting, and showed her my red notebook. I made her swear never to tell anyone, and she said best friends never tell. When she said the words 'best friends' it felt like I was glowing inside. I could feel the cockroach gurgling as it slowly drowned.

Every day at school, Cat grilled me on what I'd done the day before. She said she asked so much because she wanted to be a scientist when she grew up, and scientists needed to do that, so they could learn. She wanted to learn about Singapore, which I thought was weird. Singapore wasn't like Borneo. It was just a city, where the biggest thing that happened was when the MRT trains broke down, and everyone was outraged as they'd be late for work. Or when it rained so hard that the drains overflowed and people got mad at the government for not controlling the weather. I suppose that deep down, I sensed there was another layer to Singapore, one I couldn't find on my own. If PoPo had only still been there, she would know. She knew where to look, just like Cat knew where to look to find the magic in the little things, the magic that hid in old, chipped-on-the-edge things, not the new shiny ones most people preferred. Most people saw only the marble and the rubble.

When I told Cat about PoPo, about being Peranakan, she loved it. But when I told her about Opa, secretly proud about that one fourth of me was Dutch like her, she wasn't interested.

'I have two opas already,' she said. 'I don't have a PoPo.'

I don't have a PoPo either, not anymore, I wanted to say; but then I realised I still had her inside me. Cat wanted to have a grandmother like PoPo, and I wanted a dad that was a proboscis monkey expert.

'Do you want to be a monkey scientist?' I asked.

'No,' said Cat, 'I want to be an anthropologist, like Mama. They study people, not animals. I want to study your aunties.'

It made me think about the aunties, and Mama's fieldwork. I'd never studied them; I'd just tried to be their friend. I was fascinated by Cat, like she was fascinated by my aunties.

25

After Ronalyn, I'd been too terrified to eavesdrop – but Cat gave me my courage back with her talk of science and research. PoPo used to say that little pitchers had big ears whenever Mama, who was never sensitive to these things, was going on about something that PoPo felt I shouldn't hear. It meant I had to scram.

As for me, I'd learned to make myself invisible, and to recognise the change in tone that signalled a subject was coming up that was so interesting it wasn't suitable for me. Many adults were too short-sighted to see the little pitchers lurking in the corner.

Cat's parents let us take the public bus home together, and after we alighted near her place we'd hang out at the food court, spending our pocket money on milo dinosaurs. Scooping the sweet powder off the iced chocolate malt drinks, we were scientists, anthropologists, doing research about gossiping. Cat's fascination for the domestic workers had ignited something in me too, and rather than just helping individuals, I was keen to learn about the bigger picture. The question that inevitably arose next was *why?* Why did people treat others like that?

We wedged in between people in the queue, next to tables with groups of women, or even sneaking up on people from behind, dawdling with big innocent eyes, on the prowl for spicy words. Sometimes conversations that seemed promising were hard to follow: people would speak fast, mumbling, and in any of Singapore's accents and dialects. Cat, with her knack for languages, was fast becoming more fluent in Singlish than me, and the back of her red notebook was now a dictionary of phrases.

Cat taught me to appreciate the language of my own country, the one that my mother looked down her nose at. It was much richer that I had imagined, so much deeper than yelling aiyoh, or sticking lah at the end of your sentences. Economical to the bare bones, one word of Singlish could say more than a whole string of them in conventional English. How to translate shiok, a word easily heard at a food stall? Delicious? Pleasurable? Amazing? Nah, the prata flatbreads we ordered at our favourite stall were just shiok, no other word for them.

My best stories to listen to were still the ones about domestic workers. But they were hard to find; people didn't hang about at food courts complaining about their maids all day. Some afternoons we'd be there for an hour, and all we got was boring stuff. Other days, we'd chance upon a conversation that was a sheer gem of nastiness.

One afternoon, we managed to get seats right next to two women discussing a bad maid. One lady, dressed in a flowery skirt and green blouse and with a pile of shopping next to her feet, said she'd had one that was fine at first, but now, after two years, was always forgetting everything. She said, 'That seems to be the norm, work performance drops drastically after contract renewal. Constantly forgetting stuff, dirty rooms . She now sibeh kayu. My washing machine, spoilt already. I told her to wash all by hand. I'm not buying her new one already. She spends so much time in the toilet oso. I need to send her home. This maid terok terok, *annoying* for me.'

The other one, in track suit and trainers, replied, 'Tsk, either they are ignorant of the consequences their absentmindedness could cause, or they simply lack a care attitude leh.'

I wasn't sure what on earth she was saying. With their jumble of dialect, long fancy words and random colloquialisms, Cat and I struggled to understand most of what these women were talking about – but our ears turned red nevertheless.

Sporty lady added, as an afterthought, 'Aiyoh, if they are blur, *lost in their own world*, it can mean she pregnant, and lost what to do, so can't concentrate at work. That one blur like a sotong. There are signs to look out for. I think she busy using the hand phone in the toilet. Make sexy selfies for the boyfriend.' She sighed. 'I hope can get better one.'

Flower skirt lady sipped her kopi and said, 'No, all sama-sama. And I cannot tahan interviews. The agencies and the MOM, they don't care about how employers feel, as long as you got a maid, money goes in their pocket, job is done. They tell you this maid has been trained how to take care of newborn baby, but in fact was just half-day course. Having own kids is not experience. These women, wah lau eh, so suaku. Don't know how to do civilised way.'

'True,' nodded sporty one. 'And the maid lie too. My last maid told me she loves kids, but after a while I found out she is a good cook, not interested my kids at all. They all lie. But you can tell from their attitude during interview already.'

She shoved the plate of fried carrot cake in front of her towards her friend. 'Want or not?'

Flower skirt shook her head. 'Nah. These Ang Moh, you know, they spoil the market. Easy for them, in their big houses. When I interviewed last time, they asked me if they will have private room. I told them nicely no, it depends where I want you to sleep. Sometimes in the study room alone, sometimes with my kids if required, though I never like a maid to sleep with my kids. After that I replied, if you not happy with my answer, you want a private room, you can pay me rental lah.'

Sporty woman laughed. 'Steady lah! Me same, don't have space for private room. How big is my house? Am I a millionaire foreigner? No, just simple Singaporean. These maids, need money, so come to Singapore to work, right, to earn more? In their country, if it is so good, why not stay there? If they want a private room and eat like a queen, that means she not here to work. She want to be some ya ya queen? Can! Go stay at their own house and have an early night lor. Maybe it will come true in their dream.'

They were now both laughing. Cat and I looked at each other.

When we got to Cat's house, we went over the conversation. We hadn't understood everything but one thing was clear to us.

'Those women talk as if the aunties are not human. Animals,' Cat said.

I nodded. 'Shouldn't the rules be the same for all people?'

Cat grinned. 'All people, and monkeys, and maids.'

'I'm not sure whether you'd want the same rules for the monkeys. You'd have no bananas left.'

'Or toothpaste,' Cat added. 'They stole it again yesterday. My teeth feel dirty, I had to brush without. They especially like Ollie's strawberry-flavoured one. My mother said she'll buy a box they can't open to keep it in. The monkeys can't just take what they want. '

I remembered the strawberry jam story, and how the Cynthia had bought the more expensive pineapple jam, just to spite her maid.

'Wah adults so crazy lah,' Cat said, overdoing her own attempt at Singlish when I told her.

'They are,' I said. 'It's like they don't think about things. It's no benefit to her to not get the jam. Why can't she just go and buy her own jam? It's not fair.'

'You know what my mother always says?' Cat said.

'Well?' I asked.

Cat looked at me pointedly. 'She says: *Life's not fair. Get used to it.*' She jumped up. 'But anyway, adults are stupid, this goes to show. Let's do something else.'

She spotted some ants walking in a long file up the leg of the table, aiming to cross. 'Look, ants. Let's eat them!'

There was a small nag in my stomach.

Cat grinned. 'You wanna go first?'

I thought back at the cockroach incident. 'Nah. You go first.'

Cat shrugged. 'Okay.'

She laid her hand in front of the column, and several ants hiked up the hill of her thumb. She licked them up in one swoop.

'They taste like nothing.'

I squashed some on the tip of my index finger, and put them in my mouth. Cat was right. They were tasteless, so when I went home I had pineapple jam on my mind, not ants.

26

Mama's good moods got more and more rare. She was irritable most of the time now. She kept complaining about her boss, asking Dad how she could prove herself if they didn't give her any responsibility.

Dad's optimistic day-out-on-Sunday scheme was also wearing thin. Since dinners with the whole family were scarce, breakfast time had been appointed quality family time by Mama. The idea was nice, but I wasn't a morning person and there was little real conversation. Aunty M would have her breakfast in the kitchen and Dad was forbidden his phone. Not that he stuck to that; his work too important to leave it further than a thumb's length away.

And then, for some reason, the school bus started coming twenty minutes earlier and breakfast was squeezed into half an hour of Mama yelling at me to hurry up, yelling more frantically with every minute that passed. I hated the school bus. My main goal in the morning was to miss it, but Mama would never let that happen. She'd run around like a sheep dog, trying to get me to eat breakfast, get dressed, brush my teeth, put on shoes, comb my hair, wash my face, at the same time checking PE schedules, library books that had to be returned, and days overdue homework folders, stuffing them all into my too-heavy bag, often on the wrong days. Then she'd run out herself, just a few minutes before the bus arrived.

Aunty M made my packed lunch, which was always sitting on the kitchen table before I got up, together with a full water bottle. For a while, she'd managed the packing of my bag too. She'd known exactly which days I had PE, or swimming, or the library. She even knew which books I'd finished and which I was still reading, leaving the half-read ones next to my bed to finish. This apparently offended Mama so much that she'd decided she would oversee the bag packing herself. She was my mother, after all, not Aunty M.

But I never had enough time in the morning, and whilst Mama could manage a team of bankers without a struggle, which day I had PE eluded her. Aunty M would look on from behind the kitchen door, silently shaking her head without even moving it.

One morning, Mama exploded. I was sat at the table with my eyes half shut, wearing my pyjamas because Mama didn't trust me to keep my uniform clean, as if I were still a baby like Chloe. Dad was on the toilet, and had been for a while.

Mama was yelling, and I shoved the Weetabix around the bowl to the rhythm.

'You'd think half an hour is enough to eat breakfast! Seriously. Eat. Can you please put a bite in your mouth?'

I looked up. The spoon was halfway to my mouth when she started again.

'Sure, in your own time, take it easy. It's not as if the bus will be here in ten minutes. Ah, wait, yes, it will be! And you're not even dressed!'

With every word the volume and pitch went up. But I knew it wouldn't become really bad until the yelling stopped. That happened after I'd taken that one bite.

'Eat. Your. Weetabix. Now.'

I swallowed angrily. 'I am eating already.'

'No, not already. You didn't do it already for the last fifteen minutes! You only did it just now. Already? You are nowhere near all ready!'

She started a tirade about how eating one bite of Weetabix in ten minutes was perfectly normal, sure, while I tried not to listen and slowly ate a little bit faster.

She pulled the bowl from under my nose.

'Hey! I didn't finish yet.'

'There's no time. Bus comes in five. Get dressed.'

She did my pigtails after I'd dressed, and she did them roughly. When I looked into Mama's eyes it was not her staring back, it was the Mamamonster. A Mamamonster who would scream me into getting dressed and my hair brushed in under four minutes. The Mamamonster wasn't sensible. She knew no patience.

'Stop, Mama, you're pulling my hair!' I screamed.

'If you'd hold your head still I wouldn't have to,' she said, pulling harder.

In the mirror, I could see her thoughts puffing in angry red clouds from her ears: *I will pull your hair, your ears, till there is no scream left in you, I will kick you flying over the balcony, I will box your ears till they pound more than mine.*

But she didn't. Mama must have reached into the depths of

her soul to drag out her last ounce of self-control. She growled, shoving me into the hallway: 'The Bus. Is. There. Shoes! Now!' The last word was spoken in her deepest, darkest voice, all those terrible thoughts shining from her piercing eyes. 'Now! Or....'

The silence that followed was the scariest. I was half-afraid she'd hurt me, but she just turned away. Afterwards, huddled in my corner at the back of the bus and hoping no one else would have a go at me that morning, I tried to tell myself it was the pig-boss's fault Mama was like this. Mama had needed PoPo to keep her sane, and now I needed to become a feminist to help Mama. I hadn't had any proper conversations with her since the one about Ah Feng, and I felt guilty.

If she made it home in time, Mama always made up for breakfast at bedtime. She and Dad aimed for one of them to be there for the bed time ritual, the tooth brushing, the tucking in, and, most important, story time. Mama was more relaxed in the evenings, although I suspected her of wanting to get me to bed quickly so she could sink into oblivion in front of the TV. I asked Mama to tell me her own stories instead of reading from a book, like PoPo had, but she would make something up that lasted less than a minute, and involved a princess of some kind that rebelled against her prince, demanding the crown for herself. Dad's stories would be even shorter and, even when not broken up by his ever-present phone, they didn't really make sense. Often he resorted to silly jokes and tickling, but that was good too.

Falling asleep was difficult for me. There was so much to process, and after Mama or Dad left, I would tell myself PoPo's old stories again and again, remembering and embellishing. Now that I had a friend, I needed even more to make sure not to forget about PoPo. The stories about her past had helped me become who I was; they gave a backdrop to my own confusing life that she and I would chew over together. Chronicling events, characterising strange people, exaggerating or condensing, it all helped me make sense of the things I saw.

Occasionally, there was a night when neither Mama nor Dad were there, and Aunty M would put me to bed. Aunty M knew how to tell a story. Her stories flowed between Indonesian folk tales and people we both knew, condo children, aunties. She stirred them all up into a fantasy world that exceeded even my imagination. She tried to include lessons to be learned; sometimes it worked, but often the morals got lost somewhere along the way.

Aunty M told me about Kanchil. He came from Indonesia and was famous there, Aunty M said, like a movie star. Kanchil was a queer creature, a cross between a mouse and a deer, small, swift, without horns but with teeth that pointed from his snout like tiny daggers. Kanchil's English name, mousedeer, was less inspiring. I'd thought he was a fantasy made up by Aunty M until I saw the real thing in the zoo. It would have been a big disappointment, if the little creature with its pencil legs and black bead eyes hadn't been unspeakably cute. I stared at it for a long time, unbelieving, while it stood defiantly chewing some large green leaves. The noise of approaching footsteps scared the shy creature into the bushes. He wasn't what I'd expected from Aunty M's daredevil Kanchil at all.

Kanchil might look funny, small, and insignificant, Aunty M

said, but he was renowned for his cunning. All the stories about him showed that.

Kanchil was friends with Tiger. What a friend he was, that Tiger, always making plans to eat Kanchil.

'Why would he be friends with someone who tries to eat him?' I asked.

'That is a very good question,' Aunty M said, but gave no answer.

I nestled down in the pillows, eager with anticipation.

'One day, Kanchil was walking in the wood, and Tiger passed by. Tiger snuck up on Kanchil from behind, and seized his hind leg in his mouth. Mousedeer was stuck.

'"Good morning, breakfast," Tiger said, speaking through teeth clenched around Kanchil's tiny paw.

'"I'm not breakfast," said mousedeer.'

Kanchil spoke in Aunty M's squeakiest voice. Tiger, on the other hand, had a deep growl.

'"Of course you are," said Tiger.

'Hopping on three legs, Kanchil turned to Tiger's big yellow eyes.

'"Friend," he said, "I wouldn't eat me if I were you."

'"Why not?" asked Tiger.

'"You don't want to make the king angry," answered Kanchil.

'"The king? Why would he care?"

'Kanchil shrugged his free shoulders. "He gave me an important job today. I have to guard his cake."

'Kanchil pointed his nose at a disc of buffalo dung lying nearby.

'"A cake!" Tiger exclaimed.

'"Yes, a cake."'

By then, I'd figured out what was going to happen, but that didn't make me want to hear what followed any less.

'The Tiger growled. "Oh. Can I have a bite?"

'"No, cannot. The king will have me killed."

'Tiger laughed, almost letting go of Kanchil's leg. "And I'll eat you if you won't."

'Kanchil pretended to think long and hard. "Ok, take a bite. But you need to let me go first. I want to be far away in the forest when the king finds out."

'Tiger needed his mouth anyway to eat the cake, and he gingerly unclamped his jaw. Kanchil sprinted off.

'Tiger went to smell the cake, the musky, dungy odour wafting towards him as he approached. Tiger realised he'd been tricked. But the forest had closed behind Kanchil. He was nowhere to be seen.'

The stories were beautifully simple. Every time, Kanchil outwitted enemies that were bigger and stronger than him, seemingly without effort. 'We should be like him,' Aunty M twinkled. 'Small and smart is better than big and strong.' She tickled the soles of my feet, gave me a kiss on the forehead, and tiptoed out of the room.

'Aunty M,' I called after her. 'Is Mama the Tiger?'

Aunty M stuck her head round the doorpost. 'No sayang, Mama is your Mama. Your Mama loves you. She'd never eat you.'

I assumed the Tiger must be Jenny. But cockroaches weren't

smart, cute, or brave like a mousedeer. Aunty M looked at me and smiled, her eyes warm in the half-light that came through the crack of the door.

Aunty M seemed friendlier after that, as if she started to forgive me for the thing I didn't understand. It made me wonder whether she'd ever told Nurul and Adi these stories. Maybe over the phone? I wouldn't have minded if she had. I would have liked it, in fact. Then I thought of Mama. How would Kanchil deal with a Mamamonster?

27

A new person appeared at the playground. Cat was the one who spotted her. She nudged me and laughed: 'Is that a boy or a girl?'

He or she had short hair and a slim, gawky body. He or she wore plain shorts and a green shirt. I asked Aunty M, who seemed to think it obvious.

'Who is that? Run Vang. She's new. She lives on our floor, actually. She's from Myanmar.'

Just another aunty then, I thought, and lost some of my interest. I knew so many already. Cat was for some reason intrigued by her, and hung about to see if she could talk to her. But Run Vang didn't look very approachable. She sat apart from the other aunties, even from Moe Moe, who was from Myanmar too and was chatting to another of her countrywomen. Moe Moe still came to the playground with Harry, leaving Jenny at home (or with Meena, for all I knew).

Run Vang, the boy-girl, hovered in the corner, mostly glued to her phone. She tapped furiously away at it, switching from serious looks to bursts of giggles. Then she took out her headphones and started to watch a movie. She had a little boy and a baby in her charge, but didn't seem interested in them. She rocked the baby's stroller with her foot. The boy had run away as soon as they arrived and was scampering between the slides, the climbing frame and the seesaws with the other little ones.

Khusnul arrived with the toddlers and Snoopy in tow.

'Aunty Khusnul,' I said, 'can we play with Snoopy?'

'Sure,' Khusnul took a ball from her bag and handed it to me. It was a bright yellow plastic one, with little blue bones embossed on it.

I threw the ball and Snoopy fetched it, bringing it back for a pat and a fondle of her frizzy fur. I threw the ball towards Cat now, and Snoopy ran over, barking her high-pitched yap. But Cat looked the other way, pointing at the boy standing on top of the climbing frame yelling, holding on with one hand and flapping the other as if he were flying. Weaving his legs through the bars of the frame, he released his second hand, spreading his arms like wings.

'Is he going to fall?' Cat asked.

Behind him another boy climbed upwards, challenging for the top position.

The aunties were looking too, Jenalyn pointing and flustered. We all looked at Run Vang, who was still on her phone.

The boy was starting to swing down, dangling from one leg, bending backwards and using his hands to defend his top spot.

'He will fall,' Jenalyn cried, and ran over; but Cat beat her to it, grabbing him just as he started to topple. She hoisted him down and dragged him to Run Vang, who finally looked up.

Cat shouted at Run Vang, who glared back, not understanding the fuss. Moe Moe and her friend, who'd been watching from a distance, came over and took over the shouting in Burmese. Run

Vang stuffed her phone in her back pocket. She grabbed the boy and with an angry look pushed both him and the stroller out of the playground.

Cat walked back to the benches. 'She's just like my sister, that stupid girl. Always on the phone.'

I was a bit apprehensive that Cat was stepping in like that, and looked for Aunty M's response; but she didn't seem to notice Cat. Instead she mumbled something about Run Vang's irresponsible behaviour.

Jenalyn nodded. 'It's true. We should teach her. Someone took a photo of my friend when she was on her phone at the playground, and put it on Facebook. Everybody saw and her employer was furious. Now the employer took her phone.'

Cat grinned, and asked Jenalyn if she could borrow her phone next time they saw Run Vang. Neither of us were allowed phones yet.

'No,' said Aunty M, 'don't. It's nasty to expose someone publicly.'

Moe Moe adopted the look of a schoolteacher. 'No need. I show her,' she nodded. 'That girl, she better not here.'

'What do you mean?' Aunty M asked.

'She only fifteen. How can she do job? She no responsible.'

'Fifteen?' Jenalyn said, 'How is that possible? How did she get her work pass approved?'

'She has passport says she already twenty-five,' Moe Moe said. 'Passport fake.'

'Really?' Jenalyn said. 'But that's ten years more.'

Khusnul shrugged. 'Mine is false too. It says I'm thirty-four, but I'm only twenty-eight.

'How long have you been in Singapore?' Cat asked Khusnul.

It had taken me a long time to join the conversations of the aunties, and even now I rarely did so unless they spoke to me first. And here was Cat, diving straight in.

'Ten years. When I was nineteen, I first came. So I had to buy fake passport, so I was twenty-three already or I could not get the work pass.

'In the Philippines, you can't get it so easy,' Jinky pondered.

'It was, maybe, two hundred,' Khusnul said.

Moe Moe added, 'In Myanmar, easy too. All the girls have. Agent gets it for you. They tell you no problem.'

She looked at Run Vang again. 'This one, you can see she teenager. Giggling. Always on the hand phone.'

Cat laughed. 'Like I said, just like my sister. When she babysits me, she acts so stupid.'

Aunty M looked dismayed. 'She is a child herself, how can she look after children? The employer should take her phone.'

'Maybe they don't want,' Jenalyn pointed out. 'Mine want me to bring my hand phone everywhere. When my employer calls, I make sure to answer, otherwise I will be scolded.'

'Mine too,' Jinky said. 'I think we need our hand phones.'

'Yes,' said Khusnul, 'But some employers are not like that. They give no off day, and no hand phone. They say, no phone during work hours. But we work every day, every hour. You know, my sister, she came to Singapore this year, she is not allowed hand phone, not even Sundays. They took it from her. She has two kids, she needs to call home. I passed by when the employer was away, and gave her a phone. Now she can text me. Call her husband. But she needs to hide it.'

Jenalyn giggled. 'She is just learning how to become naughty, haha.'

Cat said, 'It's ridiculous. That's stealing. She should call the police.'

Aunty M shook her head. 'It is not that easy. Who knows which side the police will take? She would risk her job.'

Cat wanted to say more, but I nudged her to stay quiet.

'Yes,' Khusnul said, 'you don't know with the police. My sister is very nervous now. What if the employer find the illegal phone? But what choice she have? If she does not call her husband, how can she check on him? And her kids?'

Moe Moe said, 'If I had phone in first months, maybe they send me back Myanmar. I was still learning. The work. The stress. Maybe better no phone?'

But Jenalyn said, 'No. We are not small kids they can control, or can confiscate what we have.'

Moe Moe didn't have enough words to fight this battle. I suspected Cat wanted to say more, so I whispered into her ear: 'Let's just listen. It's research, right?'

Grudgingly, she stayed quiet.

Jinky pitched in instead. 'Most Singaporean employers are considerate.'

'Are they?' Jenalyn asked. 'I think they are selfish. Every move we make they want to control, especially us talking to others.'

Jinky said, 'Rules is rules. We want the job, we should just obey. Especially if we are newcomers. '

Jenalyn stood up from the bench and walked to the climbing frame, where her little boy was trying to perch dangerously on the top again. 'Some treat their helper like a garbage!' she yelled over her shoulder.

Jinky shook her head. 'Why can we not be considerate a bit? Patient. I had issue with previous employer. She did not get angry because I talked to her nicely. You know, the conversation depends on how you deliver your words. You must talk to her about your rights, and at the same time you must make her feel that you still respect her as your employer.'

Jenalyn grabbed the boy and carried him to his stroller under her arm. 'You are too nice,' she said. 'We have a right to complain if they are treating us wrong.'

Jinky answered, 'Better stay in Philippines if you come here and keep complaining, ate. It's not right, but they do that because some of us abuse the use of our phone. It affects our work performance. Some of us are addicted to social media .'

Moe Moe said, 'Like Run Vang.'

Aunty M and Khusnul laughed. 'Like Run Vang.'

Jinky and Khusnul left, leaving me and Cat without Snoopy, or a reason to sit there and play. We made ourselves small.

'How old are you?' Aunty M asked Moe Moe.

'Me?' she replied. 'Me thirty already.'

'How long have you been in Singapore? Is this your first employer?'

'Three years. This is first employer. Ma'am very difficult first. I never understand. My English, not so good. She very strict. Now

I know how to do, it is ok.' Moe Moe looked pensive. 'You know, the problem is not the ma'am. She is away a lot.'

'What is the problem then?' Aunty M asked. She gave me a sidelong look, and I realised she knew I was listening. But she kept talking. 'Is it sir? Does he look at you bad?'

Moe Moe shook her head. 'No, sir ok too. It's the kids. They mean.'

Now Aunty M turned to me. She was quiet for a minute, then turned back to Moe Moe. 'What do they do?'

'Girl, she always talk back. Stupid maid, bad maid, I'll tell ma if you don't give. She not allowed chocolate on the bread, but if I don't give she lie to Mama about me.'

I cringed in my crouched position next to the bench. Cat punched me on the arm, and looked like she wanted to say something, but I put my finger to my lips. We needed to hear the rest.

Moe Moe continued, 'But the boy is the worst. He bite me.'

'He bites you?' Aunty M exclaimed.

Moe Moe raised the leg of her shorts to reveal a purple mark on her thigh.

'How old is that boy?'

'He five already. I showed my ma'am, but boy says he did not do. Girl told Mama I hurt myself because I stupid, I always bump things.'

Aunty M said something I couldn't hear.

Moe Moe continued. 'But not so bad job. Food is good. I have my phone, my off day. Ma'am is away a lot, so no problem me.'

A tickle rose up from my stomach, and I burst out in a coughing fit. Aunty M looked up startled, and now it was Cat that pulled my hand, tore me away. We ran to the swings and sat on them, barely moving. Under Cat's silence I could hear her processing what we'd heard, trying to make sense of it all. I wasn't sure whether she was thinking about the aunties, their phones, Rung Vang, or that other thing, that thing that made something shift in my stomach. A few times it seemed like she wanted to say something but wasn't sure where to start. When she finally spoke, it wasn't about the aunties but about Jenny.

'That Jenny, she is such a bitch. Did you know I saw her on my first day at school? I was waiting at student services, and the lady who worked there introduced us, and said we were in the same year, and were sure to become good friends. As if. When Jenny found out what class I was in – not with her, thank God – she said there was a cockroach in that class. That's what made me want to know you.'

I said nothing and started swinging. I didn't want to talk about Jenny, so instead I asked Cat what she thought of Run Vang, and Jenalyn, and Jinky. Cat said that as she was not allowed a phone either, she understood exactly how they felt. We talked a long time. The aunties were treated like little children. And aside from Run Vang, they weren't children at all. Just before she left, Cat said: 'We need to do something about that Jenny.'

Cat was like a dog with a bone, she never let go, and the determined look in her eyes left me feeling somewhat uncertain. Anxious, excited – or perhaps both. I wasn't sure what to say, so I just said goodbye.

28

Mama and her friend Lisa were drinking tea in the living room on Saturday afternoon. I sat there too, reading a book.

They were talking about schools. Lisa's children went to a Singaporean school, unlike me. I was glad I went to my school, as Singaporean primary schools had this final exam called the PSLE. It made the kids stressed out of their minds. Mama said that it was of paramount importance – if you didn't do well on the PSLE, you wouldn't get into a good secondary school, and if you didn't get into a good secondary, you wouldn't do well in your O levels... Or was it A levels? Or B levels? I wasn't sure. But whichever one it was, if you didn't do well, you wouldn't get into the right course in university. How would you ever get a good job? A good salary? A career? Singapore as a country was highly successful, and that success started at school, with hard work.

Mama always stressed the importance of a good education. Singapore parents were like that, and, international school or not, my mother was still Singaporean. And Dad supported her.

Her friend Lisa sighed at the sight of me reading.

'How relaxed does she look? Is that for her school reading?'

Mama looked up. 'Erm, library, I think. Maya reads everything. All the time.'

'I wish my kids read more,' Lisa said. 'But there's simply no time. Max has tutoring now for both maths and Mandarin. And Julie for English. The PSLE is breathing down our necks.'

'Aiyoh,' my mother said. 'You are so kiasu. The PSLE is not for two more years.'

'One year, for Max,' Lisa said. 'I can't not do this. Everybody else has tutors. They'll miss out if they don't.'

Ugh. Homework was bad enough without tutors. I flipped a page in my book and then turned back again, since I hadn't read it.

Mama said: 'Sometimes, I think we should switch Maya, and some time soon. The results in the local system are much better than those in the international ones. Did you see that last ranking? Singapore scoring top in the world in education! Maybe we made a mistake. Costs a ton too, that school. She'll never get into a good local secondary if we don't switch her now, in time before the exams. She would still have time to prepare for the PSLE.'

I stopped pretending to read altogether. Switch schools? I'd never thought about that possibility, not without moving to another country. I pondered. I could be free of Jenny, of the morning bus hell. But the tutors? The homework? The PSLE? And what about Cat?

Julie always complained about the school work, and whenever my mother tried to set us up with a playdate, she wanted to, really, Lisa said, but no time.

Mama stared at me, so I buried my eyes in the book.

Lisa laughed. 'You are more kiasu than you think. But that Ang Moh husband of yours, will he agree?'

'I don't know. It's a good school she's in. I don't know which local primary I'd get her into now. And it's a lot of work, for me too. You know, it's different for you. You are independent, you work part-time. You can coach your kids. Who will coach mine? The maid? She is relatively literate, for a maid, but still. My job is more than full-time. I teach her by setting an example.'

As an afterthought, she added, 'No, she can do the IB diploma. It's very robust too. And she can always go to university abroad if she needs to. We can afford it.'

I buried my face deeper in the book. I wasn't sure what an IB diploma was, but it sounded ominous.

'Yes,' Mama added, 'Maya can stay where she is. It's just her Mandarin. It's absolutely rubbish. I don't know what teachers they have, and what they do. I don't have time to check her work every day.'

'Get a tutor,' Lisa said.

Panic struck. No way. If it was a new school, and no bus with Jenny, I'd take the tutors into the bargain. But not both. Jenny would have all sorts to say on that matter: *stupid cockroach, can't do it alone.* Obviously Jenny's Mandarin was perfect – but she was PRC, mainland Chinese, from Beijing; she spoke it at home. Her dad had a thick accent in English, so bad I barely understood, and he'd often tried to speak to me in Mandarin, expecting me to understand. Jenny's mother spoke English well – she could pass off for Singaporean any day. I was only a quarter Chinese, and that was Peranakan Chinese, so why did I have to learn stupid Mandarin anyhow? Peranakans spoke Malay.

A tutor would make me study, where now I managed to

mostly get away with pretending. My eyes were pinned on the same line, the one I hadn't read for the last ten minutes.

'I might,' Mama said, her eyes sweeping over me and then to the kitchen. I could see her heart wasn't in it. With a bit of luck, she'd forget about this whole conversation.

First I got Aunty M. Now she wanted to give me tutors? What next? Was she going to send me to boarding school?

With her friends, especially those from school or university, Mama could suddenly be kiasu, afraid to lose out on anything from an education to a must-have bag. But when her friends left the house, the attitude went too, or most of it. When she spoke to Dad, she sounded like a different person than when she spoke to her friends. She would agree with him on the international school system, no nonsense; and the funny thing was, both of these Mamas seemed real. It wasn't as if she wasn't sure who to be, like I was, but as if both versions, although contradictory, were a part of her. They did tear her in the middle though.

Her career always stayed top of the list, being the one thing Mama really feared for. She'd never used to be that bad. Once, she'd come home from work happy, tired but energised, speaking about her day enthusiastically. I hadn't minded her working then. But after PoPo died, Chloe was born, and she'd had her extra long maternity leave, something had snapped. Career-monster-mama took possession. Why did she have Chloe? If it was just me, she might have had enough to give, but it seemed as if there were not enough of her for the job, husband and two daughters. Some days, she went from quiet to crazy and shouting at us, then back to withdrawn.

Where had the real Mama gone? Was she still hiding somewhere in the monster's stomach? Sometimes we saw a glimpse. But anything could set her off – Aunty M baking a nice cake, or cleaning the fridge without Mama asking her to; things that were supposed to be good, so I didn't understand why they made Mama furious. She tried to keep it on the inside, of course. Even Mama knew you couldn't get mad at someone for baking a cake.

My education came and went in Mama's mind, from the top of the list to falling right off the bottom. Her haphazard interest in my future seemed closely related to her stress-at-work-levels. It was the one positive side effect of her going crazy, and I happily read my books and neglected my schoolwork. As for Dad? He must have disliked this Mama too, since he was home so little that year.

29

Cat came to my place often, hoping more research could be done, or better yet, that she could join us on a case when we were called out. She said she wanted to be a researcher, but she was more action than contemplation.

We spent some time gossiping about Jenny, joking that she and her brother were little devils, with teeth as big and sharp as the monkeys in her garden. Cat wanted to plan revenge, but every plan we came up with was as impractical as it was imaginative. I was secretly glad, and steered the conversation away from Jenny and back to our research. We begged Aunty M to take us somewhere interesting.

'Sayang, I can't make someone call me. Nothing happening today.'

Lately a lot of the casework Aunty M did was on the phone, via Whatsapp and Facebook. Not many domestic workers could meet up during weekdays, and we'd seen them all around the condo. Aunty M was starting to become more and more organised in the way she went about helping them. You could see a difference in her attitude too, especially when we were home alone or at the playground. She no longer had that meek, downward-looking gaze most domestic workers had. I started to understand what

Mama had meant when she said that her career defined who she was. Aunty M had become more and more defined by her second job, which gave her more and more confidence. She rarely mentioned her children, and I figured she put all her energy into helping other people, to help her forget about her own problems. I knew that trick from experience. If she was still upset she hid it well; outwardly I had never seen her more poised and self-assured than she was now. But most of that poise disappeared as soon as Mama came home. And she still had her day job to do. Today that meant cleaning out the fridge, with no time for us.

Cat and I brooded for a bit.

'Can we go to the playground, maybe we can find something to do there?' I asked Aunty M.

'It is too hot, it's all in the sun. Why not go swimming?'

Cat sprung up. 'Yes. Let's.'

She had monkeys and snakes, but not a pool.

We put on swimsuits. Mine was a bit tight on Cat, but she didn't care. When we were stood there towel-wrapped, Chloe piped up, 'Sim, sim.' She toddled to her room to grab her own suit.

'She's so cute,' said Cat.

But I took the swimsuit out of Chloe's hand. 'You can't go. You know that, only with Mama.'

'Why not?' asked Cat.

'She can't swim yet. Mama doesn't trust me to take care of her. You need to hold her all the time, so it's annoying anyway. She can stay with Aunty M.'

'Can't Aunty M go in the pool with her?'

I hesitated a moment before I answered. 'Aunty M can't swim.'

I didn't dare tell Cat the real reason Aunty M wouldn't, couldn't, take Chloe in the pool. There'd been a massive row. Mama was upset, and Dad was furious and had wanted to storm the management office. What had stopped him in the end?

Aunty M had been mortified when Mama had suggested she could take Chloe and me swimming. 'Ma'am,' she'd said, 'I don't think it's a good idea.'

'Sure, Chloe will love it. It's so hot. And I really need to finish some work, so you'd help me a lot if you would just take them off my hands for a bit. The pool is lovely. Cool.'

'Ma'am –' Aunty M had tried again.

'What?'

'I can't swim.'

'Oh, of course. You wouldn't, not in central Java.'

I thought about Aunty M's lake, the cool volcano mirror where she'd spent her childhood weekends. Why was she lying?

Aunty M had stared at her feet.

'Never mind. You can go in the baby pool, it's not deep. Just make sure Chloe doesn't go anywhere near the big pool. Maya is a good swimmer. She'll be fine.'

Aunty M had turned red, seemingly shrunk, her chin to her chest.

Mama had sighed. 'What else?' She rolled her eyes. 'Of course. Stupid of me. You don't have a bathing suit. Never mind. I have plenty. We're about the same size.'

She went to her room and came back with an old black one-piece. 'Here you go. You can keep it. Is it ok?'

The silence hurt my ears.

Mama hit her forehead. 'I forgot, you're Muslim. Is it too revealing? You can wear a shirt over it, if you like. Oh no, no clothes allowed in the pool.'

Aunty M looked up, a deeper shade of red. 'No ma'am, it's ok.'

'Well then. That's it.'

'No, ma'am. That's not it. It's just, you see, it's not allowed.'

Mama's eyes had grown big. 'What do you mean, not allowed?'

It turned out there was a sign by the pool saying maids weren't allowed to swim. Mama went berserk, saying it was a crazy, archaic rule, and that Aunty M should just go and send any guards that complained her way.

'No ma'am, I'd rather not.'

Mama called Dad and he was angrier still, saying it was ridiculous that maids weren't allowed to swim, and that Aunty M had to swim for the safety of his child, and would they rather Chloe drowned? What if she fell in, could Aunty M at least jump in to save her? I could hear him talking right through the phone, that's how loud he spoke. 'She's a resident here, right? She might want to do some laps on her Sunday off, and why not?'

He said he would visit the management office when he got home, but maybe he forgot, for I don't think he ever went; or perhaps it was Aunty M that stopped him. The shame had dripped from her downward-pointing chin, her eyes smaller than I'd ever seen them. Aunty M was never asked to swim again.

So when Cat turned to Aunty M, I felt the heat creeping into my face. 'Cat,' I said. 'Let it go.'

Aunty M kept her cool. She took Chloe's hand and said, 'I'll take her to the playground.'

Later, as we floated together on a lilo, Cat asked me what that had all been all about. When I told her, she reacted exactly as I'd expected. I let it flow over me, off the lilo into the blue chlorine of the pool, hoping Aunty M was out of earshot.

But afterwards, she targeted Aunty M directly. Aunty M smiled one of those special smiles, the ones she'd once used a lot on Mama. There was a mixture of pity, deference, sadness and contempt.

'Just leave it. I don't mind. I don't even like to swim. Too much chlorine in the water. It's not good for your skin.'

'It will bleach you,' Cat said, guessing correctly that Aunty M liked whitening creams.

'No. I don't want to make trouble.'

'You help all these women, how come you don't want to fight for yourself? Make a stand?' Cat said.

Aunty M got uncharacteristically annoyed with Cat. 'It is easy for you to say. I could lose my job.'

I felt worried. This was the type of trouble I didn't want, the type where I had to pick a side.

Uncertain, I pitched in anyway. 'But Aunty M, Mama and Dad agree that you should be able to swim, don't you remember? They wouldn't fire you.'

'I know, but there's more to it than that. I have other things to protect. Let's leave it. Please,' Aunty M said firmly.

'Ok,' Cat shrugged. But to me she said, 'For now.'

I wasn't sure whether I hoped she'd forget about it.

When we were changing, Cat started again. 'Maya, you need to learn how to do stuff. You can't just keep observing and making notes. Aunty M wants to be careful – alright; but you need to force your parents to act. This swimming thing is completely unacceptable.'

I tried to argue with her, but I wasn't sure how. I mean, how would I know what the right thing to do was? And how to have the courage? I was saved by the bell, or more accurately, Aunty M's phone. The swimming pool slipped from Cat's mind. We had bigger fish to fry.

It was Maricel. She had a new neighbour, who had a new helper who was locked inside. Maricel had been shouting to her over the wall, but hadn't got much of a response. Cat's eyes twinkled.

'She does not speak any English. I tried Tagalog too. Then I tried apa kabar, terimah kasih, the only words of Malay I know, but I don't think she is Indonesian.'

'She might be Burmese,' I said. 'Let's get Win.'

I grabbed my red notebook, and noticed that Cat pulled one out of her backpack that was exactly the same. We all went to Maricel's house, and trooped onto the balcony. Maricel had set a chair next to the wall facing toward the neighbours' balcony. Win climbed onto it. Her head did not reach anywhere near the top of the wall. I looked around. All the aunties were as short as Win. The tallest on the balcony was Cat. We all stared at her.

'Dutch genes,' Cat mumbled. 'They gave me a lot of milk growing up. You should see my dad.'

'How old is she?' Maricel whispered.

'Eleven,' I whispered back.

Cat climbed on the chair. The tip of her nose reached the top of the wall. 'There's no-one here,' said Cat. 'Hello!' she yelled.

'Shh,' said Maricel, 'I don't know if the employer is there.'

Cat turned to us. 'Actually, we should get my dad. He's really tall. And he speaks Burmese.'

'Really?' I asked. I was impressed and piqued at the same time. What was he, Superdad?

'He used to study snub-nosed monkeys in Myanmar, before I was born.'

'No. You promised not to tell your parents. You can't.'

Cat had promised she wouldn't tell her mother and father to avoid the risk of them telling mine. She was my friend, and I needed to be able to trust her. I swallowed the tickling on my tongue and kept still. We heard a sound on the other side of the wall. Cat tried to peek over again, but was a few centimetres short. Win called something out in Burmese. There was a reply, unintelligible, but still. I looked at Win, but she shook her head.

'Don't you have anything higher?' Cat asked. 'A table?'

Maricel and Cat brought out the kitchen table. They put the chair on top and Win climbed onto it, Cat supporting the chair from behind. Win could now lean over the wall, resting her elbows comfortably on top. She started to talk to someone on the other side.

After what felt like several long minutes, she turned around.

'She hungry,' she said.

Cat looked me straight in the eye. I guessed this was the time. I had to act decisively, something I hadn't done since the paper planes that hadn't worked. I walked past Maricel and resolutely pulled open the fridge. I rummaged around until Maricel tapped on my shoulder. 'Maya, please. That is my employer's food.'

'Are they hungry? I'm sure they can spare some.'

Maricel smiled. 'Yes, they can. But let me pick, before they start accusing me of eating all their expensive food.' She took the apple and packet of cheese I'd been holding, and put the cheese back in the fridge. 'Do you know how much cheese costs? Myanmar people don't even like cheese.'

'You don't know that,' I muttered, my cheeks glowing red.

Maricel got a Tupperware bowl and spooned in some rice. She added cherry tomatoes, two slices of chicken breast, and a dash of chilli sauce. Of course that was what someone from Myanmar wanted. Rice and chilli. Maricel handed the bowl to me, and I passed it to Cat on the table. 'Here.'

While the person on the other side was eating, we got Win to interrogate her. Her name, it seemed, was Nee Nee – at least, that's what it sounded like to me.

Win managed to report back a few words; her English had improved, but was still limited to simple observations. Nee Nee started work at five in the morning. At ten, she would get breakfast, which was a slice of bread and a glass of water. Lunch, if any, was instant noodles. Dinner was a scoop of rice. Only rice.

It wasn't the first time Aunty M and I had heard of malnutrition. But it was the worst. Win talked on, and every so often turned around to share more details with us.

'I smell good cooking wafting over the wall every day,' Maricel said.

'Nee Nee cook for ma'am and sir,' said Win. 'Chicken curry today. She get, erm, left over. But they eat all. She only rice, sauce some time. Bones from the chicken.'

'Is she very skinny?' asked Cat.

'Yes,' nodded Win. 'And, she says, pain go toilet.'

'We need to feed her,' said Aunty M. 'She needs vegetables and meat.'

We came up with a schedule to bring her food that Maricel would hand over the wall. I resolved that I would get the right food, at the right time, and to take things my parents wouldn't notice. I would do this properly.

Win promised to stop by regularly to chat, as Nee Nee needed companionship as much as food. Win had tears in her eyes when she tried to convey the way in which Nee Nee had hugged the wall.

'He need food. He need friend,' she summed it up.

I did not correct the use of the pronoun.

When we got home, I'd expected Cat to start analysing and giving me all her opinions, but she mostly looked confused and brooding. I wanted to discuss courses of action, make plans for what else we could do on top of our research, but I said nothing. We watched TV. Then she said she was thirsty and went to the kitchen for some water. I had barely noticed her get up until I heard loud voices from the kitchen.

I rushed over, but the only thing I could still hear was Aunty M telling Cat she needed to mind her own business. Aunty M had never said such a thing to me, or anything in that tone, and I couldn't believe her being defiant like that. She and Cat were standing silently, eyes locked, until Aunty M broke off and handed Cat her water. When we were back in the living room I asked Cat what it had all been about. 'I told her I felt she should use the pool. Fight for it.'

I gasped. 'And what did she say?'

'She said that it was easy for me to talk, that I was privileged. That I didn't understand, and something about not risking a good thing, that it wasn't worth it. And then I said I was happy to help her, and that we should all go together and I would talk to the guard. Or your parents would. But she got mad. I don't understand why.'

I thought I did, but I didn't know how to explain it to Cat.

After Cat had been picked up by her father, Aunty M and I stood watching them from the kitchen window. I wanted to say something, but Aunty M beat me to it.

'She is a nice girl,' she said. 'She means well, just sometimes a bit too much. She will be a better friend than that Jenny.'

Anyone would be a better friend than Jenny, I thought. But I felt relieved.

30

School was good again with Cat, but bus rides were as bad as ever, especially after Jenny and Meena found out that Cat and I were friends. They had a new obsession, new ways of hurting me. Cockroach and monkey, they sang. *Cockroach and monkey are best pals, BFF, what the F, it's a gaff. Monkey see, monkey do, monkeys pee, monkeys poo. Who eats the monkey poo? Cockroaches do!*

Meena had real poetic talent.

I hesitated whether to tell Cat. Did shared pain make it less, or double the load? In the end, I told her and she just laughed, making me repeat all the rhymes, saying they were hilarious.

Cat didn't understand why I was upset, offended even. 'Why would you care about what they think? You don't need them anymore, do you? You have me now. Rhyme back at them. Start a duel. I told you, you need to fight back.'

For Cat, insults bounced off her like a ball against a wall. With me, it was jelly against a glass window, slowly slithering down, leaving a slimy trail behind. But when Cat saw the tears that the cockroach stampeding in my stomach pushed out of my eyes, she began to brood again. 'Don't worry,' she said. 'We'll get her. I just need time to plan. Revenge is best served cold, you know?'

I didn't know what she meant, so I waited it out.

Some days, Cat's mother would pick us up in their battered old station wagon. Mimi would serve us Ribena and Oreos on the patio, while we sat at the large dining table colouring, writing, playing games, and dodging palm nuts slung at us by Ollie.

One day, we were comparing notes in our red notebooks. Most of the time Cat wasn't there when Aunty M and I were called out on rare case visits. I trusted Cat, but I preferred to go out alone with Aunty M, like we had before. Things were easier without Cat, who, as Aunty M described it, could be a bit too much. She always looked like she expected me to do things I wasn't sure how to do. I was happy being supportive rather than taking the lead.

Cat always asked to visit Nee Nee and Win when we were at mine, handing Nee Nee food saved from her school lunch. It was cheese sandwiches mostly, proving the point that Burmese women liked cheese just fine. Starving ones did, at least. Cat's new passion was to learn Burmese, and with Nee Nee she exchanged snacks bought at the corner shop from her pocket money for words. With Win the trade was simply words for words, English for Burmese. She treasured those words, and spelled them out phonetically in the back of her notebook, as the Burmese script defied her. She did care, but in her own way, on her own terms.

One day, when Cat had Dutch lessons after school, I went back to Maricel's to give some food to Nee Nee.

I had bought leftover goreng pisang, a bottle of Fanta, and

a Tupperware box with papaya slices I was happy to get rid of. I hoped Nee Nee liked them better than I did; this ya ya papaya didn't care for the mealy texture.

But when Maricel and I climbed the table and softly called to Nee Nee, there was no response.

'I saw her this morning,' Maricel said. 'And she can't go out, so she must be there. You want to wait?'

I nodded.

Maricel pointed to the kitchen table. 'Do you want a drink?'

'Just water, thanks.'

I had known Maricel for years, but never been alone with her. I wasn't sure what to say. I looked at her, suddenly realising Maricel was a lot older than most of the aunties.

'Maricel,' I said.

'Yes?'

'How old are you?'

Maricel laughed. 'Did your mother not tell you it's rude to ask a lady?'

I blushed, and fell quiet.

'You're lucky, girl, I'm no lady. And I'm fifty-five.'

Fifty-five? That was properly old, not old like PoPo, but a lot older than Mama. And Aunty M, I thought, though I didn't actually know her age.

'So old? Wow. Are you going to keep working? Or will you retire?'

Maricel shook her head. 'How can I retire? I have no money. And I am too old to get a job at home, in the Philippines. I have been working in Singapore for twenty-five years, and I will do so as long as they let me. My employers are good, my job is easy, just the dog. I hope they will keep me. Finding another job, at my age, I can't.'

'But what about your family? Your kids?'

Maricel smiled, a little sad. 'I was the oldest of six children. When my father died, someone had to make money to support the little ones. I was twelve already. So I went to work. First, in Manila, I cleaned houses. But I heard from my friend that the salary will be better here. So when I was twenty, I came to Singapore. My friends, my life, it is here now. Why I would want to go back?'

I understood. 'Are you going to stay here forever?'

'No, when my contract ends and my employer will not renew me, I cannot stay. No more work pass. Too old. I'll go back. My youngest brother, he will take me.'

'But what about your salary? Didn't you save any?'

Maricel laughed. 'The money in Singapore has wings. It flies back to the Philippines. First, my brothers had to go to school. There are five. Then, university, two of them. My mother, she needed a house to live in. My brother's children, they need school too. Uniforms, books.'

'So you still send it home? How much did you keep?'

'I kept some. I bought a lot, and built a house on it, where my mother lived. And then, my mother was very old, sick. The hospital bills were high. And my youngest brother, he had an accident, so he cannot work. He lives in the house.'

I looked stricken.

'Don't you worry about me, little girl, I'll be ok. I don't need much.'

She looked brave. Optimistic. It was a strange expression to see on such an old face.

'My mother is dead, so I will start saving for the retirement soon. I hope my family, my brothers, my cousins, they will be healthy, and I can keep my money. If I get sick, who else will pay?'

'Your employer,' I pointed out, glad I'd learned that rule.

Maricel grinned. 'Right. That's why I need to stay in Singapore as long as I can. Actually, it will be nice to live with my brother. His kids are cute. If I live alone I'll be, well, alone.'

If there was one thing Maricel loved, it was having people around her.

Toy-toy ran up, yapping. 'I can always get a dog, hehe. Toy-toy says Nee Nee is back.'

It was true, when I climbed the table, I saw Nee Nee on her balcony. She took the food and thanked me, in English and with a smile. Then she signalled. She hurried back inside.

'I guess she's busy,' I said.

I said goodbye to Maricel, and went home. Of course I had to start thinking about Mama now, and her kind of feminism that was a financial kind. Maricel's story seemed to confirm what Mama always said, about money being important, and that you couldn't count on others to take care of you. I hated it when Mama was right. That night, the Mamamonster was there again, so that made it easy to dismiss any thoughts of talking to her about Maricel.

31

One morning I woke up to noise in the living room. Mama exploding and yelling was no news, although she didn't usually do it this early in the day. What was more worrying was that Dad was yelling back. Dad didn't yell.

My room wasn't far from the living room, and there was no way not to hear them. The screaming had stopped, but they were still speaking with raised voices.

'Why don't you just quit?' Dad asked.

The question dropped like a bomb. I sat up with a jolt. I had been thinking Mama should quit ever since she went back to work, but somehow hearing Dad say it, I had a revelation: not only was it clear to me it was never going to happen, but I didn't want her to. Mama's job was different from the jobs of the aunties. They worked because they had to – obviously, nobody would do that job if they had a choice. Mama worked because she wanted to. I understood it now, feminism and all that, and it wasn't about being financially independent. Mama was wrong about that. It wasn't about money. I'd seen Aunty M grow from a shy, meek servant to a strong and independent woman when she started running the helpdesk, and the helpdesk didn't even pay her.

What Mama needed was a better boss so she could create a job she enjoyed. So she could relax and work things out. I'd seen a glimpse of that Mama when she spoke about the role in Myanmar, and I knew that was the Mama I needed.

How could Dad even suggest her quitting? Didn't he know her at all? No wonder Mama screamed.

'Quit? Quit? Are you mad? I need to prove that I can do this. I've had to work hard for everything, unlike some.'

'To whom do you need to prove that? Why?'

Mama was quiet for a second. 'To myself. Who else?'

'We're doing well financially. We can afford it if you take a break.'

'I just had a break! I had nine months of break. It didn't do me much good, did it?'

It was when she'd had the break that everything had started to go wrong with Mama.

'That wasn't a break and you know it. I mean a break without people dying or being born. A break where you can rest. Maybe we need a change of scenery. Release the pressure this city puts you under. Why don't we move to the UK? That role in the Surrey office is still open for me.'

'So that's what this is about? It's not about me. I should have guessed. It's about you. You want me to quit, make me dependent on you, and then move me away. We decided not to go there. But you never gave up, and now you want to use this to force me?'

'We did say we'd put it back on the table eventually. Why not now? You didn't want to leave your mother, well, she's gone.'

'I know she's gone, don't remind me. And it's not all about

you, you know, or even me. Do you think pulling Maya out of school right now, uprooting her and sending her to a new country is a good idea? Can't you see what a rough time she's having already, how much she misses her PoPo? She's not who she was before.'

I wasn't? Who was I? I felt an upsetting tickle in my tummy.

'Yes. I can see that. Can you? I'm not sure you can be there for her, for Chloe, when you're like this.'

'Like this?'

I wished I could see them, but the gap in the door let through only sound. I had to picture Mama in my mind, which was easy enough. The popping eyes. The brownish redness of her lips that would get darker. Her back rigid. Her hands, that would flop for a while next to her body before she would slowly, menacingly, raise them. That is when I would usually duck, even though she never really hit me. She'd aim a slap in my general direction, and I didn't take any chances with being close enough for her to connect. Would she do the same with Dad?

She was still silent. Was she counting to ten before she answered?

Very slowly, in her monstervoice, she said, 'What do you mean, *like this*?'

Papa sighed so hard I thought I could feel the breeze in my room. 'I mean, you're obviously not happy. You come home, you're stressed, you yell at the kids. In the evening you have no energy to do anything. Nobody in this house dares to mention your mother's name, for fear of you falling apart. Something needs to change. I thought maybe, since my promotion, we could manage on my salary.'

Mama said nothing.

'Especially in the UK. We could send them to a good state school, save a bundle on fees. We could have a house with a garden.'

'I don't want a garden,' Mama said. 'I want my job. I can turn this around, and get back where I was before. I loved my job. I can get that back.'

'You could get a new job there. A better one.'

Once I'd dreamed about moving to the UK. I mean, at school everyone moved everywhere all the time, so why shouldn't we? But I always felt the dreams were better than the reality when we visited. In any case, it seemed I didn't need to think about it anymore, as Mama was very clear.

'I don't want to move. Not now.'

'You always say that. Always, but not now will become not ever.'

I heard footsteps, and I pictured Dad staring out of the window, over the balcony to the row of condo blocks opposite.

'I'm sick of it all. The long work hours, the materialism. Rules everywhere. Don't you people get sick of the rules?'

When Mama didn't respond, he continued, 'There are too many rules, written and unwritten. And then there's the grey area, the manoeuvrability that we foreigners don't see between the lines. The times I've had to hear a face-saving yes, and didn't guess the real no.'

Mama snorted. 'It's easy to judge from the side-lines. But this is my country. You knew that when you married me.'

Dad spoke softer now, and I had to strain to understand him. 'It was exciting at first, exotic. But now? I feel like we live in a bubble. On the surface, Singapore looks like this Disneyland state, all sparkly marble, but underneath it's the opposite. No fun but work, work, work. And shopping or eating to spend the hard earned money on the weekend. Isn't there more to life? Do you want to raise our kids like that?'

'You know there's more to Singapore.'

'I used to think so, but lately, I can't see it. You've changed. You've become the clichéd Singapore career-woman. It's all about the money. You have your 'five Cs'; what are they again? Condo, cash, credit card, car – and what else do you want now? Should we join a country club? Can we stop after that, and decide we're there? Or will there be more, more, more?'

Mama was not counting to ten this time.

The first sentences she screeched so hard I could only hear a few words – Ang Moh, judgemental, crazy, mean. She ended with, 'If you hate it so much here, just leave! Go! I'm not stopping you.'

Then, more intelligibly, 'Why are you Ang Mohs always so hung up about 'real life'? What is this so called reality? Would you rather go and live in some longkang like Jakarta? You can taste reality there in a slum, with no running water or electricity, no waste collection or sewers. Will that make you see what really counts? You grew up in luxury. You don't understand.'

'Maybe I don't,' Dad said, 'but I know how this place makes me feel. I've been here sixteen years, you know. I use to love it, but the veneer is wearing thin.'

You could hear the offence streaked through Mama's words.

'Every single Singaporean is proud to be part of this nation that they created with their bare hands. People like my mother. Maybe sixteen years isn't enough to get to know us. It's not about the money, it's about what it stands for. Taking responsibility. Independence. Safety.'

'I know you,' Dad said. 'I mean you, as a person, not as a Singaporean. You're compassionate. You used to be creative, and confident, a collaborator who built bridges. But you've lost it. You're burning out and you need a break.'

'Maybe it would be easier for me to take a break if my husband was actually at home sometimes. Maybe he should quit himself. Or when he's home, maybe he should be married to me and not his phone!'

That shut Dad up.

I imagined Mama looking at Dad defiantly, adding up points in her head towards winning the battle. But the war wasn't over.

'Well, maybe if my wife was more fun to be around, I *would* be home more.'

The last thing I heard was a door slamming.

There was no way I could get up after that. It was a Saturday, and I reached under my bed for a book, trying to read away the sentences echoing in my head, the ones that overshadowed thoughts about feminism and quitting jobs.

Why was our life not real? This was the only life I'd ever known, and it was real enough to me. I felt offended and confused. I kept thinking about the suggestion that if you didn't like your life you could just pick up and try somewhere else. Would it be a cowardly thing to do or a brave one? It would mean being rid of Jenny, but also of Cat. And Cat, the foreigner, had just started to make me love Singapore again – its natural world, the lively markets, the quirky and contradictory people, and, of course, the best food ever. Cat's wish to explore them all reminded me of when Dad once said that he loved having visitors, as then you finally went to see all the nice sights in your own town.

But my thoughts kept going back to the shouting, the unhappiness that echoed through the house. The whole argument had split me down the middle, shutting up even the cockroach, the cockroach that my parents couldn't see.

It was clear what we needed: PoPo. PoPo could show Dad the real Singapore, the one he needed to see to love us, to love Singapore, Mama and me, so maybe together we could chase out the cockroach. But PoPo was dead.

When I finished my book I couldn't do much else but get up. The house was quiet. Dad played tennis on Saturday mornings and Mama must have left too and taken Chloe with her. It was safe to come out.

Aunty M was in the kitchen washing up the breakfast things. I wanted to ask her about Dad, about the bubble and real life, but she didn't hear me. I asked her again, and she started and turned around with wild eyes.

'Aunty M,' I began, but my questions seemed wrong suddenly. 'Where's Mama?' I asked instead.

'She went to the shops with Chloe. She needs new shoes.'

Her eyes were wet and red. Something felt terribly wrong.

'Aunty M, what's the matter?'

She walked to the kitchen table and slumped down in a chair. She was still holding the washing up sponge and it dripped over her lap.

'Nurul has gone missing.'

32

I stared at Aunty M, pondering how to react to this bombshell. Aunty M looked back at me and sighed.

'My mother called last night. She left yesterday morning, and nobody knows where she is.'

We sat there for a few minutes, neither of us knowing what to say. Aunty M went back to the sink and squeezed the rest of the water from the sponge.

'Did you call her Dad?'

She turned around and looked at me. 'Why would I do that?'

I shrugged. It just seemed like she should.

I took some rice crackers from the cabinet, and decided it was best to go back to bed.

When Mama came home and I knew Dad could get back at any minute, I asked if I could go to Cat's house. I was bored of reading in bed, and I didn't want to face Mama, or Dad, or Aunty M right now. They were all too difficult to deal with.

I'd pondered enough about Nurul, about running away myself, trying to decide whether it was a smart thing to do or not. I needed out. At Cat's place you could never be bored, like you could in our stacking block condo apartment. It was such a different world; it was a good place to forget things.

We were on the veranda playing Uno when Mimi ran out the side of the house waving a broom and shouting. A group of little monkeys was sitting in the orchid pots, chomping on the flowers. Mimi swung the broom and shouted at them, chasing them away. What she couldn't see was that there was one little baby monkey sitting behind her, not in the orchids but the frangipani tree. The rest of the family, including a large and imposing daddy, were by the fence. The baby squeaked. Mimi, shaking her broom after the culprits, started to turn. But suddenly the daddy charged towards her. Mimi shrunk back, stumbling away with hurried steps. As soon as the way to the frangipani tree was clear, the baby jumped out to the safety of the family.

Mimi shouted what sounded like swear words, but Cat was unperturbed. 'Aren't you afraid, living with monkeys?' I asked.

'Nah,' said Cat, 'Bob's ok. He was just protecting the baby. Perfectly normal monkey behaviour.' I remembered this was a family of monkey experts.

'Bob?' I said.

'Yes, Bob. He's the alpha male. He's a decent guy. It's Harry that's the problem.'

'Harry?' I asked. Who the heck was Harry?

'Harry's been giving us grief. In this group of macaques, there are two large males. We had a monkey war last week.'

Seriously? 'What do you mean, a monkey war?'

Cat sounded like her dad right now. He would tell amazing stories about the proboscis monkeys. He was a bit like my dad, in the sense that if he started talking about a subject he kept going, as if he were in teacher mode, everything a lecture. But where with Dad it always sounded like he got all his information from his phone, with Cat's dad, you could see he'd experienced it. He would never live in a bubble.

I'd hang on his every word when he spoke about monkeys, jungles, Borneo and Burma. Cat got bored after a while, but I couldn't get enough. Whenever he spoke like that, Cat's mother looked at him lovingly. No Mamamonster there. Sometimes Cat's dad looked at me as if I were a specimen under a magnifying glass, and I imagined him slicing me up and looking at the fragments under a microscope. Would he see the cockroach in my stomach? But a minute later he'd have forgotten I even existed, and go back to his monkeys. He was scary and fascinating at the same time.

Their family was so much noisier than ours. Ollie alone could produce more decibels than Chloe when she was hungry. Talking was done at high volume, heatedly and passionately, but it never became a fight. My family made less noise – at least in between Mamamonster visits – but with us, the things that weren't said were the loudest.

I'd never heard Cat's dad mention the macaques. I'd thought they were too plain to be interesting. Most people regarded them a pest, rather than wildlife.

'Macaques live in large family groups, with one male, the alpha male. He's the boss,' Cat lectured. 'But sometimes another male wants to be boss, and they fight. That happened last week. They were fighting up there.' Cat pointed at the large rain tree past the gate.

'It was early evening. They screamed and screeched and made such a racket that all the neighbours came out. It was a bit scary, but Dad said it was amazing and we were lucky to see it. There have been more clashes since. One time Harry fell out of the tree. But he ran straight back in to take revenge.'

Wow. Who could imagine such a thing in their own garden?

'So who won?' I asked.

'Bob. Look, he's with the family now. He's a nice guy. He was just protecting his baby. He's quite shy with people. But Harry...'

'What about Harry?'

'Harry has been kicked out of the group. He's on his own and sulking. He's a bad loser. He's aggressive. He needs to start a new group somewhere, but that means competing with Bob for territory around here. Singapore is paved with concrete, not much monkey space left. He's been coming into the house a lot. Mama is scared of him. She bought a water gun to shoot him.'

'A water gun?'

Sometimes I couldn't believe Cat and her family were for real, let alone living in the same town I was.

'Yes, they hate it when you squirt water at them. It's fun. Mama gets freaked out, because sometimes Harry will tiptoe into the house when she's working. He just sits there until she turns around. He gives her the creeps. She bought a handgun for indoors and a big super soaker for outside. But Ollie usually hoards the super soaker.'

'And shooting them with water, does it work?'

'Usually. They'll scatter if you do it. Dad says we need to make sure they know who's boss. He calls it power play. Harry is competing with us for territory, and we need to show him this is our territory and we are alpha people. We keep shooting to try and enforce that.'

'Cool. Can we shoot some monkeys?'

'Sure. Mama says only to spray them when they're on the ground, close to the house. Only she can shoot inside. She says we'll ruin the furniture.'

Cat stood up. 'We'll have to wrestle Ollie for it, though.'

Most of the monkeys were trooping around the gate, blocking the way with their toothy grins and swinging, sticklike tails. Nobody could pass, so the gate had to be human territory not monkey. As soon as we shot water at them, they all scrambled for the safety of the trees. We tried hitting them high, but it was hard to aim upwards. Cat's mother came running out. 'Don't shoot them in the trees! I told you Cat, this is about territory. The house, patio, and ground around it are ours. The tree is theirs.'

'But they were on the gate,' Cat countered.

'They aren't anymore,' her mother said drily.

When her mother had gone back inside, Cat said, 'Next time we go to your place, we should bring these guns. We need to teach Jenny and her brother something about territory too. And about good manners.'

From the way she looked, it didn't seem like she was joking at all. I thought about the power play, and the employers as well as Jenny. Maybe Cat had a point.

I had dinner at Cat's place that evening, and when I came home

Aunty M was in her room. Mama, Dad and I watched a movie. We didn't speak much, and I went to bed straight after. When I woke up, I felt really bad. Guilty, for ignoring Aunty M all day yesterday. For being more interested in the monkeys than her daughter.

It was Sunday morning, and Aunty M was in her room. I thought about knocking on her door, even though I wasn't supposed to. But I needed to know. I was standing there, pondering, when Dad passed by. 'Maya, leave Aunty M alone on Sundays, please.'

'But Dad, Nurul, her daughter, she's missing.'

'I know. We were all so worried, sweetie. Good news last night, she's been found.'

I realised my heart was racing and my stomach had clenched. 'Where was she?'

Dad pulled my hand away from the door. 'She'd run away to her father. Aunty M is very upset. Just let her be today.'

One of the knots in my stomach loosened. At least she was safe. 'Will she be ok? Is she going to stay there?'

'She will for now, until Aunty M can speak to her and sort things out.'

Would Aunty M be able to fix this? I thought about yesterday morning, when I had considered running away myself, away from the tension in the house that was thick as porridge. But Dad was right there, so where could I go?

'Dad, can I go to Cat again? We started a game of Monopoly yesterday and we need to finish it.'

'Sure,' Dad said. 'Give me half an hour to get dressed, and

I'll drop you off.'

Cat and I were in the living room playing Monopoly when she jumped up. Harry's grinning face popped over the windowsill. Cat signalled with big arms and shouts that he shouldn't come in. Harry ignored her, climbed onto the table below the window, and sat there. He looked at us, unflustered.

'Mama,' Cat yelled. 'Harry's inside again!'

To me, she said, 'Don't look him in the eye, and especially don't show your teeth. He'll take that as a challenge.'

Cat's mum came in, swearing under her breath, aiming at Harry with her small water pistol. Harry looked annoyed, protected his face with his hand, waving like he was swatting a fly, and then calmly went out the way he had come.

'That monkey is getting out of control. We need to talk to your dad about what we can do about him.'

Harry's quiff popped above the windowsill again. He bared his teeth in a scary grin. Cat's mum took aim, shouting, 'You stupid bully. Go. This is my house! Out!'

She hit him right in the face.

Harry ran off into a tree at the back of the house. Cat's mother went back to the kitchen, muttering.

Cat and I looked at each other and laughed. 'Did you know,' I said, 'that Jenny's brother is called Harry?'

We laughed even harder.

'That makes sense,' said Cat.

Afterwards I felt sad for Harry. Cat knew all about monkeys, but little about people. Harry the monkey was the loser, yes, but

Jenny wasn't. She was Bob. She'd won. She was the real alpha. Like Harry the monkey, I had been kicked out, having to fend for myself. I'd have tried to cuddle him, if only he didn't have such big teeth.

33

Cat and I did more research by eavesdropping. Not all of it was interesting; mostly employers just complained about slow maids, lazy maids, maids with attitude (which was a bad thing, if you weren't a pop star), maids that talked back, broke things, stayed out late on their day off and generally couldn't be trusted. How much of it was true? I started to see that truth was different things to different people.

The aunties complained as much about their employers as the employers did about them, and the playground was the perfect spot to listen in on the gossip. The aunties talked about being shouted at, called stupid, not allowed to go out. About having to hide the fact that they had boyfriends, and having curfew on their day off at five in the afternoon. They grumbled about eating only leftovers, or only being allowed to go out after the Sunday breakfast table was cleared up. Employers were stingy, mean and generally couldn't be trusted. How much of that was true?

It was like there were two versions of the world: the one in which domestic workers had abusive employers, and the one where employers had lazy maids. Were they both real, or two different bubbles?

Some of the conversations stayed with me for days, rolling

around my mind as I tried to make sense of them.

Two ladies at the market, sipping their kopi. Lady one said she had just had to send her maid home. She was insolent, this one. She demanded to get a day off every week. 'You know, I have a job, I work six days a week, long hours too. On Sunday, I need my day off. How can I look after the children? The company needs me back well rested on Monday.'

Her friend nodded in agreement. 'Of course. You need your rest.'

Lady one went on: 'Also, if she goes out all day on Sunday, how is she going to be fit to work on Monday? She will tire herself. No. I need her to watch my kids on Sunday.'

'The government is so soft these days, always protecting the maids. This new law, you have to give the day off, right?' lady two pondered.

'Yes, but you can decide to let them work. So I told her, I had agreed when I hired her that she should work on Sundays. That was two years ago and to be fair, she never complained, she did the work, she did it well. But now, I was kind, offered to renew her contract, and she takes advantage of my kindness by demanding a day off. So I sent her home.'

She continued. 'It's not really her fault, you know. These maids, these countries they are from, they just don't have the work ethics we have here in Singapore.'

Lady two nodded vigorously.

Was it right to even try to look for logic? There was no way I could have gone up to them and addressed them, even if I'd found the words. And the other side did not necessarily make more sense.

It was an aunty I didn't know; she came to the playground occasionally but wasn't one of our regular crowd.

'My employers are easy,' she said. 'Ma'am never checks the receipt. So when I go to the market, I always buy the nice things. Some snack, my lunch, or something else.' She giggled with her mouth covered, not letting on what the something else was. 'She is nice to me, but the nicer she is, the less I believe her. It is better if I just take.'

I replayed the statement in my mind.

The aunty went on. 'She told me I could go out sometimes if I wanted, in the evening, but now I told her I will go out Wednesday and Friday, she can do other days. She did not like, hehe. But she is afraid to say so, or I think she is a bad employer. If I leave, she worries the kids will be very upset. So I can do what I want.'

Afterwards, Aunty M had tutted that she was a spoilt child, that women like her gave domestic workers a bad reputation. 'With such an attitude, she is asking for it. Trouble will come. She can't appreciate a good thing. Many would be happy to take that job.'

The world would have been easier in plain black and white.

I ran into Aunty M that Sunday evening. She did not say much, just that Nurul was fine, and would stay with her dad for a few months, at least until the summer, when Aunty M would go home on leave and sort things out. He lived in a village a few miles away, but he had promised to make sure to send Nurul to school every day. He had a motorcycle. Aunty M said that as long as

Nurul could attend school, things would be fine. But her eyes told a different story.

Since I knew now that things were grey and complicated and not black and white, I started to make lists in my mind. Reasons for Nurul to be mad at her mother. And reasons for Aunty M to leave her and Adi. Both lists were long. I briefly started making a similar list for Mama and me, but stopped as it made me feel bad.

I wasn't sure whether how I did at school really mattered to my parents. Now and then Dad asked whether I'd done my homework without checking. Mama believed in hard work and graft, and would occasionally get fanatical about school work – but then she forgot about it, and as long as my report card was good neither of them were really on my back. I found out that not doing my homework had little effect on my results. Doing my own science project, I told myself – studying people, domestic workers – was a much better subject to spend my time on.

Cat was worse than me; she did even less schoolwork, and her parents let it go. Her mother believed kids developed best when left to their own devices after school, to learn through play, preferably outdoors. She practised what she preached and left us alone, even though she was there most of the time, at work behind her laptop.

I loved hanging out at their jungle house. I had managed to convince my parents that, like Cat, I could take the public bus home from her place. That meant I was always back before Mama, and if Aunty M missed me she never said so. It never occurred to me that it was mean what I did, deserting Aunty M when she needed me most; but I guess I wasn't sure whether my presence comforted her or just made things worse. She rarely mentioned Nurul, and only commented on Adi now and then. In any case, she had plenty of friends of her own.

The only time I still spent time with Aunty M was when something came up at the helpdesk. We both loved losing ourselves in a case, and Cat joined us whenever she could. And if there was nothing active to be done, Cat and I did our research. My favourite fantasy was that we grew up to be famous anthropologists and Mama was so proud. Would she be? I wasn't sure who Mama was these days.

One afternoon Aunty M gave us some papers to study. It was a photocopy of a schedule and a set of rules. One of the women who had come to the Sunday helpdesk had given it to her.

The woman's name was Mindy, as was written at the top of the first page, and Mindy's schedule of daily chores started with a cheerful 'rise and shine' at six in the morning.

'She would have had to get up earlier than that,' Cat pointed out, 'as she'd need to shower first.' She flicked ahead to rule one in segment D, headed personal hygiene and cleanliness. *You must bathe at least ONCE a day.*

'And do those,' Cat added, pointing at numbers two to four – *brush your teeth, put your hair up in a bun,* and *change your clothes daily* respectively.

The whole schedule was a minute description of things to do, set out in blocks of half an hour. They included feeding the kids, cleaning various parts of the house, and cooking lunch for Ma'am and the baby boy. There was a half an hour slot for Mindy's lunch, but it wasn't clear whether she would have to prepare her own food in that time, or whether she could eat some of Ma'am's food. For dinner, there was a similar set up: dinner had to be ready at six, but the maid's eating time was after washing up, at eight. Breakfast wasn't mentioned.

'She gets at least two meals a day, and time to eat them,' I said.

'But we can't see what she eats,' Cat complained, turning the paper in her hand. However precise the schedule was, outlining the details of the kids' snacks and water bottle content, it made no mention of Mindy's food.

The evening was reserved for ironing and the schedule finished at eleven, when, as clearly outlined, the maid had to go to bed.

Aunty M said the schedule was good evidence for this woman to make a complaint to MOM about excessive working hours. Cat got very interested in MOM and questioned Aunty M on the rules, and how to make a complaint. Aunty M explained that the best way was for the domestic worker to go to MOM herself, in person, and try to prove her case.

'Can't someone else do that?' Cat asked.

'Someone else can complain, but it is better if she does it herself. A complaint will get back to the employer, so she needs to be sure she wants to lodge it.'

Cat pondered this. 'But anyone can go there to complain?'

'Yes,' Aunty M nodded. 'Or you can call. They have a helpline for domestic worker matters.'

Cat picked up the papers again. 'So this Mindy, did she go there?'

'Yes,' said Aunty M, 'she went, and now MOM is investigating. The working hours are too long, and she has the schedule to prove it.'

Cat and I added it all up, and Mindy's total working hours were seventeen. Minus the two half hour breaks that still left sixteen, more than even Mama and Dad worked. Aunty M said there were no working hours set by MOM for domestic workers, so it was up to the case officer to decide if this was too much. The paper stated that Mindy would get an off-day after she completed her first six months, but that she could not leave the house before 11am, nor arrive home after 7pm. If she was late, the next off-day would be forfeited. The off-day segment further stipulated that she was not allowed to bring any items in or out of the house without the ma'am knowing, and that her bag would be searched, both on leaving and arriving.

The daily chore schedule seemed tiring even to read, and Cat and I quickly flipped to the two pages of rules. The first eleven rules were on the subject of laundry and ironing. An hour and a half every evening was assigned to ironing, so it must have been an important matter to this ma'am. The rules were very specific. First, all ironing had to be done on a progressive basis. We had no clue what that meant, and we wondered whether Mindy would have had.

The rules went on, stating Mindy could not mix her laundry with her employers', and that although she was allowed to use the family's soap powder for her personal clothes, she should by no means use the softener. The next rule listed which items had to be hand washed.

Rules four and five were back on ironing; no sitting down when ironing, and no fan.

'I never iron,' Cat said, 'but if I ever were to do it, I'd do it sitting down, with the fan on high.'

I agreed. 'Look what they need her to iron.'

The items listed included T-shirts, pyjamas and underwear. There was one notable exception: Mindy's personal home wear need not be ironed.

After personal hygiene and cleanliness, there was a long list of rules on personal conduct. It stated that the hand phone was to be used only between ten and eleven thirty in the evening; but, as Cat pointed out, the ironing didn't finish until eleven, and bedtime was straight after – so how would there be time for phone calls, especially if the mandatory showering and tooth brushing were to be observed?

The list went on and on. Cat and I marvelled specifically over *do not be fussy with your food, do not eat at the dining table, do not 'bad mouth' your employer, do not engage in an argument with the children, do not gossip, never allow the child to hit you, do not show 'black face'*, and lastly, *do not go on a diet*.

Cat and I looked at each other, and were, rare enough, lost for words.

'So,' Cat said finally, 'it must be great for the kids. It sounds like they can control their aunty easily.'

'I suppose so,' I said.

I couldn't imagine ever controlling Aunty M. Even Mama

couldn't do that. Cat and I guffawed over the paper, making up crazy rules we imagined Jenny had for Moe Moe. After that, we came up with a list of rules we wanted Jenny to stick to, which was even more hilarious. For me, this imaginary revenge was safe enough.

34

Another afternoon at the playground started off calm. Jenny was playing with Meena behind the bushes, but I managed to duck past them unseen, and went up to Mary Grace who stood alone behind the slide staring at her phone. Since the make-up incident I'd felt like there was a special bond between us. I wanted to talk to her about the thing I'd been worrying about, especially since that morning when Dad had yelled and Nurul ran away. I checked over my shoulder to see whether Aunty M was around. The coast was clear and Mary Grace just pocketed her phone.

'How is your husband?'

Mary Grace's affable eyes clouded over. 'He has a girlfriend. I spoke to my daughter the other day; the slut wants her to call her mother. My daughter refused. She stays with my mother now.'

'What are you going to do?' I asked.

'I don't know. Divorce him? Ma'am Tan gave me a ticket to go there, speak to him, sort it out. When I came, he cried, was on his knees, said he'd come back to me. He pleaded me to forgive him. He also asked for money, saying he needed to turn around the business. So did I give the money?'

My eyes grew big. 'Did you?'

'Hehe. I'm not that stupid. I gave him only a little bit. He got angry. I told him it was all I had, he threw it in my face. If he only wants my money, well, he does not get it.'

'You did well. You don't need a guy like that.'

Mary Grace looked dejected. 'I know. But I still miss him. He is angry at my daughter now too, because she picked my side.'

I wasn't sure what to answer to this. I had no notes in my red notebook for this scenario.

We walked together back to the benches. Aunty M was telling us about an Indian girl, Indira, who had been staying in the shelter a very long time, but had finally got a new employer. 'A friendly Indian family, and guess what? They have moved into our condo.'

'Does she have kids?' I asked.

'No, she is very young,' Aunty M said. 'She is not married.'

I blushed. 'I meant, does her employer have kids? Will she come to the playground?'

'Actually, I think she does. Wait, let me message her. She might come down.'

Indira appeared with two dark-haired boys dragging behind her, one my age, the other a bit older. They greeted us shyly. Aunty M hinted I should play with them, being my age and all, but luckily they spotted the football boys and were off. I much preferred to hear Indira.

Everybody was full of questions, and we gathered in a circle. I sat on the floor towards the back, out of sight of Aunty M, just in case. Indira seemed at ease in the middle of her audience. She looked like a supermodel, long slim legs in skinny jeans, a waterfall of curly brown hair, and the biggest green brown eyes.

I would have loved to have had wavy hair, and once had tried hot curlers to get the effect. It must have been the Chinese genes kicking in, but the curls would droop within five minutes. My hair just frizzed. I stared at Indira jealously as she regaled us with her once-upon-a-time.

'My mother died when I was only six months old. My father did not want me. He threw me away. He threw me in the river.'

We weren't sure we'd understood correctly. 'Where did he throw you?' Aunty M asked.

Indira repeated, 'You know, the river. Where water goes?'

'What happened then?' Mary Grace asked.

'Some people picked me up. They gave me back to my father, and told him he could not do that. That he had to take care of me.'

Indira's father had had no idea what to do with the baby, and soon after he married a widow with three sons.

The stepmother was fairy tale evil. Favouring her own children, the three she already had and a baby boy she had with Indira's father, she had no love left for Indira. After school Indira wasn't allowed out of the house, and had to occupy herself with the housework. She didn't have any friends; how could she, if she couldn't go out? The only person in her life who was nice to her was her baby brother. She was beaten, not just by her parents but by her older stepbrothers too. By the time she was sent to Singapore to work, she was all skin and bone, and happy to get out of there.

The tale darkened further. Her first employers, Indian like herself, did not treat her any better. They locked her up in the storeroom for days on end, letting her out only to clean. Once when they were out of town, she was shut in for six days in a row. They had taken away her hand phone, but when she found it while cleaning, she smuggled it into her storeroom. She texted her younger brother in India, who in his turn contacted the Singapore police. They sent an officer to rescue her, minus the white horse. The officer, a young bloke, felt for the pretty Cinderella he'd released, brought her to the shelter, and helped her press charges against her employer.

We had sat in silence, waiting for the *they-lived-happily-ever after*.

'And, now, you have a good employer? You are happy?' Maricel finally asked.

Indira shook her head. 'It took a long time. Actually, I stayed at the shelter until the police finished, and then I got a new job. I thought I was lucky, as I worked with an Ang Moh family. First, they were nice. Then they did not pay me, and deserted me when they left the country. They asked me to come to Malaysia, but I did not want. So they put me on the bus back over the causeway, with 200 dollar only, not my whole salary. So I went back to the shelter for help. And finally I was lucky. Now I am with good people, from India. But you know what the best thing is? I made friends at the shelter. Merpati here, she is my friend too.'

'We all your friends,' Jinky added.

After everyone split up, I went to Indira. I can be your friend too, if you'll have me, I wanted to say. But instead, I said to her that she ought to sign up for Asia's Next Top Model. She didn't wear the standard domestic worker uniform of shirt and shorts, but was modern and stylish in her black skinny jeans and white T-shirt, several colourful armbands wound around her thin wrists which were, on closer inspection, rosaries.

She shook her head at my suggestion. 'My parents would never allow it,' she sighed. She said that in any case, in India she was not considered good-looking. Way too skinny. Way too tall. In rural India beauty was voluptuous curves and full hips. Indira's spindly legs might do well on a Paris catwalk, but at home she was ugly.

'So what do you want to do when you grow up?' I asked. Adults to me seemed all the same, grownup, bigger than me; but Indira, even though she must have been at least twenty, acted closer to me in age than to the other aunties.

'My parents will make me get married. They have someone arranged, after I have sent enough money home to satisfy them.'

The gap between us gaped wide open again.

I mulled this over for a while. Jenny and Meena always giggled over boys, but me, I preferred to play with girls. Boys only talked sports, Minecraft or their favourite football team.

'Is he cute, the guy you'll marry?'

'I don't know. I've never met him. He is young, only like thirty something, I think. My cousin married a fifty-year-old one. Thing is, once I finish my job here, I'm old. Actually, I'm old already. I'm lucky to get a young husband.'

'You're not old.' I stammered, and changed the subject. 'Do you send all your salary home?'

'Yes,' she shrugged. 'They expect that. It's what you do. What do you want to do when you grow up?'

'I want to be a scientist, I think.'

'Cool. I have a dream too. I want to be a lawyer. At the shelter, people helped me. I want to help others. There was a lawyer, she had only just finished law school. She had a job at this high profile law firm but still helped people like me. I want to be like her. Make money. Help people.'

'Yes. You should do that. Go to university. Why not?' I said.

'How would I pay for it? I need to send my salary home. It's never enough for law school anyway.'

'There must be a way. I'll find out,' I said. 'I'll ask my mother, she knows these things.' But then I realised I wasn't sure anymore whether she did.

We sat watching the boys play football for a while.

'You know what I really want in my future. I want a house of my own. And to be alone. No one bothering me.'

'All alone?' I asked, 'No one else?'

'Yes. I like alone. You know, on Sundays, I like to go to East Coast Park. I go to the jetty, just me, and I sit there and stare at the sea all day long. I love the sea and its rhythm; it makes my mind quiet. So, my house should be by the sea.'

I loved the sea too, so I nodded. But it still didn't make complete sense.

We stared at the bushes for a while. There was a sort of rhythm in how they swayed in the wind. I remembered how Win had blossomed just from me visiting. Being alone wasn't good.

'But you said the best thing in your life was that you'd made friends.'

Indira's eyes clouded with thoughts. 'Yes. Yes, you are right.

Actually, you know, one day, at the shelter, I went to East Coast Park with my two best friends. We wandered, chatted, shared stories, had some food. It was the best day of my life.'

'So maybe you don't want to be all alone really? What about your brother, the one who saved you?'

Indira's face lit up when she spoke about her little brother. He was the light of her life, the only person that loved her, and she loved him, she said.

I pondered a while. It seemed some of my mother's feminism was needed here. I said, as if my mother spoke through my mouth, 'I don't think you want to be alone, really. I think what you want is to be independent. Have your own house, your own money, look after yourself. And then nobody can beat you, or lock you up.'

The clouds blew away from her eyes. 'That's it. But how do I do it?'

'I think you should start by stopping sending all of your salary to your family. They treated you badly, so why do you help them?'

Indira looked doubtful. 'I'm from India. It's what we do. Your parents are not like that, you won't understand. You're a little girl, anyway. What do you know?'

That hurt, and I got up to leave. 'I still think you should save a little. I'll buy you a piggy bank.'

She smiled wryly. 'Ok.'

35

Speaking with Maricel, Mary Grace and Indira had made me realise that the migrant women's problems were bigger than Singapore. Their real, long term worries were further away. Singapore was just a stepping-stone for them, part of a long journey. And if it was a risky step, they took it anyway.

People like Dad had taken a step too. He had come to Singapore on his own, when he was just out of university. Yet now, years later, he'd made a life here. He'd met Mama, found a good job, bought a house, had kids.

I realised there was a big difference between Dad, Ah Feng and the migrant domestic workers. That last group were never really here, never allowed to settle, marry, have their own home. They lived in a corner of someone else's house, sometimes for decades on end, and as soon as their employer decided they should be repatriated, they had no say in when they would be put on a plane. Ah Feng and Dad had been allowed to become Singaporeans. Ah Feng's life was hers, and if she hadn't married it was because she hadn't wanted to, not because there were laws against it.

Relief flooded into me knowing that girls like me, whether from Singapore or England, would never have to become migrant domestic workers. But pinches of guilt told me that Nurul, who I'd never even met, had no such comfort.

But what about Mama? She was born here, but things didn't look easy for her.

That career ladder she always talked about, the one that ended at the glass ceiling, was a version of the stepping stones of the domestic workers. Mama was also on a journey. Hers was perhaps more comfortable, less lonely, and up a ladder rather than across dangerous water – but her stress showed clearly that it was nevertheless a tough one. Were things really harder for women? At school, I'd never noticed it, at least not in my Singapore. Feminism must be for grownups.

Thinking it through a bit more, I had another idea: maybe feminism was about standing up for yourself and your choices. It was something I needed very badly. But how could I do it? There was so much I didn't yet understand.

The last time I'd had a real conversation with Mama was when we spoke about Ah Feng. She'd seemed so happy, proud to talk with me like I was an adult. But since then the gap between us had widened, and I was afraid to say anything to her, worried I'd scare her back into the Mamamonster. I needed a way to get Mama back, the real Mama.

Indira's real life fairy tale had been haunting me for days. She had no children to provide for, just a cold-hearted stepmother who took her hard earned money. Her salary wouldn't even pay for her own education. And then there was the not-too-old stranger she had to marry. Indira seemed to think it was pretty normal. Aunty

M had commented that it was a cultural thing, and that was how things were done in India. Indira had a nice job now, she added, with a friendly Indian family that treated her well, and that was good enough for her. But I needed another perspective.

Mama would know about India, her Indian half beating my quarter, even if she had hardly known her father. I always felt more Chinese, because of PoPo, and western, not because of Dad but because Mama acted like that's what we were. But looking in the mirror told me a different story.

'Mama,' I asked on a tranquil Saturday morning.

'Yes?' She seemed in a good mood.

'Do you know about India?'

'India? Why? What do you want to know?'

'Is it normal that someone has to marry whoever their parents tell them to? And that twenty something is an old spinster?'

I'd been right, it caught Mama's interest. She perked up, then settled down in her chair, back straight. 'Interesting topic. Why are you asking?'

'One of the aunties at the playground,' I said, 'Indira, she's from India, and when she goes home she has to marry this guy. She says she's lucky he's only in his mid-thirties. Her friend had to marry one that was fifty. She says she'll be an old spinster already when she goes back, but she's the youngest of all the aunties.'

Mama nodded. 'She's probably from a village. Rural girls in India marry very young. They see girls as a cost, so they'd rather get rid of them as soon as they can. Then the husband has to pay for her food.'

'But Indira isn't a cost. She sends all her salary to her parents, and they're not even nice to her. Her stepmother beats her.'

Mama said, 'That would be why she's not married yet. As long as she makes them money, they'll milk her for what she's worth.'

'Milk her? She's not a cow.'

Mama laughed. 'It's an expression. It means to take advantage of someone, to take something from them in little bits, slowly, like you express milk from the udder of a cow in slow squeezes. They won't marry her off until the milk has run dry.'

I contemplated that. 'Maybe it's better for her to be here? If she can work, and doesn't have to get married?'

'Yes, possibly. But if she keeps sending all her money home, she'll never gain her independence.'

'That's what I said!' I exclaimed.

'Because you're a smart girl. My girl.'

She patted my hair and sunshine filled my head.

Mama continued, 'But it would be hard for her to break free from tradition. Family bonds can be tight, and she still needs them if she goes back.'

'She says she wants to be a lawyer. She's very smart.' I left out the bit about the shelter, and helping people. 'Do you think she can study here?'

'I think law school might be far-fetched for a girl from her background. India is very much a class society. It's hard to move up when you're born low. Even here in Singapore things are harder when you're not Chinese, but hard work and perseverance count for a lot. We have meritocracy. That means people are judged on merit, not where they come from.'

She had a pensive look on her face. I wondered whether Mama found things more difficult at work because she was half Indian, and that she was thinking about that. But before I had the chance to ask, she said something completely unexpected.

'You know what, there are some Sunday schools offering classes for maids. Maybe that would be a good idea for her. I can look it up and print some stuff out for her.'

My heart started beating fast. Mama was still there, underneath the monster.

But then she added: 'Yes, I'll do that, and you can pass it to her. But...'

She was silent for a while. 'You think I don't pay attention, but I do, you know. I noticed how you hang out a lot with the aunties. I don't want you to do that so much. It's better for you to play with kids your own age. You're becoming a queer child.'

So she thought I was the crazy one?

'What's going on with Jenny?' Mama continued. 'We hardly ever see her anymore.'

I felt the little cockroach feet wriggle in my stomach. I hadn't felt them in a while, not since Cat was in my life. I swallowed deep and mumbled that I didn't like her anymore. She was no longer my friend.

The half-lie made the cockroach do a little dance. Would Mama guess that Jenny was the one doing the not-liking? But then the cockroach froze. It *wasn't* a lie. Cat was right. I didn't need Jenny. She was mean, and I really didn't like her anymore.

Clearer, I said: 'I have a new friend.'

Mama didn't pursue it. 'Yes, Cat. She's a bit queer too, but a nice girl, I suppose. Why don't you bring her over tomorrow? You're always at their place.'

I nodded, and pushed away the comments Mama had made about not hanging around with the aunties. I had another question on my mind. I needed to milk the nice Mama as long as I could, before the Mamamonster came back.

'Mama?'

'Yes?'

'Does it happen in Singapore too?'

'Does what happen?'

'Girls having arranged marriages? And marrying young? There are many Indian people here too.'

Some of which were our own family.

'Luckily, there are no child marriages here. Educated Indians and Singaporeans don't do that anymore. But I had a friend in school, Jasmeen, and she married a guy her parents picked for her. She wasn't forced, but she said her parents knew best, and how would she know who was right for her when she met a guy in a bar? She has three kids now and seems happy. She is a stay at home mum. I don't know. It's not for me. I believe women should make their own choices.'

'PoPo didn't pick Dad, did she?' I snickered.

Mama laughed too. 'I'm visualising PoPo liaising with Opa and Grandma in England. No. Don't think so. He wouldn't be whom she would have picked. Parents usually pick a partner for their child who's from their own community, similar to them.'

Would Mama and Dad find it easier if they'd been more alike? Or at least from the same country? Their fight still resonated in my ears sometimes. They must have made up later, because the last few days Dad had been home more than usually and they were uncharacteristically cuddly. Was that why Mama could control the Mamamonster? Still, I wondered if things would be easier if they were more alike.

Mama seemed so comfortable that the words slipped out of my mouth just like that: 'Who would PoPo have picked?'

'Who knows? She was hardly conventional choosing appa herself.'

We looked at each other. 'I miss PoPo,' we said at the same time. Mama didn't cry, but she closed her arms around me.

And I had missed Mama, I thought, hugging her tight, and hoping she would stay like this for a while. The feminism talk had worked, but I had also realised I had to be careful with my work for the aunties. Mama could not find out.

I felt so good after my conversation with Mama that when I saw Aunty M I ran to her and hugged her tight too. Somehow the good feeling made me want to cry. Aunty M hugged me back, and stroked my hair. 'What is the matter, sayang?'

I said something about Mama being nice.

'But why would you feel bad about that?'

'I don't, I just.' I stuttered. 'I wanted to say how sorry I was about Nurul. Have you spoken to her?'

'No, she is still not talking to me. But I spoke to her dad. She is fine, she goes to school. She went to see her brother at my mother's house.'

I needed to say something, but what could I say? I wanted

to ask Aunty M how she felt, but her eyes showed that perfectly.

We didn't speak for a while. I suppose she must have thought about Nurul, but I thought about Mama.

'Aunty M?'

'Yes?'

'Do you think Mama would be nicer if she didn't work? I mean nicer all the time? Like she was before.'

I realised Aunty M never knew Mama before. 'I mean, you know. Mama was not always like this. She used to scream less. Dad says she is still not over missing PoPo, because when she was young PoPo was all she had. And that her work gives her so much stress she can't grieve properly.'

I wasn't completely sure what stress was, but I assumed it was pretty similar to cockroach feet dancing in your stomach whenever you saw your former best friend who was now mean. Not something I was hoping a grownup would feel. If her boss made Mama feel like that, and Dad said she could easily quit, why shouldn't she? I hoped that grownups had more control over their lives.

Aunty M nodded. 'Yes, your Mama has some stress. She works too hard. But I think if she did not work, she would be even less happy. It is who she is. Some women like to sit by the pool and sip wine, but not your Mama. What would I do if I had a rich husband?' She giggled. 'I'd stop work forever. I have worked enough. But your mother, her job is not cleaning the house. She has an important job. She wants to work.'

After a short break she added: 'She will get better. Just wait.'

I sighed. Aunty M was the same as all adults. Stupid. That

was the advice we gave people when we didn't know what to say. Did she think I'd fall for that?

'People have to work hard to support their children,' Aunty M said.

'Like you. You had to leave Nurul and Adi to make money for their future.' I had learned a lot the last few months about desperation.

Aunty M nodded sadly. 'I wish Nurul would understand too.'

36

I asked Cat to come by the next day, as Mama had suggested. We spent some time playing cards, but since Mama wasn't home there was no point in staying in. We decided to catch up with Nee Nee. Aunty M stayed at home with Chloe, and no one opened the door at Win's place, so we went over to Maricel's on our own. She was home, and opened the door covered in flour. 'I'm baking a pie,' she said, pointing with her elbow. 'Go through. She's at the back, I just saw her.'

Cat climbed onto the table that was now permanently underneath the wall. What did Maricel's employers think about that, I wondered. Did they know what was happening next door? Did they question it?

It looked as if Cat had managed to pick up quite a few words of Burmese. I was jealous. It was better than my Mandarin. Better than Cat's Mandarin too.

'We need to come more often,' Cat said, hanging over the wall from Maricel's place, her face turned back to me. 'She's still too hungry. She ate the dog food yesterday.'

'The dog food? Are you sure you understood right?'

Maricel came up to the kitchen door.

'It's my fault. I was away for a few days with my employer. So we could not feed her.'

'Did she really eat the dog food?'

Maricel raised her shoulders slightly, her white pasty hands in the air. 'I don't know. She wouldn't be the first maid to do that.'

Cat passed a parcel of food to Nee Nee and exchanged a few more words.

'She says it tasted quite nice.'

I wasn't sure Cat wasn't making this up. Maricel said that it was true, it tasted fine. She had eaten cat food herself.

'It was the fancy kind. Very expensive. The employer I had only gave me a little meat, so I stole a spoon each time I fed the cat. It was chicken. In jelly. Very nice.'

We both stared at Maricel in disbelief.

'You know, once we sat in the agency, waiting for a job, maybe ten of us. We spoke about food that day.'

We waited for Maricel to continue, as we knew she would. She licked the dough off her fingers first, then rubbed her hands together.

'One woman had lost fifteen kilos at her last job. It hurt when she sat down, no fat on her bum, all bones. So we started to share experiences. We did a count. Out of ten, only two had always had enough food in all their jobs.'

'Wow,' Cat remarked. 'Why do people do that? It's like not putting petrol in your car. It won't go.'

Maricel gesticulated, *what can you do?* She went on. 'Some people give the maid one slice of bread for breakfast. My former employer did that. If I took more, she would scold me.'

'How did she know how much you took?' I asked.

'She would count the slices in the pack. One friend, they gave her leftovers, but only after two or three days, if no one else wanted them. If she took anything from the fridge herself, it was stealing. She did it once, when she was very hungry. She felt so guilty. She is a very strict catholic, so she had to go to confession. Several others took food from the bin. But that was not allowed either.'

I wondered whether any of them had ever eaten chichak. Or cockroach, even. But I was afraid to ask, lest the one in my stomach woke up.

When we got home, we interrogated Aunty M about her former employers. Had she always had enough to eat?

'No, I was never hungry. My second ma'am, I stayed with her many years. The English teacher. The family was very good to me, treated me like part of the family. I ate separately, but good food, meat too. I did not have a day off, but on Sunday they would take me out, to the park, or dinner. After a year, I got so fat. I knew I was lucky with a good employer, but every night I would cry myself to sleep for missing my kids.'

They weren't there to see, but I felt the tears on her face. Who did she think about when she tucked me in? Me or them?

I pushed the thoughts down. 'Did you speak to them often? Or were they too little then?'

Aunty M replied, 'I did not have a phone, so I could only call once a month on my employer's phone. My family did not have a phone either, so they had to go visit a relative in the next village and wait until I called. Sometimes, I was not allowed to use the phone on the agreed time. My employer would need me, and said I could only call the next day. But my family would have spent that day waiting near the phone. They could not go back the next day. We'd have to wait another month.'

Cat looked at Aunty M blankly. 'Why did you not just tell her you needed to use the phone at that specific time? You said she was nice.'

Aunty M shook her head. 'I was not like now, I was very shy. Just new in Singapore. I was afraid to talk back.'

I thought about the special smiles Aunty M reserved for Mama, and asked myself, would she talk back now? To me, yes, but to Mama?

Aunty M must have read my thoughts, as she smiled a different smile. 'You need not worry about me. I have everything I need here. Your mother is a good employer.'

I hoped she wasn't just saying that. I did worry though, lying awake at night, not just about Aunty M and all the others, but also about Mama and Dad, and sometimes Nurul. Was this growing up? If so, I wanted to stay a child, but only at Cat's place in the jungle. There we'd run around chasing monkeys and Ollie with sticks, build huts and splatter in mud pools. We were never bored there like I was in our condo, with its playground, pool, tennis and squash courts. There was always something happening, and if it not, we made it happen. Most kids at school and in the condo barely played outside anymore at our age. They played computer games or watched TV. Those things left you the wrong kind of tired. In Cat's jungle, PoPo's kampong came alive, with all its games and adventures, and I got a glimpse of what life had been like before concrete took over. Inspiring and energising instead of numbing. I had slowly learned to be rebellious, and inside me bubbled a need to shake things up – in my own life, or better, the whole city state, with MOM on top. Perhaps I'd been wrong about Singapore, and there was a fire mountain hiding underneath the surface of polite society. Could little girls make it erupt?

A week later, on a dull afternoon when I was so bored I'd watched TV all afternoon, there was a sharp rapping on the door. It was Maricel.

'Come, please, something is wrong with Nee Nee. She can't stop crying, for two days now. She does not look hurt, I can't see any injuries, but I'm not sure. I messaged Win, but no answer. I tried her door yesterday already, but no answer too.'

Aunty M put Chloe in the stroller and we took off. We tried Win again, and this time the door opened seconds after we knocked. A stout Filipina opened.

Taken aback, Maricel stumbled over her words. 'Sorry. Is Win home?'

The woman stared blankly. 'Win? Who? Don't know her.'

Aunty M cut in. 'She works here. Win, from Myanmar.'

The Filipina shook her head. 'Never heard of her. I work here. They told me not to talk to people. No visitors. So don't make noise, don't give me trouble.'

She started closing the door.

'Wait,' said Maricel, and rattled on in Tagalog. The other woman gave curt replies, then closed the door completely.

'She knows nothing about Win,' Maricel said. 'She just started working there, and is not allowed visitors when the ma'am is out. They must have fired Win, sent her back to Myanmar. No-one has seen her in over a week.'

'But she didn't even say goodbye,' I protested. 'They can't do that!'

'Looks like they just did,' said Maricel.

'They can,' said Aunty M. 'MOM says employers have to give reasonable notice when they send someone home. Some employers say half an hour to pack your bag is reasonable.'

'Maybe they found out that she was starting to have a social life and they did not like us visiting?' Maricel pondered. 'That's why they told this one, no visitors?'

Us visiting? Or me visiting? Was it my fault Win was gone? The thought pricked the lining of my stomach.

'Who knows what employers think,' said Aunty M. 'Let's think of Nee Nee now.'

We went over to Maricel's place, where Nee Nee sat with her back to the wall, sniffing. We tried to ask her what the problem was, but she just cried and mumbled words we didn't understand through her tears.

'We can ask Cat,' I suggested. She'd kill me if she missed being part of whatever this was, and she did know some Burmese.

Cat arrived half an hour later, having begged her mother for taxi money and claiming a life or death emergency. She climbed on the table and spoke to Nee Nee in a soft voice for a few minutes. Then she climbed down and shook her head. 'I have no idea what she's saying.'

'I thought you spoke Burmese,' I cried out.

Cat looked busted. 'Not really. Just a few words. Yes, no, hello, that sort of thing. We mostly use sign language. Miming eating dog food is easy. But this? No clue. Sorry.'

We all sat down on the kitchen chairs.

'Now what?'

Maricel got up. 'Let's get Moe Moe. Her English is good, and at least Nee Nee has someone to talk to, even if Moe Moe cannot translate. She needs a friend.'

I sprung up. 'No. You can't!'

Maricel glared at me. 'Why not?'

Aunty M looked at me sympathetically, and I wondered how much she knew.

Enough, it seemed, when she said, 'I think Maya does not like it that she might bring Jenny.'

Cat jumped up too. 'Oh, grow up already, Maya. This isn't about you.'

She was about to storm out, but Aunty M stopped her. 'You girls wait here with Chloe and Maricel. I'll go.'

I'd seen Jenny that morning, and I'd got used to coping with her on the bus, as well as the twinge in my tummy I experienced in the hallways, always fearing that I might run into her. The thing that had got me through all those months, especially those before Cat, was my secret life: the helping of the helpers. It made me feel I was special, and being special made me strong. I didn't want Jenny to know about it and ruin that too. It was too important.

The cockroach inside me grew bigger, and I opened my mouth to say something to make it stop, but then Cat grabbed my hand.

The cockroach shrunk back, still there, like a ball in my belly, but manageable. She squeezed. 'Don't worry. I'm here.'

When Aunty M came back, she'd brought Moe Moe but not Jenny. 'She stayed at home with her little brother,' she whispered to me.

The cockroach shrunk smaller until it was just the nauseating wriggle I'd become accustomed to when I was getting ready for the bus. I was able to focus again on Nee Nee.

Moe Moe spoke with her a long time. When she finally came down off the table, we all sat down again.

'Nee Nee mother very sick,' Moe Moe said. 'He die soon.'

'He? Do you mean her father?' I asked.

'She, I say, Nee Nee mother,' Moe Moe repeated. Like Win, she mixed up her pronouns.

'That's bad,' Aunty M said. 'Will she go see her?'

Moe Moe shook her head. 'No go home. Employer says no possible. Need Nee Nee to work.'

'No wonder she is crying. They won't let her go,' Maricel said. 'Is there anything we can do?'

Cat added, 'Does she need anything? Money?'

Moe Moe shook her head again. 'No need. Employer offer send money already. Employer nice. No need. Mother die anyway, doctor say.'

I felt surprised. Employer nice? Why would they offer to pay for treatment, if that were true, but not let her go? They barely fed her.

'They offered her money?' Aunty M said, who must have

thought the same.

'Yes. Money, her salary, next month. They take it out again.'

'So they offered her a loan, to pay a doctor,' Maricel said.

'She no want loan,' Moe Moe said. 'She want go home. Say goodbye mother.'

'So there's nothing we can do?' Maricel asked again.

Aunty M looked solemn. 'We can ask MOM if she can go home. They will probably let her, but it means she will lose the job. And it might take a week or so. It will likely be too late.'

'No. She need job. She stay. Tomorrow, I come back?' Moe Moe asked. 'Is ok? I talk her.'

'Yes, please do. My employers are out all day. Come when you like,' Maricel said.

Moe Moe went to say goodbye to Nee Nee across the wall. The sobbing had abated.

'At least she has been able to talk to someone. She looks a bit better,' Aunty M said. We all slunk out, following Moe Moe down the hall.

When we came to the elevator, my heart stopped.

'Look who's here,' Jenny grimaced. 'If it isn't little Cockroach, with her monkey friend. And her other mates, the maids. You always did like to mingle with your own kind, didn't you?'

Aunty M looked at Moe Moe, like it had been her talking. But Moe Moe just stood there.

'Why were you away so long?' Jenny's brother Harry bawled.

'I had to bring him to look for you, he was becoming such a nuisance. You can't just take off like this,' Jenny scolded Moe Moe. 'You need to watch him. I have homework. Come now, or

I'll tell Mum.'

Moe Moe hung her head and trudged towards Harry.

Cat pushed me towards the elevator. 'Ignore her,' she hissed.

'See you tomorrow in the bus,' Jenny sing-sang after me, in a sugary tone.

The door pinged shut behind us. 'Jenny doesn't let herself be ignored,' I murmured, but I didn't think Cat heard me.

I didn't sleep that night. The best thing in my life was now tainted by the worst. My bed had turned itself into a giant cockroach and I lay there in the middle of it, waiting. Waiting for the bus.

37

The bus ride wasn't worse than anything I'd expected, but that was bad enough. It was the usual stuff: that I was a cockroach, that a monkey and a bunch of maids were just the right friends for me. Jenny and Meena had cornered me in the back row, each sitting on one side of me. Luckily no-one else sat near us, so no-one had to witness my plight. Jenny had interrogated Moe Moe to find out exactly what my role had been in Operation Rescue Nee Nee. Moe Moe might not have been articulate enough to convey all the details, but Jenny knew enough.

'Is it a bird? Is it a plane? No, it's super cockroach! Superroach to the rescue! And Supermaid. Any scum, rat, lowlife or maid needs help? Superroach and Supermaid will come! We should get you a cape and mask. A brown one, with antennae.' They giggled quite a while after that one.

Then Jenny dealt her final blow. 'Does your mother know you're Superroach? And that your Aunty is a Supermaid? Your mother seems fairly respectable. I can't imagine she'd agree to these Supermaid activities during work time. She'd kick that maid back to Indonesia before you could say *super*.'

I wanted to say yes, of course, she knew. But my red face said it all.

'Well, what do you think?' Jenny said over me to Meena. 'Maybe we should tell Superroach's mummy a little tale about her daughter and her maid.'

'No, you can't do that!' I yelped.

Jenny and Meena laughed. 'Of course we can. Let's see if you can rescue yourself, Superroach, and that stinking aunty of yours.'

I felt like a giant shoe had stomped on me when I realised Jenny was right. Aunty M would lose her job, like Win had. Helping others during work hours, and dragging ten-year-old me into it too. Would Mama find it reasonable to give her at least enough time to say goodbye? Nurul, the one I'd despised, would have to leave school when her mother was unemployed, the shiny new school uniform sold for hard cash. The guilt folded in so many layers, from my foul jealousy, to the fact that I'd taken her mother away, to finally making her mother lose her job. It was too much to bear. I had already cost Win her livelihood.

The feeling of being eaten by a cockroach had gone. I'd been swallowed and digested, my flesh absorbed in its body full of bile. Jenny was right. I felt tiny. A real life insect, hiding in a corner of the sewer.

That day, of all days, Cat was home sick with a fever. I didn't sleep that night, nor the one following. I just waited. Waited for the bomb to drop, hoping for it to be over, for the plaster to be ripped off in one painful, spiteful pull.

But nothing happened. The next morning in the bus, Jenny and Meena were preoccupied with some new boy that was sitting in the front, and was, admittedly, very cute (not that I would have noticed if it hadn't been for them). Nothing happening was the worst.

In the afternoon, I phoned Cat. She sounded far-off, her voice weak and floating. She sounded so sick I couldn't tell her what had happened. She told me that she had a disease called chikungunya.

'Chicken-what?' I said.

'Chikungunya,' Cat repeated. 'It's a virus, like dengue. A lot like dengue. I have this rash, red nasty spots all over, and it itches like crazy. I can't sleep from scratching. My mother wound towels around my hands to stop me. My knees hurt so much I can't walk. And I have a fever. I had to go to the doctor to have a blood test. Dad has it too, it's mosquitoes that spread it.'

'That sounds terrible. Shall I come over?'

'No. You can't. There are mosquitoes here that are infected. You could get it too.'

'I'll slather on the DEET. I'll be ok.' I really needed her right now.

'Sorry. Not allowed. My mum says no way.'

Cat sounded so jaded I wished her well, and rung off.

The next week lasted a year without Cat to support me. I buried myself in my room, shielded by the IPad, library books, in a sheet-tent that must have made the worst bomb shelter ever. But still nothing happened. Had Jenny not found an opportune moment yet? Or did she prefer to torture me slowly, keeping the can of insecticide spray hovering above me for as long as she could?

Aunty M was withdrawn that week, still brooding over Nurul. How could I burden her with what Jenny had threatened when she had more pressing things to worry about?

The only time we spoke was after she'd received a phone call. There was a woman on the other end of the line, and it sounded like she was in hysterics. Aunty M spoke to her in soft, consoling tones.

'Where are you? Which terminal?' Aunty M scribbled some notes on a scrap of paper. 'Did they say why they are sending you back?'

I couldn't hear much, despite leaning in – just sobbing, and more hysterics.

'No? Are you sure? And when was this?' She tapped the pen on the scrap of paper. 'Listen, ate, this is important. Did they give you all your salary?'

She jotted down a few figures, then looked up again. 'Don't worry. Tell me exactly, which terminal, which desk you are. I will call someone. What are you wearing?

'Ok. Now stay there, don't move. Someone will come for you. If they want to take you through customs, don't go.

'Let them threaten with the police. Don't worry about police, just tell them you have the right to go to MOM. And that someone will come to help you.'

Aunty M hung up, and looked at me. I had understood enough. It was about the reasonable notice.

'What happened,' I asked Aunty M. 'Do they want to send her home?'

'Wait, sayang,' Aunty M said. 'I need to make a phone call first.'

'Sister, it's Merpati, I need your help. Someone is at the

airport. Her employer wants to send her to the Philippines, just told her pack your bag, let's go now. But she did not have her last month of the salary. They say they used it to pay for the ticket. It's wrong, right? Can you go?'

Aunty M shared the details of her notes, the terminal, flight number, amounts of salary owed. She hung up.

I looked at her, expectantly. 'What will happen?'

'I don't know, but sister will try. They will demand to go to MOM. Make a scene at the airport. It's not allowed to send her home without her salary.'

'But can they send her home at all? Is this reasonable notice?'

Aunty M grinned. 'Reasonable? What do you think? Reason has nothing to do with it.'

If only I hadn't neglected Win because I had a new friend, we might have been able to help her too. It was my fault she was gone, and Aunty M would be next.

A week later, Cat was back, and things went back to normal – normal being that Jenny and Meena restarted their jeering at me in the bus with new vigour. I felt as if I was permanently submerged in cockroach bile. Jenny would wink at me, whispering through the bus, 'Is it a bird? Is it a plane? No, it's...' and then she'd cackle.

For some reason it hurt more than before, like something important was at stake. I felt stranded above an abyss, on a rope bridge that could break at any minute. Could roaches fly? They had wings, but I'd never seen one take off. Even if they could, Jenny had her string tied to my leg. If I tried to fly away, she'd pull me back like the green beetle PoPo's brothers had kept.

In class there was Cat, and when I was with her I felt safer. I wanted to tell her what was happening but I didn't. Maybe if I didn't talk about it I could pretend it wasn't real. But the wanting to tell her still burned in my wriggling stomach.

Aunty M had spoken on the phone to Nurul, which had dramatically improved her mood. One Saturday, she offered to take Cat and me to a park near the shelter to meet up with Sri.

Sri was agitated. Her investigating officer at the police had finally made a decision: they would charge both Ah Mah and her former employers with abuse. The case would now be handed over to the prosecutors and the courts. Aunty M called it good news, but she also admitted it was far from over. The court case could take years. Sri seemed more pre-occupied with something else.

'We have this girl in shelter, Anissa, I met her Sunday. She stole from her employer.'

'Why did she steal?' I asked.

'How matter, sayang? Is it ok to steal, for a hospital bill for child? Or because your employer not pay you?'

I pondered that. It seemed quite understandable.

'Will she go to jail?' Cat asked.

Sri nodded. 'Yes, tomorrow she go to police station. But my employers not in jail yet. And me? I'm stuck in shelter.'

I wondered what jail was like. Would rats nibble your toes? Or was that just in poor countries like Indonesia?

Sri went on. 'You know, the employer good to her. When they

suspected her, they want to be sure, they put a trap.'

'A trap? How?' I wondered.

Sri said, 'When they went away, they put money in a bag. That same bag, money gone from before. When the money was gone, they called the police, and Anissa admitted.'

I nodded. Cat looked excited and I nudged her to stay quiet.

Sri grumbled some more. 'Some people so bad, they don't deserve the good employer. Why I get the bad one?'

Cat, who had only just met Sri but acted like she'd known her forever, said: 'It's just bad luck, right?'

Sri shot her a dirty look. 'It is not fair. I am punished more than Anissa. She go to jail for four weeks, then go home. I already waiting for many months, and it might be many more. My employer, will they ever go to jail?'

Aunty M tried to reason with Sri, but there was very little we could say. There was nothing we could do to help her, so we walked with her on the beach and had iced lemon tea at the food court. Right and wrong had never seemed more confusing.

38

Cat and I were on the swings in our condo playground. I was almost happy, doing my favourite thing with my favourite person. Until *she* showed up.

She stood in front of the swings and laughed. She didn't need to do more; her presence and the look in her eyes were enough to spoil everything.

I slid off the swing and signalled to Cat to follow. We wandered over to the benches, where the aunties sat. Jenny followed, probably bored and in need of fun. Her kind of fun. When we got close, Moe Moe, who was wearing longer shorts than normal, guiltily pulled down the hem over one knee. I stared at her. The shorts couldn't hide the purple mark at the bottom of her thigh. Suddenly, I could no longer take it. I felt the cockroach grow inside, brace his legs and burst out of my mouth.

I turned to and shouted. 'Can't you control that horrible brother of yours? Look what he's done to her. He's an animal!'

Jenny stood there and shrugged. 'Who cares? She's just a maid, I slap her sometimes. She's a pussy. She'll never tell mom.'

Jenny left for the swings. I looked at Moe Moe, who turned her red face away.

'We need to do something,' I said to Aunty M.

Aunty M looked at Moe Moe too. 'Maya, we need to be very careful here. It is up to Moe Moe.'

Moe Moe shook her head. She looked sad and empty.

Cat, who for once had stayed quiet, grabbed my hand and pulled me away. Together we ran for the bushes. She squatted next to me to the ground and we spoke at the same time.

Cat said: 'We need to do something about Jenny.'

I said: 'We need to help Moe Moe.'

Cat shrugged and was the first to speak again. 'It's the same thing. Either way, we need to act. Aunty M won't. You saw her.'

I sat on the muddy ground. Cat was right. We had to do something about Jenny, and if that helped Moe Moe at the same time, that would be perfect. Even just thinking about doing something made me braver, and I finally told Cat what had happened in the bus just before she got sick with the disease with the difficult name. The superroach comments, how Jenny was going to get Aunty M sent back to Indonesia – it all came out so easily, as if I hadn't been struggling to tell her for so long. Cat didn't seem surprised. She wasn't one to ponder. She liked to act.

'So that settles it,' she said. 'We can't let that happen. We need to do something.'

'But what?'

Cat grinned. 'I have a plan.' She sat down too. 'We'll report her. Her and her brother.'

'What do you mean? Report where?'

Cat's lips became a straight line and she said, serious now, 'They are maid abusers. We'll report them to MOM. Remember when Aunty M said you could call them on the phone?'

As soon as she said it, it seemed completely right. We went upstairs before Aunty M and Chloe got back, pulled out our notebooks with the MOM helpline number in them, and Cat grabbed the phone and dialled. We didn't give our names. We said we were concerned neighbours, that we had seen the marks on her legs, and that we suspected that Moe Moe was being abused by her employers. We gave the address, even the home phone number. Afterwards, Cat slapped the notebook closed. 'Now we wait. Let's get some Ribena.'

We didn't tell anyone, particularly not Aunty M.

39

Aunty M had become quite cheerful lately, and she was not paying much attention to Cat or me. I pretended things were normal. But inside me, the cockroach waited, tiny fists clenched. Aunty M was busy with a new project; a celebration for Kartini day that she was organising with some other volunteers from the helpdesk. There was to be Indonesian food, Indonesian dancing, music, and much more.

'Can I come?' I asked.

'Sure,' said Aunty M, 'but it's on a Sunday. You need to ask your Mama.'

I sighed. 'I don't want to ask.' Yesterday had been a Mamamonster day. I didn't want to risk it.

Aunty M smiled. 'Sayang, you think your mother is evil, but she is not. She is just stressed. I'm sure she will be fine with it.'

'Really?' I asked.

'Yes. And when you ask her, tell her... Wait. Do you actually know why we celebrate Kartini day?'

I had no idea.

'Kartini was a famous Indonesian feminist.'

A celebration for a feminist? Maybe Mama wanted to come too. I googled Kartini. She was born in 1879, in Central Java, like Aunty M, but in a rich family, and was allowed to attend a Dutch language primary school. When she turned twelve she was 'secluded' at home, in preparation for her marriage, as was the tradition for aristocratic Javanese girls. Kartini became pen friends with several Dutch women who sent her magazines, books and letters. Kartini started to write too. She saw that women's struggles for equal rights and education were part of a wider movement. I read some fragments on emancipation of the Javanese as well as women, but none of them I understood.

At twenty-three Kartini was married, as a fourth wife to an older man. I made a mental note to ask Aunty M about that later. Kartini was 'lucky' – her new husband allowed her to start a school for women in the village. A year later she died in childbirth. After her death, some people started a foundation in her name to build schools for women all over the country. Even later Indonesia, by then independent from the Dutch, decided to dedicate a national holiday in her honour.

After I'd memorised as much as I could, I went to talk to Mama.

'Mama, have you heard of Kartini? She was this famous Indonesian feminist.'

'Yes, I've heard of her. Didn't they name a holiday after her?'

'Yes,' I enthused, 'that's the one. Did you know she wanted to send all the girls to school? She wrote a book about it.'

Mama nodded. 'It's great that they still celebrate her, although these days the Indonesian government tries to make her look more like a model housewife than the activist she really was.'

She was quiet for a bit. 'When I was younger, I wanted to do social studies not finance. My teachers said better not, I was too good at maths.' Her eyes turned dreamy. But then, 'Where did you hear about Kartini?'

I panicked. I couldn't tell Mama that Aunty M was involved with the helpdesk. I stammered, 'From Aunty M. They celebrate in Singapore too. Aunty M is going. Can I go with her?'

'Sure. When is it?'

'Next Sunday,' I said, crossing my fingers behind my back.

Mama calculated on her fingers.

'Perfect,' she said, 'Dad is away that weekend, and I have an important presentation on Monday. Ask her if she can take Chloe too.'

I was disappointed Mama didn't want to join us, but elated that I could go.

'Aunty M, Mama says I can come to Kartini day, and she says can we please take Chloe too? She needs to work.'

Aunty M beamed back at me. She loved showing off Chloe to her friends.

'Aunty M,' I said, 'can I ask something else?' She nodded. 'Kartini had to marry an older man, as a fourth wife even. Do they still do that, in Indonesia? Did your parents make you marry your husband? Is that why you didn't like him and split up?'

Aunty M smiled. 'No. Not really. It was a bit different. I met him myself. I was very young and thought he was cute. And then we went out, just the two of us. Some people in the village saw us together, holding hands. That's all we did, hold hands, we didn't even kiss.'

Gross. I hadn't needed that sort of detail.

'Anyway, my father said people would gossip, and I should marry him, which I did. But I found he was not the right man for me. That is why we split up when Adi was one. He could not provide for the family.'

'So do other girls have arranged marriages in Indonesia?'

'No, not anyone I know. Maybe rich families like Kartini's. Her father was nobility, very important in government. For them marriage is like politics.'

That I knew from fairy tales. 'Like the princess having to marry the prince of the neighbouring country, to join the two and get bigger.'

'Exactly,' said Aunty M. 'Not in the villages. I think rich people don't do it anymore either on Java.'

'But Indira is from the village. Hardly a princess?'

Aunty M sighed. 'They do things differently in India.'

A few days later Aunty M was called out to another case. Cat wasn't there, and I didn't want to go. I had to stop risking Aunty M's job. Jenny still hadn't done anything, but who knew when she would. Cat asked me every day whether there was any news. 'Not yet,' I'd reply. 'You know MOM is slow.'

Cat suggested that maybe we should call the police, that they would act quicker; but a nagging feeling in my stomach told me to convince her to be patient.

Aunty M knew nothing about my worries. 'Come on Maya, let's go. We need to catch the bus.'

'I have a lot of homework. Can I stay here?'

'No, I promised you mother I wouldn't leave you alone in

the condo. You can stay in when we go to the playground. Not if I take a bus somewhere. It isn't far, just next to the Botanic Gardens.'

I supposed I could pretend that we were just going to the park. It turned out not even to be an interesting case, just someone overworked, shouted at. Nothing we hadn't heard before.

When we got back, Khusnul approached us in front of our block. She had red eyes. 'Help me sister, help me! I have been so stupid!'

Khusnul started stuttering about how stupid she'd been, and that it was an accident, she'd never meant to hurt him, and that it really, really had only happened once. Yesterday.

'Calm down,' said Aunty M. 'I don't understand you at all.'

The story came out in fits and starts. Khusnul had hit one of the kids in her care.

'Only one time, believe me, only the one time. He was screaming, and I had not slept that night. He had been awake at night too. Then, he didn't want to eat breakfast. He threw the food in my eye, poked the spoon in my eye. I was so tired, my eyes was almost closed. I got very angry. Very stupid. I hit him in the head. Then he stopped crying.'

Aunty M had a serious look on her face. 'Was the child hurt? Where is he now?'

Khusnul pointed at a playground behind her. Both her kids were playing happily. They seemed fine.

'He is okay. He did not cry after. He sleep more last night. But I, I still don't sleep from worry. I should not hit him. They will fire me. Or worse, call the police. I will never, ever do again.'

'But how will they find out?' I asked. The boy was too little to talk properly.

Khusnul cried out. 'It's on the camera.' She started crying.

'Did they see it yet?' I asked.

Khusnul shuddered. 'They always watch in the weekend only. What do I do?'

Aunty M said, 'Tell them. Tell them before they see the film. That it happened only once, and that you know it is wrong, that you will never do it again. And say sorry.'

'But what if they don't believe me? Can they send me to jail?'

'That will be for the judge to decide. If they will see it anyway, being honest is the best way. Show them they can trust you.'

Khusnul had started crying again.

I wondered whether Jenny's parents had cameras. If they did, maybe we could find proof of Harry biting Moe Moe.

40

We all went together to Kartini Day, Aunty M, Khusnul, Chloe and I. Khusnul had cheered up. She had told her employers everything and they had reacted surprisingly well. She was on probation now, but because the kids loved her so, she was allowed to stay. Her sir had mentioned that he was considering putting a camera in the bedroom Khusnul shared with the little girl, and Khusnul had been worrying about it all week. 'If he does that, I will leave,' she said. But she was scared they would not sign the transfer papers after what happened. She told us she didn't want to discuss it further. 'Today I have fun,' she said.

There were at least a hundred Indonesian women, and none of them in the usual aunty uniform of shirt and shorts. Some wore long sleeved dresses and headscarves. Others wore straight skirts in colourful batik prints that fell to the floor, or short, pretty dresses. Aunty M and Khusnul were wearing batik too, Aunty M a simple knee length dress in purple with butterflies, and Khusnul a similar one in green. Aunty M had put a batik dress on Chloe, which I remembered from when I was little. PoPo had bought it for me, and there was a photo where I was wearing it, held in PoPo's arms. Seeing it on Chloe that morning had stung my eyes. I felt plain in my shorts and yellow T-shirt.

The programme for the day was full of singing, dancing, and a fashion show, alternated with speeches. One of the speeches was about Kartini, but it was in Indonesian and I couldn't understand it. Aunty M translated some but stopped after the question, 'What would Kartini have to say about the rights of domestic workers in Singapore?'

My thoughts drifted away on the cadence of the speaker. What would she have to say? Would she be proud of all that had been achieved, or disappointed in what had not? Kartini had been rich, would have had her own servants. Had she treated them well? Being rich had not made her life much easier – I mean, being married off to an old guy as wife number four. I shivered in the chill of the aircon. If life wasn't easy at that level of society, I could only begin to imagine what Kartini's servants' lives had been like. Hopefully they were the lucky ones, like Aunty M. Mama was a good employer, and the thought warmed me a bit.

The speaker was still going on and I was starting to get bored. I imagined being Kartini, helping other girls go to school, fighting for their rights, and now, more than a hundred years later, having people still celebrate my birthday. *Helping is interfering,* Mama had said. But Kartini and Mother Teresa were both famous, and where was she? Home alone, doing a stupid presentation that everybody would have forgotten in less than a month. Cat and I had done the right thing.

In the break, I went to the toilet together with Khusnul. One of the competitors in an amazing dress was ahead of us in the line. Khusnul fingered the dress appreciatively. 'Where did you get it?'

The woman looked at her as if about to tell her a secret. 'This one I made. These ones,' she said, pointing at other dressed-up women in front of her, 'many people buy, very expensive. But I made this one myself. I got the fabric in Sumatra cheap. Then I make it here.'

I looked her up and down. 'It's beautiful. It's batik too?'

She nodded. 'This is the theme of the fashion show, you see? Everyone has batik.'

Only now I noticed; all the dresses were batik. Not plain like ours, but special gold-threaded batik.

Khusnul looked shy suddenly, but excited too. 'Actually, I sew too. I made this one.' She pointed at her own dress, much simpler, but also batik and still pretty.

The other woman looked at the fabric admiringly, inspecting the seams. 'Good job.'

Khusnul pointed, 'But I cannot make a dress like that. I need to learn.'

'Then take classes,' the other lady said. 'I do, on Sundays, here in Singapore.'

The two of them chatted some more and exchanged numbers.

'Did you make Aunty M's dress too?' I asked, having noticed the similarities.

'Yes,' Khusnul beamed.

'It's very pretty.'

'Thank you. I think I will take this classes. You know, I plan to go back to Java in two years to start my sewing business. I have my savings and I will open a shop. I need to go back so I can find a husband.'

'Can't you find a husband here?' I asked.

Khusnul huffed. 'In Singapore, very difficult. Many guys, they don't treat us maid serious, they just want to have fun. I don't want fun. I want a family.'

I smiled. 'Fun is fun too.'

'Yes,' Khusnul smiled, 'but not that kind of fun. You are too young to understand. Four years ago, I went back to my village. I was fed up with the work here, the cleaning, the screaming babies, not even my own. I went back to Java. But the village, it was so boring. No cinema. No shops. And worse, no jobs. Now I am old already. I have money, so I can make my own job. I will start the sewing business with my savings, and then I will find a husband.'

'Don't give him your money though.'

'What do you mean? If he is my husband, we can work together. And have many babies...'

Khusnul started to look dreamy and I grabbed her hand, pulling her back to the hall.

It had been such a fun day that I almost forgot about everything else. But it hadn't gone away: Jenny, superroach, MOM, or that I'd been drowning in cockroach bile. I felt dread mixed with excitement. I dreamed of fame, like Kartini's, and being the hero that saved Moe Moe. Why then did my stomach hurt when I thought of her?

I slept well that Sunday night, and woke up feeling happy for almost a whole minute. Then I realised the bus was due in forty-five minutes, and there was no way of knowing what it was going to be like. The worst thing was the anticipation, which made everything taste vile at breakfast. I fantasised about breaking and snapping to Jenny, throwing MOM in her face, *just you wait, they're coming for you...* But she could never know what we'd done. She'd go straight to Mama, and it would be over for sure for Aunty M.

Why had nothing happened yet? Had MOM even investigated? Had they decided there was no problem? Or were they just being bureaucratic and slow? Something needed to happen before Jenny went to tell my parents or hers about superroach. I didn't understand why she hadn't done it already.

She'd hinted she was going to do it several times already on the bus. Once I'd blurted out, 'Well why don't you? Are you scared? I might be a roach but at least I have guts.'

Those guts pumped out a torrent of vile acid, and I tried hard to swallow it down without choking.

Jenny just grinned. 'Why would I do it straight away? Where's the fun in that? I'm waiting for the right time. In the meantime, it's much more fun to watch you squirm.'

I wanted MOM to make *her* squirm more than anything in the world.

Meena added, 'How you'll miss your precious aunty! But don't worry, monkey might still like you. They eat shit. Yes, perhaps she'll still like you. You never know.'

I swallowed, swallowed, swallowed until I could speak. 'Cat knows everything. She doesn't care. She's not a coward like you.'

I stopped myself telling them that Cat had come up with the perfect revenge. I curled up in my corner. What could I do but wait? Wait and hope for a diversion to take my mind off things.

The playground had been my second living room when I was younger, and now it seemed to have turned into our office. Aunty M would sit on the bench in front of the orchid tree like a doctor hosting a free clinic, and people stopped by for advice. Today, it was Indira.

'You need to help me,' Indira said to Aunty M. 'Remember when I told you about my former employer? They still have not paid me.'

'Okay,' said Aunty M, 'but you need to remind me. Where is that employer?'

Indira spat out the words. 'They left the country.'

'They left?' said Aunty M. 'Where to?'

'Malaysia, Johor they live now. They owe me my salary. Sir Tom's company went bankrupt. They said had to sell their house in England. After, they could pay my salary. I waited. First, they moved to a smaller house, I had to sleep in the bomb shelter. Before, when they were rich, they were generous. They gave me good food. I had big room. Then, all stopped.' Indira accentuated everything she said with florid hand movements. At the word 'stopped' she slammed the fingers of her right hand into the palm of her left.

'How much do they owe you?' Aunty M asked.

'Nine thousand.'

'Nine thousand dollars?' I asked.

Indira nodded. 'Sir got a new job here and they moved to Johor, because it's cheaper there. The kids changed schools. First I stayed with them, but I did not like it there. I wanted my salary and then transfer. Ma'am Tamsin bought a bus ticket to Singapore and gave me two hundred dollar. Because I did not know what to do, I went back to the shelter. I only have a small suitcase. The rest of my stuff is still in Johor.'

Indira looked at me as well as Aunty M now.

'MOM allowed me to get a new job. Ma'am's phone, she does not answer. I called her many times. MOM is supposed to ask them to pay me, but I want my money now. It has been eight months already I wait. Also my luggage.'

Aunty M said that if MOM was already on the case, she didn't know what else to do. MOM was very busy. Indira had to be patient.

A few days later, at breakfast, something weird happened. Dad said to Mama: 'Do you remember my mate Tom, the one I played footie with? They've moved to Johor, months ago, without telling anyone. It seems he went bankrupt, and there were some rumours about fiddling the books. He tried to hide it for months, possibly years, but then MOM found out. He got a new job here, but moved Tamsin and the kids to Malaysia. He didn't tell anybody! I mean, we knew they'd moved to a small flat last year. But still. They didn't tell anyone.'

I hadn't really been listening; but when Aunty M poked me with her elbow I realised what it meant. 'Dad!' I exclaimed.

'Yes, honey, what is it?'

'Did they have a helper called Indira? From India?'

'I have no idea. Why?'

'Mama, remember Indira, I told you about her. The one who has to get married. She says her sir Tom, and ma'am Tamsin went to Malaysia suddenly. They owe her nine thousand dollars.'

Dad looked at Aunty M. 'Is that true?'

'Yes, sir. She went to MOM, but they have not forced them to pay yet. She has a new job but needs her money. And also her belongings are still with them.'

Aunty M told about how they had put her on a bus, without her salary, and Mama looked shocked. She glared at Dad. 'Tom and Tamsin? Stuck up, that Tamsin, always looks down her nose, like a blonde I-am-better-than-you. If they couldn't pay her, why did they not let her go a year ago? Stiff upper lip, pretend everything's alright when really it isn't? Can't they get their hands on nine thousand some way? You need to do something. Shame them into paying up.'

Dad said nothing but looked at his plate, nodding. 'Erm. Yes. I guess.'

'Put your money where your mouth is, Mr British. You think that Ang Moh treat their servants better, right,' Mama laughed.

Dad grinned sheepishly. 'I suppose I ought to, then. Defend our honour.'

You know how in some fairy tales, miracles do happen, and there's an unexpected happy ending? I'm not sure what Dad did, but it worked. They paid. Dad said his friend was very embarrassed, and had pinned all the blame on his wife. She'd planned to completely ignore the whole thing. MOM hadn't really pressured her, and she'd thought she could get away with waiting a bit longer to pay Indira. But now the story was out in public and they were ashamed. Mama looked very smug when Dad her told that.

Aunty M had looked at Dad with a proud, almost maternal expression.

41

I started spending most afternoons after school at Cat's place to avoid having to do the school bus ride more than once a day. Spending less time with Aunty M and the other aunties seemed less risky anyway. Mama and Dad knew I went to Cat's a lot, but they didn't mind. As long as I finished my homework at Cat's, Dad said – which I rarely did, but no one checked. I did a bit more homework than before, especially for Mandarin, as the threat of the tutor still haunted me.

Cat had now decided she was completely opposed to homework. To support her case she'd found research online proving that homework at primary schools was bad for kids. She hadn't yet dared present it at school, but planned on doing that the next time she was asked to write an essay on a free subject.

One evening when I came home just before dinner, Aunty M was frantic. She pulled me into the kitchen, and in loud whispers said: 'Did you see Jenny today? MOM officers came to her house. Someone reported them to MOM, claiming Moe Moe was being abused. They interrogated Moe Moe, the brother – I guess Jenny too. The mother is crazy angry. She says Moe Moe called them. She will send Moe Moe away as soon as MOM finishes the investigations. She says the accusations are ridiculous and they won't do anything.'

Aunty M stared at me with piercing eyes. 'Maya. You need to tell me the truth. Do you know anything about this?'

I was the worst liar in the world. I leaned into the wall, trying to disappear into the concrete and stammered. 'I know Harry bites her. And Jenny slaps her. Isn't it good that MOM is going to help?'

Aunty M's look pushed me further into the wall. 'Don't you understand? Moe Moe will lose a well-paid job. She will be sent back to Myanmar. She has been crying all day.'

Tears began to well in my eyes too.

Aunty M asked again. 'Maya. Did you call MOM?'

I blinked away the tears, and looked her in the eye. 'No,' I said. Cat had been the one on the phone that day.

I ran to my parents' bedroom and called Cat, tears pouring down my face. Between hiccups I told her that MOM had been round and was now officially investigating Jenny's family.

Cat was elated. 'No way! That's great. Why do you sound so weird? She's finally getting what she deserves. And this is just the beginning. Tomorrow at school…'

'You don't understand,' I cut in. 'We've been stupid. Moe Moe is going to lose her job now. It's our fault.'

'Moe Moe will be fine. She'll get a new job. I'll ask Mama, she'll have some friends looking to hire.'

'Jenny's mother will never allow her to transfer. She can't apply for a new job without signed transfer papers. When she is back in Myanmar, how can she interview with your mother's friend?'

'You're such a worrier. This is the best news ever. I'm so happy.'

The way Aunty M kept looking at me that evening made me feel the opposite.

In the morning, I stepped onto the bus with trepidation. Jenny didn't say much. She simply gave me a dirty look and said, 'I suppose it was you, Superroach, you and your superaunty? This isn't over. You can count on that.'

She went to sit on the other side of the bus, alone, as Meena wasn't there that morning. She didn't say another word for the entire bus ride.

At school, Cat was as excited as on the phone the night before, and before lunch she'd told most people in our class. She said that Jenny was a bully at home as well as here, and that officials were going to sort her out, as being a bully was unacceptable. She'd wanted to tell them about us too, that we were the ones that had made it happen, and I'd had to beg her not to.

'Think about me,' I said. *And Aunty M,* I thought. 'I'll be in so much trouble if Mama finds out.' We, I meant. And Aunty M especially.

Cat looked at me like I was talking nonsense, but she kept her mouth shut about that part of the story. When Meena, who'd shown up around lunchtime after a dentist appointment, confirmed, snickering, that it was true about Jenny and MOM, something about Jenny seemed to shrink. Like she'd been wrapped in cling film that made it difficult for her to breathe. On the bus home, she sat alone whilst Meena chatted with the older kids. They sometimes gave Jenny sidelong glances. Once, I picked up the words *biter* and MOM, and I saw laughing and shocked looks. I felt almost happy, and if it hadn't been for Moe Moe, things would have been perfect.

Both Mama and Dad were home early that day and in a good mood, and we all sat together for dinner. Aunty M ate in the kitchen. The table was still small, and Dad insisted on quality time together on some days, so I didn't speak to Aunty M much, at least not about the things that mattered. I felt happy, but at the same time selfish and guilty for feeling that way. And still there was a nagging worry. Jenny was right. It wasn't over yet.

Jenny looked tired and miserable the morning after. I'm not sure how the rest of her day was, but she looked even worse in the afternoon. On the bus home she hissed to me that Moe Moe was so fired, and that she knew it had been me, and that getting Aunty M fired was the next thing she was going to do. MOM had found nothing, and she wasn't going to tell her mother that it was me and not Moe Moe who had called them, because Moe Moe was stupid and had got what she deserved. 'I was bored of her anyway,' she said.

I didn't know what to do. Aunty M seemed to believe that I'd had nothing to do with reporting Jenny to MOM. She'd just got off the phone with Nurul when I came in, and started telling me about her plans for the summer, when she was going back to Indonesia for her holiday. Her eyes glimmered with anticipation about seeing her children for the first time in almost three years. When I asked whether she knew anything about Moe Moe, she said she hadn't spoken to her that day. 'I'm worried about her,' she said; but to her it was just another case. She couldn't get upset about everything, I supposed. She had no guilty conscience.

I called Cat, but Cat was more occupied with whether it was true that MOM wouldn't do anything about Jenny. Jenny's public exposure at school was good, but Cat wanted more. But when I told her about Jenny's threat to get Aunty M fired, she stopped me. 'Maya, there's only one thing to do about that. It's simple.'

'What?'

'You need to tell your mother first. Tell her as it is, and it will be fine.'

I started thinking up all sorts of excuses, reasons, fears, for doing anything but that; but before I could voice any of them, Aunty M put her head around the door. 'Maya, I'm going to see Mary Grace to pick up a recipe. Do you want to come?'

My head was spinning so much I took the escape route.

'Coming.'

Instead of Mary Grace, it was an old lady who answered the door. I froze, and Aunty M stuttered, looking at her feet.

'Oh, hello,' the lady said, 'you must be Merpati. Mary Grace said you'd stop by. The recipe you need is on the kitchen table. Do come in.'

She opened the door wide, signalling us in with her hand. 'Mary Grace went on an errand, she'll be right back.'

Almost as shy as I was, Aunty M stepped over the threshold, but I hovered by the door.

'Maya, do come through. Do you want some milo? Hot or cold?'

I took a few steps forward. Mary Grace had said her ma'am was nice, the best, even. She'd asked me to come in herself, so I had to suppose I wasn't putting anyone's job on the line.

'How do you know my name?' I asked.

'Don't you remember me? Aunty Tan?' The lady smiled down at me. 'I was a friend of your dear old PoPo.'

42

I looked up from my toes and stared at ma'am Tan. Suddenly I remembered four old ladies in our living room, grouped around a small green table full of mah-jong tiles.

Aunty Tan beckoned me over to the kitchen table where Aunty M was standing, turning the paper with the recipe around in her hands. Chloe had climbed out of Aunty M's arms, and was toddling around the table.

'Why don't both of you sit down, I'll make a nice milo. And biscuits. It's been so long since I've seen you, Maya, but Mary Grace has been telling me all about you. It makes me very happy to see you; you make me think of your PoPo. She was very dear to me. I hope you don't mind having a quick milo with an old lady, to please me? Sit down. You too,' she said, nodding at Aunty M.

'Of course,' Aunty M said, taking a chair, and pointing to me to do the same. 'Maya loves milo.'

Aunty Tan put two steaming cups in front of us, together with a plate of pineapple biscuits. It was hot in the room, where only a ceiling fan whizzed the thick air around, yet it was comforting to warm my hands around the chocolaty drink.

'You've got so big! How long has it been since I saw you last?'

PoPo's funeral, I thought. I didn't think I'd seen Aunty Tan after that. That was more than a year ago. Chloe was not yet born, and now she could walk and was learning to talk.

Aunty Tan must have thought the same. 'How old is your sister now?'

We all looked at Chloe, who was under the table munching a biscuit.

'Chloe turned one last month,' I said. We hadn't really celebrated. Aunty M had made a small cake, but Mama had been too busy to come up with anything more than a few presents and Chloe's favourite dinner of spaghetti. That other day, that had also marked a one-year anniversary, but no one had commented on that. My eyes were drawn to a small cabinet in the corner of Aunty Tan's room. On it were a few old statues, photographs, an incense burner, a candle, a little vase of flowers, a cup of water, and five beautifully stacked oranges. Aunty Tan's eyes followed mine. She smiled quietly.

'You must miss your PoPo a lot.'

She looked at me in a way that made me feel so full I was going to spill over, and tears welled up in my eyes. One slid into my mouth, salty after the sweet milo.

I tried to memorise all the items on the cabinet. My own little altar for PoPo didn't have more than a photo and a candle. After I had repeated the items three times in my mind, I turned back to Aunty Tan.

'I sometimes worry I'm forgetting her. She had so much more to tell me, I only know half her stories. Mama never talks about her because every time she tries to, she starts to cry. In any case, Mama is too busy working. She thinks work is the only important thing. PoPo was different. PoPo lived life...' I paused to think of the words. 'She lived life like it just was. Sorry, that's a bit vague,' I added, 'but do you see?'

Aunty M pushed a tissue box in a crocheted cover towards me. She and Aunty Tan both smiled, but it was Aunty Tan that spoke.

'Do you know, sweetie, that people are the way they are for a reason. Their upbringing, their experiences, and also where they are in their life. By the time you knew your PoPo she was an old woman. Older than me even.' She paused and laughed. 'She could rest in her memories. Life was not always like that for her. When your mother was young, PoPo had a hard life, trying to bring up a daughter on her own. Her family wasn't helping her, her husband died too young.'

We sat in silence for a short time.

'Can you tell me about PoPo?' I asked. 'Did you know her already when she was young like that?'

'No, I only met her when your mother was already in secondary school. Your PoPo was so proud of her, her smart, successful daughter.'

'I don't know anything. Did PoPo have a job?'

'Yes, and that was hard at first. She had been brought up a Peranakan lady, raised to be a good wife, not a breadwinner. She went to the kind of school that did not teach the skills to do anything more than find a good husband. Even after the war, her family did well. They were well off, but PoPo was stubborn, and refused to marry what her parents considered 'a good match'. She chose your grandfather, from a different culture as well as poor.

And when he died she was all alone with your mother.'

This I knew already. 'And then?' I asked. 'What did she do?'

'She had to find a job. First, she worked in a shop. She studied in the evenings. You think your mother is always busy working and PoPo was always there for you, but when your mother was young it was different. To make money to support her child, your PoPo became a school teacher.'

How could it be I never knew this? I felt small.

Aunty Tan continued. 'That is when I met your PoPo. We worked together at a primary at Henry Park. Your mother was smart, and managed to get a scholarship for university. But before that, PoPo had to work hard to get herself and your mother out of poverty. Later, when your great-grandparents died, your PoPo's brothers, your great-uncles, were generous, but still. Your mother learned the value of money the hard way.'

Things started to make more sense. 'Mama told me that she wanted to do social studies, but chose business instead.'

Aunty Tan nodded. She pushed the plate my way. 'Here, take another biscuit.'

At that point, Mary Grace came home, and the atmosphere changed. We sat around a bit longer, eating biscuits, chatting about random things, until Aunty M said she had to make dinner and we went home.

I didn't know how, but somehow Aunty Tan had reduced my fear – of Jenny, of getting caught, even of costing someone a job. Aunty Tan was like PoPo: she gave things a background, a reason and a purpose, which made understanding the world easier. When you understood things they became less scary.

That evening I lay in bed and tried to add it all up in my mind. I put Mama together again from all the information I'd heard, then added the Mamamonster, and Dad being away so much. I felt everything was connected, but struggled to join the dots. I still missed PoPo, but meeting Aunty Tan was like getting back a piece of her. And if I had just a little bit of PoPo, maybe I could find a way out of all of this.

The next day I stepped onto the bus more confidently. I looked at Jenny and not the ground for the first time in a long time. She said nothing.

At school I heard the rumours repeated through others now. Since I lived in the same condo, people asked me if I knew more about what Jenny had done. Cat, always beside me, was happy to give them the details. I felt like a real Superroach, but in a good way. Jenny had got her due. I just had to fix the Moe Moe problem, and things would be good. Maybe Cat was right. Maybe I could tell Mama, and ask for help. Not the monster, but the real Mama beneath, the one that Aunty Tan had revealed. If only I could be sure I could reach her.

Cat came home with me to see a manual that Aunty M had brought home from the helpdesk, which helped answer questions that we couldn't. We went through it, trying to find answers on what could or would happen to Jenny, and how we could save Moe Moe.

The manual clearly listed the rules that employers had to stick to, but there was nothing there that told us what to do next. We went through the cases we'd seen over the months. In many of them, the women wanted to transfer, because they didn't like their job, their employer, the way they were treated. But often, no matter how many questions we asked, we hadn't been able to find anything we could use to file a complaint with MOM. Since domestic workers didn't have the right to quit, their only hope was to get permission from their employer, or, if they didn't give it, to appeal to MOM. We knew that already, and the manual confirmed it. It seemed that only MOM could help Moe Moe.

'Shall we get a photo of the bites,' Cat suggested, 'and email it to them?'

'Wouldn't they have seen it when they interviewed her? And they'd know who sent the email.'

We had done enough. If Moe Moe had wanted to go on with the complaint, she would have told MOM herself. But we studied on regardless. What else could we do?

We copied the items on the list into our notebooks. An employer of a domestic worker in Singapore had to give adequate food and rest, acceptable accommodation, cover medical costs, provide safe working conditions, pay the salary – on time. What they must not do was take away their workers' permits and passports, or ill-treat them. Ill-treatment, it added, included abuse, abandonment, neglect and the causing of injury. With regards to the weekly day off, MOM, stated that every worker had the right to a weekly day of rest, but pro rata salary could be paid in lieu by the employer if she agreed this with the domestic worker. *Mutual consent,* it said.

Many of the rules we barely understood. Others seemed simple at first glance, yet talking to the aunties had proved otherwise. Many women complained about the food they got, but what was an 'adequate' amount? Instant noodles at every meal? One slice of bread at breakfast? Whatever the employer left after they'd had their fill?

Acceptable accommodation was a dubious term as well. We'd heard of women sleeping on the floor in a common room, in the hallway, with the elderly, on the floor of the kitchen, and even, Aunty M told me, on a balcony. It wasn't allowed, but it still happened. How could MOM look into people's private houses to check?

MOM would deal with complaints about violations, like they were doing now with Moe Moe, but could only do this if someone alerted them. Even then, they didn't always act. Anything to do with safety would be given priority, Aunty M had said, but taking away passports was as common as mosquitoes in this country, and there was no point complaining about either.

Just being there, listening, doling out advice and the helpdesk phone numbers was what we did to help the domestic workers we spoke to. They then had to make up their minds to either accept what they were dealt, or decide to throw in the towel and go home. A lot of them put up with it. *We came here to work, we need the money,* they said, and decided not to risk going to MOM, not to risk that much-needed salary.

But none of this was helping Moe Moe.

43

Mary Grace said Aunty Tan wanted me to come and have milo again. I went up with Mary Grace, hoping we could talk more about PoPo.

We sat at the table and Aunty Tan put a bowl of white rabbit sweets in front of me. She must have bought them specially for me, as if I were still a little girl. But Aunty Tan didn't mention PoPo. Instead she asked about Sri, who was still at the shelter, waiting for her case to progress and her employer to be convicted for physical abuse. She commented how unfair it was that this might take many more years, and Sri stuck in Singapore all that time.

I was in shock. How did she know? Did she know about my involvement too? But Aunty Tan was so friendly that I just answered her probing questions. After Sri, she asked about Julia, who had gone back to the Philippines, and when her rash had cleared came back to Singapore with a new employer.

Mary Grace told Aunty Tan how Aunty M had heard from Bella, the domestic worker who had filed a complaint about her employers making her wash all their clothes by hand, till Bella's hands bled. It was Aunty M's first success story, and Mary Grace proudly told us how MOM had approved the transfer for Bella, and how she was now happy in her new job. Then I myself told Aunty Tan about Nee Nee. When she knew all about that already too, I realised the food that Mary Grace regularly brought over came from Aunty Tan herself. She asked sharp questions.

After that, Aunty Tan looked me in the eye. 'You know Maya, sometimes I think, what has Singapore come to? When I was young, things were different. We had our amahs, and they were respected by their employers. They were trusted with the household, with the children, whom they were supposed to help raise. Nobody felt the need to put up cameras, even if they had existed then. The amahs were treated like human beings. '

I thought of Ah Feng. Had it been like that for her? Or did Aunty Tan have that rose-coloured filter Mama had mentioned? I remembered that Ah Feng had felt in charge of her own destiny. I opened my mouth to tell Aunty Tan about Ah Feng, but Aunty Tan had her own answer already.

'You know, in the old days, people knew their neighbours. We had kampong spirit. We did not live in these anonymous apartments, where everybody sits in their air-conditioned room, and nobody even knows who lives next door. Do people know if the neighbours abuse the maid? Do they care? No more kampong spirit these days, no more gotong royong. We all live stacked in buildings like sardines in a tin, but we close our eyes. We close our ears. Not our problem, stick to your own. You know about gotong royong, Maya?'

I had no idea. 'Is it Malay?'

'Of course it is Malay. Community spirit. Last time, everybody knew each other. Everybody helped each other. People made other people do their best. Do they do gotong royong at your school?'

I'd never heard of it, so I shook my head.

'It means everybody helps. With cleaning, cooking, looking after the kids. Not everyone for themselves. We all need to help flag suspicions of maid abuse, domestic abuse, child abuse. We should worry about helping others, out of genuine concern, instead of worrying to be seen as busybodies. We should have a national campaign for this purpose.'

I grinned. Singapore loved campaigns like that. There would be funny films with songs and dance. Everybody laughed at them, but did they work?

Aunty Tan went on: 'Singapore is obsessed with survival and success. Our society has become so competitive, we have neglected kindness and helpfulness. Many of us have become used to being cold and apathetic to the plight of others. Or are we just too busy working all the time to even see?'

Aunty Tan fell silent and looked around the table to Mary Grace and me. Nobody dared comment.

'Why?' she asked, but again no one answered, not even Aunty Tan herself. She went on: 'And how do we change this? For most of us Singaporeans, it is not in our nature to intrude, to be the kaypoh neighbour, we prefer to – how do you call that? – mind our own business.'

Aunty Tan sounded like the schoolteacher she'd once been, and a preachy one too. Mary Grace had sat quiet during her monologue, and now she stood up, collecting the empty milo cups and taking them to the kitchen.

In the silence that followed, I thought about what Aunty Tan had said. 'That is what Mama says, mind your own business. If she found out I went out with Aunty M, helping the helpers, she'd be so mad.'

It had slipped out before I could even think. I clasped my hands in front of my mouth. Aunty Tan had probably not known the extent of my involvement. She knew about the visits to Nee Nee, and that I sometimes went with Aunty M. But not that Mama would disapprove. She would consider it her duty to intervene, to not mind her own business, and to tell Mama.

My face froze. Aunty Tan looked at me quizzically.

'Your mother is a busy woman. A business women. But she has a good heart. Why would she object? It is sweet of you, helping your Aunty M, helping others. Your PoPo would be proud. And I'm sure your Mama too.'

I swallowed deep. 'No, she wouldn't. She told me. She said I should not be a busybody, just do my homework. But that's not the worst.'

I stumbled over my tongue, trying to put the worst into words. 'Mama would fire Aunty M if she found out. She hates even Mother Teresa.'

Aunty Tan smiled. 'She has a point there, actually. You know, Mother Teresa is worshipped in the west, but she has been criticised too. They say that what she did glorified suffering instead of relieving it. Some people like to make themselves seem bigger, by making the ones they help smaller. I don't believe in saints. Everyone is human, with good traits as well as flaws. Your mother too.'

I couldn't control my words; they all streamed out of me –

Jenny's threats, Win losing her job, Moe Moe, my fear for Aunty M, Nurul's future. I didn't say that it was us who'd probably caused Moe Moe to lose her job. There was enough to feel guilty about already.

'Maya, sweetie,' said Aunty Tan. 'Trust your parents. Tell them. Don't wait for Jenny to paint a distorted picture of you. Tell them yourself, your way. The right way.'

It was the same advice that Cat had given. Aunty Tan offered me another sweet, but I felt I was too old for one. Sweets didn't make everything right anymore.

I lay in bed, going over what Aunty Tan had said. I'd been afraid of her too before, but she'd turned out to be more understanding than I'd expected. It was time I lived up to that special feminism I'd invented, the one that was about standing up for yourself. The first step was being honest about who you were, and what you did. I had to tell Mama.

But actually doing it was harder. Should I tell Dad first? Maybe he would react better. But he was on a business trip, so that would mean postponement. No, I knew it had to be Mama.

Having decided to tell her – knowing that whatever happened, it would at least be over – I felt something close to relief. But Mama was moody at breakfast, hurrying me along to get ready for the bus. I knew it wasn't the right time.

At school, the ruckus around Jenny had died down, but she was still quiet and unhappy, and people occasionally sniggered behind her back. Her nickname now was 'biter', and I felt so bad

I even told some of her classmates that it wasn't her, but her baby brother that had bitten their helper. Jenny overheard and looked at me bitterly. She hadn't mentioned telling Mama again.

When I told Cat, she laughed, and had to point out what should have been clear to me. Jenny was a coward, and Meena just blew with the strongest wind. They'd been empty threats all along. Jenny wouldn't risk her own hide by shooting mine.

If Jenny were not going to tell Mama, need I do it? I considered backing out, but since my visit to Aunty Tan it felt like the world had shifted and many things looked different. Easier. All the things I was scared about before no longer seemed that bad. As PoPo had always done with her stories and explanations, Aunty Tan had opened my eyes and made me think.

Finally, I thought of Moe Moe, and Aunty M, and realised I couldn't ignore this. I couldn't be weak like Jenny. Someone had to tell Jenny's mother that it had been us, not Moe Moe, who had called MOM; and Jenny's mother was way more scary than my own.

I decided that if Mama was home in the evening to put me to bed, I would tell her then. If she wasn't, I wouldn't. On the way back from school I was nervous, not sure what I was hoping for. I asked Aunty M several times whether Mama would be home that night.

'I don't know, sayang, stop asking me. She'll be home when she is home.'

That night, I heard Mama return from the cocoon of my sheets. It was late and I was supposed to be asleep. When she came in, I pretended that I was, not even stirring when she straightened the sheet over me. She stroked my hair, and I kept my eyes squeezed shut. The touch of her hand was cool, and I vowed never to tell her. Maybe I could run away, and go live with Nurul in her yellow house. I was afraid to own up to my parents, to my mother, who I really was.

The next day was a blur and somehow I just knew that, that evening, Mama would be home on time and I would tell her. I had to anyway, because Cat had said that if I didn't, she would. Cat had spent a good few days fuming that Jenny had received no punishment from MOM, but I'd managed to get her to see that Jenny being embarrassed in front of the whole school was much better, and that the more time she spent provoking Jenny, the bigger the risk that she'd do something dangerous. Cat reluctantly agreed, and then promised me she'd drop the whole thing if I told my mother that night.

She looked at me sternly and said, 'You'll tell her, and then you'll save Moe Moe.'

'And Aunty M,' I added quietly.

Dad was home from abroad and Mama was home for an early dinner. They chatted about summer holiday plans, visiting Europe to see Opa and Grandma, going to France. The mood was much too happy and relaxed. But I kicked myself mentally; there was no more time for excuses. I would tell her that night.

44

Dad tucked me in and cuddled me before he went out to deal with a wailing Chloe. Mama came in and sat on my bed. 'Story or book?' she asked. 'Why don't I tell you about a princess that saved the palace from, erm, a galloping herd of, erm, of elephants?'

'Actually, Mama, can I tell a story tonight? I have a good princess one.'

'Of course.'

I took a deep breath and swallowed. 'Once, there were a princess and a prince. They were very poor. Their father, the king, had left to fight worthless wars, and they lived with their mother in a chicken shed.'

Mama giggled.

'Don't,' I said, 'it's a sad story.'

She straightened her face.

'Since the prince and princess had no money to go to school, their mother, the queen, went to another country to work. The prince and princess stayed with their grandmother, who was even poorer, and lived in a pig shed.

'The queen cleaned and cooked for an evil stepmother. But the country was full of dragons. The queen wanted to slay the dragons, but she also needed to do her job, so she slayed them secretly. But one day, a stable boy found out, and threatened to tell the evil stepmother. If he did, the queen would lose her job, and be sent back to the chicken shed, and the prince and princess would have to leave school.'

I had to swallow a few times again, struggling to find more words.

'Maya, sweetie, stop the story for a minute,' Mama said. 'What are you trying to tell me? Where did this story come from?'

I started to cry.

'Are you talking about Aunty M? That she left her children to come and work here? And what about those dragons? I don't understand. Please Maya, tell me what's bothering you.'

Slowly it trickled out. The dragons, the abusive employers, and Aunty M fighting them.

'But Maya, what did you think, that I was such an evil stepmother? That I wouldn't allow that? That I didn't know? Aunty M asked my permission to volunteer at that helpdesk. I admit, I was worried at first. We agreed that it could never interfere with her work. And it hasn't. She does her job well, better than I'd ever hoped.'

Mama pulled me towards her and cuddled me. 'Were you worried about that? That I would fire Aunty M for helping others? Why would you think that?'

'You said that, that time with Cynthia, you said you hated busybodies, and Mother Teresa.'

'Did you hear that? Were you eavesdropping again? Don't do that. You hear things you don't understand,' Mama scolded.

She continued in a softer voice. 'I was very stressed at that time. I felt like everyone was judging me. At work, my friends, and Aunty M at home. Maybe I was jealous of Aunty M. She seems so calm and efficient, like she always knows what to do. She can look at me when I'm screaming, not saying anything, in a way that makes me feel like a bad mother. And I missed you girls.'

I thought of my own irrational jealousy of Nurul.

Mama said, 'I know that things have been bad at home lately. But that's going to change. When Dad was away this week, he went to see his boss in England. He's made some changes to his job. He's going to be home more and travel less. And I'm going to try not to worry as much about work too. Things will be better. Less shouting. I promise.'

So no moving to England? I felt relieved.

'You know, Aunty M's life is difficult, more so than ours, and still she is strong. I need to learn from someone like her, not feel threatened by her. But she runs our home like, like I never could, and what does she do in her spare time? Help others. It's not easy to take in. But I honestly think we're very lucky to have her. You like her, don't you?'

I nodded.

'So stop worrying, I won't fire her. As long as she does her work well, she can do what she likes in her spare time.'

'Thanks Mama. I'm happy Nurul can get her yellow house.'

'Her yellow house?' Mama asked.

'Aunty M is building her and Adi a house to live in, so they won't have to live in a bamboo hut anymore. She's using her salary to start building this year. It was Nurul's fantasy to have it painted yellow.'

'That's so sweet. I'm glad that we can give her the opportunity to build that.'

I smiled invisibly in the half dark. 'She told me she'll start building when she goes home this summer,' I said.

But I had one more thing on my mind. 'But Mama, I want to know. Would you build me a yellow house? One with a garden and swings?'

Mama laughed. 'What do you mean? We have a house. We live in a luxury condo we own, not a bamboo hut. Why do you need a yellow one?'

How could I even begin to explain? That a condo wasn't a house, that I wanted one like the Blue House that PoPo had had, with a garden and lotus pond and barking frogs, a house that make you feel special, not one where you were stacked in a pile with so many others just like you. A garden with its own swing where you could always feel safe because it was yours, even if it had monkeys stealing your toothpaste.

Mama said, 'I do want to give you everything, but it needs to be reasonable. You do realise that with five million people on a tiny island, not everyone can have a house with a garden? Singapore isn't Java.'

I thought about that for a while until I realised that I didn't actually need all of that, I just wanted Mama to *want* to give it to me, if that was what I wanted most. She had to love me for who I was, so I could love me too. I tried to say that, but it was too complex so I said, 'I know, I don't want a house. I want my mother to build me something.'

Mama was quiet for a while, and I was scared that I'd made

her sad.

'Do you think that? Do you think I don't care, that I don't want to give you what you need?'

I didn't know what to say, so I said nothing.

Mama went on. 'I loved it when we had our talks, about feminism, about these impressive women, like Kartini, Ah Feng. Hell, I would even discuss Mother Teresa with you happily. I loved it when you were interested in those things, and I knew I was doing something right. They are role models. That's what I want to give you. That's what I want to be to you.'

I crawled onto her lap and we sat there. 'We need to talk more about these things. About the important things. Make time for it. But now you need to sleep. School tomorrow. That's the most important thing I will give you: an education.'

She started to lay me back in bed. 'It was a very good story, dear. Let's agree on a happy ending. The stepmother was not so evil after all, and the queen worked happily ever after.'

She hugged me.

For a few seconds, I was tempted to leave it at that. But that ending was too easy. Not real.

'Mama?' I said.

'Yes, honey?'

'Actually, there's more.'

'More? What do you mean?'

'Well, the stepmother had a daughter, and she, well, me, helped.'

'Helped what?'

'She, I, helped Aunty M with the helping. Helping the helpers.'

Mama's eyes turned big in the half-light of the room. 'What do you mean?'

I told her everything. How we had first helped Sri, how after that, we went out on afternoons after school, how I had taught Win English, how we hosted our own little helpdesk in the playground. How Cat and I had eavesdropped at the food court. And, finally, how we had called MOM to report Jenny. It felt like a zit being squeezed; it hurt, but the messy stuff was pouring out and I felt that it would be ok after. Mama would kiss me and we would live happily ever after. After all, she'd said she loved the role models doing good, and now I could be one too, with her help.

But that ending was too easy too.

'What do you mean, you went out with Aunty M on school afternoons, to see other domestic workers in trouble? What about your schoolwork? And what on earth makes you think it is a good idea to report your own schoolmate to MOM?'

I cringed.

Mama cried out, 'Maya, you can't do these things without telling us. You're only ten. These things, they are complicated, grownup! Do you even understand them? And Aunty M let this happen without telling me? I need to discuss this with your father.'

And all the worry poured back in.

Mama said, 'You go to sleep. We'll speak in the morning.'

I lay down and she kissed me curtly on the forehead. Before she closed the door, I asked in a little voice, 'Mama?'

'Yes?'

'Promise you won't fire Aunty M. Please?'

Mama grunted. 'We'll talk in the morning.'

I was so exhausted I fell asleep straight away. When I woke up I felt refreshed. Then the hammer hit me.

I wanted to roll back into the cocoon, but getting out of the house to school seemed safer. Even if that meant facing Jenny and my guilt.

It would be so wrong, so cynical, if Aunty M got fired after helping all those people. I asked myself if it would have been worth it, to sacrifice one for the others, but I had no answer. I kicked myself for letting her in so deep, for not listening to myself when she first arrived, when I had promised not to let her into my heart. It was too late now. She'd leave me, and it would be my own fault.

Reluctantly, I went to the kitchen. Mama and Dad were already at the table, eating breakfast calmly. Chloe was eating dry cereal straight from the table top. I realised it was Saturday. Mama had been wrong, no school today. They didn't look angry.

'Good morning,' Dad said. 'Toast or cereal?'

'Marmite toast, please,' I said, and sat down.

They chatted again about the summer plans again, as if I wasn't sitting there, my heart in my mouth.

'Mama,' I started. 'About last night...'

Dad answered. 'You know, Maya, we are deeply disappointed in you. We're still debating your punishment, but for starters, you're grounded on school afternoons. You don't go anywhere without our specific permission. Not even to go see Cat.'

I cringed. 'I know,' I said. 'I'll stop. But please...'

Dad interrupted. 'How could you not tell us something like that? This is government business. You calling MOM like that, do you realise you could get me in trouble? What if they kick me out of the country for something you do? Have you thought about that?'

I hadn't.

'That you want to help people is nice, but you need to be careful. If you were worried about Jenny and her helper, you should have told us. We could have gone and talked to her parents,' Mama continued. 'After breakfast, you will sit down, and tell us everything, every detail. We need to sort out this mess.'

'I wasn't alone,' I started; but all I could think of was Aunty M. 'I'll tell you, but please, tell me, you won't fire her, will you?'

'Who? Aunty M?'

Mama was quiet a while, and she looked at Dad, who nodded. 'It's a trust issue. If she knew about all of this and didn't tell me, I don't know if I can trust her anymore.'

My heartbeat thudded in my throat. 'She didn't know about calling MOM. It was Cat's idea. I lied to Aunty M. She told me not to do it.'

Dad said, 'Yes, we'll need to speak to Cat's parents too. You understand that, don't you? But Aunty M, she took you out to see maids in distress, didn't she? And neither she nor you told us.'

'You were away,' I blurted out. 'And Mama was at work.'

They looked at each other. They looked mad, and unsure at whom.

Chloe cried, and threw her cup to the floor. Mama looked annoyed, and sprinkled more cereal on the table in front of her.

She left the cup on the floor. Dad still said nothing, but looked the other way.

Mama was the first to speak. 'We know. We should have seen this coming. But I thought things were better. You seemed so happy lately, with Cat, and well... It's our fault too. I told you last night, we'll make some changes. All of us. We'll eat together every evening, and talk about our days. And tell each other everything.'

She looked at me pointedly. 'Okay,' I nodded. 'But what about Aunty M?'

'We still need to decide,' Mama said. 'To be honest, I can't imagine life without her anymore, and who knows what kind of replacement we'd get, but she knows she's on probation. She can only continue the helpdesk work in her spare time, on Sundays. Some phone calls during the week, fine, or some playground advice, but that's it. We've made it clear she needs to open up more, especially where you girls are concerned. She likes to sit in that clam of hers, and doesn't open up until you boil her. She'll need to win my trust again.'

'Does that mean...' I stammered.

Mama said, 'I don't want to do anything rash.'

I sighed in relief. 'So she can stay?'

Mama looked at Dad, who shrugged. 'Well, yes. But no more secrets,' Dad said.

I felt like a weight had been lifted off my head. I was ready for my punishment now.

'So what about me? I'll stop. Don't worry.'

Mama looked at Dad again. She said, 'We don't mind you teaching someone English, going to celebrations like the

Kartini one. But being a helpdesk? You're too young. You have schoolwork. For now, you stay in in the afternoon, and need permission from Dad or me when you want to do something else. We'll be home more too, to check on you. If you feel the urge to help someone in distress, you come to us, and we'll do it together.'

Dad nodded. His phone rang. He looked at the screen, but shoved it back into his pocket.

45

After breakfast I brought out my notebook. Together, we went through all the cases, and I told them what had happened to Sri, Bella, Julia, just as I'd told Aunty Tan before. Like Aunty Tan, Mama and Dad were full of questions, and I felt proud and smart that I was able to answer most of them. I explained deductions, transfer papers, and the MOM regulations. I told them about Win and how she'd disappeared one day, and about Nee Nee, who chose to stay. I told them about Khusnul, who'd admitted to her employers that she had slapped the child, just once, and who'd been given a second chance.

Looking at all those notes, seeing the names written down and remembering the unwritten ones like Cat and Aunty Tan, I felt rich. Even if I lost Aunty M now, if she chose not to take her second chance, and even if I never saw any of the other aunties again, I could never lose the memories they'd given me, any more than I could lose those of PoPo. I was secretly glad my parents hadn't known from the start; they would only have allowed the boring parts. It might be wrong to do the right thing sometimes, but that didn't make it less important.

The only story I left out was Ronalyn's. There were no notes of that in my notebook. It was something I'd have to figure out on my own, when I was older.

When I'd told them everything – the food court conversations, the MOM procedures, the police investigations, and even about Aunty Tan, who'd been the one who told me to tell them the truth – I looked at Mama. Could Aunty Tan have been right? Proud was too strong a word for the look in her eyes, but she seemed pleased. But still she didn't say anything.

Dad's reaction was simpler. 'Wow,' he said. 'Wow. You're quite something. Did you do all of this, with Aunty M?'

'And Cat,' I added.

'I had no idea. It's really fascinating, and you guys have been so thorough. I mean, my God, you're ten! If you only applied yourself like this at school, you'd be a star student. Did you know this?' he said, looking at Mama, 'These rules, these women being exploited? That they can't quit? I always figured that they could just quit if they didn't like it. And that they were happy that things were at least better than they were used to.'

Mama sighed. 'It's complicated.'

'It isn't really,' I said. 'Why can't they just get the right to quit and transfer?'

'You need to look at it from the employers' perspective too,' Mama said. 'You talk about the deductions, but the employers pay the agency as well. Quite a lot. So if all the helpers kept changing jobs, it would be very expensive for the employer. Every time someone transfers, the agency makes money.'

'We should start an agency,' I said. 'We'd be rich!'

We all laughed.

'And it's not just the money, you invest other things too. You train a helper, get attached to her, and your kids do too. So the employers need some protection. I've heard of many situations where helpers were insolent, lazy, or just wanted to change employers on a whim. Some are stupid. They'll always feel that the grass is greener somewhere else. It's not only the employers that can be bad, you know. There are bad helpers too.'

I supposed she was right. Something still felt wrong, though, and I tried to put my finger on it. I wondered out loud: 'But if the domestic worker is stupid, or lazy, the employer can fire her, can't she? Or go to the police if she steals?'

Mama nodded.

'So aren't they protected enough?'

Mama shrugged, and said nothing, so I went on.

'Why should rules be different for domestic workers?'

Mama thought for a while. She said, a bit snappily, 'Because they're different. I don't know Maya. I need to think about this.'

Dad laughed. 'I think Maya has some interesting points. You're just like your mother when she was younger. I think, in the last few years, Mama's perspective just changed a bit. Spending too much time with her friend Cynthia, and in the big, bad world of finance will do that to a person. Maybe you can rekindle the old idealist spark in your mother.' He winked at Mama, who looked indignant.

Dad continued: 'It's ironic that a child needs to point out these things to us. All of us in Singapore are too serious. The government here has always been protective of its people. That was understandable when it was a fledgling nation, with race riots and poverty. But isn't it time to realise that, like our

Maya here, the country has grown up? I'm thinking we should give Maya some freedom to pursue these things and we might be amazed where she leads us. Overprotective parents, however well meaning, raise unimaginative, irresponsible children who are afraid to take risks.'

Mama looked at him with a puzzled expression, and I was too stunned to say anything. Did he just say I should continue with the helpdesk?

'But what does all of that have to do with domestic workers?' Mama asked.

Dad shrugged. 'This country needs to grow up when it comes to humanity. They only need to look at their own history. Exploiting others, migrants from poor countries, to become rich, is exactly what the colonials did. Yes, my people too, you don't need to point it out. But this is the twenty-first century. Haven't we learned from the past?'

Mama grinned with one side of her mouth. 'You're picturing the government as this tiger mom, fiercely protecting its pups at the expense of others,' she said. 'The thing is, those tiger moms raise highly successful children. Not always happy maybe, but successful. The question is, which is the more important?'

Dad looked at me, and I felt he would give the same answer I would. We said nothing, as Mama needed to find her own answer. She went on, 'I know this country of ours is a complicated one. It's the cleanest and safest in the world, has top ranking schools and hospitals. Everybody can and will read everything online, and still the government wants to protect us – but from what? Ourselves? The weird thing is most of us like it when they do that.

I guess I gave up fighting it.'

She looked at me directly and said, 'Your dad is right. That doesn't mean you should.'

I wanted to say something, but before I could get my thoughts straight, Mama spoke again. 'Singaporeans are so stubbornly conservative on social issues. I don't think we understand why ourselves. Is it to protect what we've achieved?'

This discussion was becoming more complex, and I wasn't sure what to say anymore.

Dad spoke instead. 'Now you're the one straying from the subject of domestic workers. How do they tie into your branch of feminism?'

Mama said, 'Domestic workers allow mothers like me to work outside of the home, which is essential to the growth of the country.'

We were back at Mama's favourite subject, one that I could relate to now. I was glad that I'd done what I had: the eavesdropping research, the helpdesk, the busy bodying. Yes, we'd taken risks, gambled with other people's jobs – calling MOM about Moe Moe was perhaps a step too far. But if you never took any risks, you would never change things. The final penny dropped: what would have become of me if I'd never taken the risk of letting Aunty M in?

The thought emboldened me, and I cleared my throat to pitch in. 'But I don't think the aunties shouldn't be here. They're also important to their own countries. They bring in money to start businesses, and to send their children to school. I just want them to be treated better.'

Dad laughed. 'Thankfully they have you to fight for them. I see a bright destiny for you, Maya, and a promising future for this country with young Singaporeans like you.'

I glowed when he said that. Mama smiled too, then looked sternly at me. 'But not on school days, and not without you telling us every juicy detail.'

From the gleam in her eye I could tell Dad's words had touched her more than she would admit.

Dad closed the conversation by putting his hands on top of the notebook. 'So, all these ladies have been taken care of?'

'Most of them. Well, Sri, she's still waiting in the shelter. Her case is taking a very long time.'

'But they're helping her now. You have nothing to do with that anymore. Cases closed?'

I shook my head. 'One isn't. Moe Moe and Jenny.'

I told them again about what Cat and I did, and why; a little bit about the bullying too, leaving out the nastier bits, leaving those for later, for when I felt comfortable enough to own up to the disgusting thing I'd done. I explained that we'd known for sure that Jenny and her brother had been abusive, not just to me but to Moe Moe too, that we'd seen the bite marks. And that Aunty M didn't want to do anything, so we'd felt we had to. That it was justice. But later, I'd realised that we'd forgotten about Moe Moe, about how it would affect her. I looked at Mama and Dad. 'I need to fix this. Please help me.'

Mama turned to Dad. 'God, that woman, the mother. She's terrible. I so don't want to deal with her.'

Dad sniggered. 'Remember Tom and that Indian girl? I

stepped up. You want the juicy details, it's time to earn them.'

Mama blushed. She took out her phone, scrolled through her contacts, and stared at it for a while. 'I'll ask her to meet me for coffee this afternoon. We need to hear her side of the story first.'

As soon as Jenny's mother answered the phone, we could hear her loud voice from across the table. 'No, I'm not prying, that's not it. I'm worried that Maya might be involved in all of this. Can we maybe meet and discuss it? It's friendlier in person.'

The voice on the other side became louder and angrier. Mama held her hand over the phone and walked outside, closing the balcony door behind her.

When she came back she said, 'They've been given a warning from MOM, but nothing official since it was the kids who did it. Moe Moe didn't want to take it any further.'

Oh. I felt a small pang of disappointment.

'Jenny and Harry are in a lot of trouble. She's furious. At Moe Moe too, for not coming to her when it happened. She first thought that Moe Moe had called MOM, but after Moe Moe asked MOM not to take it further, she wasn't so sure. But she said she still had to fire her if she couldn't trust her anymore. What is it with these helpers? Why can't they just tell us important stuff?'

I felt a tiny wriggle in my stomach. 'Did you tell her..?'

Mama looked at me. 'That you did it? I suppose I would have, if I'd needed to, to save Moe Moe. But I won't expose you to that madwoman unless I really have to. She now thinks it was one of the neighbours. I reminded her that Moe Moe had always worked very hard, and tried to convince her to let her transfer. She said she'd think about it.'

Think about it? I must have looked sad and confused. Mama came up to me, and squatted in front of me. 'Maya, I've tried my best. It's all I could do. It's up to her now. Let's hope she'll do the right thing and let her transfer. And Moe Moe will be better off with another family. One with nicer kids. She'll be fine in the end. And you stay clear of that Jenny from now on.'

I didn't need any encouragement there.

Dad came over and pulled Mama to her feet. He hugged her and looked at me over his shoulder. 'I'm proud of my two ladies. A bit unconventional and extreme sometimes, but they mean well.'

I got up and weaselled myself in for a group hug. It seemed the old Mama and Dad were back today, and were planning to stay.

Mama giggled. 'Is this our Mary Poppins moment? Is Aunty M unfolding her umbrella, to fly away on the west wind, so we can go fly our kites?'

Dad and I looked at her, baffled.

'Come on, you must know Mary Poppins? That was my favourite movie growing up. The parents are both too busy, him with his job at the bank, her being a suffragette, but the nanny saves the kids, and the family, they all go and fly kites, singing, and Mary Poppins flies off in the sunset. Happy ending.'

Dad and I still looked baffled.

'We need to watch that movie,' Mama said. 'You'll love it, Maya.'

'Hi Cat, good to see you,' Mama said when Cat came in that afternoon. She'd phoned me earlier, but I'd wanted to tell her the news to her face and asked her to come over. Cat looked at Mama with a question mark on her face, and I pulled her upstairs to my room.

'I haven't heard your mother greet me so nicely, ever,' Cat said. 'I take it you told her nothing yet?'

She looked at me, her brow furrowed. I didn't know what to say for a moment, so I hugged her instead. Then I told her everything, from my confession to Mama talking to Jenny's mother.

Cat nodded. 'Well done, Maya.'

I beamed, and wondered what we should do now. Was it really over, or was this just the beginning?

Cat shrugged. 'You know, I'm bored of all of this. Let's go for a swim.'

I didn't think she was bored at all, but I agreed. A swim would freshen us up.

That afternoon we watched 'Mary Poppins,' together – me, Dad, Mama, Chloe, Cat, and even Aunty M, who made a big bowl of popcorn.

Mama was right, I loved it, down to the feminist mother, the Dad preoccupied at the bank, the magic, the adventures, and the crazy friends. At the end, when the happy family were flying their kites, and Mary Poppins swallowed a tear before she set off under her flying umbrella, I looked at Aunty M. She would go too one day. Like PoPo, I would never forget her, but she was needed by two other kids, a prince and princess in a pig shed, and I needed to share her.

Dad jumped up. 'I have a great idea. Tomorrow we'll go to Marina Barrage. It's been too long!'

I remembered the afternoon that we did makan angin, flying kites on top of the barrage building. There had been fights, a Mamamonster, Dad had sworn, Chloe had wailed. But there'd been satay too. And fun. Even fun didn't come in black and white.

Aunty M didn't come with us to the Barrage that Sunday. She was helping others, or having a picnic with friends, I wasn't sure which. Mama was right; Aunty M could be close as an oyster. But when she came home that evening she came into my room, something she never did on a Sunday. I was half asleep in my bed, dreaming of kites and picnics. I nodded when she asked if I wanted a story.

Aunty M began telling one of her Kanchil stories, in a soft, whispering voice that made the story merge with my dream.

Kanchil, the mousedeer, had been stealing cucumbers again and the farmer had had enough. He made a scarecrow out of old clothes, and smeared it with glue to trap Kanchil. I saw the scarecrow, in a batik dress, swaying gently between the cucumbers. The Kanchil, still greedy for cucumber, got stuck, one leg after the other. The farmer rejoiced, put Kanchil in a cage, and sharpened his knives for mousedeer satay.

In my half sleep, I could taste the peanut gravy, the same one I'd eaten earlier that day, with cucumber cubes on the side. But before we could eat, a dog passed by.

Cunning little Kanchil told the dog he was a prince, staying the night at the farm as a guest. Tomorrow, he would wed the farmer's daughter. Could the dog smell the peanut gravy for the satay feast that they would throw?

The dog laughed, but the gravy smelled too good not to be true. Kanchil convinced the dog to open the cage and swap places with him, so the dog could wed the farmer's daughter instead, and feast on satay.

I imagined the wedding in a yellow house, Nurul in her pink, frilly dress. But then I heard Kanchil laughing in the distance, flying away on the string of a green beetle-shaped kite. I felt the wind licking my hair, and saw that below me there was nothing left but a cockroach in a cage.

Aunty M stood up, moving her chair backwards, the sound waking me properly. The whole story swirled away like water down a plughole. I felt Aunty M was trying to tell me something in her own, complicated way. But I had no idea what it was. I wasn't even sure which part was hers, and which part I had dreamt.

Aunty M smiled her special smile, and closed the bedroom door behind her.